FROM THE PAGES OF
THE MAYOR OF CASTERBRIDGE

She had the hard, half-apathetic expression of one who deems any-thing possible at the hands of Time and Chance except, perhaps, fair play.
(page 6)

"Before you go further, Michael, listen to me. If you touch that money, I and this girl go with the man. Mind, it is a joke no longer."
(page 14)

"That meekness has done me more harm than the bitterest temper!"
(page 18)

To birds of the more soaring kind Casterbridge must have appeared on this fine evening as a mosaic-work of subdued reds, browns, greys, and crystals, held together by a rectangular frame of deep green. To the level eye of humanity it stood as an indistinct mass be-hind a dense stockade of limes and chestnuts, set in the midst of miles of rotund down and concave field. The mass became gradually dissected by the vision into towers, gables, chimneys, and casements, the highest glazings shining bleared and bloodshot with the coppery fire they caught from the belt of sunlit cloud in the west. (page 28)

"When you take away from among us the fools and the rogues, and the lammigers and the wanton hussies, and the slatterns, and such like, there's cust few left to ornament a song with in Casterbridge, or the country round."
(page 51)

"You see now that the Mayor of Casterbridge is not so thriving in his mind as it seems he might be from the state of his pocket." (page 77)

Altogether the time was an exciting one; sex had never before as-serted itself in her so strongly, for in former days she had perhaps been too impersonally human to be distinctively feminine.
(page 92)

"All her shining keys will be took from her, and her cupboards opened; and little things a' didn't wish seen, anybody will see; and her wishes and ways will all be as nothing!"　　　　(page 114)

He was the kind of man to whom some human object for pouring out his heat upon—were it emotive or were it choleric—was almost a necessity.　　　　(page 117)

"It is not by what is, in this life, but by what appears, that you are judged."　　　　(page 166)

It was hardly in human nature to keep the eyes averted when the door slammed.　　　　(page 211)

His quality was such that he could have annihilated them both in the heat of action; but to accomplish the deed by oral poison was beyond the nerve of his enmity.　　　　(page 229)

" 'Tis not our greatest doings that the world gets wind of."
　　　　(page 238)

"Who is such a reprobate as I! And yet it seems that even I be in Somebody's hand!"　　　　(page 275)

He had no wish to make an arena a second time of a world that had become a mere painted scene to him.　　　　(page 293)

"I'll never trouble 'ee again, Elizabeth-Jane—no, not to my dying day!"　　　　(page 300)

THE MAYOR OF CASTERBRIDGE

Thomas Hardy

With an Introduction by Phillip Lopate

Notes by David Kurnick

George Stade
Consulting Editorial Director

BARNES & NOBLE CLASSICS
NEW YORK

𝒥ℬ

BARNES & NOBLE CLASSICS

NEW YORK

Published by Barnes & Noble Books
122 Fifth Avenue
New York, NY 10011

www.barnesandnoble.com/classics

The Mayor of Casterbridge was serialized in The Graphic and published
in book form in 1886.

Published in 2004 by Barnes & Noble Classics with new Introduction,
Notes, Biography, Chronology, Inspired By, Comments & Questions,
and For Further Reading.

The Mayor of Casterbridge
ISBN-13: 978-1-59308-309-0
ISBN-10: 1-59308-309-2
LC Control Number 2004102768

Produced and published in conjunction with:
Fine Creative Media, Inc.
322 Eighth Avenue
New York, NY 10001
Michael J. Fine, President and Publisher

Printed in the United States of America
QM
7 9 10 8

THOMAS HARDY

Thomas Hardy was born on June 2, 1840, in the village of Higher Bockhampton, near Dorchester, a market town in the county of Dorset. Hardy would spend much of his life in his native region, transforming its rural landscapes into his fictional Wessex. Hardy's mother, Jemima, inspired him with a taste for literature, while his stonemason father, Thomas, shared with him a love of architecture and music (the two would later play the fiddle at local dances). As a boy Hardy read widely in the popular fiction of the day, including the novels of Scott, Dumas, Dickens, W. Harrison Ainsworth, and G. P. R. James, and in the poetry of Scott, Wordsworth, Byron, Shelley, Keats, and others. Strongly influenced in his youth by the Bible and the liturgy of the Anglican Church, Hardy later contemplated a career in the ministry; but his assimilation of the new theories of Darwinian evolutionism eventually made him an agnostic and a severe critic of the limitations of traditional religion.

Although Hardy was a gifted student at the local schools he attended as a boy for eight years, his lower-class social origins limited his further educational opportunities. At sixteen he was apprenticed to architect John Hicks in Dorchester and began an architectural career primarily focused on the restoration of churches. In Dorchester Hardy was also befriended by Horace Moule, eight years Hardy's senior, who acted as an intellectual mentor and literary advisor throughout his youth and early adulthood. From 1862 to 1867 Hardy worked in London for the distinguished architect Arthur Blomfield, but he continued to study—literature, art, philosophy, science, history, the classics—and to write, first poetry and then fiction.

By the early 1870s Hardy's first two published novels, *Desperate Remedies* and *Under the Greenwood Tree*, appeared to little acclaim or sales. With his third novel. *A Pair of Blue Eyes*, he began the practice of serializing his fiction in magazines prior to book publication, a method that he would utilize throughout his career as a novelist. In 1874, the year of his marriage to Emma Gifford of St. Juliot, Cornwall, Hardy enjoyed his first significant commercial and critical success with the book publication of *Far from the Madding Crowd* after its serialization in the *Cornhill Magazine*.

Hardy and his wife lived in several locations in London, Dorset, and Somerset before settling in southwest London for three years in 1878. During the late 1870s and early 1880s Hardy published *The Return of the Native, The Trumpet-Major, A Laodicean,* and *Two on a Tower* while consolidating his place as a leading contemporary English novelist. He would also eventually produce four volumes of short stories: *Wessex Tales, A Group of Noble Dames, Life's Little Ironies,* and *A Changed Man and Other Tales.*

In 1883 Hardy and his wife moved back to Dorchester where Hardy wrote *The Mayor of Casterbridge,* set in a fictionalized version of Dorchester, and went on to design and construct a permanent home for himself, named Max Gate, completed in 1885. In the later 1880s and early 1890s Hardy wrote three of his greatest novels, *The Woodlanders, Tess of the d'Urbervilles,* and *Jude the Obscure,* all of them notable for their remarkable tragic power. The latter two novels were both initially published as magazine serials in which potentially objectionable moral and religious content was removed by the author, only to be restored in book publication; both novels nevertheless aroused public controversy for their criticisms of Victorian sexual and religious mores. The appearance of *Judge the Obscure* in 1895 in particular precipitated harsh attacks on Hardy's alleged pessimism and immorality, contributing to his decision to abandon the writing of fiction after the appearance of his last-published novel, *The Well-Beloved.*

In the later 1890s Hardy returned to the writing of poetry that he had abandoned for fiction thirty years earlier. *Wessex Poems* appeared in 1898, followed by several volumes of poetry at regular intervals over the next three decades. Between 1904 and 1908 Hardy published a three-part epic verse drama. *The Dynasts,* based on the Napoleonic Wars of the early nineteenth century. Following the death of his first wife in 1912 Hardy married his literary secretary Florence Dugdale in 1914. Receiving a variety of public honors in the last two decades of his life, Hardy continued to publish poems until his death at Max Gate on January 11, 1928. His ashes were interred in the Poets' Corner of Westminster Abbey in London and his heart in Stinsford outside Dorchester. Regarded as one of England's greatest authors in both fiction and poetry, Hardy has inspired such notable twentieth-century writers as Marcel Proust, John Cowper Powys, D. H. Lawrence, Theodore Dreiser, and John Fowles.

TABLE OF CONTENTS

THE WORLD OF THOMAS HARDY AND THE MAYOR OF CASTERBRIDGE

1840 The eldest of four children, Thomas Hardy is born on June 2 in Higher Bockhampton, near Dorchester in the county of Dorset. His father, Thomas, is a builder and master stonemason, and his mother, Jemima, is a former domestic servant with literary interests who teaches her son to read at an early age. Hardy's frail health prevents him from entering the village school until age eight.

1848 Hardy enters the newly established National School in his parish. His early reading includes Samuel Johnson's *Rasselas*, John Dryden's translation of Virgil's *Aeneid*, Bernardin de Saint-Pierre's *Paul and Virginia*, and many of the popular novelists and poets of the day. He cultivates his love of music, playing the fiddle with his father in the parish choir and at local dances.

1850 Jemima enrolls her son in a school in Dorchester, where for the next six years he studies under a distinguished local schoolmaster, Isaac Last; he will begin the study of Latin at age twelve.

1856 After helping his father design renovations for a country church, Hardy is awarded an apprenticeship to the Dorchester architect John Hicks. He studies Greek and other subjects in his free time and develops a close friendship with Horace Moule, a vicar's son who becomes his mentor.

1862 Hardy leaves Dorset to work for a prominent architect, Arthur Blomfield, in London. In addition to his professional duties, he attempts to develop his talents as a poet but fails to publish any poetry at this time. He visits museums, goes to the theater, takes French lessons, and attends a reading by Charles Dickens.

1863 Hardy becomes engaged to Eliza Nicholls. He is awarded a prize from the Architectural Association for his design of a country mansion, and a Silver Medal from the Royal Institute of British Architects for an essay on architecture.

1865   Hardy's humorous prose sketch "How I Built Myself a House" appears in Chambers's Edinburgh Journal. Several of his earliest surviving poems date from this time.

1866   The engagement to Eliza Nicholls is broken off.

1867   Failing health necessitates a return to Dorchester, where Hardy again works for John Hicks. He writes his first novel, The Poor Man and the Lady (authored by "the Poor Man").

1869   The Poor Man and the Lady is rejected for publication because of its subversive depiction of English class relations. Hardy takes a position in Weymouth as an architect specializing in church restoration.

1870   Hardy meets his future wife, Emma Lavinia Gifford, while on a trip to Cornwall.

1871   Tinsley Brothers publishes the novel Desperate Remedies at Hardy's expense and without the author's name. The novel is barely noticed and sells poorly.

1872   Hardy moves back to London, where he creates architectural plans for schools. Emma's father refuses to allow Hardy to marry her. Hardy publishes Under the Greenwood Tree with Tinsley; another novel, A Pair of Blue Eyes, is serialized in Tinsley's Magazine and the New York Tribune.

1873   Shortly after he begins work on Far From the Maddening Crowd, to be serialized in Cornhill Magazine, Hardy is devastated by the suicide of his close friend Horace Moule.

1874   Far from the Madding Crowd, Hardy's first commercially successful novel, appears. Hardy and Emma marry. Over the next several years the two live in several locations in Dorset, Somerset, and London.

1878   The Return of the Native, another novel, is published, marking Hardy's debut as a tragic novelist.

1880   The Trumpet-Major, a historical novel set in the Napoleonic era, is published. Hardy suffers from an undiagnosed debilitating illness and is confined to bed for many months. During this time, he dictates a novel, A Laodicean, to his wife.

1881   Hardy and his wife, their marriage strained, leave London for the town of Wimborne in Dorset. Hardy researches a novel on astronomy to be titled Two on a Tower; it will be published in 1882.

1883   The Hardys move to Dorchester, where Hardy designs and begins construction of a house; his father and brother perform the construction work.

1885   The Hardys move into Max Gate, henceforth his permanent residence, a mile outside Dorchester and two miles from his birthplace; here he will write some of his greatest novels.

1886   Another novel, *The Mayor of Casterbridge*, is published (Casterbridge is Hardy's name for Dorchester). Hardy sets about completing *The Woodlanders*, an unfinished narrative begun a decade earlier; the novel will appear in 1887.

1888   *Wessex Tales*, Hardy's first collection of short stories, is published; three more volumes of stories will follow.

1891   *Tess of the d'Urbervilles* appears in a bowdlerized version for serial publication in *The Graphic*, but is then restored to the author's intended version for book publication. While the novel raises a storm of controversy for its treatment of marriage and religion, it is popular with the public. Many praise Hardy as England's greatest novelist.

1892   Hardy's father dies. Serialization of *The Pursuit of the Well-Beloved* begins; it will be published in volume form as *The Well-Beloved* in 1897.

1893   On a trip to Dublin, Hardy meets Florence Henniker, with whom he has a long-term literary and sentimental relationship. Marital troubles between Hardy and Emma are ongoing.

1895   *Jude the Obscure* is serialized in bowdlerized form in *Harper's New Monthly Magazine*, but is restored to its original form for book publication. Like *Tess*, *Jude* is highly controversial and precipitates harsh attacks for its alleged pessimism and immorality. Hardy turns to the writing of poetry; his first volume will appear in 1898.

1904   Hardy's mother dies. The first part of *The Dynasts*, an epic poetic drama on the Napoleonic Wars, is published, with two more parts appearing over the next three years.

1912   Hardy receives the Gold Medal of the Royal Society of Literature. Emma Hardy dies, inspiring the highly personal *Poems of 1912–13*.

1914   Hardy marries his longtime secretary, Florence Dugdale. The onset of World War I seems to confirm Hardy's tragic philosophy of life, most recently dramatized in The Dynasts and depicted in much of his poetry and fiction.

1919   *Collected Poems* is published. Three more volumes of poetry will appear during the last decade of Hardy's life.

1920   Hardy is celebrated in England and abroad on his eightieth birthday.

1928   Hardy dies of a heart attack on January 11 at Max Gate. His ashes are placed in the Poets' Corner of Westminster Abbey in London; his heart is buried next to the remains of his first wife, Emma, in Stinsford, outside Dorchester.

INTRODUCTION

The Mayor of Casterbridge is a consistently wilder and stranger book than its status as a late-Victorian secondary school classic would suggest. It was completed in 1886, in the middle of Thomas Hardy's greatest period as a novelist. *Far From the Madding Crowd* (1874) and *The Return of the Native* (1878) had appeared during the previous decade; *The Woodlanders* (1887), *Tess of the d'Urbervilles* (1891), and *Jude the Obscure* (1895) would all arrive in the next ten years. The advertising cliché that a writer is "at the height of his powers" was strictly true in this case, which may help explain why the novel brims over with invention, pungency, vitality, and wit. For all its darkness, it has brio to spare, making it enormously entertaining, especially for those readers attuned to its oddness and complexity, and its refusal to be pinned down to any one interpretation.

"The business of the poet and novelist is to show the sorriness underlying the grandest things, and the grandeur underlying the sorriest things," wrote Hardy, in a note to himself while working on *The Mayor of Casterbridge*. Virginia Woolf, who admired Hardy and especially this novel, called him "the greatest tragic writer among English novelists." Certainly, the models of Greek and Shakespearian tragedy were never far from his mind. But Hardy also meant to add on to that already capacious mansion, the nineteenth-century English realist novel. One way to view *The Mayor of Casterbridge*, in fact, is as a contest between Hardy the would-be tragedian, who kept trying to impose a tight five-act structure on his material, and Hardy the more open-ended novelist, who kept inserting quirky narrative twists, asides, historical background, and droll minor characters, altogether conveying reality at its most waywardly robust.

The Character of Michael Henchard

Inevitably, in analyzing this book, we must start with the novel's protagonist, since no other Hardy novel is quite so dominated by a single character. Michael Henchard has rightly been hailed as one of the unforgettable characters in fiction. "He takes his place at once with certain towering and possessed figures of Melville, Hawthorne, and Dostoevsky," wrote Albert Guerard (in *Thomas Hardy*; see "For Further Reading"). The novel's subtitle, "The Story of a Man of Character," is meant to lead us directly into the knot of Henchard's personality. Some of Hardy's contemporary critics took exception to this formulation, since Michael Henchard errs so often that he seems precisely to lack what Victorian moralists would have called "character." However, we should remember what Hardy's contemporary, Friedrich Nietzsche, once wryly asserted: that making the same mistake over and over was a true sign of character. In any case, Hardy clearly uses the word "character" here less as approbation than as shorthand for the set of habits, traits, and foibles that may determine a person's destiny. To drive home that point, he even inserts in his text a quote from Novalis: "Character is Fate" (p. 109).

When we first meet Michael Henchard, he is a young, disgruntled itinerant farmhand, unemployed and saddled with a wife and child. He is also a heavy drinker, which leads him into an appalling folly: He sells his wife, Susan, and baby girl, Elizabeth-Jane, at a county fair. In his book *Thomas Hardy*, Irving Howe comments on the shocking but also outrageously liberating undercurrents of this act, at least for some male readers: "To shake loose from one's wife; to discard that drooping rag of a woman, with her mute complaints and maddening passivity; to escape not by a slinking abandonment but through the public sale of her body to a stranger, as horses are sold at a fair; and thus to wrest, through sheer amoral willfulness, a second chance out of life—it is with this stroke, so insidiously attractive to male fantasy, that *The Mayor of Casterbridge* begins. In the entire history of European fiction there are few more brilliant openings." Elaine Showalter, in "The Unmanning of the Mayor of Casterbridge," has correctively pointed out that Howe and many other male critics neglect to mention an aspect of the wife-sale that is potentially much more disturbing to women readers: It included their child as well.

Awakening from his drunken stupor, he vows not to touch a drop of alcohol for the next twenty years. But he remains, as the novelist Rick Moody has shrewdly observed, "a dry drunk," with all the unresolved inner impulses of alcoholic sentimentality and hostility, now barely held in check by sobriety. Hardy skips over the next two decades, during which, we learn, Henchard has risen to become a wealthy, powerful grain merchant, and gotten himself elected Mayor of Casterbridge, the thriving town to which he has resettled. Initially, the sale of his family seems to have had just the sort of positive effect on the burdened Henchard that he intended. It releases his energies and talents, so that he is able to carve out a position of financial power and respect in a new place. True, he is alone, cut off from love and intimacy, but this seems to him a fair price to pay, on the whole.

When his rejected wife Susan returns and seeks him out, he re-marries her, mostly out of duty and penance. After she dies, a former lover of Henchard's, Lucetta, arrives on the scene, and a Hardyesque romantic triangle ensues between Lucetta, Henchard, and his Scottish assistant, Donald Farfrae. Eventually the wife-sale episode of twenty years earlier comes to light by happenstance in a police court at which Henchard is presiding. "On that day—almost at that minute— he passed the ridge of prosperity and honour, and began to descend rapidly on the other side," Hardy tells us (p. 203), with a structurally tidy sentence that diagrams all too neatly (and deceptively) the book's narrative arc.

Summarized this way, the novel would appear to be a severe, straightforward tragedy: A man commits a shameful act in his youth, then rises to prominence, at which point the truth of his earlier mis-deed surfaces, leading to his downfall. But what makes the book so much more interesting is the way the narrative keeps slipping the noose of inevitability, even as the laws of causation and retribution bear down hard. First of all, Henchard is well into his fall from grace long before his twenty-year-old error is exposed; second, he is given countless chances after this public exposure to redeem himself, which he does and does not take up; third, public opinion in Caster-bridge soon forgets, or stops caring about, his old repellent act. The townsfolk have their own worries. Hardy uses them both as a Greek chorus commenting on its masters' actions, and as a set of idiosyn-cratic individuals, whose debates, for instance, about whether it is ap-propriate to rob the pennies from a corpse's eyelids place Henchard's tragic scandal in a more forgiving, everyday perspective.

Henchard and Casterbridge form alternating strands of narrative tension and attention. For a while, Henchard is the town's

"monarch," so to speak, and he bears on his shoulders the solitudi-
nous anxiety of a Shakespearian king. But Henchard is also lowborn,
an ex-laborer, and his dilemma about how to act, his irritable testi-
ness, derive in part from uncomfortably straddling two social classes.
A self-invented man, he is desperately in need of self-knowledge to
connect the two halves of his life.

One of the ways in which Henchard does not know himself is
that he exaggerates his self-sufficiency. He believes he can take
women or leave them alone, and even brags to Farfrae, with perverse
pride, "being by nature something of a woman-hater, I have found it
no hardship to keep mostly at a distance from the sex" (p. 75). We
ought not to take him strictly at his word: He is too considerate at
times to be a thoroughgoing misogynist. A moment later, he admits
that "the loneliness of my domestic life" leaves him vulnerable to
black spells, depressions. It was during such a low period that he fell
for the affections of Lucetta. Now he is ready to remarry. He expects
women to fall into line with his intermittent need for them, to love
him unconditionally and maternally, simply because he is who he is;
when this is not forthcoming he gives vent to a bitter disappointment, the bruised self-dramatization of the badly loved. Some of this
grandiose entitlement may issue from his being the town's mayor
and preeminent merchant. Yet the youthful Henchard's willingness to
blame his wife for all his problems and then reject her indicates that
his anger against women has deeper roots, preceding his accession to
power. He resents the fact that he needs them at all.

Another facet of Henchard's emotional life that puzzles him is
his feelings for the younger, smaller Farfrae. " 'To be sure, to be sure,
how that fellow does draw me!' he had said to himself. 'I suppose 'tis
because I'm so lonely' " (p. 55). There is an element of psychological projection in this attraction: Farfrae reminds him of his younger
brother, he admits—perhaps also of a son he never had, or of his own
younger self, though amended and unburdened by shame. Some
modern critics have not been slow to find a homoerotic undertone
in this attraction, while others have been horrified at the idea. We can
assume that Hardy meant all of these shadings—a lonely man's ide-
alized friendship, paternal feelings, homoerotic leanings—to play a
part; none need take precedence. It is precisely because Henchard
lacks self-knowledge that he can be blindsided by these feelings of

tenderness toward another man. Later, he is equally stunned to realize the depth of his attachment to his stepdaughter, Elizabeth-Jane.

In her essay, Elaine Showalter develops an intriguing interpretation that views the novel as a critique of patriarchal values and rigid
masculinity. For Hardy's tragic heroes, she argues, "maturity involves
a kind of assimilation of female suffering, an identification with a
woman which is also an effort to come to terms with their own
deepest selves." She appropriately quotes the significant passage at the
end of the wrestling match, when Henchard, by far the stronger, lies
crouching in defeat:

> The scenes of his first acquaintance with Farfrae rushed back upon
> him—that time when the curious mixture of romance and thrift in
> the young man's composition so commanded his heart that Farfrae
> could play upon as on an instrument. So thoroughly subdued was he
> that he remained on the sacks in a crouching attitude, unusual for a
> man, and for such a man. Its womanliness sat tragically on the figure
> of so stern a piece of virility (pp. 253–254).

The psychologically astute Hardy knew exactly what he was
doing by planting these seeds in the reader's mind. The question is
how much we want to seize on any of these signposts to the exclu-
sion of the others. Perhaps it is not so much that Henchard is "unmanned" as that he is forced to arrive at a more complicated
definition of what it means to be a man. For instance, when he tries
to coerce Lucetta into marriage by blackmailing her, he is made to re-
think his position: "You said to me, 'If I were a man I should not insist.' That cut me deep. I felt that there was some truth in it" (p. 195).
Henchard never abandons his goal to "act like a man"; it is the standards of masculinity that keep shifting.

Just as Henchard thinks initially he can do without women or
love, so he overestimates his capacity to suffer. He is an incomplete
stoic—admirably able to say, one moment, "I am to suffer, I perceive," only to cast about the next moment for someone else to bear
the brunt of his resentment. Throughout, Hardy stands at a remove,
offering hints on how to interpret his protagonist's impetuous re-
sponses as part of a larger pattern. "Henchard showed chagrin at
once—nobody was more quick to show that than he" (p. 165), the

narrator says. He reminds us: "There was still the same unruly volcanic stuff beneath the rind of Michael Henchard as when he had
sold his wife at Weydon Fair" (p. 107). Essentially, the novelist is giving us his theory of character, as something archaeologically layered
and geologically obdurate—much slower to undergo transformation
than the optimists among us might imagine. He calmly ticks off Henchard's flaws: He is temper-ridden, overbearing, impatient, vengeful,
uncultivated, superstitious, cruel, and insensitive at times, "constructed upon too large a scale" to perceive subtle undercurrents of
feeling between people. Even when he expresses fondness, taking his
assistant, Donald Farfrae, by the arm, there is a "rough benignity," a
"tigerish affection," and a "tendency to domineer."

Hardy's achievement is to make us this mule-headed, domineer-
ing man so sympathetic. We care about, and for, Henchard because,
for all his faults, he has an expansive, generous nature, and a noble
honesty. Take, for instance, his quick admission of guilt at the police
court, when he could have easily denied his past misdeed, or his con-
fession to Farfrae, in the midst of his grudge against the younger
man: "I—sometimes think I've wronged 'ee!" (p. 211). (Can you
imagine the more cautious, Teflon-coated Farfrae ever making such a
statement?) Henchard is always about to do the right thing and mess-
ing up the timing, or preparing some villainy and relenting at the last
moment. In the spirit of botched villainy, he embarks on a plan to ex-
pose Lucetta's past to her husband, by reading aloud from her love
letters: "But sitting here in cold blood he could not do it" (p. 228)—
that is, divulge the name of the letter-writer. He lures the smaller Farfrae into a fight, but ties one hand behind his back to even the odds.
At the climax of the fight, when he could easily kill or maim his antagonist, he lets go, and confesses his fondness for the man! His baffled tenderness, at such moments, makes him very endearing.

That Hardy himself sympathized with his character is fairly evident: He knew Henchard's nature so well because he was also a
brooding, ambitious, easily wounded man who had risen in social
station and retained a touchy class resentment. As someone from the
laboring classes who had never gone to college but, through relent-
less self-education, remade himself, and who fit but awkwardly into
the drawing rooms of high society, he must have identified with
Henchard. They had many other things in common, including a re-

served mistrust of intimacy, a worship of music, and a sense of being stalked by the sinister. Of course, the smaller, physically weaker Hardy may have been indulging his fantasies by equipping his protagonist with a muscleman's virility as well as crudity. But for all their overt differences, Hardy was drawn to Henchard's passionate nature and outsider status, his inability to make small talk or settle for a safe, humdrum existence. He had confessed to Anne Thackeray (the critic Leslie Stephens' sister-in-law) that he had little interest in the workings of society—in "manners," the usual stuff of the English realistic novel. He was interested in what he called "the substance of life," the crucial struggles of man and woman, fate and free will.

Hardy's very readiness to enumerate his protagonist's imperfections demonstrates, in part, his sympathy: Not only can Henchard take it, the man is eager to lay the blame on himself. Conversely, Hardy reins in his criticism of the other characters, so that his judgments about them sound all the more harshly when they finally do break forth. Toward the end of the novel, for example, we get Farfrae singing nostalgically, "giving strong expression to a song of his dear native country that he loved so well as never to have revisited it" (p. 297). (Among critics, Farfrae has often suffered from a bad press. Perhaps the reason is that he seems more a useful connecting rod, supporting numerous plot functions, than a fully autonomous character. Why, for instance, does he remain so dim, so puzzled at Henchard's resentment, when he has taken over the older man's whole position in life?) Lucetta—one of Hardy's fascinating enchantresses, with that characteristic tincture of French blood—brings a welcome vivacity to the story; but the vanity she shows in distancing herself from Henchard, during the visit of the Royal Personage, finally arouses the reader's dislike. Even the Cordelia-like Elizabeth-Jane is guilty of an excessive preoccupation with respectable appearances, and lacks the requisite understanding and forgiveness of Henchard when it counts most. Her mother, the "simple" (or so we keep hearing), put-upon Susan, turns out herself to be a mistress of duplicity: first palming off Henchard's stepdaughter as his real daughter, then writing an anonymous note intended to bring Farfrae and Elizabeth-Jane together.

For all their shadings, the other characters function mostly as reflections of Henchard's inner consciousness, or as obstacles in his path. He is like an action figure ready to burst into impassioned response at whatever Fate tosses him; and the game is seeing what complication Hardy will toss him next, and how he will react. The reader is given limited access to the character's psychology—we are still a long way from the inner monologues of Joyce and Woolf. Hardy is on the cusp: He draws a portrait of his protagonist largely through exterior actions, contradictory behaviors, and almost reluctant introspections. Hardy's "self-alienated" Henchard looks forward to Joseph Conrad's shamed protagonist in *Lord Jim* and D. H. Lawrence's wary Rupert in *Women in Love*.

The novel's true turning point, in terms of Henchard's mettle being tested, is probably not the public disclosure of his past shame, but an earlier scene: his discovery that Elizabeth-Jane is not his biological daughter. This is when Henchard makes his famous declaration: "I am to suffer, I perceive" (p. 118). He looks in on her when she is sleeping and decides that her features resemble someone else's, not his own. "He could not endure the sight of her, and hastened away" (p. 119). Whether his repugnance is motivated by injured pride or fear of inappropriate attraction to an appealing young woman living under his roof, he fails the human test of loving her as a stepdaughter. He becomes cold and "chiding," eventually even kicking her out with a small annuity, "so as to be independent of me— and so that I may be independent of you" (p. 134). This rejection of Elizabeth-Jane through a monetary arrangement uncannily echoes the sale of his wife two decades earlier. The man has learned nothing, it would seem. Or, as Hardy tells us, with great precision: "Misery taught him nothing more than defiant endurance of it" (p. 119). The question is: Will that condition of defiant, wounded unawareness prevail? Will the protagonist stay stuck in his ways, or will he undergo some transformation?

It has become a truism that the main character in a novel or movie must show growth. In our day, this path to moral illumination is often mechanically paved: A secondary character, some old soul, say, lectures our hero, the light bulb goes on in his head, and he realizes one of those afternoon talk-show platitudes such as "No man is an island" or "Everyone needs love." This is where, I think, *The Mayor of Casterbridge* has much to teach us today. In our quick-fix therapeutic culture, it is often assumed that a weekend intensive workshop should suffice to make us become more assertive, sensuous, spiritual, or self-actualizing. One measure of the psychological subtlety of *The Mayor of Casterbridge* is that Henchard keeps coming to a wiser self-awareness, and then losing it again, the way we all do. He is a clever businesssman, nobody's fool; but when his emotions get the better of him he forgets what he knows and turns thickheaded. So he gambles that bad weather will ruin the crop: He invests more than he should have, because he wants to ruin his one-time friend and now arch-competitor, Farfrae, with one blow; then he sells everything off too quickly when the weather momentarily turns good (bad for him) and, in the process, loses all. "He was reminded of what he had well known before, that a man might gamble upon the square green areas of fields as readily as upon those of a card-room" (p. 176).

Albert Guerard, in *Thomas Hardy*, summarizes Henchard as "a man of character obsessed by guilt and so committed to his own destruction." According to this interpretation, the novel is wholly about a conscience-laden man and his unconscious need to expiate his guilt. Yet Henchard keeps scheming for personal happiness and success. His setbacks are not entirely his fault; they are also the result of bad luck. Had they not occurred, he might have been just as pleased to settle for moderate good fortune. Henchard, I would argue, is not bent on self-destruction at all costs, though it is certainly true that his "volcanic" character regularly undermines his chances for contentment.

The book fights clear of becoming a simple narrative of redemption, just as it refuses to chart a straight course for downfall. Henchard keeps trying like a leopard to change his spots, and then reverting to type. After he leaves Casterbridge, he goes away, comes back, goes away. In a passage that may give us the key to the protagonist's moral progress, as well as the narrative's circling dynamic, Hardy writes:

> The centrifugal tendency imparted by weariness of the world was counteracted by the centripetal influence of his love for his step-daughter. As a consequence, instead of following a straight course yet further away from Casterbridge, Henchard gradually, almost unconsciously, deflected from that right line of his first intention; till, by degrees, his wandering, like that of the Canadian woodsman, became part of a circle of which Casterbridge formed the centre (pp. 292–293).

When we are finally told by the author himself, in no uncertain terms, "Henchard had become a changed man" (p. 302), it happens at the last possible moment, and the exact nature of the change is left ambiguous. It would seem to be largely a matter of illness and exhaustion. As far as the judgment Henchard renders on himself goes, while it is tempting to see that last will and testament as a proof of his finally accepting responsibility for his actions, it is also in keeping with the pattern of an egotist who has always, out of inverted pride, tended to lay too much blame on himself. That self-annihilating request is as much an act of hubris as of modesty. Who is he to call for a complete expunging of his name from the human record, when the rest of us must put up, when we die, with a combination of anonymity and smudged, palimpsest traces? Is Henchard trying to stage a preemptive strike against the leveling indignity of death? If so, Hardy has ironically subverted his character's last wishes by making him immortal.

Toward Realism and Beyond Realism

Hardy began writing The Mayor of Casterbridge in 1885. Like all of his novels from A Pair of Blue Eyes onward, it was serialized, appearing in the London Graphic from January 2 to May 15, 1886. This method of composition—doling out the story to a distracted newspaper or magazine public periodically, on strict deadlines—imposed a pressure to hold the readers' interests in each section. Early on in his career as a serializing novelist, in 1874, Hardy had expressed the fear that he might be sacrificing "the proper artistic balance of the completed work" for the sake of pleasing large numbers of readers and being considered "a good hand at a serial." This qualm about compromising his artistic integrity derived partly from feeling that his true calling was poetry, not fiction; underneath the statement's modesty may also be detected Hardy's growing pride in becoming a professional at his trade. He was learning to plot. Meanwhile, he continued mediating between the demands of realism, which called for a more muted, organic treatment, and the sensationalistic ruptures invited by serialization.

In George Gissing's classic New Grub Street (1891), which appeared

in roughly the same period as *The Mayor of Casterbridge*, a minor novelist plans to write a "pure" realist novel recounting the dull, modest
life of a grocer. Though Gissing was poking fun, there is no question
that raised expectations for a new, more thoroughgoing realism were
in the air. The advance guard of the educated reading public, disen-
chanted with melodrama and treacle, had developed a taste for the
unvarnished facts of life. Hardy was conscious of this public's demands for plausibility and verisimilitude in novels, and indeed he
signed onto them. He considered himself a member of the realist
school of fiction, at the very least an enemy of Victorian sentimentality. But he understood the need to shape and distort ordinary life to
create an artistic truth. "Art is a disproportioning—(that is, distort-
ing, throwing out of proportion)—of realities, to show more clearly
the features that matter in those realities," wrote Hardy in his journal. When the distortion "increases the sense of vraisemblance," the
result is "high art"; when it decreases that sense, the result is "low
art." By using a French word (*vraisemblance*) to mean a natural, convincing sense of reality, Hardy signaled his aspiration to the sophisticated standards of Continental fiction—Flaubert, Balzac, Zola, the
Goncourt brothers. Being largely a self-taught novelist who had wandered into the field from architecture and poetry, he felt not quite
immune from the pitfalls of "low art." On the other hand, he ratio-
nalized his occasional stylistic clumsiness or cliché in advance by refusing to strive for Flaubertian perfection: "The whole secret of a
living style . . ." he wrote, "lies in not having too much style—being,
in fact, a little careless, or rather seeming to be, here and there."

Hardy did not regard his new novel as perfect, and he was quick
to blame the constraints of serial writing for any possible defects in
it. Summarizing his feelings years later about *The Mayor of Casterbridge*,
he regretted that he may have "damaged [it] more recklessly as an
artistic whole, in the interest of the newspaper in which it appeared
serially, than perhaps any other" of his novels, by "aiming to get an
incident into almost every week's part," causing him "to add events
into the narrative somewhat too freely." But he went on to say "in
favor of the plot . . . that it was quite coherent and organic, in spite
of its complications."

After the serial version had appeared in the newspaper, Hardy
made many small improvements, structural realignments, and adjust-

ments for the final version in book form, which was published later in 1886 by Smith, Elder and Company of London. The resulting labor paid off, since later critics have called *The Mayor of Casterbridge* the most well-structured of all his novels. Initial critical reaction to it may have been lukewarm, and the book sales disappointing, but Hardy's writer friends, such as Robert Louis Stevenson and William Dean Howells, praised it highly, and in the course of time it has come to be accepted as an indispensable work of fiction.

Indeed, there is reason to be grateful for its delirious jolts, which make for a more powerful novel. One way of looking at serialization's effect on *The Mayor of Casterbridge* is that it liberated Hardy into giddy narrative invention. Hardy tells the story through a series of shocks; the pace is never permitted to flag. The wife-sale; the discovery of Susan's letter revealing Elizabeth-Jane's paternity; the testimony of the furmity seller; Lucetta and Donald's surprise marriage; the tussle between Henchard and Farfrae; the skimmity-ride—all these are vital theatrical strokes. Just as the reader is settling down to one set of circumstances, something new comes along to jog the plot—an ex-lover shows up, a bull escapes from the pen, a sailor-husband who is presumed dead returns, a Royal Personage appears in town. However sudden or arbitrary these occurrences may seem at first, the appropriateness with which Henchard responds to each one is thrilling. Hardy ultimately defended his packed plot by saying, "After all, it is not improbabilities of incident but improbabilities of character that matter." And he was quite sure that his main character was plausible and convincing, just as he was quite sure that he needed to engineer for the character a tragic fate.

When Hardy's friend and mentor, Horace Moule, committed suicide, the writer began to be obsessed with the waste of human potential, as something both awful and preordained. One of his biographers, Robert Gittings, has posited in *Young Thomas Hardy* that:

> from the time of the death of Moule, Hardy never portrayed a man who was not, in some way, maimed by fate. He did not hesitate to load the dice at every point against his tragic heroes. Even if a case can be made that their own weakness or foolishness or rashness of choice caused their downfall, Hardy also made sure that the results would be as dire as possible by introducing other elements of coincidence,

irony, and what seems like divine interference or even malevolence. He does this with absolute conviction, because, he is now fully persuaded, such things do occur, in all their extremes, in real life.

The dramatic extremes of Hardy's novels, which in another writer might seem lurid or sensationalistic, constitute, therefore, his own true sense of realism, issuing as they do from a conviction that life is authentically tragic and strange.

There is in Hardy, unlike Tolstoy or George Eliot, an utter absence of the normative, of normalcy as a baseline. He can, for instance, never muster more than grudging respect for family life. Ever the skeptic regarding marriage (while writing *The Mayor of Casterbridge*, he and his first wife, Emma, were drifting into permanent estrangement), he begins the book with the observation that you could tell the "man and woman were husband and wife" by "the atmosphere of stale familiarity." There are no Austen-like "happily-ever-after" conclusions at the altar in Hardy. Near the end, Henchard expresses wonderment during his stepdaughter's wedding that the level-headed Elizabeth-Jane, "who knew in spite of her maidenhood that marriage was as a rule no dancing matter," could manifest any "zest for this revelry" (p. 298). Farfrae's capacity to settle into normal family happiness (with whomever) is viewed somewhat contemptuously as a failure of the imagination. Elizabeth-Jane's expectations of pain and sorrow seem more realistic, and the final irony for her is that she must learn to live with more contentment than squares with her sober view of life.

Henchard is from the start a tragic figure, estranged from and unable to acquiesce to the calms of daily life. Hardy knew that his fundamental métier was tragedy. He observed in his 1911 "General Preface to the Novels and Poems":

Differing natures find their tongue in the presence of differing spectacles. Some natures become vocal at tragedy, some are made vocal by comedy, and it seems to me that to whichever of these aspects of life a writer's instinct for expression the more readily responds, to that he should allow it to respond. That before a contrasting side of things he remains undemonstrative need not be assumed to mean that he remains unperceiving."

In that last line, Hardy is suggesting that he also has an appreciation for comedy. He demonstrates, in fact, his sharp sense of the comic and ridiculous by the sly, ironic tone of *The Mayor of Casterbridge*'s commenting narrator. Henchard's attitude toward Susan during their second, compensatory marriage is described as follows: "He was as kind to her as a man, mayor, and churchwarden could possibly be" (pp. 82–83). The rural peasants, in their dialogues, often provide comic relief and a grotesque sort of humor.

Hardy's taste for the grotesque is a source feeding, simultaneously, the tragic and the comic sense of life. Grisly touches often burst forth from passages that begin innocently enough with a historical or geographic overview. No sooner does a description ensue about a certain location than Hardy digresses to mention ancient gallows that used to be on the site, or dead babies ("the pool wherein nameless infants had been used to disappear" [p. 133]). The ancient past casts a ghoulish abstract pattern over the present. Hardy's invocation of the town's rebellious past ("a old, hoary place o' wickedness," says Buzzford, the dealer) is at once amateur archeology and moral speculation: Some primordial, heinous crime seems to have set in motion a chain of events for which Henchard's afflictions are but the current representative. Every acre of this town and its surroundings has been stained with human blood: The field holds the corpses of Roman soldiers, the remains of spears yet lodged against their arms, their mouths still filled with imperial coins. The Amphitheatre has witnessed fights to the death and women burnt at the stake: References to executions become a sort of running joke or, at least, prefiguring omen. Such Gothic underpinnings counterpoint the novel's realistic agenda.

Coincidence, another nonrealist device, plays a large—some critics have felt too large—role in the plot. There are key conversations eavesdropped on through thin walls, and nemeses detected in the distance through telescopes, and wild bulls who break out of their tether and require ladies to be saved, and resentful minor characters like Joff who just happen to know Lucetta from her native Jersey, and Lucetta sending Elizabeth-Jane out for an errand on the very day that Donald comes courting the girl. Readers today tend to view these outcroppings of coincidence as a flaw, detracting from the tale's verisimilitude, or as a hoary convention. But coincidences also underscore one of the main dilemmas of the novel: What is one's responsibility for one's own destiny? Henchard keeps asking if what is befalling him is "by his fault or by his misfortune." Are these setbacks "the scheme of some sinister intelligence bent on punishing hum"? As long as he can entertain such thoughts, he can deny full responsibility for his actions. On the other hand, Hardy, who had lost his religious faith, did retain some belief in Fate. Finally, the reader may choose to view each coincidence as a charmed turning toward the story's other magnetic pole: namely, that of romance, of an old-fashioned tale.

Is there not something fairy tale-like, after all, in the novel's stark opening scene: A poor peasant goes to a fair and sells his wife and child, to be rid of the burden of their dependency? The success that follows is uncanny and ominous, like an enactment of the old fairy-tale injunction: Be careful what you wish you for. The severe, compressed style of the narration in that first scene also has a scriptural air, reminiscent of some patriarchal incident in the Bible involving Abraham palming off Sarah as his sister, or preparing to sacrifice Isaac. (Hardy admired the art of biblical narratives: "Their so-called simplicity is, in fact, the simplicity of highest cunning," he noted.)

The characters all accrue fairy-tale, super-realistic properties. Henchard is a veritable blotter accumulating animal imagery (lion, tiger, buffalo), biblical references (Job, Cain, Saul, Samson), and literary associations (Faust, Lear, Macbeth, Falstaff, Julius Caesar). He is equipped with "a grotesque grin" and a perennial "red speck of light" in his dark pupils, to give him diabolic connotations. Donald Farfrae is a Rumplestilskin figure when first we meet him, with an unearthly knack for turning bad wheat into good. He also possesses the magical art of dance (he "thoroughly understood the poetry of motion") and singing ("the poet of a new school"). The bewitching Lucetta is "a strange woman of curious fascinations. . . . there might be some devilry about her presence." Elizabeth-Jane is the good, dutiful daughter of fairy tales, separated from her father and at last reunited with him. The weather-prophet whom Henchard visits seems someone out of European folklore, Greek myth, or *Macbeth*. And Newson is the sailor of Sinbad tales, swallowed by the sea, and then washed up alive on shore.

Hardy found a way to merge realism with something larger,

more mythic, by coming up with just those details that would seem plausible and yet uncanny, resonating on a symbolic plane. Two examples of this "symbolic realism" may suffice. The effigy of himself that Henchard stumbles upon in the water, at first thinking it a premonition of his own dead body, is a marvelous invention that fuses narrative strands involving the protagonist and the town. The caged goldfinches Henchard chooses for a wedding gift—only to leave them behind without telling Elizabeth, so that by the time she finds them they have died—seem to embody and summarize the balked affections between these two.

Finally, Hardy the realist looked to history and to the physical and social environment as huge forces shaping character and destiny. It is Hardy the local historian, economist, and sociologist we shall now consider.

The Setting

One of The Mayor of Casterbridge's contemporary reviewers, the eminent critic George Saintsbury, complained that he found the story "too improbable. It is fiction stranger than truth; for, even at the comparatively distant date—some fifty years ago . . . it is impossible to believe that the public sale by a husband of his wife and child to a sailor, in a crowded booth at a village fair, could have attracted such slight attention from the many onlookers" (Saturday Review, May 29, 1886). Hardy retorted that such things did routinely occur; he had found three instances of wife-selling in the local newspapers of the day. Of course, merely because something happens in life does not necessarily make it plausible as fiction. But it is noteworthy that Hardy did a good deal of research before beginning the novel: He pored over old files of the Dorset County Chronicle, entering salient items into his notebooks and deriving plot touches—dinner tributes to important citizens, bankruptcy proceedings, bigamy cases—as well as gleaning many historical details about local fashions in dress, décor, and cuisine.

Hardy had decided around this time to move back to his native Dorchester and build a fine house, Max Gate, for himself and his wife. The decision to return to the familiar surroundings of his upbringing coincided with his plan to subsume all his fiction much more consciously into the "Wessex" scheme: a set of novels and tales placed in the same locale. "Wessex" was his invented name for Dorset County, just as "Casterbridge" (which first made its appearance in *Far From the Madding Crowd*) was his fictive name for Dorchester. Although Wessex/Dorset and Casterbridge/Dorchester were not absolutely identical (Hardy occasionally took liberties with local geography), he was essentially describing real places.

Hardy was brilliant at depicting a specific sense of place. His fresh, evocative descriptions of nature, weather, and landscape remain unsurpassed, as we see in many passages here. *The Mayor of Casterbridge*, it is true, is largely a town novel, much involved with marketplace trades and an urban instinct for temporary advantage. But Casterbridge/Dorchester is also specifically characterized as an *agricultural* town:

> There was no suburb in the modern sense, or transitional intermixture of town and down. It stood, with regard to the wide fertile land adjoining, clean-cut and distinct, like a chess-board on a green table-cloth. The farmer's boy could sit under his barley-mow and pitch a stone into the office-window of the town-clerk; reapers at work among the sheaves nodded to acquaintances standing on the pavement-corner; the red-robed judge, when he condemned a sheep-stealer, pronounced sentence to the tune of Baa, that floated in at the window from the remainder of the flock browsing hard by; and at executions the waiting crowd stood in a meadow immediately before the drop, out of which the cows had been temporarily driven to give the spectators room (pp. 87–88).

This superb passage reveals Hardy the ex-architect's genius for creating clear spatial pictures in the reader's head. The location of Lucetta's house right beside the marketplace; the two bridges at the end of town where the *misérables* contemplate their losses; the old Roman Amphitheatre; the seedy Mixen Lane—all these are described with the same vivid panache. If "character is fate," so (it would seem to Hardy) is geography.

The centrality of Casterbridge in the plot has been noted by one of Hardy's best biographers, Michael Millgate:

The whole structure of the novel, with its emphasis on arrivals and departures—Susan Henchard's, Farfrae's, Lucetta's, Newson's, Henchard's—serves to strengthen the impression of Casterbridge as a focal point, and the role played in the central action by the hay and corn trade and by the market-place itself, the town's physical and symbolic heart, works consistently to reinforce the importance of Casterbridge as what the novel calls "the pole, focus, or nerve-knot of the surrounding country life" (*Thomas Hardy: His Career as a Novelist*).

Yet for all the town's dynamism, the Casterbridgians themselves seem stuck in their ways. In order for the plot to move forward, some outsider must enter and stir things up: Henchard, Lucetta, Farfare, Elizabeth-Jane, even the villainous Jopp. Perhaps Hardy, as the returning native, felt he too had become an outsider during his years away, in London and elsewhere, and could only fully enter imaginatively the outsider's perspective.

The fact that he was more familiar with the Dorchester of several decades past than the present one may have also influenced his decision to set the story fifty or so years back, turning it into a period novel. He justified the decision in his preface to the 1912 edition:

The incidents narrated arise mainly out of three events, which chanced to range themselves in the order and at or about the intervals of time here given, in the real history of the town called Casterbridge and the neighbouring country. They were the sale of a wife by her husband, the uncertain harvests which immediately preceded the repeal of the Corn Laws, and the visit of a Royal personage to the aforesaid part of England (p. 3).

Beyond his fascination with all things past, this decision also allowed him to comment with novelistic detachment on the changing economic conditions of the area, by showing the quaint beginnings of a mechanized agricultural process that was well advanced by the time the book appeared.

In "The Dorsetshire Labourer," an article Hardy had written in 1883, a few years before he began *The Mayor of Casterbridge*, he had examined the situation of the laborer who was becoming divorced from the land and forced into more itinerant, migrant conditions.

That there were trade-offs, he scrupulously acknowledged: On the one hand, laborers were becoming worldlier and better paid; on the other hand, they were losing their roots and any attachment to a local environment and its rural culture. For decades, landowners had been tearing down workers' cottages, finding it easier to remove than repair them. "The occupants who formed the backbone of village life have to seek refuge in the boroughs. The process, which is designated by statisticians as 'the tendency of the rural population towards the large towns,' is really the tendency of water to flow uphill when forced," Hardy the essayist remarked sardonically.

Michael Henchard may be seen as Hardy's fictional representative for this sociological quandary. At the beginning, Henchard, seeking work or at least a place to stay, is told discouragingly: "Pulling down is more the nater of Weydon. There were five houses cleared away last year, and three this; and the volk nowhere to go—no, not so much as a thatched hurdle; that's the way o' Weydon-Priors" (p. 7). Freed from the pressures to be family breadwinner, Henchard transforms himself into a successful member of that small, entrepreneurial, wealthy peasant class who profited from the fluid conditions of the Corn Laws. Hardy lets us see that many farm laborers fared less well, by sharply portraying the unemployed idlers and poachers who frequent the tavern at Mixen Lane. The novel also has a passage about an old, redundant journeyman at the hiring fair that practically mirrors one in his earlier essay "The Dorsetshire Labourer."

Henchard is an ex-journeyman who has risen from the ranks to control all the grain deals in the area; when he falls from wealth, he picks up his rudimentary hay-trussing tools and returns to his ancient trade. By contrast, Farfrae, his right-hand man and ultimately his supplanter, is the one who introduces new agricultural implements, such as the horse-drill. "Then the romance of the sower is gone for good," observes Elizabeth-Jane, invoking the biblical image. Hardy is no sentimental Luddite; he sees the advent of labor-saving farm machinery as unavoidable and salutary. But he also sees that this will bring about problematic changes in managerial style. Henchard, who sprang roughly from the same class as his hirelings, alternately takes care of their aging mothers and disciplines the men personally. When Abel Whittle shows a tendency to be unpunctual, Henchard goes to the laborer's cottage one morning, pulls him out of bed and forces him to proceed to work without breeches. Such barbaric treatment horrifies the younger Farfrae, who intervenes to save the poor man's dignity. (Curiously, this same humiliated Abel later ministers to Henchard in his dying hour, like the fool attending Lear on the heath.) When Farfrae takes over the business, he pays the workers less but also frightens them less. His style is more impersonal, rational, and corporate, one might say. Sociologically, Henchard may be seen as a transitional figure who can advance only so far in the about-to-be industrialized landscape, before his old-fashioned, artisanal values get the better of him. Farfrae is the New Man, who will adjust.

That Hardy chose to write a novel about a journeyman farmhand (however high up the social ladder he ascends) was, by itself, fairly daring. There were precedents in English fiction for laborer-heroes, such as George Eliot's *Adam Bede*, but not many; and publishers were initially leery about releasing *The Mayor of Casterbridge* in a hardbound volume, as Hardy later bitterly recalled, because it was felt "the lack of gentry among the characters made it uninteresting—a typical estimate of what was, or was supposed to be, mid-Victorian taste."

Hardy did not lose heart, but continued to extend the compass of adult realism in the English novel, and to provoke the proprieties of class and sex, as we know from the controversies that attended *Tess* and *Jude*. In *The Mayor of Casterbridge*, he was faced with having to determine how explicitly he should handle the original affair between Henchard and Lucetta: Fudging their relationship in the serial version, he decided in the final book form to make it clear they had been intimate.

Virginia Woolf thought that "above all in *The Mayor of Casterbridge*, we have Hardy's impression of life as it came to him without conscious ordering" ("The Novels of Thomas Hardy"). Here he meddled least, or weighted the scales least. Woolf (and she was not alone) felt that Hardy too often had a tendency to impose large, abstractly pessimistic structures on his later novels. The criticism was not merely that he was sinning against the sunny norms of Victorian sentiment but that he brought a programmatic, mechanistic heavy-handedness to his philosophical pessimism. This is what Woolf meant when she said that "at his greatest he gives us impressions; at his weakest, arguments . . . and, above all, in *The Mayor of Casterbridge*,

The Wessex of The Novels.

THE MAYOR OF
CASTERBRIDGE

PREFACE

READERS OF THE FOLLOWING story who have not yet arrived at middle age are asked to bear in mind that, in the days recalled by the tale, the home Corn Trade, on which so much of the action turns, had an importance that can hardly be realized by those accustomed to the sixpenny loaf of the present date, and to the present indifference of the public to harvest weather.

The incidents narrated arise mainly out of three events, which chanced to range themselves in the order and at or about the intervals of time here given, in the real history of the town called Casterbridge* and the neighbouring country. They were the sale of a wife by her husband, the uncertain harvests which immediately preceded the repeal of the Corn Laws,† and the visit of a Royal personage‡ to the aforesaid part of England.

The present edition of the volume, like the previous one, contains nearly a chapter which did not at first appear in any English copy, though it was printed in the serial issue of the tale, and in the American edition. The restoration was made at the instance of some good judges across the Atlantic, who strongly represented that the home edition suffered from the omission. Some shorter passages and names, omitted or altered for reasons which no longer exist, in the original printing of both English and American editions, have also been replaced or inserted.

The story is more particularly a study of one man's deeds and character than, perhaps, any other of those included in my Exhibition of Wessex life. Objections have been raised to the Scotch language of Mr. Farfrae, the second character; and one of his fellow-countrymen went so far as to declare that men beyond the Tweed did not and never could say "warrld," "cannet," "advairrtisment," and so on. As

---

*Hardy's fictional name for Dorchester.
†Protectionist laws, in effect from 1815 to 1846, designed to restrict the importing of cheap foreign corn (grain).
‡Prince Albert, who traveled through area in which the novel is set in 1849.

this gentleman's pronunciation in correcting me seemed to my Southron ear an exact repetition of what my spelling implied, I was not struck with the truth of his remark, and somehow we did not get any forwarder in the matter. It must be remembered that the Scotchman of the tale is represented not as he would appear to other Scotchmen, but as he would appear to people of outer regions. Moreover, no attempt is made herein to reproduce his entire pronunciation phonetically, any more than that of the Wessex speakers. I should add, however, that this new edition of the book has had the accidental advantage of a critical overlooking by a professor of the tongue in question—one of undoubted authority:—in fact he is a gentleman who adopted it for urgent personal reasons in the first year of his existence.

Furthermore, a charming non-Scottish lady, of strict veracity and admitted penetration, the wife of a well-known Caledonian, came to the writer shortly after the story was first published, and inquired if Farfrae were not drawn from her husband, for he seemed to her to be the living portrait of that (doubtless) happy man. It happened that I had never thought of her husband in constructing Farfrae. I trust therefore that Farfrae may be allowed to pass, if not as a Scotchman to Scotchmen, as a Scotchman to Southerners.

The novel was first published complete, in two volumes, in May 1886.

T. H.
February 1895—May 1912.

I

ONE EVENING OF LATE summer, before the nineteenth century had reached one-third of its span, a young man and woman, the latter carrying a child, were approaching the large village of Weydon-Priors, in Upper Wessex, on foot. They were plainly but not ill clad, though the thick hoar of dust which had accumulated on their shoes and garments from an obviously long journey lent a disadvantageous shabbiness to their appearance just now.

The man was of fine figure, swarthy, and stern in aspect; and he showed in profile a facial angle so slightly inclined as to be almost perpendicular. He wore a short jacket of brown corduroy, newer than the remainder of his suit, which was a fustian* waistcoat with white horn buttons, breeches of the same, tanned leggings, and a straw hat overlaid with black glazed canvas. At his back he carried by a looped strap a rush basket, from which protruded at one end the crutch of a hay-knife, a wimble† for hay-bonds being also visible in the aperture. His measured, springless walk was the walk of the skilled country-man as distinct from the desultory shamble of the general labourer; while in the turn and plant of each foot there was, further, a dogged and cynical indifference personal to himself, showing its presence even in the regularly interchanging fustian folds, now in the left leg, now in the right, as he paced along.

What was really peculiar, however, in this couple's progress, and would have attracted the attention of any casual observer otherwise disposed to overlook them, was the perfect silence they preserved. They walked side by side in such a way as to suggest afar off the low, easy, confidential chat of people full of reciprocity; but on closer view it could be discerned that the man was reading, or pretending to read, a ballad sheet‡ which he kept before his eyes with some diffi-culty by the hand that was passed through the basket strap. Whether

---

*Thick cotton material.
†Tool for combining hay strands into ropes to be used in tying bundles of hay.
‡ Cheap printed sheet containing popular songs and news.

this apparent cause were the real cause, or whether it were an assumed one to escape an intercourse that would have been irksome to him, nobody but himself could have said precisely; but his taciturnity was unbroken, and the woman enjoyed no society whatever from his presence. Virtually she walked the highway alone, save for the child she bore. Sometimes the man's bent elbow almost touched her shoulder, for she kept as close to his side as was possible without actual contact; but she seemed to have no idea of taking his arm, nor he of offering it; and far from exhibiting surprise at his ignoring silence she appeared to receive it as a natural thing. If any word at all were uttered by the little group, it was an occasional whisper of the woman to the child—a tiny girl in short clothes and blue boots of knitted yarn—and the murmured babble of the child in reply.

The chief—almost the only—attraction of the young woman's face was its mobility. When she looked down sideways to the girl she became pretty, and even handsome, particularly that in the action her features caught slantwise the rays of the strongly coloured sun, which made transparencies of her eyelids and nostrils and set fire on her lips. When she plodded on in the shade of the hedge, silently thinking, she had the hard, half-apathetic expression of one who deems anything possible at the hands of Time and Chance except, perhaps, fair play. The first phase was the work of Nature, the second probably of civilization.

That the man and woman were husband and wife, and the parents of the girl in arms, there could be little doubt. No other than such relationship would have accounted for the atmosphere of stale familiarity which the trio carried along with them like a nimbus as they moved down the road.

The wife mostly kept her eyes fixed ahead, though with little interest—the scene for that matter being one that might have been matched at almost any spot in any county in England at this time of the year; a road neither straight nor crooked, neither level nor hilly, bordered by hedges, trees, and other vegetation, which had entered the blackened-green stage of colour that the doomed leaves pass through on their way to dingy, and yellow, and red. The grassy margin of the bank, and the nearest hedgerow boughs, were powdered by the dust that had been stirred over them by hasty vehicles, the same dust as it lay on the road deadening their footfalls like a carpet;

and this, with the aforesaid total absence of conversation, allowed every extraneous sound to be heard.

For a long time there was none, beyond the voice of a weak bird singing a trite old evening song that might doubtless have been heard on the hill at the same hour, and with the self-same trills, quavers, and breves, at any sunset of that season for centuries untold. But as they approached the village sundry distant shouts and rattles reached their ears from some elevated spot in that direction, as yet screened from view by foliage. When the outlying houses of Weydon-Priors could just be descried, the family group was met by a turnip-hoer with his hoe on his shoulder, and his dinner-bag suspended from it. The reader promptly glanced up.

"Any trade doing here?" he asked phlegmatically, designating the village in his van by a wave of the broadsheet. And thinking the labourer did not understand him, he added, "Anything in the hay-trussing line?"

The turnip-hoer had already begun shaking his head. "Why, save the man, what wisdom's in him that 'a should come to Weydon for a job of that sort this time o' year?"

"Then is there any house to let—a little small new cottage just a builded, or such like?" asked the other.

The pessimist still maintained a negative. "Pulling down is more the nater of Weydon. There were five houses cleared away last year, and three this; and the volk nowhere to go—no, not so much as a thatched hurdle; that's the way o' Weydon-Priors."

The hay-trusser, which he obviously was, nodded with some su-perciliousness. Looking towards the village, he continued, "There is something going on here, however, is there not?"

"Ay. 'Tis Fair Day. Though what you hear now is little more than the clatter and scurry of getting away the money o' children and fools, for the real business is done earlier than this. I've been work-ing within sound o't all day, but I didn't go up—not I. 'Twas no business of mine."

The trusser and his family proceeded on their way, and soon en-tered the Fair-field, which showed standing-places and pens where many hundreds of horses and sheep had been exhibited and sold in the forenoon, but were now in great part taken away. At present, as their informant had observed, but little real business remained on hand, the chief being the sale by auction of a few inferior animals, that could not otherwise be disposed of, and had been absolutely refused by the better class of traders, who came and went early. Yet the crowd was denser now than during the morning hours, the frivolous contingent of visitors, including journeymen out for a holiday, a stray soldier or two come on furlough, village shopkeepers, and the like, having latterly flocked in; persons whose activities found a congenial field among the peep-shows, toy-stands, waxworks, inspired monsters, disinterested medical men who travelled for the public good, thimble-riggers, nick-nack vendors, and readers of Fate.

Neither of our pedestrians had much heart for these things, and they looked around for a refreshment tent among the many which dotted the down. Two, which stood nearest to them in the ochreous haze of expiring sunlight, seemed almost equally inviting. One was formed of new, milk-hued canvas, and bore red flags on its summit; it announced "Good Home-brewed Beer, Ale, and Cyder." The other was less new; a little iron stove-pipe came out of it at the back, and in front appeared the placard, "Good Furmity Sold Hear." The man mentally weighed the two inscriptions, and inclined to the former tent.

"No—no—the other one," said the woman. "I always like furmity; and so does Elizabeth-Jane; and so will you. It is nourishing after a long hard day."

"I've never tasted it," said the man. However, he gave way to her representations, and they entered the furmity booth forthwith.

A rather numerous company appeared within, seated at the long narrow tables that ran down the tent on each side. At the upper end stood a stove, containing a charcoal fire, over which hung a large three-legged crock, sufficiently polished round the rim to show that it was made of bell-metal. A haggish creature of about fifty presided, in a white apron, which, as it threw an air of respectability over her as far as it extended, was made so wide as to reach nearly round her waist. She slowly stirred the contents of the pot. The dull scrape of her large spoon was audible throughout the tent as she thus kept from burning the mixture of corn in the grain, flour, milk, raisins, currants, and what not, that composed the antiquated slop in which she dealt. Vessels holding the separate ingredients stood on a white-clothed table of boards and trestles close by.

The young man and woman ordered a basin each of the mixture, steaming hot, and sat down to consume it at leisure. This was very well so far, for furmity, as the woman had said, was nourishing, and as proper a food as could be obtained within the four seas; though, to those not accustomed to it, the grains of wheat swollen as large as lemon-pips, which floated on its surface, might have a deterrent effect at first.

But there was more in that tent than met the cursory glance; and the man, with the instinct of a perverse character, scented it quickly. After a mincing attack on his bowl, he watched the hag's proceedings from the corner of his eye, and saw the game she played. He winked to her, and passed up his basin in reply to her nod; when she took a bottle from under the table, slily measured out a quantity of its contents, and tipped the same into the man's furmity. The liquor poured in was rum. The man as slily sent back money in payment.

He found the concoction, thus strongly laced, much more to his satisfaction than it had been in its natural state. His wife had observed the proceeding with much uneasiness; but he persuaded her to have hers laced also, and she agreed to a milder allowance after some misgiving.

The man finished his basin, and called for another, the rum being signalled for in yet stronger proportion. The effect of it was soon apparent in his manner, and his wife but too sadly perceived that in strenuously steering off the rocks of the licensed liquor-tent she had only got into maelstrom depths here amongst the smugglers.*

The child began to prattle impatiently, and the wife more than once said to her husband, "Michael, how about our lodging? You know we may have trouble in getting it if we don't go soon."

But he turned a deaf ear to those bird-like chirpings. He talked loud to the company. The child's black eyes, after slow, round, ruminating gazes at the candles when they were lighted, fell together; then they opened, then shut again, and she slept.

At the end of the first basin the man had risen to serenity; at the second he was jovial; at the third, argumentative; at the fourth, the qualities signified by the shape of his face, the occasional clench of

---

* The furmity woman has smuggled in her rum to avoid high import duties.

his mouth, and the fiery spark of his dark eye, began to tell in his conduct; he was overbearing—even brilliantly quarrelsome.

The conversation took a high turn, as it often does on such occasions. The ruin of good men by bad wives, and, more particularly, the frustration of many a promising youth's high aims and hopes and the extinction of his energies by an early imprudent marriage, was the theme.

"I did for myself that way thoroughly," said the trusser, with a contemplative bitterness that was well-nigh resentful. "I married at eighteen, like the fool that I was; and this is the consequence o't." He pointed at himself and family with a wave of the hand intended to bring out the penuriousness of the exhibition.

The young woman his wife, who seemed accustomed to such remarks, acted as if she did not hear them, and continued her intermittent private words on tender trifles to the sleeping and waking child, who was just big enough to be placed for a moment on the bench beside her when she wished to ease her arms. The man continued—

"I haven't more than fifteen shillings in the world, and yet I am a good experienced hand in my line. I'd challenge England to beat me in the fodder business; and if I were a free man again I'd be worth a thousand pound before I'd done o't. But a fellow never knows these little things till all chance of acting upon 'em is past."

The auctioneer selling the old horses in the field outside could be heard saying, "Now this is the last lot—now who'll take the last lot for a song? Shall I say forty shillings? 'Tis a very promising broodmare, a trifle over five years old, and nothing the matter with the hoss at all, except that she's a little holler in the back and had her left eye knocked out by the kick of another, her own sister, coming along the road."

"For my part I don't see why men who have got wives and don't want 'em, shouldn't get rid of 'em as these gipsy fellows do their old horses," said the man in the tent. "Why shouldn't they put 'em up and sell 'em by auction to men who are in need of such articles? Hey? Why, begad, I'd sell mine this minute if anybody would buy her!"

"There's them that would do that," some of the guests replied, looking at the woman, who was by no means ill-favoured.

"True," said a smoking gentleman, whose coat had the fine polish about the collar, elbows, seams, and shoulder-blades that long-continued friction with grimy surfaces will produce, and which is usually more desired on furniture than on clothes. From his appearance he had possibly been in former time groom or coachman to some neighbouring county family. "I've had my breedings in as good circles, I may say, as any man," he added, "and I know true cultivation, or nobody do; and I can declare she's got it—in the bone, mind ye, I say—as much as any female in the fair—though it may want a little bringing out." Then, crossing his legs, he resumed his pipe with a nicely-adjusted gaze at a point in the air.

The fuddled young husband stared for a few seconds at this unexpected praise of his wife, half in doubt of the wisdom of his own attitude towards the possessor of such qualities. But he speedily lapsed into his former conviction, and said harshly—

"Well, then, now is your chance; I am open to an offer for this gem o' creation."

She turned to her husband and murmured, "Michael, you have talked this nonsense in public places before. A joke is a joke, but you may make it once too often, mind!"

"I know I've said it before; I meant it. All I want is a buyer."

At the moment a swallow, one among the last of the season, which had by chance found its way through an opening into the upper part of the tent, flew to and fro in quick curves above their heads, causing all eyes to follow it absently. In watching the bird till it made its escape the assembled company neglected to respond to the workman's offer, and the subject dropped.

But a quarter of an hour later the man, who had gone on lacing his furmity more and more heavily, though he was either so strong-minded or such an intrepid toper that he still appeared fairly sober, recurred to the old strain, as in a musical fantasy the instrument fetches up the original theme. "Here—I am waiting to know about this offer of mine. The woman is no good to me. Who'll have her?"

The company had by this time decidedly degenerated, and the renewed inquiry was received with a laugh of appreciation. The woman whispered; she was imploring and anxious: "Come, come, it is getting dark, and this nonsense won't do. If you don't come along, I shall go without you. Come!"

She waited and waited; yet he did not move. In ten minutes the man broke in upon the desultory conversation of the furmity drinkers with, "I asked this question, and nobody answered to 't. Will any Jack Rag or Tom Straw among ye buy my goods?"

The woman's manner changed, and her face assumed the grim shape and colour of which mention has been made.

"Mike, Mike," said she; "this is getting serious. O!—too serious!"

"Will anybody buy her?" said the man.

"I wish somebody would," said she firmly. "Her present owner is not at all to her liking!"

"Nor you to mine," said he. "So we are agreed about that. Gentlemen, you hear? It's an agreement to part. She shall take the girl if she wants to, and go her ways. I'll take my tools, and go my ways. 'Tis simple as Scripture history. Now then, stand up, Susan, and show yourself."

"Don't, my chiel," whispered a buxom staylace dealer in voluminous petticoats, who sat near the woman; "yer good man don't know what he's saying."

The woman, however, did stand up. "Now, who's auctioneer?" cried the hay-trusser.

"I be," promptly answered a short man, with a nose resembling a copper knob, a damp voice, and eyes like button-holes. "Who'll make an offer for this lady?"

The woman looked on the ground, as if she maintained her position by a supreme effort of will.

"Five shillings," said some one, at which there was a laugh.

"No insults," said the husband. "Who'll say a guinea?"

Nobody answered; and the female dealer in staylaces interposed.

"Behave yerself moral, good man, for Heaven's love! Ah, what a cruelty is the poor soul married to! Bed and board is dear at some figures, 'pon my 'vation* 'tis!"

"Set it higher, auctioneer," said the trusser.

"Two guineas!" said the auctioneer; and no one replied.

"If they don't take her for that, in ten seconds they'll have to give more," said the husband. "Very well. Now, auctioneer, add another."

"Three guineas—going for three guineas!" said the rheumy man.

---

*Salvation.

"No bid?" said the husband. "Good Lord, why she's cost me fifty times the money, if a penny. Go on."

"Four guineas!" cried the auctioneer.

"I'll tell ye what—I won't sell her for less than five," said the husband, bringing down his fist so that the basins danced. "I'll sell her for five guineas to any man that will pay me the money, and treat her well; and he shall have her for ever, and never hear aught o' me. But she shan't go for less. Now then—five guineas—and she's yours. Susan, you agree?"

She bowed her head with absolute indifference.

"Five guineas," said the auctioneer, "or she'll be withdrawn. Do anybody give it? The last time. Yes or no?"

"Yes," said a loud voice from the doorway.

All eyes were turned. Standing in the triangular opening which formed the door of the tent was a sailor, who, unobserved by the rest, had arrived there within the last two or three minutes. A dead silence followed his affirmation.

"You say you do?" asked the husband, staring at him.

"I say so," replied the sailor.

"Saying is one thing, and paying is another. Where's the money?"

The sailor hesitated a moment, looked anew at the woman, came in, unfolded five crisp pieces of paper, and threw them down upon the table-cloth. They were Bank-of-England notes for five pounds. Upon the face of this he chinked down the shillings severally—one, two, three, four, five.

The sight of real money in full amount, in answer to a challenge for the same till then deemed slightly hypothetical, had a great effect upon the spectators. Their eyes became riveted upon the faces of the chief actors, and then upon the notes as they lay, weighted by the shillings, on the table.

Up to this moment it could not positively have been asserted that the man, in spite of his tantalizing declaration, was really in earnest. The spectators had indeed taken the proceedings throughout as a piece of mirthful irony carried to extremes; and had assumed that, being out of work, he was, as a consequence, out of temper with the world, and society, and his nearest kin. But with the demand and re-sponse of real cash the jovial frivolity of the scene departed. A lurid colour seemed to fill the tent, and change the aspect of all therein.

The mirth-wrinkles left the listeners' faces, and they waited with parting lips.

"Now," said the woman, breaking the silence, so that her low dry voice sounded quite loud, "before you go further, Michael, listen to me. If you touch that money, I and this girl go with the man. Mind, it is a joke no longer."

"A joke? Of course it is not a joke!" shouted her husband, his resentment rising at her suggestion. "I take the money: the sailor takes you. That's plain enough. It has been done elsewhere—and why not here?"

" 'Tis quite on the understanding that the young woman is willing," said the sailor blandly. "I wouldn't hurt her feelings for the world."

"Faith, nor I," said her husband. "But she is willing, provided she can have the child. She said so only the other day when I talked o't!"

"That you swear?" said the sailor to her.

"I do," said she, after glancing at her husband's face and seeing no repentance there.

"Very well, she shall have the child, and the bargain's complete," said the trusser. He took the sailor's notes and deliberately folded them, and put them with the shillings in a high remote pocket, with an air of finality.

The sailor looked at the woman and smiled. "Come along!" he said kindly. "The little one too—the more the merrier!" She paused for an instant, with a close glance at him. Then dropping her eyes again, and saying nothing, she took up the child and followed him as he made towards the door. On reaching it, she turned, and pulling off her wedding-ring, flung it across the booth in the hay-trusser's face.

"Mike," she said, "I've lived with thee a couple of years, and had nothing but temper! Now I'm no more to 'ee; I'll try my luck elsewhere. 'Twill be better for me and Elizabeth-Jane, both. So goodbye!"

Seizing the sailor's arm with her right hand, and mounting the little girl on her left, she went out of the tent sobbing bitterly.

A stolid look of concern filled the husband's face, as if, after all, he had not quite anticipated this ending; and some of the guests laughed.

"Is she gone?" he said.

"Faith, ay; she's gone clane enough," said some rustics near the door.

He rose and walked to the entrance with the careful tread of one conscious of his alcoholic load. Some others followed, and they stood looking into the twilight. The difference between the peacefulness of inferior nature and the wilful hostilities of mankind was very apparent at this place. In contrast with the harshness of the act just ended within the tent was the sight of several horses crossing their necks and rubbing each other lovingly as they waited in patience to be harnessed for the homeward journey. Outside the fair, in the valleys and woods, all was quiet. The sun had recently set, and the west heaven was hung with rosy cloud, which seemed permanent, yet slowly changed. To watch it was like looking at some grand feat of stagery from a darkened auditorium. In presence of this scene after the other there was a natural instinct to abjure man as the blot on an otherwise kindly universe; till it was remembered that all terrestrial conditions were intermittent, and that mankind might some night be innocently sleeping when these quiet objects were raging loud.

"Where do the sailor live?" asked a spectator, when they had vainly gazed around.

"God knows that," replied the man who had seen high life. "He's without doubt a stranger here."

"He came in about five minutes ago," said the furmity-woman, joining the rest with her hands on her hips. "And then 'a stepped back, and then 'a looked in again. I'm not a penny the better for him."

"Serves the husband well be-right," said the staylace vendor. "A comely respectable body like her—what can a man want more? I glory in the woman's sperrit. I'd ha' done it myself—od send if I wouldn't, if a husband had behaved so to me! I'd go, and 'a might call, and call, till his keacorn* was raw; but I'd never come back—no, not till the great trumpet,† would I!"

"Well, the woman will be better off," said another of a more deliberative turn. "For seafaring natures be very good shelter for shorn

---

*Throat.
†The trumpet heralding Judgment Day.

lambs, and the man do seem to have plenty of money, which is what she's not been used to lately, by all showings."

"Mark me—I'll not go after her!" said the trusser, returning doggedly to his seat. "Let her go! If she's up to such vagaries she must suffer for 'em. She'd no business to take the maid—'tis my maid; and if it were the doing again she shouldn't have her!"

Perhaps from some little sense of having countenanced an indefensible proceeding, perhaps because it was late, the customers thinned away from the tent shortly after this episode. The man stretched his elbows forward on the table, leant his face upon his arms, and soon began to snore. The furmity-seller decided to close for the night, and after seeing the rum-bottles, milk, corn, raisins, etc., that remained on hand, loaded into the cart, came to where the man reclined. She shook him, but could not wake him. As the tent was not to be struck that night, the fair continuing for two or three days, she decided to let the sleeper, who was obviously no tramp, stay where he was, and his basket with him. Extinguishing the last candle, and lowering the flap of the tent, she left it, and drove away.

II

THE MORNING SUN WAS streaming through the crevices of the canvas when the man awoke. A warm glow pervaded the whole atmosphere of the marquee, and a single big blue fly buzzed musically round and round it. Besides the buzz of the fly there was not a sound. He looked about—at the benches—at the table supported by trestles—at his basket of tools—at the stove where the furmity had been boiled—at the empty basins—at some shed grains of wheat—at the corks which dotted the grassy floor. Among the odds and ends he discerned a little shining object, and picked it up. It was his wife's ring.

A confused picture of the events of the previous evening seemed to come back to him, and he thrust his hand into his breast-pocket. A rustling revealed the sailor's bank-notes thrust carelessly in.

This second verification of his dim memories was enough; he knew now they were not dreams. He remained seated, looking on the ground for some time. "I must get out of this as soon as I can," he said deliberately at last, with the air of one who could not catch his thoughts without pronouncing them. "She's gone—to be sure she is—gone with that sailor who bought her, and little Elizabeth-Jane. We walked here, and I had the furmity, and rum in it—and sold her. Yes, that's what's happened, and here am I. Now, what am I to do— am I sober enough to walk, I wonder?" He stood up, found that he was in fairly good condition for progress, unencumbered. Next he shouldered his tool basket, and found he could carry it. Then lifting the tent door he emerged into the open air.

Here the man looked around with gloomy curiosity. The freshness of the September morning inspired and braced him as he stood. He and his family had been weary when they arrived the night before, and they had observed but little of the place; so that he now beheld it as a new thing. It exhibited itself as the top of an open down, bounded on one extreme by a plantation, and approached by a winding road. At the bottom stood the village which lent its name to the upland and the annual fair that was held thereon. The spot stretched downward into valleys, and onward to other uplands, dotted with barrows,* and trenched with the remains of prehistoric forts. The whole scene lay under the rays of a newly risen sun, which had not as yet dried a single blade of the heavily dewed grass, whereon the shadows of the yellow and red vans were projected far away, those thrown by the felloe† of each wheel being elongated in shape to the orbit of a comet. All the gipsies and showmen who had remained on the ground lay snug within their carts and tents, or wrapped in horse-cloths under them, and were silent and still as death, with the exception of an occasional snore that revealed their presence. But the Seven Sleepers had a dog;[1] and dogs of the mysterious breeds that vagrants own, that are as much like cats as dogs and as much like foxes as cats, also lay about here. A little one started up under one of the carts, barked as a matter of principle, and quickly lay down again. He was the only positive spectator of the hay-trusser's exit from the Weydon Fair-field.

This seemed to accord with his desire. He went on in silent

---

*A barrow is a mound of earth erected over a grave.
†Rim.

thought, unheeding the yellowhammers which flitted about the hedges with straws in their bills, the crowns of the mushrooms, and the tinkling of local sheep-bells, whose wearers had had the good fortune not to be included in the fair. When he reached a lane, a good mile from the scene of the previous evening, the man pitched his basket and leant upon a gate. A difficult problem or two occupied his mind.

"Did I tell my name to anybody last night, or didn't I tell my name?" he said to himself; and at last concluded that he did not. His general demeanour was enough to show how he was surprised and nettled that his wife had taken him so literally—as much could be seen in his face, and in the way he nibbled a straw which he pulled from the hedge. He knew that she must have been somewhat excited to do this; moreover, she must have believed that there was some sort of binding force in the transaction. On this latter point he felt almost certain, knowing her freedom from levity of character, and the extreme simplicity of her intellect. There may, too, have been enough recklessness and resentment beneath her ordinary placidity to make her stifle any momentary doubts. On a previous occasion when he had declared during a fuddle that he would dispose of her as he had done, she had replied that she would not hear him say that many times more before it happened, in the resigned tones of a fatalist. . . . "Yet she knows I am not in my senses when I do that!" he exclaimed. "Well, I must walk about till I find her. . . . Seize her, why didn't she know better than bring me into this disgrace!" he roared out. "She wasn't queer if I was. 'Tis like Susan to show such idiotic simplicity. Meek—that meekness has done me more harm than the bitterest temper!"

When he was calmer he turned to his original conviction that he must somehow find her and his little Elizabeth-Jane, and put up with the shame as best he could. It was of his own making, and he ought to bear it. But first he resolved to register an oath, a greater oath than he had ever sworn before: and to do it properly he required a fit place and imagery; for there was something fetichistic* in this man's beliefs.

He shouldered his basket and moved on, casting his eyes inquis-

---

*Superstitious.

itively round upon the landscape as he walked, and at the distance of three or four miles perceived the roofs of a village and the tower of a church. He instantly made towards the latter object. The village was quite still, it being that motionless hour of rustic daily life which fills the interval between the departure of the field-labourers to their work, and the rising of their wives and daughters to prepare the breakfast for their return. Hence he reached the church without observation, and the door being only latched he entered. The hay-trusser deposited his basket by the font, went up the nave till he reached the altar-rails, and opening the gate entered the sacrarium,* where he seemed to feel a sense of the strangeness for a moment; then he knelt upon the foot-pace.† Dropping his head upon the clamped book which lay on the Communion-table, he said aloud—

"I, Michael Henchard, on this morning of the sixteenth of September, do take an oath before God here in this solemn place that I will avoid all strong liquors for the space of twenty-one years to come, being a year for every year that I have lived. And this I swear upon the book before me; and may I be strook dumb, blind, and helpless, if I break this my oath!"

When he had said it and kissed the big book, the hay-trusser arose, and seemed relieved at having made a start in a new direction. While standing in the porch a moment he saw a thick jet of wood smoke suddenly start up from the red chimney of a cottage near, and knew that the occupant had just lit her fire. He went round to the door, and the housewife agreed to prepare him some breakfast for a trifling payment, which was done. Then he started on the search for his wife and child.

The perplexing nature of the undertaking became apparent soon enough. Though he examined and inquired, and walked hither and thither day after day, no such characters as those he described had any where been seen since the evening of the fair. To add to the difficulty he could gain no sound of the sailor's name. As money was short with him he decided, after some hesitation, to spend the sailor's money in the prosecution of this search; but it was equally in vain. The truth was that a certain shyness of revealing his conduct pre-

---

*Area surrounding the altar.
†Space immediately before the altar.

vented Michael Henchard from following up the investigation with the loud hue-and-cry such a pursuit demanded to render it effectual; and it was probably for this reason that he obtained no clue, though everything was done by him that did not involve an explanation of the circumstances under which he had lost her.

Weeks counted up to months, and still he searched on, maintaining himself by small jobs of work in the intervals. By this time he had arrived at a seaport, and there he derived intelligence that persons answering somewhat to his description had emigrated a little time before. Then he said he would search no longer, and that he would go and settle in the district which he had had for some time in his mind. Next day he started, journeying south-westward, and did not pause, except for nights' lodgings, till he reached the town of Casterbridge, in a far distant part of Wessex.

III

THE HIGHROAD INTO THE village of Weydon-Priors was again carpeted with dust. The trees had put on as of yore their aspect of dingy green, and where the Henchard family of three had once walked along, two persons not unconnected with that family walked now.

The scene in its broad aspect had so much of its previous character, even to the voices and rattle from the neighbouring village down, that it might for that matter have been the afternoon following the previously recorded episode. Change was only to be observed in details; but here it was obvious that a long procession of years had passed by. One of the two who walked the road was she who had figured as the young wife of Henchard on the previous occasion; now her face had lost much of its rotundity; her skin had undergone a textural change; and though her hair had not lost colour it was considerably thinner than heretofore. She was dressed in the mourning clothes of a widow. Her companion, also in black, appeared as a well-formed young woman about eighteen, completely possessed of that ephemeral precious essence youth, which is itself beauty, irrespective of complexion or contour.

A glance was sufficient to inform the eye that this was Susan Henchard's grown-up daughter. While life's middle summer had set its hardening mark on the mother's face, her former spring-like specialities were transferred so dexterously by Time to the second figure, her child, that the absence of certain facts within her mother's knowledge from the girl's mind would have seemed for the moment, to one reflecting on those facts, to be a curious imperfection in Nature's powers of continuity.

They walked with joined hands, and it could be perceived that this was the act of simple affection. The daughter carried in her outer hand a withy basket* of old-fashioned make; the mother a blue bundle, which contrasted oddly with her black stuff gown.

Reaching the outskirts of the village they pursued the same track as formerly, and ascended to the fair. Here, too, it was evident that the years had told. Certain mechanical improvements might have been noticed in the roundabouts and highfliers, machines for testing rustic strength and weight, and in the erections devoted to shooting for nuts. But the real business of the fair had considerably dwindled. The new periodical great markets of neighbouring towns were beginning to interfere seriously with the trade carried on here for centuries. The pens for sheep, the tie-ropes for horses, were about half as long as they had been. The stalls of tailors, hosiers, coopers,† linen-drapers, and other such trades had almost disappeared, and the vehicles were far less numerous. The mother and daughter threaded the crowd for some little distance, and then stood still.

"Why did we hinder our time by coming in here? I thought you wished to get onward?" said the maiden.

"Yes, my dear Elizabeth-Jane," explained the other. "But I had a fancy for looking up here."

"Why?"

"It was here I first met with Newson—on such a day as this."

"First met with father here? Yes, you have told me so before. And now he's drowned and gone from us!" As she spoke the girl drew a card from her pocket and looked at it with a sigh. It was edged with black, and inscribed within a design resembling a mural tablet were

---

*Basket made of willow branches.
†Barrel-makers.

the words, "In affectionate memory of Richard Newson, mariner, who was unfortunately lost at sea, in the month of November 184—, aged forty-one years."

"And it was here," continued her mother, with more hesitation, "that I last saw the relation we are going to look for—Mr. Michael Henchard."

"What is his exact kin to us, mother? I have never clearly had it told me."

"He is, or was—for he may be dead—a connection by marriage," said her mother deliberately.

"That's exactly what you have said a score of times before!" replied the young woman, looking about her inattentively. "He's not a near relation, I suppose?"

"Not by any means."

"He was a hay-trusser, wasn't he, when you last heard of him?"

"He was."

"I suppose he never knew me?" the girl innocently continued.

Mrs. Henchard paused for a moment, and answered uneasily, "Of course not, Elizabeth-Jane. But come this way." She moved on to another part of the field.

"It is not much use inquiring here for anybody, I should think," the daughter observed, as she gazed round about. "People at fairs change like the leaves of trees; and I daresay you are the only one here to-day who was here all those years ago."

"I am not so sure of that," said Mrs. Newson, as she now called herself, keenly eyeing something under a green bank a little way off. "See there."

The daughter looked in the direction signified. The object pointed out was a tripod of sticks stuck into the earth, from which hung a three-legged crock, kept hot by a smouldering wood fire beneath. Over the pot stooped an old woman, haggard, wrinkled, and almost in rags. She stirred the contents of the pot with a large spoon, and occasionally croaked in a broken voice, "Good furmity sold here!"

It was indeed the former mistress of the furmity tent—once thriving, cleanly, white-aproned, and chinking with money—now tentless, dirty, owning no tables or benches, and having scarce any customers except two small whity-brown boys, who came up and asked for "A ha'p'orth,* please—good measure," which she served in a couple of chipped yellow basins of commonest clay.

"She was here at that time," resumed Mrs. Newson, making a step as if to draw nearer.

"Don't speak to her—it isn't respectable!" urged the other.

"I will just say a word—you, Elizabeth-Jane, can stay here."

The girl was not loth, and turned to some stalls of coloured prints while her mother went forward. The old woman begged for the latter's custom as soon as she saw her, and responded to Mrs. Henchard-Newson's request for a pennyworth with more alacrity than she had shown in selling six-pennyworths in her younger days. When the *soidisant*† widow had taken the basin of thin poor slop that stood for the rich concoction of the former time, the hag opened a little basket behind the fire, and looking up slily, whispered, "Just a thought o' rum in it?—smuggled, you know—say two penn'orth— 'twill make it slip down like cordial!"

Her customer smiled bitterly at this survival of the old trick, and shook her head with a meaning the old woman was far from translating. She pretended to eat a little of the furmity with the leaden spoon offered, and as she did so said blandly to the hag, "You've seen better days?"

"Ah, ma'am—well ye may say it!" responded the old woman, opening the sluices of her heart forthwith. "I've stood in this fairground, maid, wife, and widow, these nine-and-thirty year, and in that time have known what it was to do business with the richest stomachs in the land! Ma'am, you'd hardly believe that I was once the owner of a great pavilion-tent that was the attraction of the fair. Nobody could come, nobody could go, without having a dish of Mrs. Goodenough's furmity. I knew the clergy's taste, the dandy gent's taste; I knew the town's taste, the country's taste. I even knowed the taste of the coarse shameless females. But Lord's my life—the world's no memory; straightforward dealings don't bring profit—'tis the sly and the underhand that get on in these times!"

Mrs. Newson glanced round—her daughter was still bending over the distant stalls. "Can you call to mind," she said cautiously to

---

*Half-penny's worth.
†Self-styled (French).

the old woman, "the sale of a wife by her husband in your tent eighteen years ago to-day?"

The hag reflected, and half shook her head. "If it had been a big thing I should have minded it in a moment," she said. "I can mind every serious fight o' married parties, every murder, every manslaughter, even every pocket-picking—leastwise large ones—that 't has been my lot to witness. But a selling? Was it done quiet-like?"

"Well, yes. I think so."

The furmity-woman half shook her head again. "And yet," she said, "I do. At any rate, I can mind a man doing something o' the sort—a man in a cord jacket, with a basket of tools; but, Lord bless ye, we don't gi'e it head-room, we don't, such as that. The only reason why I can mind the man is that he came back here to the next year's fair, and told me quite private-like that if a woman ever asked for him I was to say he had gone to—where?—Casterbridge—yes—to Casterbridge, said he. But, Lord's my life, I shouldn't ha' thought of it again!"

Mrs. Newson would have rewarded the old woman as far as her small means afforded had she not discreetly borne in mind that it was by that unscrupulous person's liquor her husband had been degraded. She briefly thanked her informant, and rejoined Elizabeth, who greeted her with, "Mother, do let's go on—it was hardly respectable for you to buy refreshments there. I see none but the lowest do."

"I have learned what I wanted, however," said her mother quietly. "The last time our relative visited this fair he said he was living at Casterbridge. It is a long, long way from here, and it was many years ago that he said it; but there I think we'll go."

With this they descended out of the fair, and went onward to the village, where they obtained a night's lodging.

IV

HENCHARD'S WIFE ACTED FOR the best, but she had involved herself in difficulties. A hundred times she had been upon the point of telling her daughter Elizabeth-Jane the true story of her life, the tragical crisis of which had been the transaction at Weydon Fair, when she was not much older than the girl now beside her. But she had refrained. An innocent maiden had thus grown up in the belief that the relations between the genial sailor and her mother were the ordinary ones that they had always appeared to be. The risk of endangering a child's strong affection by disturbing ideas which had grown with her growth was to Mrs. Henchard too fearful a thing to contemplate. It had seemed, indeed, folly to think of making Elizabeth-Jane wise.[2]

But Susan Henchard's fear of losing her dearly loved daughter's heart by a revelation had little to do with any sense of wrong-doing on her own part. Her simplicity—the original ground of Henchard's contempt for her—had allowed her to live on in the conviction that Newson had acquired a morally real and justifiable right to her by his purchase—though the exact bearings and legal limits of that right were vague. It may seem strange to sophisticated minds that a sane young matron could believe in the seriousness of such a transfer; and were there not numerous other instances of the same belief the thing might scarcely be credited. But she was by no means the first or last peasant woman who had religiously adhered to her purchaser, as too many rural records show.

The history of Susan Henchard's adventures in the interim can be told in two or three sentences. Absolutely helpless she had been taken off to Canada, where they had lived several years without any great worldly success, though she worked as hard as any woman could to keep their cottage cheerful and well-provided. When Elizabeth-Jane was about twelve years old the three returned to England, and settled at Falmouth, where Newson made a living for a few years as boatman and general handy shoreman.

He then engaged in the Newfoundland trade, and it was during this period that Susan had an awakening. A friend to whom she confided her history ridiculed her grave acceptance of her position; and all was over with her peace of mind. When Newson came home at the end of one winter he saw that the delusion he had so carefully sustained had vanished for ever.

There was then a time of sadness, in which she told him her doubts if she could live with him longer. Newson left home again on the Newfoundland trade when the season came round. The vague news of his loss at sea a little later on solved a problem which had become torture to her meek conscience. She saw him no more.

Of Henchard they heard nothing. To the liege subjects of Labour,* the England of those days was a continent, and a mile a geographical degree.†

Elizabeth-Jane developed early into womanliness. One day, a month or so after receiving intelligence of Newson's death off the Bank of Newfoundland, when the girl was about eighteen, she was sitting on a willow chair in the cottage they still occupied, working twine nets for the fishermen. Her mother was in a back corner of the same room, engaged in the same labour; and dropping the heavy wood needle she was filling she surveyed her daughter thoughtfully. The sun shone in at the door upon the young woman's head and hair, which was worn loose, so that the rays streamed into its depths as into a hazel copse. Her face, though somewhat wan and incomplete, possessed the raw materials of beauty in a promising degree. There was an under-handsomeness in it, struggling to reveal itself through the provisional curves of immaturity, and the casual disfigurements that resulted from the straitened circumstances of their lives. She was handsome in the bone, hardly as yet handsome in the flesh. She possibly might never be fully handsome, unless the carking‡ accidents of her daily existence could be evaded before the mobile parts of her countenance had settled to their final mould.

The sight of the girl made her mother sad—not vaguely, but by logical inference. They both were still in that strait-waistcoat of poverty from which she had tried so many times to be delivered for the girl's sake. The woman had long perceived how zealously and constantly the young mind of her companion was struggling for enlargement; and yet now, in her eighteenth year, it still remained but little unfolded. The desire—sober and repressed—of Elizabeth-Jane's heart was indeed to see, to hear, and to understand. How could she become a woman of wider knowledge, higher repute—"better," as she termed it—this was her constant inquiry of her mother. She

---

*Workers.
†Unit of measuring distance: 72 miles.
‡Fretting, wearying.

sought further into things than other girls in her position ever did, and her mother groaned as she felt she could not aid in the search.

The sailor, drowned or no, was probably now lost to them; and Susan's staunch, religious adherence to him as her husband in principle, till her views had been disturbed by enlightenment, was demanded no more. She asked herself whether the present moment, now that she was a free woman again, were not as opportune a one as she would find in a world where everything had been so inopportune, for making a desperate effort to advance Elizabeth. To pocket her pride and search for the first husband seemed, wisely or not, the best initiatory step. He had possibly drunk himself into his tomb. But he might, on the other hand, have had too much sense to do so; for in her time with him he had been given to bouts only, and was not a habitual drunkard.

At any rate, the propriety of returning to him, if he lived, was unquestionable. The awkwardness of searching for him lay in enlightening Elizabeth, a proceeding which her mother could not endure to contemplate. She finally resolved to undertake the search without confiding to the girl her former relations with Henchard, leaving it to him if they found him to take what steps he might choose to that end. This will account for their conversation at the fair and the half-informed state in which Elizabeth was led onward.

In this attitude they proceeded on their journey, trusting solely to the dim light afforded of Henchard's whereabouts by the furmity-woman. The strictest economy was indispensable. Sometimes they might have been seen on foot, sometimes on farmers' waggons, sometimes in carriers' vans; and thus they drew near to Casterbridge. Elizabeth-Jane discovered to her alarm that her mother's health was not what it once had been, and there was ever and anon in her talk that renunciatory tone which showed that, but for the girl, she would not be very sorry to quit a life she was growing thoroughly weary of.

It was on a Friday evening, near the middle of September, and just before dusk, that they reached the summit of a hill within a mile of the place they sought. There were high-banked hedges to the coach-road here, and they mounted upon the green turf within, and sat down. The spot commanded a full view of the town and its environs.

"What an old-fashioned place it seems to be!" said Elizabeth-

Jane, while her silent mother mused on other things than topography. "It is huddled all together; and it is shut in by a square wall of trees, like a plot of garden ground by a box-edging."

Its squareness was, indeed, the characteristic which most struck the eye in this antiquated borough, the borough of Casterbridge—at that time, recent as it was, untouched by the faintest sprinkle of modernism. It was compact as a box of dominoes. It had no suburbs—in the ordinary sense. Country and town met at a mathematical line.

To birds of the more soaring kind Casterbridge must have appeared on this fine evening as a mosaic-work of subdued reds, browns, greys, and crystals, held together by a rectangular frame of deep green. To the level eye of humanity it stood as an indistinct mass behind a dense stockade of limes and chestnuts, set in the midst of miles of rotund down and concave field. The mass became gradually dissected by the vision into towers, gables, chimneys, and casements, the highest glazings shining bleared and bloodshot with the coppery fire they caught from the belt of sunlit cloud in the west.

From the centre of each side of this tree-bound square ran avenues east, west, and south into the wide expanse of corn-land and coomb* to the distance of a mile or so. It was by one of these avenues that the pedestrians were about to enter. Before they had risen to proceed two men passed outside the hedge, engaged in argumentative conversation.

"Why, surely," said Elizabeth, as they receded, "those men mentioned the name of Henchard in their talk—the name of our relative?"

"I thought so too," said Mrs. Newson.

"That seems a hint to us that he is still here."

"Yes."

"Shall I run after them, and ask them about him——"

"No, no, no! Not for the world just yet. He may be in the workhouse, or in the stocks, for all we know."

"Dear me—why should you think that, mother?"

" 'Twas just something to say—that's all! But we must make private inquiries."

---

*Deep hollow on the side of a hill.

Having sufficiently rested they proceeded on their way at evenfall. The dense trees of the avenue rendered the road dark as a tunnel, though the open land on each side was still under a faint daylight; in other words, they passed down a midnight between two gloamings. The features of the town had a keen interest for Elizabeth's mother, now that the human side came to the fore. As soon as they had wandered about they could see that the stockade of gnarled trees which framed in Casterbridge was itself an avenue, standing on a low green bank or escarpment, with a ditch yet visible without. Within the avenue and bank was a wall more or less discontinuous, and within the wall were packed the abodes of the burghers.

Though the two women did not know it these external features were but the ancient defences of the town, planted as a promenade.

The lamplights now glimmered through the engirdling trees, conveying a sense of great snugness and comfort inside, and rendering at the same time the unlighted country without strangely solitary and vacant in aspect, considering its nearness to life. The difference between burgh and champaign* was increased, too, by sounds which now reached them above others—the notes of a brass band. The travellers returned into the High Street, where there were timber houses with overhanging stories, whose small-paned lattices were screened by dimity curtains on a drawing-string, and under whose bargeboards old cobwebs waved in the breeze. There were houses of brick-nogging,† which derived their chief support from those adjoining. There were slate roofs patched with tiles, and the roofs patched with slate, with occasionally a roof of thatch.

The agricultural and pastoral character of the people upon whom the town depended for its existence was shown by the class of objects displayed in the shop window. Scythes, reap-hooks, sheep-shears, bill-hooks, spades, mattocks, and hoes at the ironmonger's; beehives, butter-firkins, churns, milking stools and pails, hay-rakes, field-flagons, and seed-lips at cooper's; cart-ropes and plough-harness at the saddler's; carts, wheel-barrows, and mill-gear at the wheelwright's and machinist's; horse-embrocations at the chemist's;

---

*Town and country.
†*Barge-boards* covered protruding support beams; *brick-nogging* was timber framework filled in with brick.

at the glover's and leather-cutter's, hedging-gloves, thatchers' knee-caps, ploughmen's leggings, villagers' pattens* and clogs.

They came to a grizzled church, whose massive square tower rose unbroken into the darkening sky, the lower parts being illuminated by the nearest lamps sufficiently to show how completely the mortar from the joints of the stonework had been nibbled out by time and weather, which had planted in the crevices thus made little tufts of stone-crop and grass almost as far up as the very battlements. From this tower the clock struck eight, and thereupon a bell began to toll with a peremptory clang. The curfew was still rung in Casterbridge, and it was utilized by the inhabitants as a signal for shutting their shops. No sooner did the deep notes of the bell throb between the house-fronts than a clatter of shutters arose through the whole length of the High Street. In a few minutes business at Casterbridge was ended for the day.

Other clocks struck eight from time to time—one gloomily from the gaol, another from the gable of an almshouse, with a preparative creak of machinery, more audible than the note of the bell; a row of tall, varnished case-clocks from the interior of a clockmaker's shop joined in one after another just as the shutters were enclosing them, like a row of actors delivering their final speeches before the fall of the curtain; then chimes were heard stammering out the Sicilian Mariners' Hymn;† so that chronologists of the advanced school were appreciably on their way to the next hour before the whole business of the old one was satisfactorily wound up.

In an open space before the church walked a woman with her gown-sleeves rolled up so high that the edge of her under-linen was visible, and her skirt tucked up through her pocket hole. She carried a loaf under her arm from which she was pulling pieces of bread, and handing them to some other women who walked with her; which pieces they nibbled critically. The sight reminded Mrs. Henchard-Newson and her daughter that they had an appetite; and they inquired of the woman for the nearest baker's.

---

*Bill-hooks: hooked knives; *mattocks*: tools used to loosen hard ground; *butter-firkins*: small casks for butter; *field-flagons*: bottles in which field workers carried beer; *seed-lips*: baskets used to carry seed; *horse-embrocations*: medicinal ointments used on diseased horses; *pattens*: wooden overshoes.

†Traditional tune to which various religious lyrics were set.

"Ye may as well look for manna-food* as good bread in Caster-bridge just now," she said, after directing them. "They can blare their trumpets and thump their drums, and have their roaring dinners"—waving her hand towards a point further along the street, where the brass band could be seen standing in front of an illuminated build-ing—"but we must needs be put-to for want of a wholesome crust. There's less good bread than good beer in Casterbridge now."

"And less good beer than swipes,"† said a man with his hands in his pockets.

"How does it happen there's no good bread?" asked Mrs. Hen-chard.

"Oh, 'tis the corn-factor‡—he's the man that our millers and bakers all deal wi', and he has sold 'em growed wheat,§ which they didn't know was growed, so the say, till the dough ran all over the ovens like quicksilver; so that the loaves be as flat as toads, and like suet pudden inside. I've been a wife, and I've been a mother, and I never see such unprincipled bread in Casterbridge as this before.—But you must be a real stranger here not to know what's made all the poor volks' insides plim‖ like blowed bladders this week?"

"I am," said Elizabeth's mother shyly.

Not wishing to be observed further till she knew more of her fu-ture in this place, she withdrew with her daughter from the speaker's side. Getting a couple of biscuits at the shop indicated as a temporary substitute for a meal, they next bent their steps instinctively to where the music was playing.

---

*Food given to the Isrealites by God as they fled Egypt (Exodus 16:14–26).
†Weak beer.
‡Grain-dealer.
§Wheat that has already sprouted; bread made from this wheat is of poor quality.
‖Swell.

V

A FEW SCORE YARDS brought them to the spot where the town band was now shaking the window-panes with the strains of "The Roast Beef of Old England."*

The building before whose doors they had pitched their music-stands was the chief hotel in Casterbridge—namely, the King's Arms. A spacious bow-window projected into the street over the main portico, and from the open sashes came the babble of voices, the jingle of glasses, and the drawing of corks. The blinds, moreover, being left unclosed, the whole interior of this room could be surveyed from the top of a flight of stone steps to the road-waggon office opposite, for which reason a knot of idlers had gathered there.

"We might, perhaps, after all, make a few inquiries about—our relation Mr. Henchard," whispered Mrs. Newson who, since her entry into Casterbridge, had seemed strangely weak and agitated. "And this, I think, would be a good place for trying it—just to ask, you know, how he stands in the town—if he is here, as I think he must be. You, Elizabeth-Jane, had better be the one to do it. I'm too worn out to do anything—pull down your fall† first."

She sat down upon the lowest step, and Elizabeth-Jane obeyed her directions and stood among the idlers.

"What's going on to-night?" asked the girl, after singling out an old man and standing by him long enough to acquire a neighbourly right of converse.

"Well, ye must be a stranger sure," said the old man, without taking his eyes from the window. "Why, 'tis a great public dinner of the gentle-people and such-like leading volk—wi' the Mayor in the chair. As we plainer fellows bain't invited, they leave the winder-shutters open that we may get jist a sense o't out here. If you mount the steps you can see 'em. That's Mr. Henchard, the Mayor, at the end of the table, a facing ye; and that's the Council men right and left. . . . Ah, lots of them when they begun life were no more than I be now!"

"Henchard!" said Elizabeth-Jane, surprised, but by no means

---

*Song from Henry Fielding's *Grub-Street Opera* (1731).
†Veil.

32

suspecting the whole force of the revelation. She ascended to the top of the steps.

Her mother, though her head was bowed, had already caught from the inn-window tones that strangely riveted her attention, before the old man's words, "Mr. Henchard, the Mayor," reached her ears. She arose, and stepped up to her daughter's side as soon as she could do so without showing exceptional eagerness.

The interior of the hotel dining-room was spread out before her, with its tables, and glass, and plate, and inmates. Facing the window, in the chair of dignity, sat a man about forty years of age; of heavy frame, large features, and commanding voice; his general build being rather coarse than compact. He had a rich complexion, which verged on swarthiness, a flashing black eye, and dark, bushy brows and hair. When he indulged in an occasional loud laugh at some remark among the guests, his large mouth parted so far back as to show to the rays of the chandelier a full score or more of the two-and-thirty sound white teeth that he obviously still could boast of.

That laugh was not encouraging to strangers; and hence it may have been well that it was rarely heard. Many theories might have been built upon it. It fell in well with conjectures of a temperament which would have no pity for weakness, but would be ready to yield ungrudging admiration to greatness and strength. Its producer's personal goodness, if he had any, would be of a very fitful cast—an occasional almost oppressive generosity rather than a mild and constant kindness.

Susan Henchard's husband—in law, at least—sat before them, matured in shape, stiffened in line, exaggerated in traits; disciplined, thought-marked—in a word, older. Elizabeth, encumbered with no recollections as her mother was, regarded him with nothing more than the keen curiosity and interest which the discovery of such unexpected social standing in the long-sought relative naturally begot. He was dressed in an old-fashioned evening suit, an expanse of frilled shirt showing on his broad breast; jewelled studs, and a heavy gold chain. Three glasses stood at his right hand; but, to his wife's surprise, the two for wine were empty, while the third, a tumbler, was half full of water.

When last she had seen him he was sitting in a corduroy jacket, fustian waistcoat and breeches, and tanned leather leggings, with a basin of hot furmity before him. Time, the magician, had wrought much here. Watching him, and thus thinking of past days, she became so moved that she shrank back against the jamb of the waggon-office doorway to which the steps gave access, the shadow from it conveniently hiding her features. She forgot her daughter till a touch from Elizabeth-Jane aroused her. "Have you seen him, mother?" whispered the girl.

"Yes, yes," answered her companion hastily. "I have seen him, and it is enough for me! Now I only want to go—pass away—die."

"Why—O what?" She drew closer, and whispered in her mother's ear, "Does he seem to you not likely to befriend us? I thought he looked a generous man. What a gentleman he is, isn't he? and how his diamond studs shine! How strange that you should have said he might be in the stocks, or in the workhouse, or dead! Did ever anything go more by contraries! Why do you feel so afraid of him? I am not at all; I'll call upon him—he can but say he don't own such remote kin."

"I don't know at all—I can't tell what to set about. I feel so down."

"Don't be that, mother, now we have got here and all! Rest there where you be a little while—I will look on and find out more about him."

"I don't think I can ever meet Mr. Henchard. He is not how I thought he would be—he overpowers me! I don't wish to see him any more."

"But wait a little time and consider."

Elizabeth-Jane had never been so much interested in anything in her life as in their present position, partly from the natural elation she felt at discovering herself akin to a coach;* and she gazed again at the scene. The younger guests were talking and eating with animation; their elders were searching for titbits, and sniffing and grunting over their plates like sows nuzzling for acorns. Three drinks seemed to be sacred to the company—port, sherry, and rum; outside which old-established trinity few or no palates ranged.

A row of ancient rummers† with ground figures on their sides,

---

*That is, related to someone who rides in the mayoral coach.
†Large drinking glasses.

and each primed with a spoon, was now placed down the table, and these were promptly filled with grog at such high temperatures as to raise serious considerations for the articles exposed to its vapours. But Elizabeth-Jane noticed that, though this filling went on with great promptness up and down the table, nobody filled the Mayor's glass, who still drank large quantities of water from the tumbler behind the clump of crystal vessels intended for wine and spirits.

"They don't fill Mr. Henchard's wine-glasses," she ventured to say to her elbow acquaintance, the old man.

"Ah, no; don't ye know him to be the celebrated abstaining worthy of that name? He scorns all tempting liquors; never touches nothing. O yes, he've strong qualities that way. I have heard tell that he sware a gospel oath in by-gone times, and has bode by it ever since. So they don't press him, knowing it would be unbecoming in the face of that; for yer gospel oath is a serious thing."

Another elderly man, hearing this discourse, now joined in by inquiring, "How much longer have he got to suffer from it, Solomon Longways?"

"Another two year, they say. I don't know the why and the wherefore of his fixing such a time, for'a never has told anybody. But 'tis exactly two calendar years longer, they say. A powerful mind to hold out so long!"

"True. . . . But there's great strength in hope. Knowing that in four-and-twenty months' time ye'll be out of your bondage, and able to make up for all you've suffered, by partaking without stint—why, it keeps a man up, no doubt."

"No doubt, Christopher Coney, no doubt. And 'a must need such reflections—a lonely widow man," said Longways.

"When did he lose his wife?" asked Elizabeth.

"I never knowed her. 'Twas afore he came to Casterbridge," Solomon Longways replied with terminative emphasis, as if the fact of his ignorance of Mrs. Henchard were sufficient to deprive her history of all interest. "But I know that'a's a banded teetotaller, and that if any of his men be ever so little overtook by a drop he's down upon 'em as stern as the Lord upon the jovial Jews."*

---

*Reference to the God's anger at the Jews who worshiped a golden calf and celebrated while Moses was receiving the Commandments on Mount Sinai (see Exodus 32).

"Has he many men, then?" said Elizabeth-Jane.

"Many! Why, my good maid, he's the powerfullest member of the Town Council, and quite a principal man in the country round besides. Never a big dealing in wheat, barley, oats, hay, roots, and such like but Henchard's got a hand in it. Ay, and he'll go into other things too; and that's where he makes his mistake. He worked his way up from nothing when 'a came here; and now he's a pillar of the town. Not but what he's been shaken a little to-year* about this bad corn he has supplied in his contracts. I've seen the sun rise over Durnover Moor these nine-and-sixty year, and though Mr. Henchard has never cussed me unfairly ever since I've worked for'n, seeing I be but a little small man, I must say that I have never before tasted such rough bread as has been made from Henchard's wheat lately. 'Tis that growed out that ye could a'most call it malt, and there's a list† at bottom o' the loaf as thick as the sole of one's shoe."

The band now struck up another melody, and by the time it was ended the dinner was over, and speeches began to be made. The evening being calm, and the windows still open, these orations could be distinctly heard. Henchard's voice arose above the rest; he was telling a story of his hay-dealing experiences, in which he had outwitted a sharper who had been bent upon outwitting him.

"Ha-ha-ha!" responded his audience at the upshot of the story; and hilarity was general till a new voice arose with, "This is all very well; but how about the bad bread?"

It came from the lower end of the table, where there sat a group of minor tradesmen who, although part of the company, appeared to be a little below the social level of the others; and who seemed to nourish a certain independence of opinion and carry on discussions not quite in harmony with those at the head; just as the west end of a church is sometimes persistently found to sing out of time and tune with the leading spirits in the chancel.

This interruption about the bad bread afforded infinite satisfaction to the loungers outside, several of whom were in the mood which finds its pleasure in others' discomfiture; and hence they echoed pretty freely, "Hey! How about the bad bread, Mr. Mayor?" Moreover, feeling

---

*This year.
†Inedible layer of bread caused by the use of inferior wheat.

none of the restraints of those who shared the feast, they could afford to add, "You rather ought to tell the story o' that, sir!"

The interruption was sufficient to compel the Mayor to notice it. "Well, I admit that the wheat turned out badly," he said. "But I was taken in in buying it as much as the bakers who bought it o' me."

"And the poor folk who had to eat it whether or no," said the inharmonious man outside the window.

Henchard's face darkened. There was temper under the thin bland surface—the temper which, artificially intensified, had banished a wife nearly a score of years before.

"You must make allowances for the accidents of a large business," he said. "You must bear in mind that the weather just at the harvest of that corn was worse than we have known it for years. However, I have mended my arrangements on account o't. Since I have found my business too large to be well looked after by myself alone, I have advertised for a thorough good man as manager of the corn department. When I've got him you will find these mistakes will no longer occur—matters will be better looked into."

"But what are you going to do to repay us for the past?" inquired the man who had before spoken, and who seemed to be a baker or miller. "Will you replace the grown flour we've still got by sound grain?"

Henchard's face had become still more stern at these interruptions, and he drank from his tumbler of water as if to calm himself or gain time. Instead of vouchsafing a direct reply, he stiffly observed—

"If anybody will tell me how to turn grown wheat into wholesome wheat I'll take it back with pleasure. But it can't be done."

Henchard was not to be drawn again. Having said this, he sat down.

VI

NOW THE GROUP OUTSIDE the window had within the last few minutes been reinforced by new arrivals, some of them respectable shopkeepers and their assistants, who had come out for a whiff of air after putting up the shutters for the night; some of them of a lower class. Distinct from either there appeared a stranger—a young man of remarkably pleasant aspect—who carried in his hand a carpet-bag of the smart floral pattern prevalent in such articles at that time.

He was ruddy and of a fair countenance,[3] bright-eyed, and slight in build. He might possibly have passed by without stopping at all, or at most for half a minute to glance in at the scene, had not his advent coincided with the discussion on corn and bread; in which event this history had never been enacted. But the subject seemed to arrest him, and he whispered some inquiries of the other bystanders, and remained listening.

When he heard Henchard's closing words, "It can't be done," he smiled impulsively, drew out his pocketbook, and wrote down a few words by the aid of the light in the window. He tore out the leaf, folded and directed it, and seemed about to throw it in through the open sash upon the dining-table; but, on second thoughts, edged himself through the loiterers, till he reached the door of the hotel, where one of the waiters who had been serving inside was now idly leaning against the door-post.

"Give this to the Mayor at once," he said, handing in his hasty note.

Elizabeth-Jane had seen his movements and heard the words, which attracted her both by their subject and by their accent—a strange one for those parts. It was quaint and northerly.

The waiter took the note, while the young stranger continued—

"And can ye tell me of a respectable hotel that's a little more moderate than this?"

The waiter glanced indifferently up and down the street.

"They say the Three Mariners, just below here, is a very good place," he languidly answered; "but I have never stayed there myself."

The Scotchman, as he seemed to be, thanked him, and strolled on in the direction of the Three Mariners aforesaid, apparently more concerned about the question of an inn than about the fate of his note, now that the momentary impulse of writing it was over. While he was disappearing slowly down the street the waiter left the door, and Elizabeth-Jane saw with some interest the note brought into the dining-room and handed to the Mayor.

Henchard looked at it carelessly, unfolded it with one hand, and glanced it through. Thereupon it was curious to note an unexpected effect. The nettled, clouded aspect which had held possession of his face since the subject of his corn-dealings had been broached, changed itself into one of arrested attention. He read the note slowly, and fell into thought, not moody, but fitfully intense, as that of a man who has been captured by an idea.

By this time toasts and speeches had given place to songs, the wheat subject being quite forgotten. Men were putting their heads together in twos and threes, telling good stories, with pantomimic laughter which reached convulsive grimace. Some were beginning to look as if they did not know how they had come there, what they had come for, or how they were going to get home again; and provisionally sat on with a dazed smile. Square-built men showed a tendency to become hunchbacks; men with a dignified presence lost it in a curious obliquity of figure, in which their features grew disarranged and one-sided, whilst the heads of a few who had dined with extreme thoroughness were somehow sinking into their shoulders, the corners of their mouths and eyes being bent upwards by the subsidence. Only Henchard did not conform to these flexuous changes; he remained stately and vertical, silently thinking.

The clock struck nine. Elizabeth-Jane turned to her companion. "The evening is drawing on, mother," she said. "What do you propose to do?"

She was surprised to find how irresolute her mother had become. "We must get a place to lie down in," she murmured. "I have seen—Mr. Henchard; and that's all I wanted to do."

"That's enough for to-night, at any rate," Elizabeth-Jane replied soothingly. "We can think to-morrow what is best to do about him. The question now is—is it not—how shall we find a lodging?"

As her mother did not reply Elizabeth-Jane's mind reverted to the words of the waiter, that the Three Mariners was an inn of moderate charges. A recommendation good for one person was probably good for another. "Let's go where the young man has gone to," she said. "He is respectable. What do you say?"

Her mother assented, and down the street they went.

In the meantime the Mayor's thoughtfulness, engendered by the note as stated, continued to hold him in abstraction; till, whispering to his neighbour to take his place, he found opportunity to leave the chair. This was just after the departure of his wife and Elizabeth.

Outside the door of the assembly-room he saw the waiter, and beckoning to him asked who brought the note which had been handed in a quarter of an hour before.

"A young man, sir—a sort of traveller. He was a Scotchman seemingly."

"Did he say how he had got it?"

"He wrote it himself, sir, as he stood outside the window."

"Oh—wrote it himself. . . . Is the young man in the hotel?"

"No, sir. He went to the Three Mariners, I believe."

The Mayor walked up and down the vestibule of the hotel with his hands under his coat tails, as if he were merely seeking a cooler atmosphere than that of the room he had quitted. But there could be no doubt that he was in reality still possessed to the full by the new idea, whatever that might be. At length he went back to the door of the dining-room, paused, and found that the songs, toasts, and conversation were proceeding quite satisfactorily without his presence. The Corporation,* private residents, and major and minor tradesmen had, in fact, gone in for comforting beverages to such an extent that they had quite forgotten, not only the Mayor, but all those vast political, religious, and social differences which they felt necessary to maintain in the daytime, and which separated them like iron grills. Seeing this the Mayor took his hat, and when the waiter had helped him on with a thin holland† overcoat, went out and stood under the portico.

Very few persons were now in the street; and his eyes, by a sort of attraction, turned and dwelt upon a spot about a hundred yards further down. It was the house to which the writer of the note had gone—the Three Mariners—whose two prominent Elizabethan gables, bow-window, and passage-light could be seen from where he stood. Having kept his eyes on it for a while he strolled in that direction.

This ancient house of accommodation for man and beast, now,

---

*Town council.
†Linen.

unfortunately, pulled down, was built of mellow sandstone, with mullioned* windows of the same material, markedly out of perpendicular from the settlement of foundations. The bay window projecting into the street, whose interior was so popular among the frequenters of the inn, was closed with shutters, in each of which appeared a heart-shaped aperture, somewhat more attenuated in the right and left ventricles than is seen in Nature. Inside these illuminated holes, at a distance of about three inches, were ranged at this hour, as every passer knew, the ruddy polls† of Billy Wills the glazier, Smart the shoemaker, Buzzford the general dealer, and others of a secondary set of worthies, of a grade somewhat below that of the diners at the King's Arms, each with his yard of clay.‡

A four-centred Tudor arch was over the entrance, and over the arch the signboard, now visible in the rays of an opposite lamp. Hereon the Mariners, who had been represented by the artist as persons of two dimensions only—in other words, flat as a shadow—were standing in a row in paralyzed attitudes. Being on the sunny side of the street the three comrades had suffered largely from warping, splitting, fading, and shrinkage, so that they were but a half-invisible film upon the reality of the grain, and knots, and nails, which composed the signboard. As a matter of fact, this state of things was not so much owing to Stannidge the landlord's neglect, as from the lack of a painter in Casterbridge who would undertake to reproduce the features of men so traditional.

A long, narrow, dimly-lit passage gave access to the inn, within which passage the horses going to their stalls at the back, and the coming and departing human guests, rubbed shoulders indiscriminately, the latter running no slight risk of having their toes trodden upon by the animals. The good stabling and the good ale of the Mariners, though somewhat difficult to reach on account of there being but this narrow way to both, were nevertheless perseveringly sought out by the sagacious old heads who knew what was what in Casterbridge.

Henchard stood without the inn for a few instants; then lower-

---

*Divided by stone bars; a characteristic feature of Gothic architecture.
†Heads.
‡Clay pipe.

ing the dignity of his presence as much as possible by buttoning the brown holland coat over his shirt-front, and in other ways toning himself down to his ordinary everyday appearance, he entered the inn door.

VII

ELIZABETH-JANE AND HER MOTHER had arrived some twenty minutes earlier. Outside the house they had stood and considered whether even this homely place, though recommended as moderate, might not be too serious in its prices for their light pockets. Finally, however, they had found courage to enter, and duly met Stannidge the landlord; a silent man, who drew and carried frothing measures to this room and to that, shoulder to shoulder with his waiting-maids—a stately slowness, however, entering into his ministrations by contrast with theirs, as became one whose service was somewhat optional. It would have been altogether optional but for the orders of the landlady, a person who sat in the bar, corporeally motionless, but with a flitting eye and quick ear, with which she observed and heard through the open door and hatchway the pressing needs of customers whom her husband overlooked though close at hand. Elizabeth and her mother were passively accepted as sojourners, and shown to a small bedroom under one of the gables, where they sat down.

The principle of the inn seemed to be to compensate for the antique awkwardness, crookedness, and obscurity of the passages, floors, and windows, by quantities of clean linen spread about everywhere, and this had a dazzling effect upon the travellers.

" 'Tis too good for us—we can't meet it!" said the elder woman, looking round the apartment with misgiving as soon as they were left alone.

"I fear it is, too," said Elizabeth. "But we must be respectable."

"We must pay our way even before we must be respectable," replied her mother. "Mr. Henchard is too high for us to make ourselves known to him, I much fear; so we've only our own pockets to depend on."

"I know what I'll do," said Elizabeth-Jane after an interval of waiting, during which their needs seemed quite forgotten under the press of business below and leaving the room, she descended the stairs and penetrated to the bar.

If there was one good thing more than another which characterized this single-hearted girl it was a willingness to sacrifice her personal comfort and dignity to the common weal.

"As you seem busy here to-night, and mother's not well off, might I take out part of our accommodation by helping?" she asked of the landlady.

The latter, who remained as fixed in the arm-chair as if she had been melted into it when in a liquid state, and could not now be unstuck, looked the girl up and down inquiringly, with her hands on the chair-arms. Such arrangements as the one Elizabeth proposed were not uncommon in country villages; but, though Casterbridge was old-fashioned, the custom was well-nigh obsolete here. The mistress of the house, however, was an easy woman to strangers, and she made no objection. Thereupon Elizabeth, being instructed by nods and motions from the taciturn landlord as to where she could find the different things, trotted up and down stairs with materials for her own and her parent's meal.

While she was doing this the wood partition in the centre of the house thrilled to its centre with the tugging of a bell-pull upstairs. A bell below tinkled a note that was feebler in sound than the twanging of wires and cranks that had produced it.

" 'Tis the Scotch gentleman," said the landlady omnisciently; and turning her eyes to Elizabeth, "Now then, can you go and see if his supper is on the tray? If it is you can take it up to him. The front room over this."

Elizabeth-Jane, though hungry, willingly postponed serving herself awhile, and applied to the cook in the kitchen, whence she brought forth the tray of supper viands, and proceeded with it upstairs to the apartment indicated. The accommodation of the Three Mariners was far from spacious, despite the fair area of ground it covered. The room demanded by intrusive beams and rafters, partitions, passages, staircases, disused ovens, settles, and four-posters, left comparatively small quarters for human beings. Moreover, this being at a time before home-brewing was abandoned by the smaller victuallers, and a house in which the twelve-bushel strength* was still religiously adhered to by the landlord in his ale, the quality of the liquor was the chief attraction of the premises, so that everything had to make way for utensils and operations in connection therewith. Thus Elizabeth found that the Scotchman was located in a room quite close to the small one that had been allotted to herself and her mother.

When she entered nobody was present but the young man himself—the same whom she had seen lingering without the windows of the King's Arms Hotel. He was now idly reading a copy of the local paper, and was hardly conscious of her entry, so that she looked at him quite coolly, and saw how his forehead shone where the light caught it, and how nicely his hair was cut, and the sort of velvet-pile or down that was on the skin at the back of his neck, and how his cheek was so truly curved as to be part of a globe, and how clearly drawn were the lids and lashes which hid his bent eyes.

She set down the tray, spread his supper, and went away without a word. On her arrival below the landlady, who was as kind as she was fat and lazy, saw that Elizabeth-Jane was rather tired, though in her earnestness to be useful she was waiving her own needs altogether. Mrs. Stannidge thereupon said with a considerate peremptoriness that she and her mother had better take their own suppers if they meant to have any.

Elizabeth fetched their simple provisions, as she had fetched the Scotchman's, and went up to the little chamber where she had left her mother, noiselessly pushing open the door with the edge of the tray. To her surprise her mother, instead of being reclined on the bed where she had left her, was in an erect position, with lips parted. At Elizabeth's entry she lifted her finger.

The meaning of this was soon apparent. The room allotted to the two women had at one time served as a dressing-room to the Scotchman's chamber, as was evidenced by signs of a door of communication between them—now screwed up and pasted over with the wall paper. But, as is frequently the case with hotels of far higher preten-

---

*Strong; refers to the proportion of malt in the ale.

sions than the Three Mariners, every word spoken in either of these rooms was distinctly audible in the other. Such sounds came through now.

Thus silently conjured Elizabeth deposited the tray, and her mother whispered as she drew near, " 'Tis he."

"Who?" said the girl.

"The Mayor."

The tremors in Susan Henchard's tone might have led any person but one so perfectly unsuspicious of the truth as the girl was, to surmise some closer connection than the admitted simple kinship as a means of accounting for them.

Two men were indeed talking in the adjoining chamber, the young Scotchman and Henchard, who, having entered the inn while Elizabeth-Jane was in the kitchen waiting for the supper, had been deferentially conducted upstairs by host Stannidge himself. The girl noiselessly laid out their little meal, and beckoned to her mother to join her, which Mrs. Henchard mechanically did, her attention being fixed on the conversation through the door.

"I merely strolled in on my way home to ask you a question about something that has excited my curiosity," said the Mayor, with careless geniality. "But I see you have not finished supper."

"Ay, but I will be done in a little! Ye needn't go, sir. Take a seat. I've almost done, and it makes no differrence at all."

Henchard seemed to take the seat offered, and in a moment he resumed: "Well, first I should ask, did you write this?" A rustling of paper followed.

"Yes, I did," said the Scotchman.

"Then," said Henchard, "I am under the impression that we have met by accident while waiting for the morning to keep an appointment with each other? My name is Henchard; ha'n't you replied to an advertisement for a corn-factor's manager that I put into the paper—ha'n't you come here to see me about it?"

"No," said the Scotchman, with some surprise.

"Surely you are the man," went on Henchard insistingly, "who arranged to come and see me? Joshua, Joshua, Jipp—Jopp—what was his name?"

"You're wrong!" said the young man. "My name is Donald Farfrae. It is true I am in the corren trade—but I have replied to no advairrtisment, and arranged to see no one. I am on my way to Bristol—from there to the other side of the warrld, to try my fortune in the great wheat-growing districts of the West! I have some inventions useful to the trade, and there is no scope for developing them heere."

"To America—well, well," said Henchard, in a tone of disappointment, so strong as to make itself felt like a damp atmosphere. "And yet I could have sworn you were the man!"

The Scotchman murmured another negative, and there was a silence, till Henchard resumed: "Then I am truly and sincerely obliged to you for the few words you wrote on that paper."

"It was nothing, sir."

"Well, it has a great importance for me just now. This row about my grown wheat, which I declare to Heaven I didn't know to be bad till the people came complaining, has put me to my wits' end. I've some hundreds of quarters* of it on hand; and if your renovating process will make it wholesome, why, you can see what a quag† 'twould get me out of. I saw in a moment there might be truth in it. But I should like to have it proved; and of course you don't care to tell the steps of the process sufficiently for me to do that, without my paying ye well for't first."

The young man reflected a moment or two. "I don't know that I have any objection," he said. "I'm going to another country, and curing bad corn is not the line I'll take up there. Yes, I'll tell ye the whole of it—you'll make more out of it heere than I will in a foreign country. Just look heere a minute, sir. I can show ye by a sample in my carpetbag."

The click of a lock followed, and there was a sifting and rustling; then a discussion about so many ounces to the bushel, and drying, and refrigerating, and so on.

"These few grains will be sufficient to show ye with," came in the young fellow's voice; and after a pause, during which some operation seemed to be intently watched by them both, he exclaimed, "There, now, do you taste that."

"It's complete!—quite restored, or—well—nearly."

"Quite enough restored to make good seconds out of it," said the

---

*One quarter is 8 bushels, or 64 gallons.
†Quagmire; that is, quandary.

Scotchman. "To fetch it back entirely is impossible; Nature won't stand so much as that, but heere you go a great way towards it. Well, sir, that's the process; I don't value it, for it can be but of little use in countries where the weather is more settled than in ours; and I'll be only too glad if it's of service to you."

"But hearken to me," pleaded Henchard. "My business, you know, is in corn and in hay; but I was brought up as a hay-trusser simply, and hay is what I understand best, though I now do more in corn than in the other. If you'll accept the place, you shall manage the corn branch entirely, and receive a commission in addition to salary."

"You're liberal—very liberal; but no, no—I cannet!" the young man still replied, with some distress in his accents.

"So be it!" said Henchard conclusively. "Now—to change the subject—one good turn deserves another; don't stay to finish that miserable supper. Come to my house; I can find something better for 'ee than cold ham and ale."

Donald Farfrae was grateful—said he feared he must decline—that he wished to leave early next day.

"Very well," said Henchard quickly, "please yourself. But I tell you, young man, if this holds good for the bulk, as it has done for the sample, you have saved my credit, stranger though you be. What shall I pay you for this knowledge?"

"Nothing at all, nothing at all. It may not prove necessary to ye to use it often, and I don't value it at all. I thought I might just as well let ye know, as you were in a difficulty, and they were harrd upon ye."

Henchard paused. "I shan't soon forget this," he said. "And from a stranger! . . . I couldn't believe you were not the man I had engaged! Says I to myself, 'He knows who I am, and recommends himself by this stroke.' And yet it turns out, after all, that you are not the man who answered my advertisement, but a stranger!"

"Ay, ay; that's so," said the young man.

Henchard again suspended his words, and then his voice came thoughtfully: "Your forehead, Farfrae, is something like my poor brother's—now dead and gone; and the nose, too, isn't unlike his. You must be, what—five foot nine, I reckon? I am six foot one and a half out of my shoes. But what of that? In my business, 'tis true that strength and bustle build up a firm. But judgment and knowledge are what keep it established. Unluckily, I am bad at science, Farfrae; bad at figures—a rule o' thumb sort of man. You are just the reverse—I can see that. I have been looking for such as you these two year, and yet you are not for me. Well, before I go, let me ask this: Though you are not the young man I thought you were, what's the difference? Can't ye stay just the same? Have you really made up your mind about this American notion? I won't mince matters. I feel you would be invaluable to me—that needn't be said—and if you will bide and be my manager, I will make it worth your while."

"My plans are fixed," said the young man, in negative tones. "I have formed a scheme, and so we need na say any more about it. But will you not drink with me, sir? I find this Casterbridge ale warreming to the stomach."

"No no; I fain would, but I can't," said Henchard gravely, the scraping of his chair informing the listeners that he was rising to leave. "When I was a young man I went in for that sort of thing too strong—far too strong—and was well-nigh ruined by it! I did a deed on account of it which I shall be ashamed of to my dying day. It made such an impression on me that I swore, there and then, that I'd drink nothing stronger than tea for as many years as I was old that day. I have kept my oath; and though, Farfrae, I am sometimes that dry in the dog days that I could drink a quarter-barrel to the pitching,* I think o' my oath, and touch no strong drink at all."

"I'll no' press ye, sir—I'll no' press ye. I respect your vow."

"Well, I shall get a manager somewhere, no doubt," said Henchard, with strong feeling in his tones. "But it will be long before I see one that would suit me so well!"

The young man appeared much moved by Henchard's warm convictions of his value. He was silent till they reached the door. "I wish I could stay—sincerely I would like to," he replied. "But no—it cannet be! it cannet! I want to see the warrld."

---

*To the bottom; the bottom of barrels were lined with pitch.

VIII

THUS THEY PARTED; AND Elizabeth-Jane and her mother remained each in her thoughts over their meal, the mother's face being strangely bright since Henchard's avowal of shame for a past action. The quivering of the partition to its core presently denoted that Donald Farfrae had again rung his bell, no doubt to have his supper removed; for humming a tune, and walking up and down, he seemed to be attracted by the lively bursts of conversation and melody from the general company below. He sauntered out upon the landing, and descended the staircase.

When Elizabeth-Jane had carried down his supper tray, and also that used by her mother and herself, she found the bustle of serving to be at its height below, as it always was at this hour. The young woman shrank from having anything to do with the ground-floor serving, and crept silently about observing the scene—so new to her, fresh from the seclusion of a seaside cottage. In the general sitting-room, which was large, she remarked the two or three dozen strong-backed chairs that stood round against the wall, each fitted with its genial occupant; the sanded floor; the black settle which, projecting endwise from the wall within the door, permitted Elizabeth to be a spectator of all that went on without herself being particularly seen.

The young Scotchman had just joined the guests. These, in addition to the respectable master-tradesmen occupying the seats of privilege in the bow-window and its neighbourhood, included an inferior set at the unlighted end, whose seats were mere benches against the wall, and who drank from cups instead of from glasses. Among the latter she noticed some of those personages who had stood outside the windows of the King's Arms.

Behind their backs was a small window, with a wheel ventilator in one of the panes, which would suddenly start off spinning with a jingling sound, as suddenly stop, and as suddenly start again.

While thus furtively making her survey the opening words of a song greeted her ears from the front of the settle, in a melody and accent of peculiar charm. There had been some singing before she came down; and now the Scotchman had made himself so soon at home that, at the request of some of the master-tradesmen, he, too, was favouring the room with a ditty.

Elizabeth-Jane was fond of music; she could not help pausing to listen; and the longer she listened the more she was enraptured. She had never heard any singing like this; and it was evident that the majority of the audience had not heard such frequently, for they were attentive to a much greater degree than usual. They neither whispered, nor drank, nor dipped their pipe-stems in their ale to moisten them, nor pushed the mug to their neighbours. The singer himself grew emotional, till she could imagine a tear in his eye as the words went on:—

> "It's hame, and it's hame, hame fain would I be,
> O hame, hame, hame to my ain countree!
> There's an eye that ever weeps, and a fair face will be fain,
> As I pass through Annan Water with my bonnie bands again;
> When the flower is in the bud, and the leaf upon the tree,
> The lark shall sing me hame to my ain countree!"[4]

There was a burst of applause, and a deep silence which was even more eloquent than the applause. It was of such a kind that the snapping of a pipe-stem too long for him by old Solomon Longways, who was one of those gathered at the shady end of the room, seemed a harsh and irreverent act. Then the ventilator in the window-pane spasmodically started off for a new spin, and the pathos of Donald's song was temporarily effaced.

" 'Twas not amiss—not at all amiss!" muttered Christopher Coney, who was also present. And removing his pipe a finger's breadth from his lips, he said aloud, "Draw on with the next verse, young gentleman, please."

"Yes. Let's have it again, stranger," said the glazier, a stout, bucket-headed man, with a white apron rolled up round his waist. "Folks don't lift up their hearts like that in this part of the world." And turning aside, he said in undertones, "Who is the young man?— Scotch, d'ye say?"

"Yes, straight from the mountains of Scotland, I believe," replied Coney.

Young Farfrae repeated the last verse. It was plain that nothing so pathetic had been heard at the Three Mariners for a considerable time. The difference of accent, the excitability of the singer, the intense local feeling, and the seriousness with which he worked himself up to a climax, surprised this set of worthies, who were only too prone to shut up their emotions with caustic words.

"Danged if our country down here is worth singing about like that!" continued the glazier, as the Scotchman again melodized with a dying fall, "My ain countree!" "When you take away from among us the fools and the rogues, and the lammigers* and the wanton hussies, and the slatterns, and such like, there's cust few left to ornament a song with in Casterbridge, or the country round."

"True," said Buzzford, the dealer, looking at the grain of the table. "Casterbridge is a old, hoary place o' wickedness, by all account. 'Tis recorded in history that we rebelled against the King one or two hundred years ago, in the time of the Romans,[5] and that lots of us was hanged on Gallows Hill, and quartered, and our different jints sent about the country like butcher's meat; and for my part I can well believe it."

"What did ye come away from yer own country for, young maister, if ye be so wownded about it?" inquired Christopher Coney, from the background, with the tone of a man who preferred the original subject. "Faith, it wasn't worth your while on our account, for, as Maister Billy Wills says, we be bruckle† folk here—the best o' us hardly honest sometimes, what with hard winters, and so many mouths to fill, and God-a'mighty sending his little taties‡ so terrible small to fill 'em with. We don't think about flowers and fair faces, not we—except in the shape o' cauliflowers and pigs' chaps."§

"But, no!" said Donald Farfrae, gazing round into their faces with earnest concern; "the best of ye hardly honest—not that surely? None of ye has been stealing what didn't belong to him?"

"Lord! no, no!" said Solomon Longways, smiling grimly. "That's only his random way o' speaking. 'A was always such a man of underthoughts." (And reprovingly towards Christopher): "Don't ye be so over-familiar with a gentleman that ye know nothing of—and that's travelled a'most from the North Pole."

---

*Physically disabled people.
†Rough.
‡Potatoes.
§Pigs' cheeks.

Christopher Coney was silenced, and as he could get no public sympathy, he mumbled his feelings to himself: "Be dazed, if I loved my country half as well as the young feller do, I'd live by claning my neighbour's pigsties afore I'd go away! For my part I've no more love for my country than I have for Botany Bay!"*

"Come," said Longways; "let the young man draw onward with his ballet, or we shall be here all night."

"That's all of it," said the singer apologetically.

"Soul of my body, then we'll have another!" said the general dealer.

"Can you turn a strain to the ladies, sir?" inquired a fat woman with a figured purple apron, the waist-string of which was overhung so far by her sides as to be invisible.

"Let him breathe—let him breathe, Mother Cuxsom. He hain't got his second wind yet," said the master glazier.

"O yes, but I have!" exclaimed the young man; and he at once tendered "O Nannie"† with faultless modulations, and another or two of the like sentiment, winding up at their earnest request with "Auld Lang Syne."‡

By this time he had completely taken possession of the hearts of the Three Mariners' inmates, including even old Coney. Notwithstanding an occasional odd gravity which awoke their sense of the ludicrous for the moment, they began to view him through a golden haze which the tone of his mind seemed to raise around him. Casterbridge had sentiment—Casterbridge had romance; but this stranger's sentiment was of differing quality. Or rather, perhaps, the difference was mainly superficial; he was to them like the poet of a new school who takes his contemporaries by storm; who is not really new, but is the first to articulate what all his listeners have felt, though but dumbly till then.

The silent landlord came and leant over the settle while the young man sang; and even Mrs. Stannidge managed to unstick herself from the framework of her chair in the bar and get as far as the door-post, which movement she accomplished by rolling herself

---

*Convict settlement in Australia.
†Scottish song (1773) written by Thomas Carter.
‡Poem and song by Scottish poet Robert Burns.

round, as a cask is trundled on the chine* by a drayman without losing much of its perpendicular.

"And are you going to bide in Casterbridge, sir?" she asked.

"Ah—no!" said the Scotchman, with melancholy fatality in his voice, "I'm only passing thirrough! I am on my way to Bristol, and on frae there to foreign parts."

"We be truly sorry to hear it," said Solomon Longways. "We can ill afford to lose tuneful wynd-pipes like yours when they fall among us. And verily, to mak' acquaintance with a man a-come from so far, from the land o' perpetual snow, as we may say, where wolves and wild boars and other dangerous animalcules be as common as blackbirds hereabout—why, 'tis a thing we can't do every day; and there's good sound information for bide-at-homes like we when such a man opens his mouth."

"Nay, but ye mistake my country," said the young man, looking round upon them with tragic fixity, till his eye lighted up and his cheek kindled with a sudden enthusiasm to right their errors. "There are not perpetual snow and wolves at all in it!—except snow in winter, and—well—a little in summer just sometimes, and a 'gaberlunzie'† or two, stalking about here and there, if ye may call them dangerous. Eh, but you should take a summer jarreny to Edinboro', and Arthur's Seat,‡ and all round there, and then go on to the lochs, and all the Highland scenery—in May and June—and you would never say 'tis the land of wolves and perpetual snow!"

"Of course not—it stands to reason," said Buzzford. " 'Tis barren ignorance that leads to such words. He's a simple home-spun man, that never was fit for good company—think nothing of him, sir."

"And do ye carry your flock bed,§ and your quilt, and your crock and your bit of chiney? or do ye go in bare bones, as I may say?" inquired Christopher Coney.

"I've sent on my luggage—though it isn't much; for the voyage is long." Donald's eyes dropped into a remote gaze as he added: "But

---

*Rim of a cask.

†Person who traveled from town to town, receiving money in exchange for delivering news (Scots).

‡Hill overlooking Edinburgh.

§Bed stuffed with cotton or wool.

I said to myself, 'Never a one of the prizes of life will I come by unless I undertake it!' and I decided to go."

A general sense of regret, in which Elizabeth-Jane shared not least, made itself apparent in the company. As she looked at Farfrae from the back of the settle she decided that his statements showed him to be no less thoughtful than his fascinating melodies revealed him to be cordial and impassioned. She admired the serious light in which he looked at serious things. He had seen no jest in ambiguities and roguery, as the Casterbridge toss-pots* had done; and rightly not—there was none. She disliked those wretched humours of Christopher Coney and his tribe; and he did not appreciate them. He seemed to feel exactly as she felt about life and its surroundings—that they were a tragical rather than a comical thing; that though one could be gay on occasion, moments of gaiety were interludes, and no part of the actual drama. It was extraordinary how similar their views were.

Though it was still early the young Scotchman expressed his wish to retire, whereupon the landlady whispered to Elizabeth to run upstairs and turn down his bed. She took a candlestick and proceeded on her mission, which was the act of a few moments only. When, candle in hand, she reached the top of the stairs on her way down again, Mr. Farfrae was at the foot coming up. She could not very well retreat; they met and passed in the turn of the staircase.

She must have appeared interesting in some way—notwithstanding her plain dress—or rather, possibly, in consequence of it, for she was a girl characterized by earnestness and soberness of mien, with which simple drapery accorded well. Her face flushed, too, at the slight awkwardness of the meeting, and she passed him with her eyes bent on the candle-flame that she carried just below her nose. Thus it happened that when confronting her he smiled; and then, with the manner of a temporarily light-hearted man, who has started himself on a flight of song whose momentum he cannot readily check, he softly tuned an old ditty that she seemed to suggest—

> "As I came in by my bower door,
>   As day was waxin' wearie,

---

*Drunkards.

> Oh wha came tripping down the stair
> But bonnie Peg my dearie."*

Elizabeth-Jane, rather disconcerted, hastened on; and the Scotchman's voice died away, humming more of the same within the closed door of his room.

Here the scene and sentiment ended for the present. When, soon after, the girl rejoined her mother, the latter was still in thought—on quite another matter than a young man's song.

"We've made a mistake," she whispered (that the Scotchman might not overhear). "On no account ought ye to have helped serve here tonight. Not because of ourselves, but for the sake of him. If he should befriend us, and take us up, and then find out what you did when staying here, 'twould grieve and wound his natural pride as Mayor of the town."

Elizabeth, who would perhaps have been more alarmed at this than her mother had she known the real relationship, was not much disturbed about it as things stood. Her "he" was another man than her poor mother's. "For myself," she said, "I didn't at all mind waiting a little upon him. He's so respectable, and educated—far above the rest of 'em in the inn. They thought him very simple not to know their grim broad way of talking about themselves here. But of course he didn't know—he was too refined in his mind to know such things!" Thus she earnestly pleaded.

Meanwhile, the "he" of her mother was not so far away as even they thought. After leaving the Three Mariners he had sauntered up and down the empty High Street, passing and repassing the inn in his promenade. When the Scotchman sang his voice had reached Henchard's ears through the heart-shaped holes in the window-shutters, and had led him to pause outside them a long while.

"To be sure, to be sure, how that fellow does draw me!" he had said to himself. "I suppose 'tis because I'm so lonely. I'd have given him a third share in the business to have stayed!"

---

*Variation of a song by Robert Burns.

IX

WHEN ELIZABETH-JANE OPENED THE hinged casement next morning the mellow air brought in the feel of imminent autumn almost as distinctly as if she had been in the remotest hamlet. Casterbridge was the complement of the rural life around; not its urban opposite. Bees and butterflies in the cornfields at the top of the town, who desired to get to the meads at the bottom, took no circuitous course, but flew straight down High Street without any apparent consciousness that they were traversing strange latitudes. And in autumn airy spheres of thistledown floated into the same street, lodged upon the shop fronts, blew into drains; and innumerable tawny and yellow leaves skimmed along the pavement, and stole through people's doorways into their passages with a hesitating scratch on the floor, like the skirts of timid visitors.

Hearing voices, one of which was close at hand, she withdrew her head and glanced from behind the window-curtains. Mr. Henchard—now habited no longer as a great personage, but as a thriving man of business—was pausing on his way up the middle of the street, and the Scotchman was looking from the window adjoining her own. Henchard, it appeared, had gone a little way past the inn before he had noticed his acquaintance of the previous evening. He came back a few steps, Donald Farfrae opening the window further.

"And you are off soon, I suppose?" said Henchard upwards.

"Yes—almost this moment, sir," said the other. "Maybe I'll walk on till the coach makes up on me."

"Which way?"

"The way ye are going."

"Then shall we walk together to the top o' town?"

"If ye'll wait a minute," said the Scotchman.

In a few minutes the latter emerged, bag in hand. Henchard looked at the bag as at an enemy. It showed there was no mistake about the young man's departure. "Ah, my lad," he said, "you should have been a wise man, and have stayed with me."

"Yes, yes—it might have been wiser," said Donald, looking microscopically at the houses that were furthest off. "It is only telling ye the truth when I say my plans are vague."

They had by this time passed on from the precincts of the inn, and Elizabeth-Jane heard no more. She saw that they continued in conversation, Henchard turning to the other occasionally, and emphasizing some remark with a gesture. Thus they passed the King's Arms Hotel, the Market House, St. Peter's churchyard wall, ascending to the upper end of the long street till they were small as two grains of corn; when they bent suddenly to the right into the Bristol Road, and were out of view.

"He was a good man—and he's gone," she said to herself. "I was nothing to him, and there was no reason why he should have wished me good-bye."

The simple thought, with its latent sense of slight, had moulded itself out of the following little fact: when the Scotchman came out at the door he had by accident glanced up at her; and then he had looked away again without nodding, or smiling, or saying a word.

"You are still thinking, mother," she said, when she turned inwards.

"Yes; I am thinking of Mr. Henchard's sudden liking for that young man. He was always so. Now, surely, if he takes so warmly to people who are not related to him at all, may he not take as warmly to his own kin?"

While they debated this question a procession of five large waggons went past, laden with hay up to the bedroom windows. They came in from the country, and the steaming horses had probably been travelling a great part of the night. To the shaft of each hung a little board, on which was painted in white letters, "Henchard, corn-factor and hay-merchant." The spectacle renewed his wife's conviction that, for her daughter's sake, she should strain a point to rejoin him.

The discussion was continued during breakfast, and the end of it was that Mrs. Henchard decided, for good or for ill, to send Elizabeth-Jane with a message to Henchard, to the effect that his relative Susan, a sailor's widow, was in the town; leaving it to him to say whether or not he would recognize her. What had brought her to this determination were chiefly two things. He had been described as a lonely widower; and he had expressed shame for a past transaction of his life. There was promise in both.

"If he says no," she enjoined, as Elizabeth-Jane stood, bonnet on, ready to depart; "if he thinks it does not become the good position he has reached to in the town, to own—to let us call on him as—his distant kinsfolk, say, 'Then, sir, we would rather not intrude; we will leave Casterbridge as quietly as we have come, and go back to our own country.' . . . I almost feel that I would rather he did say so, as I have not seen him for so many years, and we are so—little allied to him!"

"And if he say yes?" inquired the more sanguine one.

"In that case," answered Mrs. Henchard cautiously, "ask him to write me a note, saying when and how he will see us—or *me*."

Elizabeth-Jane went a few steps towards the landing. "And tell him," continued her mother, "that I fully know I have no claim upon him—that I am glad to find he is thriving; that I hope his life may be long and happy—there, go." Thus with a half-hearted willingness, a smothered reluctance, did the poor forgiving woman start her unconscious daughter on this errand.

It was about ten o'clock, and market-day, when Elizabeth paced up the High Street, in no great hurry; for to herself her position was only that of a poor relation deputed to hunt up a rich one. The front doors of the private houses were mostly left open at this warm autumn time, no thought of umbrella stealers disturbing the minds of the placid burgesses. Hence, through the long, straight, entrance passages thus unclosed could be seen, as through tunnels, the mossy gardens at the back, glowing with nasturtiums, fuchsias, scarlet geraniums, "bloody warriors,"* snapdragons, and dahlias, this floral blaze being backed by crusted grey stone-work remaining from a yet remoter Casterbridge than the venerable one visible in the street. The old-fashioned fronts of these houses, which had older than old-fashioned backs, rose sheer from the pavement, into which the bow-windows protruded like bastions, necessitating a pleasing *chassez-déchassez*† movement to the time-pressed pedestrian at every few yards. He was bound also to evolve other Terpsichorean‡ figures in respect of door-steps, scrapers, cellar-hatches, church buttresses, and the over-hanging angles of walls which, originally unobtrusive, had become bow-legged and knock-kneed.

---

*Wallflowers.
†French term for a dance step involving quick steps to either side.
‡Relating to dance; Terpsichore was the Greek muse of choral dance.

In addition to these fixed obstacles which spoke so cheerfully of individual unrestraint as to boundaries, movables occupied the path and roadway to a perplexing extent. First the vans of the carriers in and out of Casterbridge, who hailed from Mellstock, Weatherbury, The Hintocks, Sherton-Abbas, Kingsbere, Overcombe, and many other towns and villages round. Their owners were numerous enough to be regarded as a tribe, and had almost distinctiveness enough to be regarded as a race. Their vans had just arrived, and were drawn up on each side of the street in close file, so as to form at places a wall between the pavement and the roadway. Moreover every shop pitched out half its contents upon trestles and boxes on the kerb, extending the display each week a little further and further into the roadway, despite the expostulations of the two feeble old constables, until there remained but a tortuous defile for carriages down the centre of the street, which afforded fine opportunities for skill with the reins. Over the pavement on the sunny side of the way hung shopblinds so constructed as to give the passenger's hat a smart buffet off his head, as from the unseen hands of Cranstoun's Goblin Page,[6] celebrated in romantic lore.

Horses for sale were tied in rows, their forelegs on the pavement, their hind legs in the street, in which position they occasionally nipped little boys by the shoulder who were passing to school. And any inviting recess in front of a house that had been modestly kept back from the general line was utilized by pig-dealers as a pen for their stock.

The yeomen, farmers, dairymen, and townsfolk, who came to transact business in these ancient streets, spoke in other ways than by articulation. Not to hear the words of your interlocutor in metropolitan centres is to know nothing of his meaning. Here the face, the arms, the hat, the stick, the body throughout spoke equally with the tongue. To express satisfaction the Casterbridge market-man added to his utterance a broadening of the cheeks, a crevicing of the eyes, a throwing back of the shoulders, which was intelligible from the other end of the street. If he wondered, though all Henchard's carts and waggons were rattling past him, you knew it from perceiving the inside of his crimson mouth, and a target-like circling of his eyes. Deliberation caused sundry attacks on the moss of adjoining walls with the end of his stick, a change of his hat from the horizontal to the less so; a sense of tediousness announced itself in a lowering of the person by spreading the knees to a lozenge-shaped aperture and contorting the arms. Chicanery, subterfuge, had hardly a place in the streets of this honest borough to all appearance; and it was said that the lawyers in the Court House hard by occasionally threw in strong arguments for the other side out of pure generosity (though apparently by mischance) when advancing their own.

Thus Casterbridge was in most respects but the pole, focus, or nerve-knot of the surrounding country life; differing from the many manufacturing towns which are as foreign bodies set down, like boulders on a plain, in a green world with which they have nothing in common. Casterbridge lived by agriculture at one remove further from the fountain-head than the adjoining villages—no more. The townsfolk understood every fluctuation in the rustic's condition, for it affected their receipts as much as the labourer's; they entered into the troubles and joys which moved the aristocratic families ten miles round—for the same reason. And even at the dinner-parties of the professional families the subjects of discussion were corn, cattle-disease, sowing and reaping, fencing and planting; while politics were viewed by them less from their own standpoint of burgesses with rights and privileges than from the standpoint of their county neighbours.

All the venerable contrivances and confusions which delighted the eye by their quaintness, and in a measure reasonableness, in this rare old market-town, were metropolitan novelties to the unpractised eyes of Elizabeth-Jane, fresh from netting fish-seines* in a seaside cottage. Very little inquiry was necessary to guide her footsteps. Henchard's house was one of the best, faced with dull red-and-grey old brick. The front door was open, and, as in other houses, she could see through the passage to the end of the garden—nearly a quarter of a mile off.

Mr. Henchard was not in the house, but in the store-yard. She was conducted into the mossy garden, and through a door in the wall, which was studded with rusty nails speaking of generations of fruit trees that had been trained there. The door opened upon the yard, and here she was left to find him as she could. It was a place flanked by

---

*Fishing nets.

hay-barns, into which tons of fodder, all in trusses, were being packed from the waggons she had seen pass the inn that morning. On other sides of the yard were wooden granaries on stone staddles,* to which access was given by Flemish ladders, and a store-house several floors high. Wherever the doors of these places were open, a closely packed throng of bursting wheat-sacks could be seen standing inside, with the air of awaiting a famine that would not come.

She wandered about this place, uncomfortably conscious of the impending interview, till she was quite weary of searching; she ventured to inquire of a boy in what quarter Mr. Henchard could be found. He directed her to an office which she had not seen before, and knocking at the door she was answered by a cry of "Come in."

Elizabeth turned the handle; and there stood before her, bending over some sample-bags on a table, not the corn-merchant, but the young Scotchman Mr. Farfrae—in the act of pouring some grains of wheat from one hand to the other. His hat hung on a peg behind him, and the roses of his carpet-bag glowed from the corner of the room.

Having toned her feelings and arranged words on her lips for Mr. Henchard, and for him alone, she was for the moment confounded.

"Yes, what is it?" said the Scotchman, like a man who permanently ruled there.

She said she wanted to see Mr. Henchard.

"Ah, yes; will you wait a minute? He's engaged just now," said the young man, apparently not recognizing her as the girl at the inn. He handed her a chair, bade her sit down, and turned to his sample-bags again. While Elizabeth-Jane sits waiting in great amaze at the young man's presence we may briefly explain how he came there.

When the two new acquaintances had passed out of sight that morning towards the Bath and Bristol road they went on silently, except for a few commonplaces, till they had gone down an avenue on the town walls called the Chalk Walk, leading to an angle where the North and West escarpments met. From this high corner of the square earthworks a vast extent of country could be seen. A footpath ran steeply down the green slope, conducting from the shady prom-

---

*Stones to elevate the granary floor above ground level, as a protection against rodents.

enade on the walls to a road at the bottom of the scarp.* It was by this path the Scotchman had to descend.

"Well, here's success to 'ee," said Henchard, holding out his right hand and leaning with his left upon the wicket which protected the descent. In the act there was the inelegance of one whose feelings are nipped and wishes defeated. "I shall often think of this time, and of how you came at the very moment to throw a light upon my difficulty."

Still holding the young man's hand he paused, and then added deliberately: "Now I am not the man to let a cause be lost for want of a word. And before ye are gone for ever I'll speak. Once more, will ye stay? There it is, flat and plain. You can see that it isn't all selfishness that makes me press 'ee; for my business is not quite so scientific as to require an intellect entirely out of the common. Others would do for the place without doubt. Some selfishness perhaps there is, but there is more; it isn't for me to repeat what. Come bide with me—and name your own terms. I'll agree to 'em willingly and 'ithout a word of gainsaying; for, hang it, Farfrae, I like thee well!"

The young man's hand remained steady in Henchard's for a moment or two. He looked over the fertile country that stretched beneath them, then backward along the shaded walk reaching to the top of the town. His face flushed.

"I never expected this—I did not!" he said. "It's Providence! Should any one go against it? No; I'll not go to America; I'll stay and be your man!"

His hand, which had lain lifeless in Henchard's, returned the latter's grasp.

"Done," said Henchard.

"Done," said Donald Farfrae.

The face of Mr. Henchard beamed forth a satisfaction that was almost fierce in its strength. "Now you are my friend!" he exclaimed. "Come back to my house; let's clinch it at once by clear terms, so as to be comfortable in our minds." Farfrae caught up his bag and retraced the North-West Avenue in Henchard's company as he had come. Henchard was all confidence now.

"I am the most distant fellow in the world when I don't care for

---

*Steep incline.

a man," he said. "But when a man takes my fancy he takes it strong. Now I am sure you can eat another breakfast? You couldn't have eaten much so early, even if they had anything at that place to gi'e thee, which they hadn't; so come to my house and we will have a solid, staunch tuck-in, and settle terms in black-and-white if you like; though my word's my bond. I can always make a good meal in the morning. I've got a splendid cold pigeon-pie going just now. You can have some home-brewed if you want to, you know."

"It is too airly in the morning for that," said Farfræ with a smile.

"Well, of course, I didn't know. I don't drink it because of my oath; but I am obliged to brew for my work-people."

Thus talking they returned, and entered Henchard's premises by the back way or traffic entrance. Here the matter was settled over the breakfast, at which Henchard heaped the young Scotchman's plate to a prodigal fulness. He would not rest satisfied till Farfrae had written for his luggage from Bristol, and despatched the letter to the post-office. When it was done this man of strong impulses declared that his new friend should take up his abode in his house—at least till some suitable lodgings could be found.

He then took Farfrae round and showed him the place, and the stores of grain, and other stock; and finally entered the offices where the younger of them has already been discovered by Elizabeth.

X

WHILE SHE STILL SAT under the Scotchman's eyes a man came up to the door, reaching it as Henchard opened the door of the inner office to admit Elizabeth. The new-comer stepped forward like the quicker cripple at Bethesda,[7] and entered in her stead. She could hear his words to Henchard: "Joshua Jopp, sir—by appointment—the new manager."

"The new manager!—he's in his office," said Henchard bluntly.

"In his office!" said the man, with a stultified air.

"I mentioned Thursday," said Henchard; "and as you did not keep your appointment, I have engaged another manager. At first I thought he must be you. Do you think I can wait when business is in question?"

"You said Thursday or Saturday, sir," said the new-comer, pulling out a letter.

"Well, you are too late," said the corn-factor. "I can say no more."

"You as good as engaged me," murmured the man.

"Subject to an interview," said Henchard. "I am sorry for you— very sorry indeed. But it can't be helped."

There was no more to be said, and the man came out, encountering Elizabeth-Jane in his passage. She could see that his mouth twitched with anger, and that bitter disappointment was written in his face everywhere.

Elizabeth-Jane now entered, and stood before the master of the premises. His dark pupils—which always seemed to have a red spark of light in them, though this could hardly be a physical fact—turned indifferently round under his dark brows until they rested on her figure. "Now then, what is it, my young woman?" he said blandly.

"Can I speak to you—not on business, sir?" said she.

"Yes—I suppose." He looked at her more thoughtfully.

"I am sent to tell you; sir," she innocently went on, "that a distant relative of yours by marriage, Susan Newson, a sailor's widow, is in the town; and to ask whether you would wish to see her."

The rich *rouge-et-noir** of his countenance underwent a slight change. "Oh—Susan is—still alive?" he asked with difficulty.

"Yes, sir."

"Are you her daughter?"

"Yes, sir—her only daughter."

"What—do you call yourself—your Christian name?"

"Elizabeth-Jane, sir."

"Newson?"

"Elizabeth-Jane Newson."

This at once suggested to Henchard that the transaction of his early married life at Weydon Fair was unrecorded in the family history. It was more than he could have expected. His wife had behaved kindly to him in return for his unkindness, and had never proclaimed her wrong to her child or to the world.

---

*Red and black (French).

"I am—a good deal interested in your news," he said. "And as this is not a matter of business, but pleasure, suppose we go indoors."

It was with a gentle delicacy of manner, surprising to Elizabeth, that he showed her out of the office and through the outer room, where Donald Farfrae was overhauling bins and samples with the inquiring inspection of a beginner in charge. Henchard preceded her through the door in the wall to the suddenly changed scene of the garden and flowers, and onward into the house. The dining-room to which he introduced her still exhibited the remnants of the lavish breakfast laid for Farfrae. It was furnished to profusion with heavy mahogany furniture of the deepest red-Spanish hues. Pembroke tables, with leaves hanging so low that they well-nigh touched the floor, stood against the walls on legs and feet shaped like those of an elephant, and on one lay three huge folio volumes—a Family Bible, a "Josephus,"* and a "Whole Duty of Man."† In the chimney corner was a firegrate with a fluted semicircular back, having urns and festoons cast in relief thereon; and the chairs were of the kind which, since that day, has cast lustre upon the names of Chippendale and Sheraton,‡ though, in point of fact, their patterns may have been such as those illustrious carpenters never saw or heard of.

"Sit down—Elizabeth-Jane—sit down," he said, with a shake in his voice as he uttered her name; and sitting down himself he allowed his hands to hang between his knees, while he looked upon the carpet. "Your mother, then, is quite well?"

"She is rather worn out, sir, with travelling."

"A sailor's widow—when did he die?"

"Father was lost last spring."

Henchard winced at the word "father," thus applied. "Do you and she come from abroad—America or Australia?" he asked.

"No. We have been in England some years. I was twelve when we came here from Canada."

"Ah; exactly." By such conversation he discovered the circumstances which had enveloped his wife and her child in such total

---

*A copy of either The Antiquities of the Jews or History of the Jewish War, by first-century historian Flavius Josephus.
†Popular devotional manual published in 1658.
‡Famous eighteenth-century furniture designers.

obscurity that he had long ago believed them to be in their graves. These things being clear, he returned to the present. "And where is your mother staying?"

"At the Three Mariners."

"And you are her daughter Elizabeth-Jane?" repeated Henchard. He arose, came close to her, and glanced in her face. "I think," he said, suddenly turning away with a wet eye, "you shall take a note from me to your mother. I should like to see her. . . . She is not left very well off by her late husband?" His eye fell on Elizabeth's clothes, which, though a respectable suit of black, and her very best, were decidedly old-fashioned even to Casterbridge eyes.

"Not very well," she said, glad that he had divined this without her being obliged to express it.

He sat down at the table and wrote a few lines; next taking from his pocket-book a five-pound note, which he put in the envelope with the letter, adding to it, as by an after-thought, five shillings. Sealing the whole up carefully, he directed it to "Mrs. Newson, Three Mariners Inn," and handed the packet to Elizabeth.

"Deliver it to her personally, please," said Henchard. "Well, I am glad to see you here, Elizabeth-Jane—very glad. We must have a long talk together—but not just now."

He took her hand at parting, and held it so warmly that she, who had known so little friendship, was much affected, and tears rose to her aerial-grey eyes. The instant that she was gone Henchard's state showed itself more distinctly; having shut the door he sat in his dining-room stiffly erect, gazing at the opposite wall as if he read his history there.

"Begad!" he suddenly exclaimed, jumping up. "I didn't think of that. Perhaps these are impostors—and Susan and the child dead after all!"

However, a something in Elizabeth-Jane soon assured him that, as regarded her, at least, there could be little doubt. And a few hours would settle the question of her mother's identity; for he had arranged in his note to see her that evening.

"It never rains but it pours!" said Henchard. His keenly excited interest in his new friend the Scotchman was now eclipsed by this event; and Donald Farfrae saw so little of him during the rest of the day that he wondered at the suddenness of his employer's moods.

In the meantime Elizabeth had reached the inn. Her mother, instead of taking the note with the curiosity of a poor woman expecting assistance, was much moved at sight of it. She did not read it at once, asking Elizabeth to describe her reception, and the very words Mr. Henchard used. Elizabeth's back was turned when her mother opened the letter. It ran thus:—

> Meet me at eight o'clock this evening, if you can, at the Ring on the Budmouth road. The place is easy to find. I can say no more now. The news upsets me almost. The girl seems to be in ignorance. Keep her so till I have seen you.
>
> M. H.

He said nothing about the enclosure of five guineas. The amount was significant; it may tacitly have said to her that he bought her back again. She waited restlessly for the close of the day, telling Elizabeth-Jane that she was invited to see Mr. Henchard; that she would go alone. But she said nothing to show that the place of meeting was not at his house, nor did she hand the note to Elizabeth.

XI

THE RING AT CASTERBRIDGE WAS merely the local name of one of the finest Roman Amphitheatres, if not the very finest, remaining in Britain.

Casterbridge announced old Rome in every street, alley, and precinct. It looked Roman, bespoke the art of Rome, concealed dead men of Rome. It was impossible to dig more than a foot or two deep about the town fields and gardens without coming upon some tall soldier or other of the Empire, who had lain there in his silent unobtrusive rest for a space of fifteen hundred years. He was mostly found lying on his side, in an oval scoop in the chalk, like a chicken in its shell; his knees drawn up to his chest; sometimes with the remains of his spear against his arm; a fibula* or brooch of bronze on his breast

---

*Buckle or fastener (Latin).

or forehead; an urn at his knees, a jar at his throat, a bottle at his mouth; and mystified conjecture pouring down upon him from the eyes of Casterbridge street boys and men, who had turned a moment to gaze at the familiar spectacle as they passed by.

Imaginative inhabitants, who would have felt an unpleasantness at the discovery, of a comparatively modern skeleton in their gardens, were quite unmoved by these hoary shapes. They had lived so long ago, their time was so unlike the present, their hopes and motives were so widely removed from ours, that between them and the living there seemed to stretch a gulf too wide for even a spirit to pass.

The Amphitheatre was a huge circular enclosure, with a notch at opposite extremities of its diameter north and south. From its sloping internal form it might have been called the spittoon of the Jötuns.* It was to Casterbridge what the ruined Coliseum is to modern Rome, and was nearly of the same magnitude. The dusk of evening was the proper hour at which a true impression of this suggestive place could be received. Standing in the middle of the arena at that time there by degrees became apparent its real vastness, which a cursory view from the summit at noon-day was apt to obscure. Melancholy, impressive, lonely, yet accessible from every part of the town, the historic circle was the frequent spot for appointments of a furtive kind. Intrigues were arranged there; tentative meetings were there experimented after divisions and feuds. But one kind of appointment—in itself the most common of any—seldom had place in the Amphitheatre: that of happy lovers.

Why, seeing that it was pre-eminently an airy, accessible, and sequestered spot for interviews, the cheerfullest form of those occurrences never took kindly to the soil of the ruin, would be a curious inquiry. Perhaps it was because its associations had about them something sinister. Its history proved that. Apart from the sanguinary nature of the games originally played therein, such incidents attached to its past as these: that for scores of years the town-gallows had stood at one corner; that in 1705 a woman who had murdered her husband was half-strangled and then burnt there in the presence of ten thousand spectators.[8] Tradition reports that at a certain stage of the burning her heart burst and leapt out of her body, to the ter-

---

*Giants in Scandinavian mythology.

ror of them all, and that not one of those ten thousand people ever cared particularly for hot roast after that. In addition to these old tragedies, pugilistic encounters almost to the death had come off down to recent dates in that secluded arena, entirely invisible to the outside world save by climbing to the top of the enclosure, which few townspeople in the daily round of their lives ever took the trouble to do. So that, though close to the turnpike-road, crimes might be perpetrated there unseen at mid-day.

Some boys had latterly tried to impart gaiety to the ruin by using the central arena as a cricket-ground. But the game usually languished for the aforesaid reason—the dismal privacy which the earthen circle enforced, shutting out every appreciative passer's vision, every commendatory remark from outsiders—everything, except the sky; and to play at games in such circumstances was like acting to an empty house. Possibly, too, the boys were timid, for some old people said that at certain moments in the summer time, in broad daylight, persons sitting with a book or dozing in the arena had, on lifting their eyes, beheld the slopes lined with a gazing legion of Hadrian's soldiery* as if watching the gladiatorial combat; and had heard the roar of their excited voices; that the scene would remain but a moment, like a lightning flash, and then disappear.

It was related that there still remained under the south entrance excavated cells for the reception of the wild animals and athletes who took part in the games. The arena was still smooth and circular, as if used for its original purpose not so very long ago. The sloping pathways by which spectators had ascended to their seats were pathways yet. But the whole was grown over with grass, which now, at the end of summer was bearded with withered bents† that formed waves under the brush of the wind, returning to the attentive ear Æolian‡ modulations, and detaining for moments the flying globes of thistledown.

Henchard had chosen this spot as being the safest from observation which he could think of for meeting his long-lost wife, and at

---

*Hadrian was emperor of Rome from A.D. 117 to 138; he came to Britain in 122.
†Reeds.
‡Referring to Aeolus, the Greek god of the wind; the Aeolian harp, which produces song when the wind blows through its strings, is a common symbol in Romantic poetry.

the same time as one easily to be found by a stranger after nightfall. As Mayor of the town, with a reputation to keep up, he could not invite her to come to his house till some definite course had been decided on.

Just before eight he approached the deserted earthwork, and entered by the south path which descended over the débris of the former dens. In a few moments he could discern a female figure creeping in by the great north gap, or public gateway. They met in the middle of the arena. Neither spoke just at first—there was no necessity for speech—and the poor woman leant against Henchard, who supported her in his arms.

"I don't drink," he said in a low, halting, apologetic voice. "You hear, Susan?—I don't drink now—I haven't since that night." Those were his first words.

He felt her bow her head in acknowledgment that she understood. After a minute or two he again began:

"If I had known you were living, Susan! But there was every reason to suppose you and the child were dead and gone. I took every possible step to find you—travelled—advertised. My opinion at last was that you had started for some colony with that man, and had been drowned on your voyage out. Why did you keep silent like this?"

"O Michael! because of him—what other reason could there be? I thought I owed him faithfulness to the end of one of our lives— foolishly I believed there was something solemn and binding in the bargain; I thought that even in honour I dared not desert him when he had paid so much for me in good faith. I meet you now only as his widow—I consider myself that, and that I have no claim upon you. Had he not died I should never have come—never! Of that you may be sure."

"Ts-s-s! How could you be so simple?"

"I don't know. Yet it would have been very wicked—if I had not thought like that!" said Susan, almost crying.

"Yes—yes—so it would. It is only that which makes me feel 'ee an innocent woman. But—to lead me into this!"

"What, Michael?" she asked, alarmed.

"Why, this difficulty about our living together again, and Elizabeth-

Jane. She cannot be told all—she would so despise us both that—I could not bear it!"

"That was why she was brought up in ignorance of you. I could not bear it either."

"Well—we must talk of a plan for keeping her in her present belief, and getting matters straight in spite of it. You have heard I am in a large way of business here—that I am Mayor of the town, and churchwarden, and I don't know what all?"

"Yes," she murmured.

"These things, as well as the dread of the girl discovering our disgrace, make it necessary to act with extreme caution. So that I don't see how you two can return openly to my house as the wife and daughter I once treated badly, and banished from me; and there's the rub o't."*

"We'll go away at once. I only came to see——"

"No, no, Susan; you are not to go—you mistake me!" he said, with kindly severity. "I have thought of this plan: that you and Elizabeth take a cottage in the town as the widow Mrs. Newson and her daughter; that I meet you, court you, and marry you, Elizabeth-Jane coming to my house as my step-daughter. The thing is so natural and easy that it is half done in thinking o't. This would leave my shady, headstrong, disgraceful life as a young man absolutely unopened; the secret would be yours and mine only; and I should have the pleasure of seeing my own only child under my roof, as well as my wife."

"I am quite in your hands, Michael," she said meekly. "I came here for the sake of Elizabeth; for myself, if you tell me to leave again tomorrow morning, and never come near you more, I am content to go."

"Now, now; we don't want to hear that," said Henchard gently. "Of course you won't leave again. Think over the plan I have proposed for a few hours; and if you can't hit upon a better one we'll adopt it. I have to be away for a day or two on business, unfortunately; but during that time you can get lodgings—the only ones in the town fit for you are those over the china-shop in High Street—and you can also look for a cottage."

---

*The problem; see the "to be or not to be" speech in Shakespeare's *Hamlet* (act 3, scene 1).

"If the lodgings are in High Street they are dear, I suppose?"

"Never mind—you must start genteel if our plan is to be carried out. Look to me for money. Have you enough till I come back?"

"Quite," said she.

"And are you comfortable at the inn?"

"O yes."

"And the girl is quite safe from learning the shame of her case and ours?—that's what makes me most anxious of all."

"You would be surprised to find how unlikely she is to dream of the truth. How could she ever suppose such a thing?"

"True!"

"I like the idea of repeating our marriage," said Mrs. Henchard, after a pause. "It seems the only right course, after all this. Now I think I must go back to Elizabeth-Jane, and tell her that our kinsman, Mr. Henchard, kindly wishes us to stay in the town."

"Very well—arrange that yourself. I'll go some way with you."

"No, no. Don't run any risk!" said his wife anxiously. "I can find my way back—it is not late. Please let me go alone."

"Right," said Henchard. "But just one word. Do you forgive me, Susan?"

She murmured something; but seemed to find it difficult to frame her answer.

"Never mind—all in good time," said he. "Judge me by my future works—good-bye!"

He retreated, and stood at the upper side of the Amphitheatre while his wife passed out through the lower way, and descended under the trees to the town. Then Henchard himself went homeward, going so fast that by the time he reached his door he was almost upon the heels of the unconscious* woman from whom he had just parted. He watched her up the street, and turned into his house.

---

*Indicates that Susan was unaware, not that she had lost consciousness.

XII

ON ENTERING HIS OWN door after watching his wife out of sight, the Mayor walked on through the tunnel-shaped passage into the garden, and thence by the back door towards the stores and granaries. A light shone from the office-window, and there being no blind to screen the interior Henchard could see Donald Farfrae still seated where he had left him, initiating himself into the managerial work of the house by overhauling the books. Henchard entered, merely observing, "Don't let me interrupt you, if ye will stay so late."

He stood behind Farfrae's chair, watching his dexterity in clearing up the numerical fogs which had been allowed to grow so thick in Henchard's books as almost to baffle even the Scotchman's perspicacity. The corn-factor's mien was half admiring, and yet it was not without a dash of pity for the tastes of any one who could care to give his mind to such finnikin details. Henchard himself was mentally and physically unfit for grubbing subtleties from soiled paper; he had in a modern sense received the education of Achilles,* and found penmanship a tantalizing art.

"You shall do no more to-night," he said at length, spreading his great hand over the paper. "There's time enough to-morrow. Come indoors with me and have some supper. Now you shall! I am determined on't." He shut the account-books with friendly force.

Donald had wished to get to his lodgings; but he already saw that his friend and employer was a man who knew no moderation in his requests and impulses, and he yielded gracefully. He liked Henchard's warmth, even if it inconvenienced him; the great difference in their characters adding to the liking.

They locked up the office, and the young man followed his companion through the private little door which, admitting directly into Henchard's garden, permitted a passage from the utilitarian to the beautiful at one step. The garden was silent, dewy, and full of perfume. It extended a long way back from the house, first as lawn and flowerbeds, then as fruit-garden, where the long-tied espaliers, as old as the old house itself, had grown so stout, and cramped, and gnarled

---

*Greek hero of the Trojan War; that is, Henchard was trained as a warrior, not as a businessman.

that they had pulled their stakes out of the ground and stood distorted and writhing in vegetable agony, like leafy Laocoöns.[9] The flowers which smelt so sweetly were not discernible; and they passed through them into the house.

The hospitalities of the morning were repeated, and when they were over Henchard said, "Pull your chair round to the fireplace, my dear fellow, and let's make a blaze—there's nothing I hate like a black grate, even in September." He applied a light to the laid-in fuel, and a cheerful radiance spread around.

"It is odd," said Henchard, "that two men should meet as we have done on a purely business ground, and that at the end of the first day I should wish to speak to 'ee on a family matter. But, damn it all, I am a lonely man, Farfrae: I have nobody else to speak to; and why shouldn't I tell it to'ee?"

"I'll be glad to hear it, if I can be of any service," said Donald, allowing his eyes to travel over the intricate wood-carvings of the chimney-piece, representing garlanded lyres, shields, and quivers, on either side of a draped ox-skull, and flanked by heads of Apollo and Diana in low relief.

"I've not been always what I am now," continued Henchard, his firm deep voice being ever so little shaken. He was plainly under that strange influence which sometimes prompts men to confide to the newfound friend what they will not tell to the old. "I began life as a working hay-trusser, and when I was eighteen I married on the strength o' my calling. Would you think me a married man?"

"I heard in the town that you were a widower."

"Ah, yes—you would naturally have heard that. Well, I lost my wife nineteen years ago or so—by my own fault. . . . This is how it came about. One summer evening I was travelling for employment, and she was walking at my side, carrying the baby, our only child. We came to a booth in a country fair. I was a drinking man at that time."

Henchard paused a moment, threw himself back so that his elbow rested on the table, his forehead being shaded by his hand, which, however, did not hide the marks of introspective inflexibility on his features as he narrated in fullest detail the incidents of the transaction with the sailor. The tinge of indifference which had at first been visible in the Scotchman now disappeared.

Henchard went on to describe his attempts to find his wife; the oath he swore; the solitary life he led during the years which followed. "I have kept my oath for nineteen years," he went on; "I have risen to what you see me now."

"Ay!"

"Well—no wife could I hear of in all that time; and being by nature something of a woman-hater, I have found it no hardship to keep mostly at a distance from the sex. No wife could I hear of, I say, till this very day. And now—she has come back."

"Come back, has she!"

"This morning—this very morning. And what's to be done?"

"Can ye no' take her and live with her, and make some amends?"

"That's what I've planned and proposed. But, Farfrae," said Henchard gloomily, "by doing right with Susan I wrong another innocent woman."

"Ye don't say that?"

"In the nature of things, Farfrae, it is almost impossible that a man of my sort should have the good fortune to tide through twenty years o' life without making more blunders than one. It has been my custom for many years to run across to Jersey* in the way of business, particularly in the potato and root season. I do a large trade wi' them in that line. Well, one autumn when stopping there I fell quite ill, and in my illness I sank into one of those gloomy fits I sometimes suffer from, on account o' the loneliness of my domestic life, when the world seems to have the blackness of hell, and, like Job,† I could curse the day that gave me birth."

"Ah, now, I never feel like it," said Farfrae.

"Then pray to God that you never may, young man. While in this state I was taken pity on by a woman—a young lady I should call her, for she was of good family, well bred, and well educated—the daughter of some harum-scarum military officer who had got into difficulties, and had his pay sequestrated.‡ He was dead now, and her mother too, and she was as lonely as I. This young creature was staying at the boarding-house where I happened to have my lodging; and

---

*Largest of the Channel Islands.

†Much put-upon Old Testament figure who, in the Bible (Job 3:3), cries out, "Let the day perish wherein I was born" (King James Version).

‡Seized to cover outstanding debts.

when I was pulled down she took upon herself to nurse me. From that she got to have a foolish liking for me. Heaven knows why, for I wasn't worth it. But being together in the same house, and her feelings warm, we got naturally intimate. I won't go into particulars of what our relations were. It is enough to say that we honestly meant to marry. There arose a scandal, which did me no harm, but was of course ruin to her. Though, Farfrae, between you and me, as man and man, I solemnly declare that philandering with womankind has neither been my vice nor my virtue. She was terribly careless of appearances, and I was perhaps more, because o' my dreary state; and it was through this that the scandal arose. At last I was well, and came away. When I was gone she suffered much on my account, and didn't forget to tell me so in letters one after another; till, latterly, I felt I owed her something, and thought that, as I had not heard of Susan for so long, I would make this other one the only return I could make, and ask her if she would run the risk of Susan being alive (very slight as I believed) and marry me, such as I was. She jumped for joy, and we should no doubt soon have been married—but, behold, Susan appears!"

Donald showed his deep concern at a complication so far beyond the degree of his simple experiences.

"Now see what injury a man may cause around him! Even after that wrong-doing at the fair when I was young, if I had never been so selfish as to let this giddy girl devote herself to me over at Jersey, to the injury of her name, all might now be well. Yet, as it stands, I must bitterly disappoint one of these women; and it is the second. My first duty is to Susan—there's no doubt about that."

"They are both in a very melancholy position, and that's true!" murmured Donald.

"They are! For myself I don't care—'twill all end one way. But these two." Henchard paused in reverie. "I feel I should like to treat the second, no less than the first, as kindly as a man can in such a case."

"Ah, well, it cannet be helped!" said the other, with philosophic woefulness. "You mun write to the young lady, and in your letter you must put it plain and honest that it turns out she cannet be your wife, the first having come back; that ye cannet see her more; and that— ye wish her weel."

"That won't do. 'Od seize it, I must do a little more than that! I must—though she did always brag about her rich uncle or rich aunt, and her expectations from 'em—I must send a useful sum of money to her, I suppose—just as a little recompense, poor girl. . . . Now, will you help me in this, and draw up an explanation to her of all I've told ye, breaking it as gently as you can? I'm so bad at letters."

"And I will."

"Now, I haven't told you quite all yet. My wife Susan has my daughter with her—the baby that was in her arms at the fair; and this girl knows nothing of me beyond that I am some sort of relation by marriage. She has grown up in the belief that the sailor to whom I made over her mother, and who is now dead, was her father, and her mother's husband. What her mother has always felt, she and I together feel now—that we can't proclaim our disgrace to the girl by letting her know the truth. Now what would you do?—I want your advice."

"I think I'd run the risk, and tell her the truth. She'll forgive ye both."

"Never!" said Henchard. "I am not going to let her know the truth. Her mother and I be going to marry again; and it will not only help us to keep our child's respect, but it will be more proper. Susan looks upon herself as the sailor's widow, and won't think o' living with me as formerly without another religious ceremony—and she's right."

Farfrae thereupon said no more. The letter to the young Jersey woman was carefully framed by him, and the interview ended, Henchard saying, as the Scotchman left, "I feel it a great relief, Farfrae, to tell some friend o' this! You see now that the Mayor of Casterbridge is not so thriving in his mind as it seems he might be from the state of his pocket."

"I do. And I'm sorry for ye!" said Farfrae.

When he was gone Henchard copied the letter, and, enclosing a cheque, took it to the post-office, from which he walked back thoughtfully.

"Can it be that it will go off so easily!" he said. "Poor thing— God knows! Now then, to make amends to Susan!"

XIII

THE COTTAGE WHICH MICHAEL Henchard hired for his wife Susan under her name of Newson—in pursuance of their plan—was in the upper or western part of the town, near the Roman wall, and the avenue which overshadowed it. The evening sun seemed to shine more yellowly there than anywhere else this autumn—stretching its rays, as the hours grew later, under the lowest sycamore boughs, and steeping the ground-floor of the dwelling, with its green shutters, in a substratum of radiance which the foliage screened from the upper parts. Beneath these sycamores on the town walls could be seen from the sitting-room the tumuli* and earth forts of the distant uplands; making it altogether a pleasant spot, with the usual touch of melancholy that a past-marked prospect lends.

As soon as the mother and daughter were comfortably installed, with a white-aproned servant and all complete, Henchard paid them a visit, and remained to tea. During the entertainment Elizabeth was carefully hoodwinked by the very general tone of the conversation that prevailed—a proceeding which seemed to afford some humour to Henchard, though his wife was not particularly happy in it. The visit was repeated again and again with business-like determination by the Mayor, who seemed to have schooled himself into a course of strict mechanical rightness towards this woman of prior claim, at any expense to the later one and to his own sentiments.

One afternoon the daughter was not indoors when Henchard came, and he said drily, "This is a very good opportunity for me to ask you to name the happy day, Susan."

The poor woman smiled faintly; she did not enjoy pleasantries on a situation into which she had entered solely for the sake of her girl's reputation. She liked them so little, indeed, that there was room for wonder why she had countenanced deception at all, and had not bravely let the girl know her history. But the flesh is weak; and the true explanation came in due course.

"O Michael!" she said, "I am afraid all this is taking up your time and giving trouble—when I did not expect any such thing!" And she

---

*Mounds of earth marking ancient burial sites (Latin).

looked at him and at his dress as a man of affluence, and at the furniture he had provided for the room—ornate and lavish to her eyes.

"Not at all," said Henchard, in rough benignity. "This is only a cottage—it costs me next to nothing. And as to taking up here his red and black visage kindled with satisfaction—"I've a splendid fellow to superintend my business now—a man whose like I've never been able to lay hands on before. I shall soon be able to leave everything to him, and have more time to call my own than I've had for these last twenty years."

Henchard's visits here grew so frequent and so regular that it soon became whispered, and then openly discussed, in Casterbridge that the masterful, coercive Mayor of the town was captured and enervated by the genteel widow Mrs. Newson. His well-known haughty indifference to the society of womankind, his silent avoidance of converse with the sex, contributed a piquancy to what would otherwise have been an unromantic matter enough. That such a poor fragile woman should be his choice was inexplicable, except on the ground that the engagement was a family affair in which sentimental passion had no place; for it was known that they were related in some way. Mrs. Henchard was so pale that the boys called her "The Ghost." Sometimes Henchard overheard this epithet when they passed together along the Walks—as the avenues on the walls were named—at which his face would darken with an expression of destructiveness towards the speakers ominous to see; but he said nothing.

He pressed on the preparations for his union, or rather reunion, with this pale creature in a dogged, unflinching spirit which did credit to his conscientiousness. Nobody would have conceived from his outward demeanour that there was no amatory fire or pulse of romance acting as stimulant to the bustle going on in his gaunt, great house; nothing but three large resolves—one, to make amends to his neglected Susan; another, to provide a comfortable home for Elizabeth-Jane under his paternal eye; and a third, to castigate himself with the thorns which these restitutory acts brought in their train; among them the lowering of his dignity in public opinion by marrying so comparatively humble a woman.

Susan Henchard entered a carriage for the first time in her life when she stepped into the plain brougham* which drew up at the

*Closed one-horse carriage.

door on the wedding-day to take her and Elizabeth-Jane to church. It was a windless morning of warm November rain, which floated down like meal, and lay in a powdery form on the nap of hats and coats. Few people had gathered round the church door though they were well packed within. The Scotchman, who assisted as grooms-man, was of course the only one present, beyond the chief actors, who knew the true situation of the contracting parties. He, however, was too inexperienced, too thoughtful, too judicial, too strongly con-scious of the serious side of the business, to enter into the scene in its dramatic aspect. That required the special genius of Christopher Coney, Solomon Longways, Buzzford, and their fellows. But they knew nothing of the secret; though, as the time for coming out of church drew on, they gathered on the pavement adjoining, and ex-pounded the subject according to their lights.

" 'Tis five-and-forty years since I had my settlement in this here town," said Coney; "but daze me if ever I see a man wait so long be-fore to take so little! There's a chance even for thee after this, Nance Mockridge." The remark was addressed to a woman who stood be-hind his shoulder—the same who had exhibited Henchard's bad bread in public when Elizabeth and her mother entered Casterbridge.

"Be cust if I'd marry any such as he, or thee either," replied that lady. "As for thee, Christopher, we know what ye be, and the less said the better. And as for he—well, there—(lowering her voice) 'tis said 'a was a poor parish 'prentice—I wouldn't say it for all the world—but 'a was a poor parish 'prentice, that began life wi' no more belonging to 'en than a carrion crow."

"And now he's worth ever so much a minute," murmured Long-ways. "When a man is said to be worth so much a minute, he's a man to be considered!"

Turning, he saw a circular disc reticulated with creases, and rec-ognized the smiling countenance of the fat woman who had asked for another song at the Three Mariners. "Well, Mother Cuxsom," he said, "how's this? Here's Mrs. Newson, a mere skellinton, has got another husband to keep her, while a woman of your tonnage have not."

"I have not. Nor another to beat me. . . . Ah, yes, Cuxsom's gone, and so shall leather breeches!"*

---

*That is, nothing lasts forever.

"Yes; with the blessing of God leather breeches shall go."

" 'Tisn't worth my old while to think of another husband," continued Mrs. Cuxsom. "And yet I'll lay my life I'm as respectable born as she."

"True; your mother was a very good woman—I can mind her. She were rewarded by the Agricultural Society for having begot the greatest number of healthy children without parish assistance, and other virtuous marvels."

" 'Twas that that kept us so low upon ground—that great hungry family."

"Ay. Where the pigs be many the wash* runs thin."

"And dostn't mind how mother would sing, Christopher?" continued Mrs. Cuxsom, kindling at the retrospection; "and how we went with her to the party at Mellstock, do ye mind?—at old Dame Ledlow's, farmer Shinar's aunt, do ye mind?—she we used to call Toad-skin, because her face were so yaller and freckled, do ye mind?"

"I do, hee-hee, I do!" said Christopher Coney.

"And well do I—for I was getting up husband-high at that time—one-half girl, and t'other half woman, as one may say. And canst mind"—she prodded Solomon's shoulder with her finger-tip, while her eyes twinkled between the crevices of their lids—"canst mind the sherry-wine, and the zilver-snuffers,† and how Joan Dummett was took bad when we were coming home, and Jack Briggs was forced to carry her through the mud; and how 'a let her fall in Dairyman Sweetapple's cow-barton,‡ and we had to clane her gown wi' grass—never such a mess as 'a were in?"

"Ay—that I do—hee-hee, such doggery as there was in them ancient days, to be sure! Ah, the miles I used to walk then; and now I can hardly step over a furrow!"

Their reminiscences were cut short by the appearance of the reunited pair—Henchard looking round upon the idlers with that ambiguous gaze of his, which at one moment seemed to mean satisfaction, and at another fiery disdain.

"Well—there's a difference between 'em, though he do call him-

---

*Swill.
†Silver tool for putting out a candle.
‡Cow yard.

self a teetotaller," said Nance Mockridge. "She'll wish her cake dough* afore she's done of him. There's a bluebeardy† look about 'en; and 'twill out in time."

"Stuff—he's well enough! Some folk want their luck butted. If I had a choice as wide as the ocean sea I wouldn't wish for a better man. A poor twanking‡ woman like her—'tis a godsend for her, and hardly a pair of jumps or night-rail§ to her name."

The plain little brougham drove off in the mist, and the idlers dispersed. "Well, we hardly know how to look at things in these times!" said Solomon. "There was a man dropped down dead yesterday, not so very many miles from here; and what wi' that, and this moist weather, 'tis scarce worth one's while to begin any work o' consequence today. I'm in such a low key with drinking nothing but small table ninepenny‖ this last week or two that I shall call and warm up at the Mar'ners as I pass along."

"I don't know but that I may as well go with 'ee, Solomon," said Christopher; "I'm as clammy as a cockle-snail."

XIV

A MARTINMAS SUMMER# OF Mrs. Henchard's life set in with her entry into her husband's large house and respectable social orbit; and it was as bright as such summers well can be. Lest she should pine for deeper affection than he could give he made a point of showing some semblance of it in external action. Among other things he had the iron railings, that had smiled sadly in dull rust for the last eighty years, painted a bright green, and the heavy-barred, small-paned Georgian sash windows enlivened with three coats of white. He was

---

*She'll wish she'd kept her old (that is, unmarried) position.
†The legendary pirate Bluebeard was said to have married and killed a series of women.
‡Miserable.
§Corsets or nightgown.
‖Cheap ale.
#Unusually warm fall weather; Martinmas is a November holiday.

as kind to her as a man, mayor, and churchwarden could possibly be. The house was large, the rooms lofty, and the landings wide; and the two unassuming women scarcely made a perceptible addition to its contents.

To Elizabeth-Jane the time was a most triumphant one. The freedom she experienced, the indulgence with which she was treated, went beyond her expectations. The reposeful, easy, affluent life to which her mother's marriage had introduced her was, in truth, the beginning of a great change in Elizabeth. She found she could have nice personal possessions and ornaments for the asking, and, as the mediæval saying puts it, "Take, have, and keep, are pleasant words." With peace of mind came development, and with development beauty. Knowledge—the result of great natural insight—she did not lack; learning, accomplishments—those, alas, she had not; but as the winter and spring passed by her thin face and figure filled out in rounder and softer curves; the lines and contractions upon her young brow went away; the muddiness of skin which she had looked upon as her lot by nature departed with a change to abundance of good things, and a bloom came upon her cheek. Perhaps, too, her grey, thoughtful eyes revealed an arch gaiety sometimes; but this was infrequent; the sort of wisdom which looked from their pupils did not readily keep company with these lighter moods. Like all people who have known rough times, light-heartedness seemed to her too irrational and inconsequent to be indulged in except as a reckless dram now and then; for she had been too early habituated to anxious reasoning to drop the habit suddenly. She felt none of those ups and downs of spirit which beset so many people without cause; never— to paraphrase a recent poet—never a gloom in Elizabeth-Jane's soul but she well knew how it came there[10] and her present cheerfulness was fairly proportionate to her solid guarantees for the same.

It might have been supposed that, given a girl rapidly becoming good-looking, comfortably circumstanced, and for the first time in her life commanding ready money, she would go and make a fool of her self by dress. But no. The reasonableness of almost everything that Elizabeth did was nowhere more conspicuous than in this question of clothes. To keep in the rear of opportunity in matters of indulgence is as valuable a habit as to keep abreast of opportunity in matters of enterprise. This unsophisticated girl did it by an innate perceptiveness that was almost genius. Thus she refrained from bursting out like a waterflower that spring, and clothing herself in puffings* and knick-knacks, as most of the Casterbridge girls would have done in her circumstances. Her triumph was tempered by circumspection; she had still that fieldmouse fear of the coulter† of destiny despite fair promise, which is common among the thoughtful who have suffered early from poverty and oppression.

"I won't be too gay on any account," she would say to herself. "It would be tempting Providence to hurl mother and me down, and afflict us again as He used to do."

We now see her in a black silk bonnet, velvet mantle or silk spencer,‡ dark dress, and carrying a sunshade. In this latter article she drew the line at fringe, and had it plain edged, with a little ivory ring for keeping it closed. It was odd about the necessity for that sunshade. She discovered that with the clarification of her complexion and the birth of pink cheeks her skin had grown more sensitive to the sun's rays. She protected those cheeks forthwith, deeming spotlessness part of womanliness.

Henchard had become very fond of her, and she went out with him more frequently than with her mother now. Her appearance one day was so attractive that he looked at her critically.

"I happened to have the ribbon by me, so I made it up," she faltered, thinking him perhaps dissatisfied with some rather bright trimming she had donned for the first time.

"Ay—of course—to be sure," he replied in his leonine way. "Do as you like—or rather as your mother advises ye. 'Od send—I've nothing to say to't!"

Indoors she appeared with her hair divided by a parting that arched like a white rainbow from ear to ear. All in front of this line was covered with a thick encampment of curls; all behind was dressed smoothly, and drawn to a knob.

The three members of the family were sitting at breakfast one day, and Henchard was looking silently, as he often did, at this head of hair, which in colour was brown—rather light than dark. "I

---

*Decorative frills.
†Iron blade affixed to a plow.
‡Short fitted jacket.

thought Elizabeth-Jane's hair—didn't you tell me that Elizabeth-Jane's hair promised to be black when she was a baby?" he said to his wife.

She looked startled, jerked his foot warningly, and murmured, "Did I?"

As soon as Elizabeth was gone to her own room Henchard resumed. "Begad, I nearly forgot myself just now! What I meant was that the girl's hair certainly looked as if it would be darker, when she was a baby."

"It did; but they alter so," replied Susan.

"Their hair gets darker, I know—but I wasn't aware it lightened ever?"

"O yes." And the same uneasy expression came out on her face, to which the future held the key. It passed as Henchard went on:

"Well, so much the better. Now, Susan, I want to have her called Miss Henchard—not Miss Newson. Lots o' people do it already in carelessness—it is her legal name—so it may as well be made her usual name—I don't like t'other name at all for my own flesh and blood. I'll advertise it in the Casterbridge paper—that's the way they do it. She won't object."

"No. O no. But——"

"Well, then, I shall do it," said he, peremptorily. "Surely, if she's willing, you must wish it as much as I?"

"O yes—if she agrees let us do it by all means," she replied.

Then Mrs. Henchard acted somewhat inconsistently; it might have been called falsely, but that her manner was emotional and full of the earnestness of one who wishes to do right at great hazard. She went to Elizabeth-Jane, whom she found sewing in her own sitting-room upstairs, and told her what had been proposed about her surname. "Can you agree—is it not a slight upon Newson—now he's dead and gone?"

Elizabeth reflected. "I'll think of it, mother," she answered.

When, later in the day, she saw Henchard, she adverted to the matter at once, in a way which showed that the line of feeling started by her mother had been persevered in. "Do you wish this change so very much, sir?" she asked.

"Wish it. Why, my blessed fathers, what an ado you women make about a trifle! I proposed it—that's all. Now, 'Lizabeth-Jane, just please yourself. Curse me if I care what you do. Now, you understand, don't 'ee go agreeing to it to please me."

Here the subject dropped, and nothing more was said, and nothing was done, and Elizabeth still passed as Miss Newson, and not by her legal name.

Meanwhile the great corn and hay traffic conducted by Henchard throve under the management of Donald Farfrae as it had never thriven before. It had formerly moved in jolts; now it went on oiled castors. The old crude *vivâ voce** system of Henchard, in which everything depended upon his memory, and bargains were made by the tongue alone, was swept away. Letters and ledgers took the place of "I'll do't," and "you shall hae't"; and, as in all such cases of advance, the rugged picturesqueness of the old method disappeared with its inconveniences.

The position of Elizabeth-Jane's room—rather high in the house, so that it commanded a view of the hay-stores and granaries across the garden—afforded her opportunity for accurate observation of what went on there. She saw that Donald and Mr. Henchard were inseparables. When walking together Henchard would lay his arm familiarly on his manager's shoulder, as if Farfrae were a younger brother, bearing so heavily that his slight figure bent under the weight. Occasionally she would hear a perfect cannonade of laughter from Henchard, arising from something Donald had said, the latter looking quite innocent and not laughing at all. In Henchard's somewhat lonely life he evidently found the young man as desirable for comradeship as he was useful for consultations. Donald's brightness of intellect maintained in the corn-factor the admiration it had won at the first hour of their meeting. The poor opinion, and but ill-concealed, that he entertained of the slim Farfrae's physical girth, strength, and dash was more than counterbalanced by the immense respect he had for his brains.

Her quiet eye discerned that Henchard's tigerish affection for the younger man, his constant liking to have Farfrae near him, now and then resulted in a tendency to domineer, which, however, was checked in a moment when Donald exhibited marks of real offence. One day, looking down on their figures from on high, she heard the

---

*Oral (Latin).

latter remark, as they stood in the doorway between the garden and yard, that their habit of walking and driving about together rather neutralized Farfrae's value as a second pair of eyes, which should be used in places where the principal was not. "'Od damn it," cried Henchard, "what's all the world! I like a fellow to talk to. Now come along and hae some supper, and don't take too much thought about things, or ye'll drive me crazy."

When she walked with her mother, on the other hand, she often beheld the Scotchman looking at them with a curious interest. The fact that he had met her at the Three Mariners was insufficient to account for it, since on the occasions on which she had entered his room he had never raised his eyes. Besides, it was at her mother more particularly than at herself that he looked, to Elizabeth-Jane's half-conscious, simple-minded, perhaps pardonable, disappointment. Thus she could not account for this interest by her own attractiveness, and she decided that it might be apparent only—a way of turning his eyes that Mr. Farfrae had.

She did not divine the ample explanation of his manner, without personal vanity, that was afforded by the fact of Donald being the depositary of Henchard's confidence in respect of his past treatment of the pale, chastened mother who walked by her side. Her conjectures on that past never went further than faint ones based on things casually heard and seen—mere guesses that Henchard and her mother might have been lovers in their younger days, who had quarrelled and parted.

Casterbridge, as has been hinted, was a place deposited in the block upon a corn-field. There was no suburb in the modern sense, or transitional intermixture of town and down. It stood, with regard to the wide fertile land adjoining, clean-cut and distinct, like a chessboard on a green table-cloth. The farmer's boy could sit under his barley-mow* and pitch a stone into the office-window of the town-clerk; reapers at work among the sheaves nodded to acquaintances standing on the pavement-corner; the red-robed judge, when he condemned a sheep-stealer, pronounced sentence to the tune of Baa, that floated in at the window from the remainder of the flock browsing hard by; and at executions the waiting crowd stood in a meadow im-

---

*Stack of barley.

mediately before the drop, out of which the cows had been temporarily driven to give the spectators room.

The corn grown on the upland side of the borough was garnered by farmers who lived in an eastern purlieu called Durnover. Here wheat-ricks overhung the old Roman street, and thrust their eaves against the church tower; green-thatched barns, with doorways as high as the gates of Solomon's temple, opened directly upon the main thoroughfare. Barns indeed were so numerous as to alternate with every half-dozen houses along the way. Here lived burgesses who daily walked the fallow; shepherds in an intra-mural* squeeze. A street of farmers' homesteads—a street ruled by a mayor and corporation, yet echoing with the thump of the flail, the flutter of the winnowing-fan, and the purr of the milk into the pails—a street which had nothing urban in it whatever—this was the Durnover end of Casterbridge.

Henchard, as was natural, dealt largely with this nursery or bed of small farmers close at hand—and his waggons were often down that way. One day, when arrangements were in progress for getting home corn from one of the aforesaid farms, Elizabeth-Jane received a note by hand, asking her to oblige the writer by coming at once to a granary on Durnover Hill. As this was the granary whose contents Henchard was removing, she thought the request had something to do with his business, and proceeded thither as soon as she had put on her bonnet. The granary was just within the farm-yard, and stood on stone staddles, high enough for persons to walk under. The gates were open, but nobody was within. However, she entered and waited. Presently she saw a figure approaching the gate—that of Donald Farfrae. He looked up at the church clock, and came in. By some unaccountable shyness, some wish not to meet him there alone, she quickly ascended the step-ladder leading to the granary door, and entered it before he had seen her. Farfrae advanced, imagining himself in solitude; and a few drops of rain beginning to fall he moved and stood under the shelter where she had just been standing. Here he leant against one of the staddles, and gave himself up to patience. He, too, was plainly expecting some one; could it be herself?

---

*Within the walls.

if so, why? In a few minutes he looked at his watch, and then pulled out a note, a duplicate of the one she had herself received.

The situation began to be very awkward, and the longer she waited the more awkward it became. To emerge from a door just above his head and descend the ladder, and show she had been in hiding there, would look so very foolish that she still waited on. A winnowing machine stood close beside her, and to relieve her suspense she gently moved the handle; whereupon a cloud of wheat husks flew out into her face, and covered her clothes and bonnet, and stuck into the fur of her victorine.* He must have heard the slight movement for he looked up, and then ascended the steps.

"Ah—it's Miss Newson," he said as soon as he could see into the granary. "I didn't know you were there. I have kept the appointment, and am at your service."

"O Mr. Farfrae," she faltered; "so have I. But I didn't know it was you who wished to see me, otherwise I——"

"I wished to see you? O no—at least, that is, I am afraid there may be a mistake."

"Didn't you ask me to come here? Didn't you write this?" Elizabeth held out her note.

"No. Indeed, at no hand would I have thought of it! And for you—didn't you ask me? This is not your writing?" And he held up his.

"By no means."

"And is that really so! Then it's somebody wanting to see us both. Perhaps we would do well to wait a little longer."

Acting on this consideration they lingered, Elizabeth-Jane's face being arranged to an expression of preternatural composure, and the young Scot, at every footstep in the street without, looking from under the granary to see if the passer were about to enter and declare himself their summoner. They watched individual drops of rain creeping down the thatch of the opposite rick—straw after straw— till they reached the bottom; but nobody came, and the granary roof began to drip.

"The person is not likely to be coming," said Farfrae. "It's a trick

*Fur scarf worn by women.

perhaps, and if so, it's a great pity to waste our time like this, and so much to be done."

" 'Tis a great liberty," said Elizabeth.

"It's true, Miss Newson. We'll hear news of this some day, depend on't, and who it was that did it. I wouldn't stand for it hindering myself; but you, Miss Newson"——

"I don't mind—much," she replied.

"Neither do I."

They lapsed again into silence. "You are anxious to get back to Scotland, I suppose, Mr. Farfrae?" she inquired.

"O no, Miss Newson. Why would I be?"

"I only supposed you might be from the song you sang at the Three Mariners—about Scotland and home, I mean—which you seemed to feel so deep down in your heart; so that we all felt for you."

"Ay—and I did sing there—I did——But, Miss Newson"—and Donald's voice musically undulated between two semitones, as it always did when he became earnest—"it's well you feel a song for a few minutes, and your eyes they get quite tearful; but you finish it, and for all you felt you don't mind it or think of it again for a long while. O no, I don't want to go back! Yet I'll sing the song to you wi' pleasure whenever you like. I could sing it now, and not mind at all?"

"Thank you, indeed. But I fear I must go—rain or no."

"Ay! Then, Miss Newson, ye had better say nothing about this hoax, and take no heed of it. And if the person should say anything to you, be civil to him or her, as if you did not mind it—so you'll take the clever person's laugh away." In speaking his eyes became fixed upon her dress, still sown with wheat husks. "There's husks and dust on you. Perhaps you don't know it?" he said, in tones of extreme delicacy. "And it's very bad to let rain come upon clothes when there's chaff on them. It washes in and spoils them. Let me help you—blowing is the best."

As Elizabeth neither assented nor dissented Donald Farfrae began blowing her back hair, and her side hair, and her neck, and the crown of her bonnet, and the fur of her victorine, Elizabeth saying, "O, thank you," at every puff. At last she was fairly clean, though Farfrae, having got over his first concern at the situation, seemed in no manner of hurry to be gone.

"Ah—now I'll go and get ye an umbrella," he said.

She declined the offer, stepped out and was gone. Farfrae walked slowly after, looking thoughtfully at her diminishing figure, and whistling in undertones, "As I came down through Cannobie."*

XV

AT FIRST MISS NEWSON's budding beauty was not regarded with much interest by anybody in Casterbridge. Donald Farfrae's gaze, it is true, was now attracted by the Mayor's so-called stepdaughter, but he was only one. The truth is that she was but a poor illustrative instance of the prophet Baruch's sly definition: "The virgin that loveth to go gay."[11]

When she walked abroad she seemed to be occupied with an inner chamber of ideas, and to have slight need for visible objects. She formed curious resolves on checking gay fancies in the matter of clothes, because it was inconsistent with her past life to blossom gaudily the moment she had become possessed of money. But nothing is more insidious than the evolution of wishes from mere fancies, and of wants from mere wishes. Henchard gave Elizabeth-Jane a box of delicately-tinted gloves one spring day. She wanted to wear them to show her appreciation of his kindness, but she had no bonnet that would harmonize. As an artistic indulgence she thought she would have such a bonnet. When she had a bonnet that would go with the gloves she had no dress that would go with the bonnet. It was now absolutely necessary to finish; she ordered the requisite article, and found that she had no sunshade to go with the dress. In for a penny in for a pound; she bought the sunshade, and the whole structure was at last complete.

Everybody was attracted, and some said that her bygone simplicity was the art that conceals art, the "delicate imposition" of Rochefoucauld;[12] she had produced an effect, a contrast, and it had

---

*Variant of the song Farfrae sings when he first encounters Elizabeth-Jane at the Three Mariners.

been done on purpose. As a matter of fact this was not true, but it had
its result; for as soon as Casterbridge thought her artful it thought her
worth notice. "It is the first time in my life that I have been so much
admired," she said to herself; "though perhaps it is by those whose
admiration is not worth having."

But Donald Farfrae admired her, too; and altogether the time was
an exciting one; sex had never before asserted itself in her so strongly,
for in former days she had perhaps been too impersonally human to
be distinctively feminine. After an unprecedented success one day she
came indoors, went upstairs, and leant upon her bed face downwards, quite forgetting the possible creasing and damage. "Good
Heaven," she whispered, "can it be? Here am I setting up as the town
beauty!"

When she had thought it over, her usual fear of exaggerating appearances engendered a deep sadness. "There is something wrong in
all this," she mused. "If they only knew what an unfinished girl I
am—that I can't talk Italian, or use globes, or show any of the accomplishments they learn at boarding-schools, how they would despise me! Better sell all this finery and buy myself grammar-books
and dictionaries and a history of all the philosophies!"

She looked from the window and saw Henchard and Farfrae in
the hay-yard talking, with that impetuous cordiality on the Mayor's
part, and genial modesty on the younger man's, that was now so generally observable in their intercourse. Friendship between man and
man; what a rugged strength there was in it, as evinced by these two.
And yet the seed that was to lift the foundation of this friendship was
at that moment taking root in a chink of its structure.

It was about six o'clock; the men were dropping off homeward
one by one. The last to leave was a round shouldered, blinking young
man of nineteen or twenty, whose mouth fell ajar on the slightest
provocation, seemingly because there was no chin to support it. Henchard called aloud to him as he went out of the gate. "Here—Abel
Whittle!"

Whittle turned, and ran back a few steps. "Yes, sir," he said, in
breathless deprecation, as if he knew what was coming next.

"Once more—be in time to-morrow morning. You see what's to
be done, and you hear what I say, and you know I'm not going to be
trifled with any longer."

"Yes, sir." Then Abel Whittle left, and Henchard and Farfrae; and Elizabeth saw no more of them.

Now there was good reason for this command on Henchard's part. Poor Abel, as he was called, had an inveterate habit of oversleeping himself and coming late to his work. His anxious will was to be among the earliest; but if his comrades omitted to pull the string that he always tied round his great toe and left hanging out of the window for that purpose, his will was as wind. He did not arrive in time.

As he was often second hand at the hay-weighing, or at the crane which lifted the sacks, or was one of those who had to accompany the waggons into the country to fetch away stacks that had been purchased, this affliction of Abel's was productive of much inconvenience. For two mornings in the present week he had kept the others waiting nearly an hour; hence Henchard's threat. It now remained to be seen what would happen to-morrow.

Six o'clock struck, and there was no Whittle. At half-past six Henchard entered the yard; the waggon was horsed that Abel was to accompany; and the other man had been waiting twenty minutes. Then Henchard swore, and Whittle coming up breathless at that instant, the corn-factor turned on him, and declared with an oath that this was the last time; that if he were behind once more, by God, he would come and drag him out o' bed.

"There is sommit wrong in my make, your worshipful!" said Abel, "especially in the inside, whereas my poor dumb brain gets as dead as a clot afore I've said my few scrags of prayers. Yes—it came on as a stripling, just afore I'd got man's wages, whereas I never enjoy my bed at all, for no sooner do I lie down than I be asleep, and afore I be awake I be up. I've fretted my gizzard green about it, maister, but what can I do? Now last night, afore I went to bed, I only had a scantling* o' cheese and——"

"I don't want to hear it!" roared Henchard. "To-morrow the waggons must start at four, and if you're not here, stand clear. I'll mortify thy flesh for thee!"

"But let me clear up my points, your worshipful——"

Henchard turned away.

---

*Scrap.

"He asked me and he questioned me, and then 'a wouldn't hear my points!" said Abel, to the yard in general. "Now, I shall twitch like a moment-hand* all night to-night for fear o' him!"

The journey to be taken by the waggons next day was a long one into Blackmoor Vale, and at four o'clock lanterns were moving about the yard. But Abel was missing. Before either of the other men could run to Abel's and warn him, Henchard appeared in the garden door-way. "Where's Abel Whittle? Not come after all I've said? Now I'll carry out my word, by my blessed fathers—nothing else will do him any good! I'm going up that way."

Henchard went off, entered Abel's house, a little cottage in Back Street, the door of which was never locked because the inmates had nothing to lose. Reaching Whittle's bedside the corn-factor shouted a bass note so vigorously that Abel started up instantly, and beholding Henchard standing over him, was galvanized into spasmodic move-ments which had not much relation to getting on his clothes.

"Out of bed, sir, and off to the granary, or you leave my employ today! 'Tis to teach ye a lesson. March on; never mind your breeches!"

The unhappy Whittle threw on his sleeve waistcoat, and managed to get into his boots at the bottom of the stairs, while Henchard thrust his hat over his head. Whittle then trotted on down Back Street, Henchard walking sternly behind.

Just at this time Farfrae, who had been to Henchard's house to look for him, came out of the back gate, and saw something white fluttering in the morning gloom, which he soon perceived to be the part of Abel's shirt that showed below his waistcoat.

"For maircy's sake, what object's this?" said Farfrae, following Abel into the yard, Henchard being some way in the rear by this time.

"Ye see, Mr. Farfrae," gibbered Abel with a resigned smile of ter-ror, "he said he'd mortify my flesh if so be I didn't get up sooner, and now he's a-doing on't! Ye see it can't be helped, Mr. Farfrae; things do happen queer sometimes! Yes—I'll go to Blackmoor Vale half naked as I be, since he do command; but I shall kill myself afterwards; I can't outlive the disgrace; for the women-folk will be looking out of

---

*Second hand on a watch or clock.

their winders at my mortification all the way along, and laughing me to scorn as a man 'ithout breeches! You know how I feel such things, Maister Farfrae, and how forlorn thoughts get hold upon me. Yes—I shall do myself harm—I feel it coming on!"

"Get back home, and slip on your breeches, and come to wark like a man! If ye go not, you'll ha'e your death standing there!"

"I'm afeard I mustn't! Mr. Henchard said——"

"I don't care what Mr. Henchard said, nor anybody else! 'Tis simple foolishness to do this. Go and dress yourself instantly, Whittle."

"Hullo, hullo!" said Henchard, coming up behind: "Who's sending him back?"

All the men looked towards Farfrae.

"I am," said Donald. "I say this joke has been carried far enough."

"And I say it hasn't! Get up in the waggon, Whittle."

"Not if I am manager," said Farfrae. "He either goes home, or I march out of this yard for good."

Henchard looked at him with a face stern and red. But he paused for a moment, and their eyes met. Donald went up to him, for he saw in Henchard's look that he began to regret this.

"Come," said Donald quietly, "a man o' your position should ken better, sir! It is tyrannical and no worthy of you."

" 'Tis not tyrannical!" murmured Henchard, like a sullen boy. "It is to make him remember!" He presently added, in a tone of one bitterly hurt: "Why did you speak to me before them like that, Farfrae? You might have stopped till we were alone. Ah—I know why! I've told ye the secret o' my life—fool that I was to do't—and you take advantage of me!"

"I had forgot it," said Farfrae simply.

Henchard looked on the ground, said nothing more, and turned away. During the day Farfrae learnt from the men that Henchard had kept Abel's old mother in coals and snuff all the previous winter, which made him less antagonistic to the corn-factor. But Henchard continued moody and silent, and when one of the men inquired of him if some oats should be hoisted to an upper floor or not, he said shortly, "Ask Mr. Farfrae. He's master here!"

Morally he was; there could be no doubt of it. Henchard, who had hitherto been the most admired man in his circle, was the most admired no longer. One day the daughters of a deceased farmer in Durnover wanted an opinion on the value of their haystack, and sent a messenger to ask Mr. Farfrae to oblige them with one. The messenger, who was a child, met in the yard not Farfrae, but Henchard.

"Very well," he said. "I'll come."

"But please will Mr. Farfrae come?" said the child.

"I am going that way. . . . Why Mr. Farfrae?" said Henchard, with the fixed look of thought. "Why do people always want Mr. Farfrae?"

"I suppose because they like him so—that's what they say."

"Oh—I see—that's what they say—hey? They like him because he's cleverer than Mr. Henchard, and because he knows more; and, in short, Mr. Henchard can't hold a candle to him—hey?"

"Yes—that's just it, sir—some of it."

"Oh, there's more? Of course there's more! What besides? Come, here's sixpence for a fairing."*

" 'And he's better-tempered, and Henchard's a fool to him,' they say. And when some of the women were a-walking home they said, 'He's a diment†—he's a chap o' wax‡—he's the best—he's the horse for my money,' says they. And they said, 'He's the most understanding man o' them two by long chalks. I wish he was the master instead of Henchard,' they said."

"They'll talk any nonsense," Henchard replied with covered gloom. "Well, you can go now. And I am coming to value the hay, d'ye hear?—I." The boy departed, and Henchard murmured, "Wish he were master here, do they?"

He went towards Durnover. On his way he overtook Farfrae. They walked on together, Henchard looking mostly on the ground.

"You're no yoursel' the day?" Donald inquired.

"Yes, I am very well," said Henchard.

"But ye are a bit down—surely ye are down? Why, there's nothing to be angry about! 'Tis splendid stuff that we've got from Blackmoor Vale. By the by, the people in Durnover want their hay valued."

"Yes. I am going there."

"I'll go with ye."

---

*Gift.
†Diamond.
‡Good man.

As Henchard did not reply Donald practised a piece of music *sotto voce*,* till, getting near the bereaved people's door, he stopped himself with—

"Ah, as their father is dead I won't go on with such as that. How could I forget?"

"Do you care so very much about hurting folks' feelings?" observed Henchard with a half sneer. "You do, I know—especially mine!"

"I am sorry if I have hurt yours, sir," replied Donald, standing still, with a second expression of the same sentiment in the regretfulness of his face. "Why should you say it—think it?"

The cloud lifted from Henchard's brow, and as Donald finished the corn-merchant turned to him, regarding his breast rather than his face.

"I have been hearing things that vexed me," he said. " 'Twas that made me short in my manner—made me overlook what you really are. Now, I don't want to go in here about this hay—Farfrae, you can do it better than I. They sent for 'ee, too. I have to attend a meeting of the Town Council at eleven, and 'tis drawing on for't."

They parted thus in renewed friendship, Donald forbearing to ask Henchard for meanings that were not very plain to him. On Henchard's part there was now again repose; and yet, whenever he thought of Farfrae, it was with a dim dread; and he often regretted that he had told the young man his whole heart, and confided to him the secrets of his life.

XVI

ON THIS ACCOUNT HENCHARD'S manner towards Farfrae insensibly became more reserved. He was courteous—too courteous—and Farfrae was quite surprised at the good breeding which now for the first time showed itself among the qualities of a man he had hitherto thought undisciplined, if warm and sincere. The corn-factor seldom

---

*With a lowered voice (Italian); quietly.

or never again put his arm upon the young man's shoulder so as to nearly weigh him down with the pressure of mechanized friendship. He left off coming to Donald's lodgings and shouting into the passage, "Hoy, Farfrae, boy, come and have some dinner with us! Don't sit here in solitary confinement!" But in the daily routine of their business there was little change.

Thus their lives rolled on till a day of public rejoicing was suggested to the country at large in celebration of a national event* that had recently taken place.

For some time Casterbridge, by nature slow, made no response. Then one day Donald Farfrae broached the subject to Henchard by asking if he would have any objection to lend some rick-cloths† to himself and a few others, who contemplated getting up an entertainment of some sort on the day named, and required a shelter for the same, to which they might charge admission at the rate of so much a head.

"Have as many cloths as you like," Henchard replied.

When his manager had gone about the business Henchard was fired with emulation. It certainly had been very remiss of him, as Mayor, he thought, to call no meeting ere this, to discuss what should be done on this holiday. But Farfrae had been so cursed quick in his movements as to give old-fashioned people in authority no chance of the initiative. However, it was not too late; and on second thoughts he determined to take upon his own shoulders the responsibility of organizing some amusements, if the other Councilmen would leave the matter in his hands. To this they quite readily agreed, the majority being fine old crusted characters who had a decided taste for living without worry.

So Henchard set about his preparations for a really brilliant thing—such as should be worthy of the venerable town. As for Farfrae's little affair, Henchard nearly forgot it; except once now and then when, on it coming into his mind, he said to himself, "Charge admission at so much a head—just like a Scotchman!—who is going to pay anything a head?" The diversions which the Mayor intended to provide were to be entirely free.

---

*A royal birth, marriage, or anniversary; Hardy seems to have no specific event from the period in mind.

†Cloths used to shield grain-ricks from rain.

He had grown so dependent upon Donald that he could scarcely resist calling him in to consult. But by sheer self-coercion he refrained. No, he thought, Farfrae would be suggesting such improvements in his damned luminous way that in spite of himself he, Henchard, would sink to the position of second fiddle, and only scrape harmonies to his manager's talents.

Everybody applauded the Mayor's proposed entertainment, especially when it became known that he meant to pay for it all himself.

Close to the town was an elevated green spot surrounded by an ancient square earthwork—earthworks square, and not square, were as common as blackberries hereabout—a spot whereon the Casterbridge people usually held any kind of merry-making, meeting, or sheep-fair that required more space than the streets would afford. On one side it sloped to the river Froom, and from any point a view was obtained of the country round for many miles. This pleasant upland was to be the scene of Henchard's exploit.

He advertised about the town, in long posters of a pink colour, that games of all sorts would take place here; and set to work a little battalion of men under his own eye. They erected greasy-poles for climbing, with smoked hams and local cheeses at the top. They placed hurdles in rows for jumping over; across the river they laid a slippery pole, with a live pig of the neighbourhood tied at the other end, to become the property of the man who could walk over and get it. There were also provided wheelbarrows for racing, donkeys for the same, a stage for boxing, wrestling, and drawing blood generally; sacks for jumping in. Moreover, not forgetting his principles, Henchard provided a mammoth tea, of which everybody who lived in the borough was invited to partake without payment. The tables were laid parallel with the inner slope of the rampart, and awnings were stretched overhead.

Passing to and fro the Mayor beheld the unattractive exterior of Farfrae's erection in the West Walk, rick-cloths of different sizes and colours being hung up to the arching trees without any regard to appearance. He was easy in his mind now, for his own preparations far transcended these.

The morning came. The sky, which had been remarkably clear down to within a day or two, was overcast, and the weather threatening, the wind having an unmistakable hint of water in it. Henchard wished he had not been quite so sure about the continuance of a fair season. But it was too late to modify or postpone, and the proceedings went on. At twelve o'clock the rain began to fall, small and steady, commencing and increasing so insensibly that it was difficult to state exactly when dry weather ended or wet established itself. In an hour the slight moisture resolved itself into a monotonous smiting of earth by heaven, in torrents to which no end could be prognosticated.

A number of people had heroically gathered in the field, but by three o'clock Henchard discerned that his project was doomed to end in failure. The hams at the top of the poles dripped watered smoke in the form of a brown liquor, the pig shivered in the wind, the grain of the deal tables showed through the sticking tablecloths, for the awning allowed the rain to drift under at its will, and to enclose the sides at this hour seemed a useless undertaking. The landscape over the river disappeared; the wind played on the tent-cords in Æolian improvisations; and at length rose to such a pitch that the whole erection slanted to the ground, those who had taken shelter within it having to crawl out on their hands and knees.

But towards six the storm abated, and a drier breeze shook the moisture from the grass bents. It seemed possible to carry out the programme after all. The awning was set up again; the band was called out from its shelter, and ordered to begin, and where the tables had stood a place was cleared for dancing.

"But where are the folk?" said Henchard, after the lapse of half-an-hour, during which time only two men and a woman had stood up to dance. "The shops are all shut. Why don't they come?"

"They are at Farfrae's affair in the West Walk," answered a Councilman who stood in the field with the Mayor.

"A few, I suppose. But where are the body o' 'em?"

"All out of doors are there."

"Then the more fools they!"

Henchard walked away moodily. One or two young fellows gallantly came to climb the poles, to save the hams from being wasted; but as there were no spectators, and the whole scene presented the most melancholy appearance, Henchard gave orders that the proceedings were to be suspended, and the entertainment closed, the food to be distributed among the poor people of the town. In a short time nothing was left in the field but a few hurdles, the tents, and the poles.

Henchard returned to his house, had tea with his wife and daughter, and then walked out. It was now dusk. He soon saw that the tendency of all promenaders was towards a particular spot in the Walks, and eventually proceeded thither himself. The notes of a stringed band came from the enclosure that Farfrae had erected—the pavilion as he called it—and when the Mayor reached it he perceived that a gigantic tent had been ingeniously constructed without poles or ropes. The densest point of the avenue of sycamores had been selected, where the boughs made a closely interlaced vault overhead; to these boughs the canvas had been hung, and a barrel roof was the result. The end towards the wind was enclosed, the other end was open. Henchard went round and saw the interior.

In form it was like the nave of a cathedral with one gable removed, but the scene within was anything but devotional. A reel or fling of some sort was in progress; and the usually sedate Farfrae was in the midst of the other dancers in the costume of a wild Highlander, flinging himself about and spinning to the tune. For a moment Henchard could not help laughing. Then he perceived the immense admiration for the Scotchman that revealed itself in the women's faces; and when this exhibition was over, and a new dance proposed, and Donald had disappeared for a time to return in his natural garments, he had an unlimited choice of partners, every girl being in a coming-on disposition towards one who so thoroughly understood the poetry of motion as he.

All the town crowded to the Walk, such a delightful idea of a ballroom never having occurred to the inhabitants before. Among the rest of the onlookers were Elizabeth and her mother—the former thoughtful yet much interested, her eyes beaming with a longing lingering light, as if Nature had been advised by Correggio* in their creation. The dancing progressed with unabated spirit, and Henchard walked and waited till his wife should be disposed to go home. He did not care to keep in the light, and when he went into the dark it was worse, for there he heard remarks of a kind which were becoming too frequent:

"Mr. Henchard's rejoicings couldn't say good morning to this,"

---

*Italian painter Antonio Allegri, known as Correggio (1494–1534), whose work is noted for its sensual interplay of light and shade.

said one. "A man must be a headstrong stunpoll* to think folk would go up to that bleak place to-day."

The other answered that people said it was not only in such things as those that the Mayor was wanting. "Where would his business be if it were not for this young fellow? 'Twas verily Fortune sent him to Henchard. His accounts were like a bramblewood when Mr. Farfrae came. He used to reckon his sacks by chalk strokes all in a row like garden-palings, measure his ricks by stretching with his arms, weigh his trusses by a lift, judge his hay by a chaw,† and settle the price with a curse. But now this accomplished young man does it all by ciphering and mensuration. Then the wheat—that sometimes used to taste so strong o' mice when made into bread that people could fairly tell the breed—Farfrae has a plan for purifying, so that nobody would dream the smallest four-legged beast had walked over it once. O yes, everybody is full of him, and the care Mr. Henchard has to keep him, to be sure!" concluded this gentleman.

"But he won't do it for long, good-now," said the other.

"No!" said Henchard to himself behind the tree. "Or if he do, he'll be honeycombed clean out of the character and standing that he's built up in these eighteen year!"

He went back to the dancing pavilion. Farfrae was footing a quaint little dance with Elizabeth-Jane—an old country thing, the only one she knew, and though he considerately toned down his movements to suit her demurer gait, the pattern of the shining little nails in the soles of his boots became familiar to the eyes of every bystander. The tune had enticed her into it; being a tune of a busy, vaulting, leaping sort—some low notes on the silver string of each fiddle, then a skipping on the small, like running up and down ladders— "Miss M'leod of Ayr"‡ was its name, so Mr. Farfrae had said, and that it was very popular in his own country.

It was soon over, and the girl looked at Henchard for approval; but he did not give it. He seemed not to see her. "Look here, Farfrae," he said, like one whose mind was elsewhere, "I'll go to Port-Bredy Great Market to-morrow myself. You can stay and put things right in

---

*Idiot.
†Chew.
‡Favorite childhood dance tune of Hardy's.

your clothes-box, and recover strength to your knees after your vagaries." He planted on Donald an antagonistic glare that had begun as a smile.

Some other townsmen came up, and Donald drew aside. "What's this, Henchard," said Alderman Tubber, applying his thumb to the corn-factor like a cheese-taster. "An opposition randy to yours, eh? Jack's as good as his master, eh? Cut ye out quite, hasn't he?"

"You see, Mr. Henchard," said the lawyer, another good-natured friend, "where you made the mistake was in going so far afield. You should have taken a leaf out of his book, and have had your sports in a sheltered place like this. But you didn't think of it, you see; and he did, and that's where he's beat you."

"He'll be top-sawyer* soon of you two, and carry all afore him," added jocular Mr. Tubber.

"No," said Henchard gloomily. "He won't be that, because he's shortly going to leave me." He looked towards Donald, who had again come near. "Mr. Farfrae's time as my manager is drawing to a close—isn't it, Farfrae?"

The young man, who could now read the lines and folds of Henchard's strongly-traced face as if they were clear verbal inscriptions, quietly assented; and when people deplored the fact, and asked why it was, he simply replied that Mr. Henchard no longer required his help.

Henchard went home, apparently satisfied. But in the morning, when his jealous temper had passed away, his heart sank within him at what he had said and done. He was the more disturbed when he found that this time Farfrae was determined to take him at his word.

XVII

ELIZABETH-JANE HAD PERCEIVED from Henchard's manner that in assenting to dance she had made a mistake of some kind. In her simplicity she did not know what it was till a hint from a nodding acquaintance

---

*Top dog; the worker who holds the lower end of a saw gets showered with sawdust.

enlightened her. As the Mayor's stepdaughter, she learnt, she had not been quite in her place in treading a measure amid such a mixed throng as filled the dancing pavilion.

Thereupon her ears, cheeks, and chin glowed like live coals at the dawning of the idea that her tastes were not good enough for her position, and would bring her into disgrace.

This made her very miserable, and she looked about for her mother; but Mrs. Henchard, who had less idea of conventionality than Elizabeth herself, had gone away, leaving her daughter to return at her own pleasure. The latter moved on into the dark dense old avenues, or rather vaults of living woodwork, which ran along the town boundary, and stood reflecting.

A man followed in a few minutes, and her face being towards the shine from the tent he recognized her. It was Farfrae—just come from the dialogue with Henchard which had signified his dismissal.

"And it's you, Miss Newson?—and I've been looking for ye everywhere!" he said, overcoming a sadness imparted by the estrangement with the corn-merchant. "May I walk on with you as far as your street-corner?"

She thought there might be something wrong in this, but did not utter any objection. So together they went on, first down the West Walk, and then into the Bowling Walk, till Farfrae said, "It's like that I'm going to leave you soon."

She faltered. "Why?"

"Oh—as a mere matter of business—nothing more. But we'll not concern ourselves about it—it is for the best. I hoped to have another dance with you."

She said she could not dance—in any proper way.

"Nay, but you do! It's the feeling for it rather than the learning of steps that makes pleasant dancers. . . . I fear I offended your father by getting up this! And now, perhaps, I'll have to go to another part o' the warrld altogether!"

This seemed such a melancholy prospect that Elizabeth-Jane breathed a sigh—letting it off in fragments that he might not hear her. But darkness makes people truthful, and the Scotchman went on impulsively—perhaps he had heard her after all:

"I wish I was richer, Miss Newson; and your stepfather had not been offended; I would ask you something in a short time—yes, I would ask you to-night. But that's not for me!"

What he would have asked her he did not say, and instead of encouraging him she remained incompetently silent. Thus afraid one of another they continued their promenade along the walls till they got near the bottom of the Bowling Walk; twenty steps further and the trees would end, and the street corner and lamps appear. In consciousness of this they stopped.

"I never found out who it was that sent us to Durnover granary on a fool's errand that day," said Donald, in his undulating tones. "Did ye ever know yourself, Miss Newson?"

"Never," said she.

"I wonder why they did it!"

"For fun, perhaps."

"Perhaps it was not for fun. It might have been that they thought they would like us to stay waiting there, talking to one another? Ay, well! I hope you Casterbridge folk will not forget me if I go."

"That I'm sure we won't!" she said earnestly. "I—wish you wouldn't go at all."

They had got into the lamplight. "Now, I'll think over that," said Donald Farfrae. "And I'll not come up to your door; but part from you here; lest it make your father more angry still."

They parted, Farfrae returning into the dark Bowling Walk, and Elizabeth-Jane going up the street. Without any consciousness of what she was doing she started running with all her might till she reached her father's door. "O dear me—what am I at?" she thought, as she pulled up breathless.

Indoors she fell to conjecturing the meaning of Farfrae's enigmatic words about not daring to ask her what he fain would. Elizabeth, that silent observing woman, had long noted how he was rising in favour among the townspeople; and knowing Henchard's nature now she had feared that Farfrae's days as manager were numbered; so that the announcement gave her little surprise. Would Mr. Farfrae stay in Casterbridge despite his words and her father's dismissal? His occult breathings to her might be solvable by his course in that respect.

The next day was windy—so windy that walking in the garden she picked up a portion of the draft of a letter on business in Donald Farfrae's writing, which had flown over the wall from the office. The useless scrap she took indoors, and began to copy the calligraphy, which she much admired. The letter began "Dear Sir,", and presently writing on a loose slip "Elizabeth-Jane," she laid the latter over "Sir," making the phrase "Dear Elizabeth-Jane." When she saw the effect a quick red ran up her face and warmed her through, though nobody was there to see what she had done. She quickly tore up the slip, and threw it away. After this she grew cool and laughed at herself, walked about the room, and laughed again; not joyfully, but distressfully rather.

It was quickly known in Casterbridge that Farfrae and Henchard had decided to dispense with each other. Elizabeth-Jane's anxiety to know if Farfrae were going away from the town reached a pitch that disturbed her, for she could no longer conceal from herself the cause. At length the news reached her that he was not going to leave the place. A man following the same trade as Henchard, but on a very small scale, had sold his business to Farfrae, who was forthwith about to start as corn and hay merchant on his own account.

Her heart fluttered when she heard of this step of Donald's, proving that he meant to remain; and yet, would a man who cared one little bit for her have endangered his suit by setting up a business in opposition to Mr. Henchard's? Surely not; and it must have been a passing impulse only which had led him to address her so softly.

To solve the problem whether her appearance on the evening of the dance were such as to inspire a fleeting love at first sight, she dressed herself up exactly as she had dressed then—the muslin, the spencer, the sandals, the parasol—and looked in the mirror. The picture glassed back was, in her opinion, precisely of such a kind as to inspire that fleeting regard, and no more—"just enough to make him silly, and not enough to keep him so," she said luminously; and Elizabeth thought, in a much lower key, that by this time he had discovered how plain and homely was the informing spirit of that pretty outside.

Hence, when she felt her heart going out to him, she would say to herself with a mock pleasantry that carried an ache with it, "No, no, Elizabeth-Jane—such dreams are not for you!" She tried to prevent herself from seeing him, and thinking of him; succeeding fairly well in the former attempt, in the latter not so completely.

Henchard, who had been hurt at finding that Farfrae did not

mean to put up with his temper any longer, was incensed beyond measure when he learnt what the young man had done as an alternative. It was in the town-hall, after a council meeting, that he first became aware of Farfrae's *coup* for establishing himself independently in the town; and his voice might have been heard as far as the town-pump expressing his feelings to his fellow councilmen. Those tones showed that, though under a long reign of self-control he had become Mayor and churchwarden and what not, there was still the same unruly volcanic stuff beneath the rind of Michael Henchard as when he had sold his wife at Weydon Fair.

"Well, he's a friend of mine, and I'm a friend of his—or if we are not, what are we? 'Od send, if I've not been his friend, who has, I should like to know? Didn't he come here without a sound shoe to his voot? Didn't I keep him here—help him to a living? Didn't I help him to money, or whatever he wanted? I stuck out for no terms—I said 'Name your own price.' I'd have shared my last crust with that young fellow at one time, I liked him so well. And now he's defied me! But damn him, I'll have a tussle with him now—at fair buying and selling, mind—at fair buying and selling! And if I can't overbid such a stripling as he, then I'm not wo'th a varden!* We'll show that we know our business as well as one here and there!"

His friends of the Corporation did not specially respond. Henchard was less popular now than he had been when, nearly two years before, they had voted him to the chief magistracy on account of his amazing energy. While they had collectively profited by this quality of the corn-factor's they had been made to wince individually on more than one occasion. So he went out of the hall and down the street alone.

Reaching home he seemed to recollect something with a sour satisfaction. He called Elizabeth-Jane. Seeing how he looked when she entered she appeared alarmed.

"Nothing to find fault with," he said, observing her concern. "Only I want to caution you, my dear. That man, Farfrae—it is about him. I've seen him talking to you two or three times—he danced with 'ee at the rejoicings, and came home with 'ee. Now, now, no

---

*Farthing.

blame to you. But just hearken: Have you made him any foolish promise? Gone the least bit beyond sniff and snaff* at all?"

"No. I have promised him nothing."

"Good. All's well that ends well. I particularly wish you not to see him again."

"Very well, sir."

"You promise?"

She hesitated for a moment, and then said—

"Yes, if you much wish it."

"I do. He's an enemy to our house!"

When she had gone he sat down, and wrote in a heavy hand to Farfrae thus:—

Sir,—I make request that henceforth you and my stepdaughter be as strangers to each other. She on her part has promised to welcome no more addresses from you; and I trust, therefore, you will not attempt to force them upon her.

M. Henchard.

One would almost have supposed Henchard to have had policy to see that no better modus vivendi† could be arrived at with Farfrae than by encouraging him to become his son-in-law. But such a scheme for buying over a rival had nothing to recommend it to the Mayor's headstrong faculties. With all domestic finesse of that kind he was hopelessly at variance. Loving a man or hating him, his diplomacy was as wrongheaded as a buffalo's; and his wife had not ventured to suggest the course which she, for many reasons, would have welcomed gladly.

Meanwhile Donald Farfrae had opened the gates of commerce on his own account at a spot on Durnover Hill—as far as possible from Henchard's stores, and with every intention of keeping clear of his former friend and employer's customers. There was, it seemed to the younger man, room for both of them and to spare. The town was small, but the corn and hay-trade was proportionately large, and with his native sagacity he saw opportunity, for a share of it.

So determined was he to do nothing which should seem like

---

*Friendly acquaintance.
†Way of living (Latin).

trade-antagonism to the Mayor that he refused his first customer—a large farmer of good repute—because Henchard and this man had dealt together within the preceding three months.

"He was once my friend," said Farfrae, "and it's not for me to take business from him. I am sorry to disappoint you, but I cannot hurt the trade of a man who's been so kind to me."

In spite of this praiseworthy course the Scotchman's trade increased. Whether it were that his northern energy was an overmastering force among the easygoing Wessex worthies, or whether it was sheer luck, the fact remained that whatever he touched he prospered in. Like Jacob in Padan-Aram, he would no sooner humbly limit himself to the ringstraked-and-spotted exceptions of trade than the ringstraked-and-spotted would multiply and prevail.[13]

But most probably luck had little to do with it. Character is Fate, said Novalis,[14] and Farfrae's character was just the reverse of Henchard's, who might not inaptly be described as Faust has been described—as a vehement gloomy being who had quitted the ways of vulgar men without light to guide him on a better way.*

Farfrae duly received the request to discontinue attentions to Elizabeth-Jane. His acts of that kind had been so slight that the request was almost superfluous. Yet he had felt a considerable interest in her, and after some cogitation he decided that it would be as well to enact no Romeo part just then—for the young girl's sake no less than his own. Thus the incipient attachment was stifled down.

A time came when, avoid collision with his former friend as he might, Farfrae was compelled, in sheer self-defence, to close with Henchard in mortal commercial combat. He could no longer parry the fierce attacks of the latter by simple avoidance. As soon as their war of prices began everybody was interested, and some few guessed the end. It was, in some degree, Northern insight matched against Southron doggedness—the dirk against the cudgel—and Henchard's weapon was one which, if it did not deal ruin at the first or second stroke, left him afterwards well-nigh at his antagonist's mercy.

Almost every Saturday they encountered each other amid the crowd of farmers which thronged about the market-place in the weekly course of their business. Donald was always ready, and even

---

*The description of Faust is from Thomas Carlyle's essay "Goethe's Helena" (1828).

anxious, to say a few friendly words; but the Mayor invariably gazed
stormfully past him, like one who had endured and lost on his account, and could in no sense forgive the wrong; nor did Farfrae's
snubbed manner of perplexity at all appease him. The large farmers,
corn-merchants, millers, auctioneers, and others had each an official
stall in the corn-market room, with their names painted thereon; and
when to the familiar series of "Henchard," "Everdene," "Shiner,"
"Darton," and so on, was added one inscribed "Farfrae," in staring
new letters, Henchard was stung into bitterness; like Bellerophon,*
he wandered away from the crowd, cankered in soul.

From that day Donald Farfrae's name was seldom mentioned in
Henchard's house. If at breakfast or dinner Elizabeth-Jane's mother
inadvertently alluded to her favourite's movements, the girl would
implore her by a look to be silent; and her husband would say,
"What—are you, too, my enemy?"

XVIII

THERE CAME A SHOCK which had been foreseen for some time by Elizabeth, as the box passenger† foresees the approaching jerk from some
channel across the highway.

Her mother was ill—too unwell to leave her room. Henchard,
who treated her kindly, except in moments of irritation, sent at once
for the richest, busiest doctor, whom he supposed to be the best. Bed-
time came, and they burnt a light all night. In a day or two she rallied.

Elizabeth, who had been staying up, did not appear at breakfast on
the second morning, and Henchard sat down alone. He was startled to
see a letter for him from Jersey in a writing he knew too well, and had
expected least to behold again. He took it up in his hands and looked
at it as at a picture, a vision, a vista of past enactments; and then he
read it as an unimportant finale to conjecture.

---

*Legendary Greek hero who, in the *Iliad*, is said to endure a long exile in the Aleian
Plain after being deserted by the gods.
†Passenger who rides on the outside of a coach, next to the driver.

The writer said that she at length perceived how impossible it would be for any further communications to proceed between them now that his re-marriage had taken place. That such re-union had been the only straightforward course open to him she was bound to admit.

"On calm reflection, therefore," she went on, "I quite forgive you for landing me in such a dilemma, remembering that you concealed nothing before our ill-advised acquaintance; and that you really did set before me in your grim way the fact of there being a certain risk in intimacy with you, slight as it seemed to be after fifteen or sixteen years of silence on your wife's part. I thus look upon the whole as a misfortune of mine, and not a fault of yours.

"So that, Michael, I must ask you to overlook those letters with which I pestered you day after day in the heat of my feelings. They were written whilst I thought your conduct to me cruel; but now I know more particulars of the position you were in I see how inconsiderate my reproaches were.

"Now you will, I am sure, perceive that the one condition which will make any future happiness possible for me is that the past connection between our lives be kept secret outside this isle. Speak of it I know you will not; and I can trust you not to write of it. One safeguard more remains to be mentioned—that no writings of mine, or trifling articles belonging to me, should be left in your possession through neglect or forgetfulness. To this end may I request you to return to me any such you may have, particularly the letters written in the first abandonment of feeling.

"For the handsome sum you forwarded to me as a plaster to the wound I heartily thank you.

"I am now on my way to Bristol, to see my only relative. She is rich, and I hope will do something for me. I shall return through Casterbridge and Budmouth, where I shall take the packet-boat.* Can you meet me with the letters and other trifles? I shall be in the coach which changes horses at the Antelope Hotel at half-past five Wednesday evening; I shall be wearing a Paisley shawl with a red centre, and thus may easily be found. I should prefer this plan of receiving them to having them sent.—I remain still, yours ever,

"Lucetta."

Henchard breathed heavily. "Poor thing—better you had not known me! Upon my heart and soul, if ever I should be left in a po-

*Mail boat; it also carried passengers.

sition to carry out that marriage with thee, I *ought* to do it—I ought
to do it, indeed!"

The contingency that he had in his mind was, of course, the
death of Mrs. Henchard.

As requested, he sealed up Lucetta's letters, and put the parcel
aside till the day she had appointed; this plan of returning them by
hand being apparently a little *ruse* of the young lady for exchanging a
word or two with him on past times. He would have preferred not to
see her; but deeming that there could be no great harm in acquiesc-
ing thus far, he went at dusk and stood opposite the coach-office.

The evening was chilly, and the coach was late. Henchard crossed
over to it while the horses were being changed; but there was no
Lucetta inside or out. Concluding that something had happened to
modify her arrangements he gave the matter up and went home, not
without a sense of relief.

Meanwhile Mrs. Henchard was weakening visibly. She could not
go out of doors any more. One day, after much thinking which
seemed to distress her, she said she wanted to write something. A
desk was put upon her bed with pen and paper, and at her request
she was left alone. She remained writing for a short time, folded her
paper carefully, called Elizabeth-Jane to bring a taper and wax, and
then, still refusing assistance, sealed up the sheet, directed it, and
locked it in her desk. She had directed it in these words:—

"Mr. Michael Henchard. Not to be opened till Elizabeth-Jane's wedding-day."

The latter sat up with her mother to the utmost of her strength
night after night. To learn to take the universe seriously there is no
quicker way than to watch—to be a "waker," as the country-people
call it. Between the hours at which the last toss-pot went by and the
first sparrow shook himself, the silence in Casterbridge—barring the
rare sound of the watchman—was broken in Elizabeth's ear only by
the time-piece in the bedroom ticking frantically against the clock on
the stairs; ticking harder and harder till it seemed to clang like a gong;
and all this while the subtle-souled girl asking herself why she was
born, why sitting in a room, and blinking at the candle; why things
around her had taken the shape they wore in preference to every other
possible shape. Why they stared at her so helplessly, as if waiting for
the touch of some wand that should release them from terrestrial con-
straint; what that chaos called consciousness, which spun in her at this

moment like a top, tended to, and began in. Her eyes fell together; she was awake, yet she was asleep.

A word from her mother roused her. Without preface, and as the continuation of a scene already progressing in her mind, Mrs. Henchard said: "You remember the note sent to you and Mr. Farfrae—asking you to meet some one in Durnover Barton—and that you thought it was a trick to make fools of you?"

"Yes."

"It was not to make fools of you—it was done to bring you together. 'Twas I did it."

"Why?" said Elizabeth, with a start.

"I—wanted you to marry Mr. Farfrae."

"O mother!" Elizabeth-Jane bent down her head so much that she looked quite into her own lap. But as her mother did not go on, she said, "What reason?"

"Well, I had a reason. 'Twill out one day. I wish it could have been in my time! But there—nothing is as you wish it! Henchard hates him."

"Perhaps they'll be friends again," murmured the girl.

"I don't know—I don't know." After this her mother was silent, and dozed; and she spoke on the subject no more.

Some little time later on Farfrae was passing Henchard's house on a Sunday morning, when he observed that the blinds were all down. He rang the bell so softly that it only sounded a single full note and a small one; and then he was informed that Mrs. Henchard was dead—just dead—that very hour.

At the town-pump there were gathered when he passed a few old inhabitants, who came there for water whenever they had, as at present, spare time to fetch it, because it was purer from that original fount than from their own wells. Mrs. Cuxsom, who had been standing there for an indefinite time with her pitcher, was describing the incidents of Mrs. Henchard's death, as she had learnt them from the nurse.

"And she was as white as marble-stone," said Mrs. Cuxsom. "And likewise such a thoughtful woman, too—ah, poor soul—that a' minded every little thing that wanted tending. 'Yes,' says she, 'when I'm gone, and my last breath's blowed, look in the top drawer o' the chest in the back room by the window, and you'll find all my coffin clothes; a piece of flannel—that's to put under me, and the little piece is to put under my head; and my new stockings for my feet—they are folded alongside, and all my other things. And there's four ounce pennies, the heaviest I could find, a-tied up in bits of linen, for weights—two for my right eye and two for my left,' she said. 'And when you've used 'em, and my eyes don't open no more, bury the pennies, good souls, and don't ye go spending 'em, for I shouldn't like it. And open the windows as soon as I am carried out, and make it as cheerful as you can for Elizabeth-Jane.' "

"Ah, poor heart!"

"Well, and Martha did it, and buried the ounce pennies in the garden. But if ye'll believe words, that man, Christopher Coney, went and dug 'em up, and spent 'em at the Three Mariners. 'Faith,' he said, 'why should death rob life o' fourpence? Death's not of such good report that we should respect 'en to that extent,' says he."

" 'Twas a cannibal deed!" deprecated her listeners.

"Gad, then, I won't quite ha'e it," said Solomon Longways. "I say it to-day, and 'tis a Sunday morning, and I wouldn't speak wrongfully for a zilver zixpence at such a time. I don't see noo harm in it. To respect the dead is sound doxology* and I wouldn't sell skellintons— leastwise respectable skellintons—to be varnished for 'natomies, except I were out o' work. But money is scarce, and throats get dry. Why *should* death rob life o' fourpence? I say there was no treason in it."

"Well, poor soul; she's helpless to hinder that or anything now," answered Mother Cuxsom. "And all her shining keys will be took from her, and her cupboards opened; and little things a' didn't wish seen, anybody will see; and her wishes and ways will all be as nothing!"

XIX

HENCHARD AND ELIZABETH SAT conversing by the fire. It was three weeks after Mrs. Henchard's funeral; the candles were not lighted, and a restless, acrobatic flame, poised on a coal, called from the shady walls

---

*Statement of formal praise to God; Longways may be confusing the word with "theology."

the smiles of all shapes that could respond—the old pier-glass,* with gilt columns and huge entablature,† the picture-frames, sundry knobs and handles, and the brass rosette at the bottom of each riband bell-pull on either side of the chimney-piece.

"Elizabeth, do you think much of old times?" said Henchard.

"Yes, sir; often," said she.

"Who do you put in your pictures of 'em?"

"Mother and father—nobody else hardly."

Henchard always looked like one bent on resisting pain when Elizabeth-Jane spoke of Richard Newson as "father." "Ah! I am out of all that, am I not?" he said. . . . "Was Newson a kind father?"

"Yes, sir; very."

Henchard's face settled into an expression of stolid loneliness which gradually modulated into something softer. "Suppose I had been your real father?" he said. "Would you have cared for me as much as you cared for Richard Newson?"

"I can't think it," she said quickly. "I can think of no other as my father, except my father."

Henchard's wife was dissevered from him by death; his friend and helper Farfrae by estrangement; Elizabeth-Jane by ignorance. It seemed to him that only one of them could possibly be recalled, and that was the girl. His mind began vibrating between the wish to reveal himself to her and the policy of leaving well alone, till he could no longer sit still. He walked up and down, and then he came and stood behind her chair, looking down upon the top of her head. He could no longer restrain his impulse. "What did your mother tell you about me—my history?" he asked.

"That you were related by marriage."

"She should have told more—before you knew me! Then my task would not have been such a hard one. . . . Elizabeth, it is I who am your father, and not Richard Newson. Shame alone prevented your wretched parents from owning this to you while both of 'em were alive."

The back of Elizabeth's head remained still, and her shoulders did not denote even the movements of breathing. Henchard went on:

---

*Tall mirror.

†Ornamental upper portion of the mirror.

"I'd rather have your scorn, your fear, anything than your ignorance; 'tis that I hate! Your mother and I were man and wife when we were young. What you saw was our second marriage. Your mother was too honest. We had thought each other dead—and—Newson became her husband."

This was the nearest approach Henchard could make to the full truth. As far as he personally was concerned he would have screened nothing; but he showed a respect for the young girl's sex and years worthy of a better man.

When he had gone on to give details which a whole series of slight and unregarded incidents in her past life strangely corroborated; when, in short, she believed his story to be true, she became greatly agitated, and turning round to the table flung her face upon it weeping.

"Don't cry—don't cry!" said Henchard, with vehement pathos, "I can't bear it, I won't bear it. I am your father; why should you cry? Am I so dreadful, so hateful to 'ee? Don't take against me, Elizabeth-Jane!" he cried, grasping her wet hand. "Don't take against me—though I was a drinking man once, and used your mother roughly—I'll be kinder to you than *he* was! I'll do anything, if you will only look upon me as your father!"

She tried to stand up and confront him trustfully; but she could not; she was troubled at his presence, like the brethren at the avowal of Joseph.[15]

"I don't want you to come to me all of a sudden," said Henchard in jerks, and moving like a great tree in a wind. "No, Elizabeth, I don't. I'll go away and not see you till to-morrow, or when you like; and then I'll show 'ee papers to prove my words. There, I am gone, and won't disturb you any more. . . . 'Twas I that chose your name, my daughter; your mother wanted it Susan. There, don't forget 'twas I gave you your name!" He went out at the door and shut her softly in, and she heard him go away into the garden. But he had not done. Before she had moved, or in any way recovered from the effect of his disclosure, he reappeared.

"One word more, Elizabeth," he said. "You'll take my surname now—hey? Your mother was against it; but it will be much more pleasant to me. 'Tis legally yours, you know. But nobody need know that. You shall take it as if by choice. I'll talk to my lawyer—I don't know the law of it exactly; but will you do this—let me put a few lines into the newspaper that such is to be your name?"

"If it is my name I must have it, mustn't I?" she asked.

"Well, well; usage is everything in these matters."

"I wonder why mother didn't wish it?"

"Oh, some whim of the poor soul's. Now get a bit of paper and draw up a paragraph as I shall tell you. But let's have a light."

"I can see by the firelight," she answered. "Yes—I'd rather."

"Very well."

She got a piece of paper, and bending over the fender wrote at his dictation words which he had evidently got by heart from some advertisement or other—words to the effect that she, the writer, hitherto known as Elizabeth-Jane Newson, was going to call herself Elizabeth-Jane Henchard forthwith. It was done, and fastened up, and directed to the office of the *Casterbridge Chronicle*.

"Now," said Henchard, with the blaze of satisfaction that he always emitted when he had carried his point—though tenderness softened it this time—"I'll go upstairs and hunt for some documents that will prove it all to you. But I won't trouble you with them till tomorrow. Good-night, my Elizabeth-Jane!"

He was gone before the bewildered girl could realize what it all meant, or adjust her filial sense to the new centre of gravity. She was thankful that he had left her to herself for the evening, and sat down over the fire. Here she remained in silence, and wept—not for her mother now, but for the genial sailor Richard Newson, to whom she seemed doing a wrong.

Henchard in the meantime had gone upstairs. Papers of a domestic nature he kept in a drawer in his bedroom, and this he unlocked. Before turning them over he leant back and indulged in reposeful thought. Elizabeth was his at last, and she was a girl of such good sense and kind heart that she would be sure to like him. He was the kind of man to whom some human object for pouring out his heat upon—were it emotive or were it choleric—was almost a necessity. The craving of his heart for the reestablishment of this tenderest human tie had been great during his wife's lifetime, and now he had submitted to its mastery without reluctance and without fear. He bent over the drawer again, and proceeded in his search.

Among the other papers had been placed the contents of his

wife's little desk, the keys of which had been handed to him at her request. Here was the letter addressed to him with the restriction, "*Not to be opened till Elizabeth-Jane's wedding-day.*"

Mrs. Henchard, though more patient than her husband, had been no practical hand at anything. In sealing up the sheet, which was folded and tucked in without an envelope, in the old-fashioned way, she had overlaid the junction with a large mass of wax without the requisite under-touch of the same. The seal had cracked, and the letter was open: Henchard had no reason to suppose the restriction one of serious weight, and his feeling for his late wife had not been of the nature of deep respect. "Some trifling fancy or other of poor Susan's, I suppose," he said; and without curiosity he allowed his eyes to scan the letter:

My dear Michael,—For the good of all three of us I have kept one thing a secret from you till now. I hope you will understand why; I think you will; though perhaps you may not forgive me. But, dear Michael, I have done it for the best. I shall be in my grave when you read this, and Elizabeth-Jane will have a home. Don't curse me, Mike—think of how I was situated. I can hardly write it, but here it is. Elizabeth-Jane is not your Elizabeth-Jane—the child who was in my arms when you sold me. No; she died three months after that, and this living one is my other husband's. I christened her by the same name we had given to the first, and she filled up the ache I felt at the other's loss. Michael, I am dying, and I might have held my tongue; but I could not. Tell her husband of this or not, as you may judge; and forgive, if you can, a woman you once deeply wronged, as she forgives you.

Susan Henchard.

Her husband regarded the paper as if it were a window-pane through which he saw for miles. His lip twitched, and he seemed to compress his frame, as if to bear better. His usual habit was not to consider whether destiny were hard upon him or not—the shape of his ideas in cases of affliction being simply a moody "I am to suffer, I perceive." "This much scourging, then, is it for me." But now through his passionate head there stormed this thought—that the blasting disclosure was what he had deserved.

His wife's extreme reluctance to have the girl's name altered from Newson to Henchard was now accounted for fully. It furnished another illustration of that honesty in dishonesty which had characterized her in other things.

He remained unnerved and purposeless for near a couple of hours; till he suddenly said, "Ah—I wonder if it is true!"

He jumped up in an impulse, kicked off his slippers, and went with a candle to the door of Elizabeth-Jane's room, where he put his ear to the keyhole and listened. She was breathing profoundly. Henchard softly turned the handle, entered, and shading the light, approached the bedside. Gradually bringing the light from behind a screening curtain he held it in such a manner that it fell slantwise on her face without shining on her eyes. He steadfastly regarded her features.

They were fair: his were dark. But this was an unimportant preliminary. In sleep there come to the surface buried genealogical facts, ancestral curves, dead men's traits, which the mobility of daytime animation screens and overwhelms. In the present statuesque repose of the young girl's countenance Richard Newson's was unmistakably reflected. He could not endure the sight of her, and hastened away.

Misery taught him nothing more than defiant endurance of it. His wife was dead, and the first impulse for revenge died with the thought that she was beyond him. He looked out at the night as at a fiend. Henchard, like all his kind, was superstitious, and he could not help thinking that the concatenation of events this evening had produced was the scheme of some sinister intelligence bent on punishing him. Yet they had developed naturally. If he had not revealed his past history to Elizabeth he would not have searched the drawer for papers, and so on. The mockery was, that he should have no sooner taught a girl to claim the shelter of his paternity than he discovered her to have no kinship with him.

This ironical sequence of things angered him like an impish trick from a fellow-creature. Like Prester John's, his table had been spread, and infernal harpies had snatched up the food.[16] He went out of the house, and moved sullenly onward down the pavement till he came to the bridge at the bottom of the High Street. Here he turned in upon a bypath on the river bank, skirting the north-eastern limits of the town.

These precincts embodied the mournful phases of Casterbridge life, as the south avenues embodied its cheerful moods. The whole

way along here was sunless, even in summer time; in spring, white
frosts lingered here when other places were steaming with warmth;
while in winter it was the seed-field of all the aches, rheumatisms,
and torturing cramps of the year. The Casterbridge doctors must have
pined away for want of sufficient nourishment but for the configur-
ation of the landscape on the north-eastern side.

The river—slow, noiseless, and dark—the Schwarzwasser* of
Casterbridge—ran beneath a low cliff, the two together forming a
defence which had rendered walls and artificial earthworks on this
side unnecessary. Here were ruins of a Franciscan priory, and a mill
attached to the same, the water of which roared down a back-hatch
like the voice of desolation. Above the cliff, and behind the river, rose
a pile of buildings, and in the front of the pile a square mass cut into
the sky. It was like a pedestal lacking its statue. This missing feature,
without which the design remained incomplete, was, in truth, the
corpse of a man; for the square mass formed the base of the gallows,
the extensive buildings at the back being the county gaol. In the
meadow where Henchard now walked the mob were wont to gather
whenever an execution took place, and there to the tune of the roaring weir they stood and watched the spectacle.

The exaggeration which darkness imparted to the glooms of this
region impressed Henchard more than he had expected. The lugubri-
ous harmony of the spot with his domestic situation was too perfect
for him, impatient of effects, scenes, and adumbrations. It reduced
his heartburning to melancholy, and he exclaimed, "Why the deuce
did I come here!" He went on past the cottage in which the old local
hangman had lived and died, in times before that calling was mo-
nopolized over all England by a single gentleman; and climbed up by
a steep back lane into the town.

For the sufferings of that night, engendered by his bitter disappointment, he might well have been pitied. He was like one who had
half fainted, and could neither recover nor complete the swoon. In
words he could blame his wife, but not in his heart; and had he
obeyed the wise directions outside her letter this pain would have
been spared him for long—possibly for ever, Elizabeth-Jane seeming

---

*Black water (German).

to show no ambition to quit her safe and secluded maiden courses for the speculative path of matrimony.

The morning came after this night of unrest, and with it the necessity for a plan. He was far too self-willed to recede from a position, especially as it would involve humiliation. His daughter he had asserted her to be, and his daughter she should always think herself, no matter what hypocrisy it involved.

But he was ill-prepared for the first step in this new situation. The moment he came into the breakfast-room Elizabeth advanced with open confidence to him and took him by the arm.

"I have thought and thought all night of it," she said frankly. "And I see that everything must be as you say. And I am going to look upon you as the father that you are, and not to call you Mr. Henchard any more. It is so plain to me now. Indeed, father, it is. For, of course, you would not have done half the things you have done for me, and let me have my own way so entirely, and bought me presents, if I had only been your stepdaughter! He—Mr. Newson—whom my poor mother married by such a strange mistake" (Henchard was glad that he had disguised matters here), "was very kind—O so kind!" (she spoke with tears in her eyes); "but that is not the same thing as being one's real father after all. Now, father, breakfast is ready!" said she cheerfully.

Henchard bent and kissed her cheek. The moment and the act he had prefigured for weeks with a thrill of pleasure; yet it was no less than a miserable insipidity to him now that it had come. His reinstation of her mother had been chiefly for the girl's sake, and the fruition of the whole scheme was such dust and ashes as this.

XX

OF ALL THE ENIGMAS which ever confronted a girl there can have been seldom one like that which followed Henchard's announcement of himself to Elizabeth as her father. He had done it in an ardour and an agitation which had half carried the point of affection with her; yet, behold, from the next morning onwards his manner was constrained as she had never seen it before.

The coldness soon broke out into open chiding. One grievous failing of Elizabeth's was her occasional pretty and picturesque use of dialect words—those terrible marks of the beast to the truly genteel.

It was dinner-time—they never met except at meals—and she happened to say when he was rising from table, wishing to show him something, "If you'll bide where you be a minute, father, I'll get it."

" 'Bide where you be,' " he echoed sharply. "Good God, are you only fit to carry wash to a pig-trough, that ye use such words as those?"

She reddened with shame and sadness.

"I meant 'Stay where you are,' father," she said, in a low, humble voice. "I ought to have been more careful."

He made no reply, and went out of the room.

The sharp reprimand was not lost upon her, and in time it came to pass that for "fay" she said "succeed"; that she no longer spoke of "dumbledores" but of "humble bees"; no longer said of young men and women that they "walked together," but that they were "engaged"; that she grew to talk of "greggles" as "wild hyacinths"; that when she had not slept she did not quaintly tell the servants next morning that she had been "hag-rid," but that she had "suffered from indigestion."

These improvements, however, are somewhat in advance of the story. Henchard, being uncultivated himself, was the bitterest critic the fair girl could possibly have had of her own lapses—really slight now, for she read omnivorously. A gratuitous ordeal was in store for her in the matter of her handwriting. She was passing the dining-room door one evening, and had occasion to go in for something. It was not till she had opened the door that she knew the Mayor was there in the company of a man with whom he transacted business.

"Here, Elizabeth-Jane," he said, looking round at her, "just write down what I tell you—a few words of an agreement for me and this gentleman to sign. I am a poor tool with a pen."

"Be jowned,* and so be I," said the gentleman.

She brought forward blotting-book, paper, and ink, and sat down.

---

*Damned.

"Now then—'An agreement entered into this sixteenth day of October'—write that first."

She started the pen in an elephantine march across the sheet. It was a splendid round, bold hand of her own conception, a style that would have stamped a woman as Minerva's* own in more recent days. But other ideas reigned then: Henchard's creed was that proper young girls wrote ladies'-hand—nay, he believed that bristling characters were as innate and inseparable a part of refined womanhood as sex itself. Hence when, instead of scribbling, like the Princess Ida,†—

> "In such a hand as when a field of corn
> Bows all its ears before the roaring East,"

Elizabeth-Jane produced a line of chain-shot‡ and sand-bags, he reddened in angry shame for her, and, peremptorily saying, "Never mind—I'll finish it," dismissed her there and then.

Her considerate disposition became a pitfall to her now. She was, it must be admitted, sometimes provokingly and unnecessarily willing to saddle herself with manual labours. She would go to the kitchen instead of ringing, "Not to make Phoebe come up twice." She went down on her knees, shovel in hand, when the cat overturned the coal-scuttle; moreover, she would persistently thank the parlour-maid for everything, till one day, as soon as the girl was gone from the room, Henchard broke out with, "Good God, why dosn't leave off thanking that girl as if she were a goddess-born! Don't I pay her a dozen pound a year to do things for 'ee?" Elizabeth shrank so visibly at the exclamation that he became sorry a few minutes after, and said that he did not mean to be rough.

These domestic exhibitions were the small protruding needle-rocks which suggested rather than revealed what was underneath. But his passion had less terror for her than his coldness. The increasing frequency of the latter mood told her the sad news that he disliked her with a growing dislike. The more interesting that her

---

*Minerva was the Roman goddess of wisdom and war.
†The lines are from Alfred, Lord Tennyson's *The Princess* (1847); ironically, in the poem the writer is a man posing as a woman.
‡Pair of cannonballs linked by a chain.

appearance and manners became under the softening influences which she could now command, and in her wisdom did command, the more she seemed to estrange him. Sometimes she caught him looking at her with a louring invidiousness that she could hardly bear. Not knowing his secret it was a cruel mockery that she should for the first time excite his animosity when she had taken his surname.

But the most terrible ordeal was to come. Elizabeth had latterly been accustomed of an afternoon to present a cup of cider or ale and bread-and-cheese to Nance Mockridge, who worked in the yard wimbling hay-bonds. Nance accepted this offering thankfully at first; afterwards as a matter of course. On a day when Henchard was on the premises he saw his stepdaughter enter the hay-barn on this errand; and, as there was no clear spot on which to deposit the provisions, she at once set to work arranging two trusses of hay as a table, Mockridge meanwhile standing with her hands on her hips, easefully looking at the preparations on her behalf.

"Elizabeth, come here!" said Henchard; and she obeyed.

"Why do you lower yourself so confoundedly?" he said with suppressed passion. "Haven't I told you o't fifty times? Hey? Making yourself a drudge for a common workwoman of such a character as hers! Why, ye'll disgrace me to the dust!"

Now these words were uttered loud enough to reach Nance inside the barn door, who fired up immediately at the slur upon her personal character. Coming to the door she cried, regardless of consequences, "Come to that, Mr. Michael Henchard, I can let'ee know she've waited on worse!"

"Then she must have had more charity than sense," said Henchard.

"O no, she hadn't. 'Twere not for charity but for hire; and at a public-house in this town!"

"It is not true!" cried Henchard indignantly.

"Just ask her," said Nance, folding her naked arms in such a manner that she could comfortably scratch her elbows.

Henchard glanced at Elizabeth-Jane, whose complexion, now pink and white from confinement, lost nearly all of the former colour. "What does this mean?" he said to her. "Anything or nothing?"

"It is true," said Elizabeth-Jane. "But it was only——"

"Did you do it, or didn't you? Where was it?"

"At the Three Mariners; one evening for a little while, when we were staying there."

Nance glanced triumphantly at Henchard, and sailed into the barn; for assuming that she was to be discharged on the instant she had resolved to make the most of her victory. Henchard, however, said nothing about discharging her. Unduly sensitive on such points by reason of his own past, he had the look of one completely ground down to the last indignity. Elizabeth followed him to the house like a culprit; but when she got inside she could not see him. Nor did she see him again that day.

Convinced of the scathing damage to his local repute and position that must have been caused by such a fact, though it had never before reached his own ears, Henchard showed a positive distaste for the presence of this girl not his own, whenever he encountered her. He mostly dined with the farmers at the market-room of one of the two chief hotels, leaving her in utter solitude. Could he have seen how she made use of those silent hours he might have found reason to reverse his judgment on her quality. She read and took notes incessantly, mastering facts with painful laboriousness, but never flinching from her self-imposed task. She began the study of Latin, incited by the Roman characteristics of the town she lived in. "If I am not well-informed it shall be by no fault of my own," she would say to herself through the tears that would occasionally glide down her peachy cheeks when she was fairly baffled by the portentous obscurity of many of these educational works.

Thus she lived on, a dumb, deep-feeling, great-eyed creature, construed by not a single contiguous being; quenching with patient fortitude her incipient interest in Farfrae, because it seemed to be one sided, unmaidenly, and unwise. True, that for reasons best known to herself, she had, since Farfrae's dismissal, shifted her quarters from the back room affording a view of the yard (which she had occupied with such zest) to a front chamber overlooking the street; but as for the young man, whenever he passed the house he seldom or never turned his head.

Winter had almost come, and unsettled weather made her still more dependent upon indoor resources. But there were certain early winter days in Casterbridge—days of firmamental exhaustion which followed angry south-westerly tempests—when, if the sun shone, the air was like velvet. She seized on these days for her periodical visits to the spot where her mother lay buried—the still-used burial-ground of the old Roman-British city, whose curious feature was this, its continuity as a place of sepulture. Mrs. Henchard's dust mingled with the dust of women who lay ornamented with glass hair-pins and amber necklaces, and men who held in their mouths coins of Hadrian, Posthumus, and the Constantines.[17]

Half-past ten in the morning was about her hour for seeking this spot—a time when the town avenues were deserted as the avenues of Karnac.* Business had long since passed down them into its daily cells, and Leisure had not arrived there. So Elizabeth-Jane walked and read, or looked over the edge of the book to think, and thus reached the churchyard.

There, approaching her mother's grave, she saw a solitary dark figure in the middle of the gravel-walk. This figure, too, was reading; but not from a book: the words which engrossed it being the inscription on Mrs. Henchard's tombstone. The personage was in mourning like herself, was about her age and size, and might have been her wraith or double, but for the fact that it was a lady much more beautifully dressed than she. Indeed, comparatively indifferent as Elizabeth-Jane was to dress, unless for some temporary whim or purpose, her eyes were arrested by the artistic perfection of the lady's appearance. Her gait, too, had a flexuousness about it, which seemed to avoid angularity of movement less from choice than from predisposition. It was a revelation to Elizabeth that human beings could reach this stage of external development—she had never suspected it. She felt all the freshness and grace to be stolen from herself on the instant by the neighbourhood of such a stranger. And this was in face of the fact that Elizabeth could now have been writ handsome, while the young lady was simply pretty.

Had she been envious she might have hated the woman; but she did not do that—she allowed herself the pleasure of feeling fascinated. She wondered where the lady had come from. The stumpy and practical walk of honest homeliness which mostly prevailed there,

---

*Northern part of the site of the ancient city Thebes in Egypt.

the two styles of dress thereabout, the simple and the mistaken, equally avouched that this figure was no Casterbridge woman's, even if a book in her hand resembling a guide-book had not also suggested it.

The stranger presently moved from the tombstone of Mrs. Henchard, and vanished behind the corner of the wall. Elizabeth went to the tomb herself; beside it were two footprints distinct in the soil, signifying that the lady had stood there a long time. She returned homeward, musing on what she had seen, as she might have mused on a rainbow or the Northern Lights, a rare butterfly or a cameo.

Interesting as things had been out of doors, at home it turned out to be one of her bad days. Henchard, whose two years' mayoralty was ending, had been made aware that he was not to be chosen to fill a vacancy in the list of aldermen; and that Farfrae was likely to become one of the Council. This caused the unfortunate discovery that she had played the waiting-maid in the town of which he was Mayor to rankle in his mind yet more poisonously. He had learnt by personal inquiry at the time that it was to Donald Farfrae—that treacherous upstart—that she had thus humiliated herself. And though Mrs. Stannidge seemed to attach no great importance to the incident—the cheerful souls at the Three Mariners having exhausted its aspects long ago—such was Henchard's haughty spirit that the simple thrifty deed was regarded as little less than a social catastrophe by him.

Ever since the evening of his wife's arrival with her daughter there had been something in the air which had changed his luck. That dinner at the King's Arms with his friends had been Henchard's Austerlitz:* he had had his successes since, but his course had not been upward. He was not to be numbered among the aldermen—that Peerage of burghers—as he had expected to be, and the consciousness of this soured him to-day.

"Well, where have you been?" he said to her with off-hand laconism.

"I've been strolling in the Walks and churchyard, father, till I feel quite leery."† She clapped her hand to her mouth, but too late.

This was just enough to incense Henchard after the other crosses

---

*Battle that marked the high point of the career of Napoleon I (1805).
†Hungry.

of the day. "I won't have you talk like that!" he thundered. " 'Leery,' indeed. One would think you worked upon a farm! One day I learn that you lend a hand in public-houses. Then I hear you talk like a clodhopper. I'm burned, if it goes on, this house can't hold us two."

The only way of getting a single pleasant thought to go to sleep upon after this was by recalling the lady she had seen that day, and hoping she might see her again.

Meanwhile Henchard was sitting up, thinking over his jealous folly in forbidding Farfrae to pay his addresses to this girl who did not belong to him, when if he had allowed them to go on he might not have been encumbered with her. At last he said to himself with satisfaction as he jumped up and went to the writing-table: "Ah! he'll think it means peace, and a marriage portion—not that I don't want my house to be troubled with her, and no portion at all!" He wrote as follows:—

Sir,—On consideration, I don't wish to interfere with your courtship of Elizabeth-Jane, if you care for her. I therefore withdraw my objection; excepting in this—that the business be not carried on in my house.—Yours,

M. Henchard.
Mr. Farfrae.

The morrow, being fairly fine, found Elizabeth-Jane again in the churchyard; but while looking for the lady she was startled by the apparition of Farfrae, who passed outside the gate. He glanced up for a moment from a pocket-book in which he appeared to be making figures as he went; whether or not he saw her he took no notice, and disappeared.

Unduly depressed by a sense of her own superfluity she thought he probably scorned her; and quite broken in spirit sat down on a bench. She fell into painful thought on her position, which ended with her saying quite loud, "O, I wish I was dead with dear mother!"

Behind the bench was a little promenade under the wall where people sometimes walked instead of on the gravel. The bench seemed to be touched by something; she looked round, and a face was bending over her, veiled, but still distinct, the face of the young woman she had seen yesterday.

Elizabeth-Jane looked confounded for a moment, knowing she

had been overheard, though there was pleasure in her confusion. "Yes, I heard you," said the lady, in a vivacious voice, answering her look. "What can have happened?"

"I don't—I can't tell you," said Elizabeth, putting her hand to her face to hide a quick flush that had come.

There was no movement or word for a few seconds; then the girl felt that the young lady was sitting down beside her.

"I guess how it is with you," said the latter. "That was your mother." She waved her hand towards the tombstone. Elizabeth looked up at her as if inquiring of herself whether there should be confidence. The lady's manner was so desirous, so anxious, that the girl decided there should be confidence. "It was my mother," she said, "my only friend."

"But your father, Mr. Henchard. He is living?"

"Yes, he is living," said Elizabeth-Jane.

"Is he not kind to you?"

"I've no wish to complain of him."

"There has been a disagreement?"

"A little."

"Perhaps you were to blame," suggested the stranger.

"I was—in many ways," sighed the meek Elizabeth. "I swept up the coals when the servant ought to have done it; and I said I was leery;—and he was angry with me."

The lady seemed to warm towards her for that reply. "Do you know the impression your words give me?" she said ingenuously. "That he is a hot-tempered man—a little proud—perhaps ambitious; but not a bad man." Her anxiety not to condemn Henchard while siding with Elizabeth was curious.

"O no; certainly not *bad*," agreed the honest girl. "And he has not even been unkind to me till lately—since mother died. But it has been very much to bear while it has lasted. All is owing to my defects, I daresay; and my defects are owing to my history."

"What is your history?"

Elizabeth-Jane looked wistfully at her questioner. She found that her questioner was looking at her; turned her eyes down; and then seemed compelled to look back again. "My history is not gay or attractive," she said. "And yet I can tell it, if you really want to know."

The lady assured her that she did want to know; whereupon

Elizabeth-Jane told the tale of her life as she understood it, which was in general the true one, except that the sale at the fair had no part therein.

Contrary to the girl's expectation her new friend was not shocked. This cheered her; and it was not till she thought of returning to that home in which she had been treated so roughly of late that her spirits fell.

"I don't know how to return," she murmured. "I think of going away. But what can I do? Where can I go?"

"Perhaps it will be better soon," said her friend gently. "So I would not go far. Now what do you think of this: I shall soon want somebody to live in my house, partly as housekeeper, partly as companion; would you mind coming to me? But perhaps———"

"O yes," cried Elizabeth, with tears in her eyes. "I would, indeed—I would do anything to be independent; for then perhaps my father might get to love me. But, ah!"

"What?

"I am no accomplished person. And a companion to you must be that."

"O, not necessarily."

"Not? But I can't help using rural words sometimes, when I don't mean to."

"Never mind, I shall like to know them."

"And—O, I know I shan't do!"—she cried with a distressful laugh. "I accidentally learned to write round hand instead of ladies'-hand. And, of course, you want some one who can write that?"

"Well, no."

"What, not necessary to write ladies'-hand?" cried the joyous Elizabeth.

"Not at all."

"But where do you live?"

"In Casterbridge, or rather I shall be living here after twelve o'clock to-day."

Elizabeth expressed her astonishment.

"I have been staying at Budmouth for a few days while my house was getting ready. The house I am going into is that one they call High-Place Hall—the old stone one looking down the lane to the Market. Two or three rooms are fit for occupation, though not all: I sleep there to-night for the first time. Now will you think over my proposal, and meet me here the first fine day next week, and say if you are still in the same mind?"

Elizabeth, her eyes shining at this prospect of a change from an unbearable position, joyfully assented; and the two parted at the gate of the churchyard.

XXI

As a MAXIM GLIBLY repeated from childhood remains practically unmarked till some mature experience enforces it, so did this High-Place Hall now for the first time really show itself to Elizabeth-Jane, though her ears had heard its name on a hundred occasions.

Her mind dwelt upon nothing else but the stranger, and the house, and her own chance of living there, all the rest of the day. In the afternoon she had occasion to pay a few bills in the town and do a little shopping, when she learnt that what was a new discovery to herself had become a common topic about the streets. High-Place Hall was undergoing repair; a lady was coming there to live shortly; all the shop-people knew it, and had already discounted the chance of her being a customer.

Elizabeth-Jane could, however, add a capping touch to information so new to her in the bulk. The lady, she said, had arrived that day.

When the lamps were lighted, and it was yet not so dark as to render chimneys, attics, and roofs invisible, Elizabeth, almost with a lover's feeling, thought she would like to look at the outside of High-Place Hall. She went up the street in that direction.

The Hall, with its grey *façade* and parapet, was the only residence of its sort so near the centre of the town. It had, in the first place, the characteristics of a country mansion—birds' nests in its chimneys, damp nooks where fungi grew, and irregularities of surface direct from Nature's trowel. At night the forms of passengers were patterned by the lamps in black shadows upon the pale walls.

This evening motes of straw lay around, and other signs of the premises having been in that lawless condition which accompanies the entry of a new tenant. The house was entirely of stone, and formed an example of dignity without great size. It was not altogether aristocratic, still less consequential, yet the old-fashioned stranger instinctively said, "Blood built it, and Wealth enjoys it," however vague his opinions of those accessories might be.

Yet as regards the enjoying it the stranger would have been wrong, for until this very evening, when the new lady had arrived, the house had been empty for a year or two, while before that interval its occupancy had been irregular. The reason of its unpopularity was soon made manifest. Some of its rooms overlooked the market-place; and such a prospect from such a house was not considered desirable or seemly by its would-be occupiers.

Elizabeth's eyes sought the upper rooms, and saw lights there. The lady had obviously arrived. The impression that this woman of comparatively practised manner had made upon the studious girl's mind was so deep that she enjoyed standing under an opposite archway merely to think that the charming lady was inside the confronting walls, and to wonder what she was doing. Her admiration for the architecture of that front was entirely on account of the inmate it screened. Though for that matter the architecture deserved admiration, or at least study, on its own account. It was Palladian,* and like most architecture erected since the Gothic age was a compilation rather than a design. But its reasonableness made it impressive. It was not rich, but rich enough. A timely consciousness of the ultimate vanity of human architecture, no less than of other human things, had prevented artistic superfluity.

Men had till quite recently been going in and out with parcels and packing-cases, rendering the door and hall within like a public thoroughfare. Elizabeth trotted through the open door in the dusk, but becoming alarmed at her own temerity she went quickly out again by another which stood open in the lofty wall of the back court. To her surprise she found herself in one of the little-used alleys of the town. Looking round at the door which had given her egress, by the light of the solitary lamp fixed in the alley, she saw that it was arched and old—older even than the house itself. The door was stud-

---

*Pertaining to Andrea Palladio (1508–1580), whose classically inspired architectural style was popular in England into the eighteenth century.

ded, and the keystone of the arch was a mask. Originally the mask had exhibited a comic leer, as could still be discerned; but generations of Casterbridge boys had thrown stones at the mask, aiming at its open mouth; and the blows thereon had chipped off the lips and jaws as if they had been eaten away by disease. The appearance was so ghastly by the weakly lamp-glimmer that she could not bear to look at it—the first unpleasant feature of her visit.

The position of the queer old door and the odd presence of the leering mask suggested one thing above all others as appertaining to the mansion's past history—intrigue. By the alley it had been possible to come unseen from all sorts of quarters in the town—the old playhouse, the old bull-stake, the old cock-pit, the pool wherein nameless infants had been used to disappear. High-Place Hall could boast of its conveniences undoubtedly.

She turned to come away in the nearest direction homeward, which was down the alley, but hearing footsteps approaching in that quarter, and having no great wish to be found in such a place at such a time she quickly retreated. There being no other way out she stood behind a brick pier* till the intruder should have gone his ways.

Had she watched she would have been surprised. She would have seen that the pedestrian on coming up made straight for the arched doorway: that as he paused with his hand upon the latch the lamplight fell upon the face of Henchard.

But Elizabeth-Jane clung so closely to her nook that she discerned nothing of this. Henchard passed in, as ignorant of her presence as she was ignorant of his identity, and disappeared in the darkness. Elizabeth came out a second time into the alley, and made the best of her way home.

Henchard's chiding, by begetting in her a nervous fear of doing anything definable as unlady-like, had operated thus curiously in keeping them unknown to each other at a critical moment. Much might have resulted from recognition—at the least a query on either side in one and the self-same form: What could he or she possibly be doing there?

Henchard, whatever his business at the lady's house, reached his own home only a few minutes later than Elizabeth-Jane. Her plan was

---

*Pillar.

to broach the question of leaving his roof this evening; the events of the day had urged her to the course. But its execution depended upon his mood, and she anxiously awaited his manner towards her. She found that it had changed. He showed no further tendency to be angry; he showed something worse. Absolute indifference had taken the place of irritability; and his coldness was such that it encouraged her to departure, even more than hot temper could have done.

"Father, have you any objection to my going away?" she asked.

"Going away! No—none whatever. Where are you going?"

She thought it undesirable and unnecessary to say anything at present about her destination to one who took so little interest in her. He would know that soon enough. "I have heard of an opportunity of getting more cultivated and finished, and being less idle," she answered, with hesitation. "A chance of a place in a household where I can have advantages of study, and seeing refined life."

"Then make the best of it, in Heaven's name—if you can't get cultivated where you are."

"You don't object?"

"Object—I? Ho—no! Not at all." After a pause he said, "But you won't have enough money for this lively scheme without help, you know? If you like I should be willing to make you an allowance, so that you be not bound to live upon the starvation wages refined folk are likely to pay 'ee."

She thanked him for this offer.

"It had better be done properly," he added after a pause. "A small annuity is what I should like you to have—so as to be independent of me—and so that I may be independent of you. Would that please ye?"

"Certainly."

"Then I'll see about it this very day." He seemed relieved to get her off his hands by this arrangement, and as far as they were concerned the matter was settled. She now simply waited to see the lady again.

The day and the hour came; but a drizzling rain fell. Elizabeth-Jane, having now changed her orbit from one of gay independence to laborious self-help, thought the weather good enough for such declined glory as hers, if her friend would only face it—a matter of doubt. She went to the boot-room where her pattens had hung ever since her apotheosis; took them down, had their mildewed leathers blacked, and put them on as she had done in old times. Thus mounted, and with cloak and umbrella, she went off to the place of appointment—intending, if the lady were not there, to call at the house.

One side of the churchyard—the side towards the weather—was sheltered by an ancient thatched mud wall whose eaves overhung as much as one or two feet. At the back of the wall was a corn-yard with its granary and barns—the place wherein she had met Farfrae many months earlier. Under the projection of the thatch she saw a figure. The young lady had come.

Her presence so exceptionally substantiated the girl's utmost hopes that she almost feared her good fortune. Fancies find room in the strongest minds. Here, in a churchyard old as civilization, in the worst of weathers, was a strange woman of curious fascinations never seen elsewhere: there might be some devilry about her presence. However, Elizabeth went on to the church tower, on whose summit the rope of a flag-staff rattled in the wind; and thus she came to the wall.

The lady had such a cheerful aspect in the drizzle that Elizabeth forgot her fancy. "Well," said the lady, a little of the whiteness of her teeth appearing with the word through the black fleece that protected her face, "have you decided?"

"Yes, quite," said the other eagerly.

"Your father is willing?"

"Yes."

"Then come along."

"When?"

"Now—as soon as you like. I had a good mind to send to you to come to my house, thinking you might not venture up here in the wind. But as I like getting out of doors, I thought I would come and see first."

"It was my own thought."

"That shows we shall agree. Then can you come to-day? My house is so hollow and dismal that I want some living thing there."

"I think I might be able to," said the girl, reflecting.

Voices were borne over to them at that instant on the wind and raindrops from the other side of the wall. There came such words as "sacks," "quarters," "threshing," "tailing,"* "next Saturday's market,"

---

*Corn of inferior quality.

each sentence being disorganized by the gusts like a face in a cracked mirror. Both the women listened.

"Who are those?" said the lady.

"One is my father. He rents that yard and barn."

The lady seemed to forget the immediate business in listening to the technicalities of the corn trade. At last she said suddenly, "Did you tell him where you were going to?"

"No."

"O—how was that?"

"I thought it safer to get away first—as he is so uncertain in his temper."

"Perhaps you are right. . . . Besides, I have never told you my name. It is Miss Templeman. . . . Are they gone—on the other side?"

"No. They have only gone up into the granary."

"Well, it is getting damp here. I shall expect you to-day—this evening, say, at six."

"Which way shall I come, ma'am?"

"The front way—round by the gate. There is no other that I have noticed."

Elizabeth-Jane had been thinking of the door in the alley.

"Perhaps, as you have not mentioned your destination, you may as well keep silent upon it till you are clear off. Who knows but that he may alter his mind?"

Elizabeth-Jane shook her head. "On consideration I don't fear it," she said sadly. "He has grown quite cold to me."

"Very well. Six o'clock then."

When they had emerged upon the open road and parted, they found enough to do in holding their bowed umbrellas to the wind. Nevertheless the lady looked in at the corn-yard gates as she passed them, and paused on one foot for a moment. But nothing was visible there save the ricks, and the humpbacked barn cushioned with moss, and the granary rising against the church-tower behind, where the smacking of the rope against the flag-staff still went on.

Now Henchard had not the slightest suspicion that Elizabeth-Jane's movement was to be so prompt. Hence when, just before six, he reached home and saw a fly* at the door from the King's Arms,

*One-horse carriage.

and his stepdaughter, with all her little bags and boxes, getting into it, he was taken by surprise.

"But you said I might go, father?" she explained through the carriage window.

"Said!—yes. But I thought you meant next month, or next year. 'Od, seize it—you take time by the forelock! This, then, is how you be going to treat me for all my trouble about ye?"

"O father! how can you speak like that? It is unjust of you!" she said with spirit.

"Well, well, have your own way," he replied. He entered the house, and, seeing that all her things had not yet been brought down, went up to her room to look on. He had never been there since she had occupied it. Evidences of her care, of her endeavours for improvement, were visible all around, in the form of books, sketches, maps, and little arrangements for tasteful effects. Henchard had known nothing of these efforts. He gazed at them, turned suddenly about, and came down to the door.

"Look here," he said, in an altered voice—he never called her by name now—"don't 'ee go away from me. It may be I've spoke roughly to you—but I've been grieved beyond everything by you—there's something that caused it."

"By me?" she said, with deep concern. "What have I done?"

"I can't tell you now. But if you'll stop, and go on living as my daughter, I'll tell you all in time."

But the proposal had come ten minutes too late. She was in the fly—was already, in imagination, at the house of the lady whose manner had such charms for her. "Father," she said, as considerately as she could, "I think it best for us that I go on now. I need not stay long; I shall not be far away; and if you want me badly I can soon come back again."

He nodded ever so slightly, as a receipt of her decision and no more. "You are not going far, you say. What will be your address, in case I wish to write to you? Or am I not to know?"

"Oh yes—certainly. It is only in the town—High-Place Hall."

"Where?" said Henchard, his face stilling.

She repeated the words. He neither moved nor spoke, and waving her hand to him in utmost friendliness she signified to the fly-man to drive up the street.

XXII

W<small>E GO BACK FOR</small> a moment to the preceding night, to account for Henchard's attitude.

At the hour when Elizabeth-Jane was contemplating her stealthy reconnoitring excursion to the abode of the lady of her fancy, he had been not a little amazed at receiving a letter by hand in Lucetta's well known characters. The self-repression, the resignation of her previous communication had vanished from her mood; she wrote with some of the natural lightness which had marked her in their early acquaintance.

High-Place Hall.

My Dear Mr. Henchard,—Don't be surprised. It is for your good and mine, as I hope, that I have come to live at Casterbridge—for how long I cannot tell. That depends upon another; and he is a man, and a merchant, and a Mayor, and one who has the first right to my affections.

Seriously, mon ami, I am not so light-hearted as I may seem to be from this. I have come here in consequence of hearing of the death of your wife—whom you used to think of as dead so many years before! Poor woman, she seems to have been a sufferer, though uncomplaining, and though weak in intellect not an imbecile. I am glad you acted fairly by her. As soon as I knew she was no more, it was brought home to me very forcibly by my conscience that I ought to endeavour to disperse the shade which my étourderie* flung over my name, by asking you to carry out your promise to me. I hope you are of the same mind, and that you will take steps to this end. As, however, I did not know how you were situated, or what had happened since our separation, I decided to come and establish myself here before communicating with you.

You probably feel as I do about this. I shall be able to see you in a day or two. Till then, farewell.—Yours,

Lucetta.

P.S.—I was unable to keep my appointment to meet you for a moment or two in passing through Casterbridge the other day. My plans were altered by a family event, which it will surprise you to hear of.

---

*Blunder, thoughtlessness (French).

Henchard had already heard that High-Place Hall was being prepared for a tenant. He said with a puzzled air to the first person he encountered, "Who is coming to live at the Hall?"

"A lady of the name of Templeman, I believe, sir," said his informant.

Henchard thought it over. "Lucetta is related to her, I suppose," he said to himself. "Yes, I must put her in her proper position, undoubtedly."

It was by no means with the oppression that would once have accompanied the thought that he regarded the moral necessity now; it was, indeed, with interest, if not warmth. His bitter disappointment at finding Elizabeth-Jane to be none of his, and himself a childless man, had left an emotional void in Henchard that he unconsciously craved to fill. In this frame of mind, though without strong feeling, he had strolled up the alley and into High-Place Hall by the postern* at which Elizabeth had so nearly encountered him. He had gone on thence into the court, and inquired of a man whom he saw unpacking china from a crate if Miss Le Sueur was living there. Miss Le Sueur had been the name under which he had known Lucetta—or "Lucette," as she had called herself at that time.

The man replied in the negative; that Miss Templeman only had come. Henchard went away, concluding that Lucetta had not as yet settled in.

He was in this interested stage of the inquiry when he witnessed Elizabeth-Jane's departure the next day. On hearing her announce the address there suddenly took possession of him the strange thought that Lucetta and Miss Templeman were one and the same person, for he could recall that in her season of intimacy with him the name of the rich relative whom he had deemed somewhat a mythical personage had been given as Templeman. Though he was not a fortune-hunter, the possibility that Lucetta had been sublimed into a lady of means by some munificent testament on the part of this relative lent a charm to her image which it might not otherwise have acquired. He was getting on towards the dead level of middle age, when material things increasingly possess the mind.

But Henchard was not left long in suspense. Lucetta was rather

---

*Back door.

addicted to scribbling, as had been shown by the torrent of letters after the fiasco in their marriage arrangements, and hardly had Elizabeth gone away when another note came to the Mayor's house from High-Place Hall.

"I am in residence," she said, "and comfortable, though getting here has been a wearisome undertaking. You probably know what I am going to tell you, or do you not? My good Aunt Templeman, the banker's widow, whose very existence you used to doubt, much more her affluence, has lately died, and bequeathed some of her property to me. I will not enter into details except to say that I have taken her name—as a means of escape from mine, and its wrongs.

"I am now my own mistress, and have chosen to reside in Casterbridge—to be tenant of High-Place Hall, that at least you may be put to no trouble if you wish to see me. My first intention was to keep you in ignorance of the changes in my life till you should meet me in the street; but I have thought better of this.

"You probably are aware of my arrangement with your daughter, and have doubtless laughed at the—what shall I call it?—practical joke (in all affection) of my getting her to live with me. But my first meeting with her was purely an accident. Do you see, Michael, partly why I have done it?—why, to give you an excuse for coming here as if to visit her, and thus to form my acquaintance naturally. She is a dear, good girl, and she thinks you have treated her with undue severity. You may have done so in your haste, but not deliberately, I am sure. As the result has been to bring her to me I am not disposed to upbraid you.—In haste, yours always,

"Lucetta."

The excitement which these announcements produced in Henchard's gloomy soul was to him most pleasurable. He sat over his dining-table long and dreamily, and by an almost mechanical transfer the sentiments which had run to waste since his estrangement from Elizabeth-Jane and Donald Farfrae gathered around Lucetta before they had grown dry. She was plainly in a very coming-on disposition for marriage. But what else could a poor woman be who had given her time and heart to him so thoughtlessly, at that former time, as to lose her credit by it? Probably conscience no less than affection had brought her here. On the whole he did not blame her.

"The artful little woman!" he said, smiling (with reference to Lucetta's adroit and pleasant manœuvre with Elizabeth-Jane).

To feel that he would like to see Lucetta was with Henchard to start for her house. He put on his hat and went. It was between eight and nine o'clock when he reached her door. The answer brought him was that Miss Templeman was engaged for that evening; but that she would be happy to see him the next day.

"That's rather like giving herself airs!" he thought. "And considering what we——" But after all, she plainly had not expected him, and he took the refusal quietly. Nevertheless he resolved not to go next day. "These cursed women—there's not an inch of straight grain in 'em!" he said.

Let us follow the track of Mr. Henchard's thought as if it were a clue line,* and view the interior of High-Place Hall on this particular evening.

On Elizabeth-Jane's arrival she had been phlegmatically asked by an elderly woman to go upstairs and take off her things. She had replied with great earnestness that she would not think of giving that trouble, and on the instant divested herself of her bonnet and cloak in the passage. She was then conducted to the first door on the landing, and left to find her way further alone.

The room disclosed was prettily furnished as a boudoir or small drawing-room, and on a sofa with two cylindrical pillows reclined a dark-haired, large-eyed, pretty woman, of unmistakably French extraction on one side or the other. She was probably some years older than Elizabeth, and had a sparkling light in her eye. In front of the sofa was a small table, with a pack of cards scattered upon it faces upward.

The attitude had been so full of abandonment that she bounded up like a spring on hearing the door open.

Perceiving that it was Elizabeth she lapsed into ease, and came across to her with a reckless skip that innate grace only prevented from being boisterous.

"Why, you are late," she said, taking hold of Elizabeth-Jane's hands.

"There were so many little things to put up."

"And you seem dead-alive and tired. Let me try to enliven you by some wonderful tricks I have learnt, to kill time. Sit there and don't move." She gathered up the pack of cards, pulled the table in

---

*Rigging that hooks a sail to the mast.

front of her, and began to deal them rapidly, telling Elizabeth to choose some.

"Well, have you chosen?" she asked, flinging down the last card.

"No," stammered Elizabeth, arousing herself from a reverie. "I quite forgot, I was thinking of—you, and me—and how strange it is that I am here."

Miss Templeman looked at Elizabeth-Jane with interest, and laid down the cards. "Ah! never mind," she said. "I'll lie here while you sit by me; and we'll talk."

Elizabeth drew up silently to the head of the sofa, but with obvious pleasure. It could be seen that though in years she was younger than her entertainer in manner and general vision she seemed more of the sage. Miss Templeman deposited herself on the sofa in her former flexuous position, and throwing her arm above her brow—somewhat in the pose of a well-known conception of Titian's*—talked up at Elizabeth-Jane invertedly across her forehead and arm.

"I must tell you something," she said. "I wonder if you have suspected it. I have only been mistress of a large house and fortune a little while."

"Oh—only a little while?" murmured Elizabeth-Jane, her countenance slightly falling.

"As a girl I lived about in garrison towns and elsewhere with my father, till I was quite flighty and unsettled. He was an officer in the army. I should not have mentioned this had I not thought it best you should know the truth."

"Yes, yes." She looked thoughtfully round the room—at the little square piano with brass inlayings, at the window-curtains, at the lamp, at the fair and dark kings and queens on the card-table, and finally at the inverted face of Lucetta Templeman, whose large lustrous eyes had such an odd effect upside down.

Elizabeth's mind ran on acquirements to an almost morbid degree. "You speak French and Italian fluently, no doubt," she said. "I have not been able to get beyond a wretched bit of Latin yet."

"Well, for that matter, in my native isle speaking French does not go for much. It is rather the other way."

---

*Reference to the reclining nude figure in The Venus of Urbino (1538) by Tiziano Vecellio, known as Titian (c.1488–1576).

"Where is your native isle?"

It was with rather more reluctance that Miss Templeman said, "Jersey. There they speak French on one side of the street and English on the other, and a mixed tongue in the middle of the road. But it is a long time since I was there. Bath is where my people really belong to, though my ancestors in Jersey were as good as anybody in England. They were the Le Sueurs, an old family who have done great things in their time. I went back and lived there after my father's death. But I don't value such past matters, and am quite an English person in my feelings and tastes."

Lucetta's tongue had for a moment outrun her discretion. She had arrived at Casterbridge as a Bath lady, and there were obvious reasons why Jersey should drop out of her life. But Elizabeth had tempted her to make free, and a deliberately formed resolve had been broken.

It could not, however, have been broken in safer company. Lucetta's words went no further, and after this day she was so much upon her guard that there appeared no chance of her identification with the young Jersey woman who had been Henchard's dear comrade at a critical time. Not the least amusing of her safeguards was her resolute avoidance of a French word if one by accident came to her tongue more readily than its English equivalent. She shirked it with the suddenness of the weak Apostle at the accusation, "Thy speech betrayeth thee!"*

Expectancy sat visibly upon Lucetta the next morning. She dressed herself for Mr. Henchard, and restlessly awaited his call before mid-day; as he did not come she waited on through the afternoon. But she did not tell Elizabeth that the person expected was the girl's stepfather.

They sat in adjoining windows of the same room in Lucetta's great stone mansion, netting,† and looking out upon the market, which formed an animated scene. Elizabeth could see the crown of her stepfather's hat among the rest beneath, and was not aware that Lucetta watched the same object with yet intenser interest. He moved

---

*The Apostle Peter is identified as a follower of Christ with these words in Matthew 26:73.
†Doing intricate needlework.

about amid the throng, at this point lively as an ant-hill; elsewhere more reposeful, and broken up by stalls of fruit and vegetables. The farmers as a rule preferred the open *carrefour** for their transactions, despite its inconvenient jostlings and the danger from crossing vehicles, to the gloomy sheltered market-room provided for them. Here they surged on this one day of the week, forming a little world of leggings, switches, and sample-bags; men of extensive stomachs, sloping like mountain sides; men whose heads in walking swayed as the trees in November gales; who in conversing varied their attitudes much, lowering themselves by spreading their knees, and thrusting their hands into the pockets of remote inner jackets. Their faces radiated tropical warmth; for though when at home their countenances varied with the seasons, their market-faces all the year round were glowing little fires.

All over-clothes here were worn as if they were an inconvenience, a hampering necessity. Some men were well-dressed; but the majority were careless in that respect, appearing in suits which were historical records of their wearer's deeds, sun-scorchings, and daily struggles for many years past. Yet many carried ruffled cheque-books in their pockets which regulated at the bank hard by a balance of never less than four figures. In fact, what these gibbous human shapes specially represented was ready money—money insistently ready—not ready next year like a nobleman's—often not merely ready at the bank like a professional man's, but ready in their large plump hands.

It happened that to-day there rose in the midst of them all two or three tall apple-trees standing as if they grew on the spot; till it was perceived that they were held by men from the cider-districts who came here to sell them, bringing the clay of their county on their boots. Elizabeth-Jane, who had often observed them, said, "I wonder if the same trees come every week?"

"What trees?" said Lucetta, absorbed in watching for Henchard.

Elizabeth replied vaguely, for an incident checked her. Behind one of the trees stood Farfrae, briskly discussing a sample-bag with a farmer. Henchard had come up, accidentally encountering the young man, whose face seemed to inquire, "Do we speak to each other?"

She saw her stepfather throw a shine into his eye which answered "No!" Elizabeth-Jane sighed.

---

*Crossroads (French).

"Are you particularly interested in anybody out there?" said Lucetta.

"O no," said her companion, a quick red shooting over her face. Luckily Farfrae's figure was immediately covered by the apple-tree. Lucetta looked hard at her. "Quite sure?" she said.

"O yes," said Elizabeth-Jane.

Again Lucetta looked out. "They are all farmers, I suppose?" she said.

"No. There's Mr. Bulge—he's a wine merchant; there's Benjamin Brownlet—a horse dealer; and Kitson, the pig breeder; and Yopper, the auctioneer; besides maltsters, and millers—and so on." Farfrae stood out quite distinctly now; but she did not mention him.

The Saturday afternoon slipped on thus desultorily. The market changed from the sample-showing hour to the idle hour before starting homewards, when tales were told. Henchard had not called on Lucetta though he had stood so near. He must have been too busy, she thought. He would come on Sunday or Monday.

The days came but not the visitor, though Lucetta repeated her dressing with scrupulous care. She was disheartened. It may at once be declared that Lucetta no longer bore towards Henchard all that warm allegiance which had characterized her in their first acquaintance; the then unfortunate issue of things had chilled pure love considerably. But there remained a conscientious wish to bring about her union with him, now that there was nothing to hinder it—to right her position—which in itself was a happiness to sigh for. With strong social reasons on her side why their marriage should take place there had ceased to be any worldly reason on his why it should be postponed, since she had succeeded to fortune.

Tuesday was the great Candlemas* fair. At breakfast she said to Elizabeth-Jane quite coolly: "I imagine your father may call to see you to-day. I suppose he stands close by in the market-place with the rest of the corn-dealers?"

She shook her head. "He won't come."

"Why?"

"He has taken against me," she said in a husky voice.

"You have quarrelled more deeply than I know of."

---

*Feast of the Purification of the Virgin.

Elizabeth, wishing to shield the man she believed to be her father from any charge of unnatural dislike, said "Yes."

"Then where you are is, of all places, the one he will avoid?"

Elizabeth nodded sadly.

Lucetta looked blank, twitched up her lovely eyebrows and lip, and burst into hysterical sobs. Here was a disaster—her ingenious scheme completely stultified.

"O, my dear Miss Templeman—what's the matter?" cried her companion.

"I like your company much!" said Lucetta, as soon as she could speak.

"Yes, yes—and so do I yours!" Elizabeth chimed in soothingly.

"But—but——" She could not finish the sentence, which was, naturally, that if Henchard had such a rooted dislike for the girl as now seemed to be the case, Elizabeth-Jane would have to be got rid of—a disagreeable necessity.

A provisional resource suggested itself. "Miss Henchard—will you go on an errand for me as soon as breakfast is over?—Ah, that's very good of you. Will you go and order——" Here she enumerated several commissions at sundry shops, which would occupy Elizabeth's time for the next hour or two, at least.

"And have you ever seen the Museum?"

Elizabeth-Jane had not.

"Then you should do so at once. You can finish the morning by going there. It is an old house in a back street—I forget where—but you'll find out—and there are crowds of interesting things—skeletons, teeth, old pots and pans, ancient boots and shoes, birds' eggs—all charmingly instructive. You'll be sure to stay till you get quite hungry."

Elizabeth hastily put on her things and departed. "I wonder why she wants to get rid of me to-day!" she said sorrowfully as she went. That her absence, rather than her services or instruction, was in request, had been readily apparent to Elizabeth-Jane, simple as she seemed, and difficult as it was to attribute a motive for the desire.

She had not been gone ten minutes when one of Lucetta's servants was sent to Henchard's with a note. The contents were briefly:

Dear Michael,—You will be standing in view of my house to-day for two or three hours in the course of your business, so do please call and see me. I am sadly disappointed that you have not come before, for can I help anxiety about my own equivocal relation to you?—especially now my aunt's fortune has brought me more prominently before society? Your daughter's presence here may be the cause of your neglect; and I have therefore sent her away for the morning. Say you come on business—I shall be quite alone.

Lucetta.

When the messenger returned her mistress gave directions that if a gentleman called he was to be admitted at once, and sat down to await results.

Sentimentally she did not much care to see him—his delays had wearied her; but it was necessary; and with a sigh she arranged herself picturesquely in the chair; first this way, then that; next so that the light fell over her head. Next she flung herself on the couch in the cyma-recta* curve which so became her, and with her arm over her brow looked towards the door. This, she decided, was the best position after all; and thus she remained till a man's step was heard on the stairs. Whereupon Lucetta, forgetting her curve (for Nature was too strong for Art as yet), jumped up and ran and hid herself behind one of the window-curtains in a freak of timidity. In spite of the waning of passion the situation was an agitating one—she had not seen Henchard since his (supposed) temporary parting from her in Jersey.

She could hear the servant showing the visitor into the room, shutting the door upon him, and leaving as if to go and look for her mistress. Lucetta flung back the curtain with a nervous greeting. The man before her was not Henchard.

XXIII

A CONJECTURE THAT HER visitor might be some other person had, indeed, flashed through Lucetta's mind when she was on the point of bursting out; but it was just too late to recede.

---

*Concave above, convex below.

He was years younger than the Mayor of Casterbridge; fair, fresh, and slenderly handsome. He wore genteel cloth leggings with white buttons, polished boots with infinite lace holes, light cord breeches under a black velveteen coat and waistcoat; and he had a silver-topped switch in his hand. Lucetta blushed, and said with a curious mixture of pout and laugh on her face—"O, I've made a mistake!"

The visitor, on the contrary, did not laugh half a wrinkle.

"But I'm very sorry!" he said, in deprecating tones. "I came and I inquired for Miss Henchard, and they showed me up heere, and in no case would I have caught ye so unmannerly if I had known!"

"I was the unmannerly one," said she.

"But is it that I have come to the wrong house, madam?" said Mr. Farfrae, blinking a little in his bewilderment and nervously tapping his legging with his switch.

"O no, sir,—sit down. You must come and sit down now you are here," replied Lucetta kindly, to relieve his embarrassment. "Miss Henchard will be here directly."

Now this was not strictly true; but that something about the young man—that hyperborean* crispness, stringency, and charm, as of a well-braced musical instrument, which had awakened the interest of Henchard, and of Elizabeth-Jane, and of the Three Mariners' jovial crew, at sight, made his unexpected presence here attractive to Lucetta. He hesitated, looked at the chair, thought there was no danger in it (though there was), and sat down.

Farfrae's sudden entry was simply the result of Henchard's permission to him to see Elizabeth if he were minded to woo her. At first he had taken no notice of Henchard's brusque letter; but an exceptionally fortunate business transaction put him on good terms with everybody, and revealed to him that he could undeniably marry if he chose. Then who so pleasing, thrifty, and satisfactory in every way as Elizabeth-Jane? Apart from her personal recommendations a reconciliation with his former friend Henchard would, in the natural course of things, flow from such a union. He therefore forgave the Mayor his curtness; and this morning on his way to the fair he had called at her house, where he learnt that she was staying at Miss Templeman's. A little stimulated at not finding her ready and waiting—so

---

*From the far north.

fanciful are men!—he hastened on to High-Place Hall to encounter no Elizabeth but its mistress herself.

"The fair to-day seems a large one," she said when, by a natural deviation, their eyes sought the busy scene without. "Your numerous fairs and markets keep me interested. How many things I think of while I watch from here!"

He seemed in doubt how to answer, and the babble without reached them as they sat—voices as of wavelets on a lopping sea, one ever and anon rising above the rest. "Do you look out often?" he asked.

"Yes—very often."

"Do you look for any one you know?"

Why should she have answered as she did?

"I look as at a picture merely. But," she went on, turning pleasantly to him, "I may do so now—I may look for you. You are always there, are you not? Ah—I don't mean it seriously! But it is amusing to look for somebody one knows in a crowd, even if one does not want him. It takes off the terrible oppressiveness of being surrounded by a throng, and having no point of junction with it through a single individual."

"Ay! Maybe you'll be very lonely, ma'am?"

"Nobody knows how lonely."

"But you are rich, they say?"

"If so, I don't know how to enjoy my riches. I came to Casterbridge thinking I should like to live here. But I wonder if I shall."

"Where did ye come from, ma'am?"

"The neighbourhood of Bath."

"And I from near Edinboro'," he murmured. "It's better to stay at home, and that's true; but a man must live where his money is made. It is a great pity, but it's always so! Yet I've done very well this year. O yes," he went on with ingenuous enthusiasm. "You see that man with the drab kerseymere* coat? I bought largely of him in the autumn when wheat was down, and then afterwards when it rose a little I sold off all I had! It brought only a small profit to me; while the farmers kept theirs, expecting higher figures—yes, though the rats were gnawing the ricks hollow. Just when I sold the markets went

---

*Of a fine woolen cloth.

lower, and I bought up the corn of those who had been holding back at less price than my first purchases. And then," cried Farfrae impetuously, his face alight, "I sold it a few weeks after, when it happened to go up again! And so, by contenting mysel' with small profits frequently repeated, I soon made five hundred pounds—yes!"— (bringing down his hand upon the table, and quite forgetting where he was)—"while the others by keeping theirs in hand made nothing at all!"

Lucetta regarded him with a critical interest. He was quite a new type of person to her. At last his eye fell upon the lady's and their glances met.

"Ay, now, I'm wearying you!" he exclaimed.

She said, "No, indeed," colouring a shade.

"What then?"

"Quite otherwise. You are most interesting."

It was now Farfrae who showed the modest pink.

"I mean all you Scotchmen," she added in hasty correction. "So free from Southern extremes. We common people are all one way or the other—warm or cold, passionate or frigid. You have both temperatures going on in you at the same time."

"But how do you mean that? Ye were best to explain clearly, ma'am."

"You are animated—then you are thinking of getting on. You are sad the next moment—then you are thinking of Scotland and friends."

"Yes. I think of home sometimes!" he said simply.

"So do I—as far as I can. But it was an old house where I was born, and they pulled it down for improvements, so I seem hardly to have any home to think of now."

Lucetta did not add, as she might have done, that the house was in St. Helier, and not in Bath.

"But the mountains, and the mists and the rocks, they are there! And don't they seem like home?"

She shook her head.

"They do to me—they do to me," he murmured. And his mind could be seen flying away northwards. Whether its origin were national or personal, it was quite true what Lucetta had said, that the curious double strands in Farfrae's thread of life—the commercial and the romantic—were very distinct at times. Like the colours in a variegated cord those contrasts could be seen intertwisted, yet not mingling.

"You are wishing you were back again," said she.

"Ah, no, ma'am," said Farfrae, suddenly recalling himself.

The fair without the windows was now raging thick and loud. It was the chief hiring fair* of the year, and differed quite from the market of a few days earlier. In substance it was a whitey-brown crowd flecked with white—this being the body of labourers waiting for places. The long bonnets of the women, like waggon-tilts,† their cotton gowns and checked shawls, mixed with the carters' smock-frocks; for they, too, entered into the hiring. Among the rest, at the corner of the pavement, stood an old shepherd, who attracted the eyes of Lucetta and Farfrae by his stillness. He was evidently a chastened man. The battle of life had been a sharp one with him, for, to begin with, he was a man of small frame. He was now so bowed by hard work and years that, approaching from behind, a person could hardly see his head. He had planted the stem of his crook in the gutter and was resting upon the bow, which was polished to silver brightness by the long friction of his hands. He had quite forgotten where he was, and what he had come for, his eyes being bent on the ground. A little way off negotiations were proceeding which had reference to him; but he did not hear them, and there seemed to be passing through his mind pleasant visions of the hiring successes of his prime, when his skill laid open to him any farm for the asking.

The negotiations were between a farmer from a distant county and the old man's son. In these there was a difficulty. The farmer would not take the crust without the crumb of the bargain, in other words, the old man without the younger; and the son had a sweetheart on his present farm, who stood by, waiting the issue with pale lips.

"I'm sorry to leave ye, Nelly," said the young man with emotion. "But, you see, I can't starve father, and he's out o' work at Lady-day.‡ 'Tis only thirty-five mile."

The girl's lips quivered. "Thirty-five mile!" she murmured. "Ah!

*Annual fair at which agricultural laborers sought work.
†Canvas coverings.
‡Feast of the Annunciation.

'tis enough! I shall never see 'ee again!" It was, indeed, a hopeless length of traction for Dan Cupid's* magnet; for young men were young men at Casterbridge as elsewhere.

"O! no, no—I never shall," she insisted, when he pressed her hand; and she turned her face to Lucetta's wall to hide her weeping. The farmer said he would give the young man half-an-hour for his answer, and went away, leaving the group sorrowing.

Lucetta's eyes, full of tears, met Farfrae's. His, too, to her surprise, were moist at the scene.

"It is very hard," she said with strong feelings. "Lovers ought not to be parted like that! O, if I had my wish, I'd let people live and love at their pleasure!"

"Maybe I can manage that they'll not be parted," said Farfrae. "I want a young carter, and perhaps I'll take the old man too—yes; he'll not be very expensive, and doubtless he will answer my pairrpose somehow."

"O, you are so good!" she cried, delighted. "Go and tell them, and let me know if you have succeeded!"

Farfrae went out, and she saw him speak to the group. The eyes of all brightened; the bargain was soon struck. Farfrae returned to her immediately it was concluded.

"It is kind-hearted of you, indeed," said Lucetta. "For my part, I have resolved that all my servants shall have lovers if they want them! Do make the same resolve!"

Farfrae looked more serious, waving his head a half turn. "I must be a little stricter than that," he said.

"Why?"

"You are a—a thriving woman; and I am a struggling hay-and-corn merchant."

"I am a very ambitious woman."

"Ah, well, I cannet explain. I don't know how to talk to ladies, ambitious or no; and that's true," said Donald with grave regret. "I try to be civil to a' folk—no more!"

"I see you are as you say," replied she, sensibly getting the upper hand in these exchanges of sentiment. Under this revelation of insight Farfrae again looked out of the window into the thick of the fair.

---

*Master Cupid's.

Two farmers met and shook hands, and being quite near the window their remarks could be heard as others' had been.

"Have you seen young Mr. Farfrae this morning?" asked one. "He promised to meet me here at the stroke of twelve; but I've gone athwart and about the fair half-a-dozen times, and never a sign of him: though he's mostly a man to his word."

"I quite forgot the engagement," murmured Farfrae.

"Now you must go," said she; "must you not?"

"Yes," he replied. But he still remained.

"You had better go," she urged. "You will lose a customer."

"Now, Miss Templeman, you will make me angry," exclaimed Farfrae.

"Then suppose you don't go; but stay a little longer?"

He looked anxiously at the farmer who was seeking him, and who just then ominously walked across to where Henchard was standing, and he looked into the room and at her. "I like staying; but I fear I must go!" he said. "Business ought not to be neglected, ought it?"

"Not for a single minute."

"It's true. I'll come another time—if I may, ma'am?"

"Certainly," she said. "What has happened to us to-day is very curious."

"Something to think over when we are alone, it's like to be?"

"Oh, I don't know that. It is commonplace after all."

"No, I'll not say that. O no!"

"Well, whatever it has been, it is now over; and the market calls you to be gone."

"Yes, yes. Market—business! I wish there were no business in the warrld."

Lucetta almost laughed—she would quite have laughed—but that there was a little emotion going in her at the time. "How you change!" she said. "You should not change like this."

"I have never wished such things before," said the Scotchman, with a simple, shamed, apologetic look for his weakness. "It is only since coming heere and seeing you!"

"If that's the case, you had better not look at me any longer. Dear me, I feel I have quite demoralized you!"

"But look or look not, I will see you in my thoughts. Well, I'll go—thank you for the pleasure of this visit."

"Thank you for staying."

"Maybe I'll get into my market-mind when I've been out a few minutes," he murmured. "But I don't know—I don't know!"

As he went she said eagerly, "You may hear them speak of me in Casterbridge as time goes on. If they tell you I'm a coquette, which some may, because of the incidents of my life, don't believe it, for I am not."

"I swear I will not!" he said fervidly.

Thus the two. She had enkindled the young man's enthusiasm till he was quite brimming with sentiment; while he, from merely affording her a new form of idleness had gone on to wake her serious solicitude. Why was this? They could not have told.

Lucetta as a young girl would hardly have looked at a tradesman. But her ups and downs, capped by her indiscretions with Henchard, had made her uncritical as to station. In her poverty she had met with repulse from the society to which she had belonged, and she had no great zest for renewing an attempt upon it now. Her heart longed for some ark into which it could fly and be at rest. Rough or smooth she did not care so long as it was warm.

Farfrae was shown out, it having entirely escaped him that he had called to see Elizabeth. Lucetta at the window watched him threading the maze of farmers and farmers' men. She could see by his gait that he was conscious of her eyes, and her heart went out to him for his modesty—pleaded with her sense of his unfitness that he might be allowed to come again. He entered the market-house, and she could see him no more.

Three minutes later, when she had left the window, knocks, not of multitude but of strength, sounded through the house, and the waiting-maid tripped up.

"The Mayor," she said.

Lucetta had reclined herself, and was looking dreamily through her fingers. She did not answer at once, and the maid repeated the information with the addition, "And he's afraid he hasn't much time to spare, he says."

"Oh! Then tell him that as I have a headache I won't detain him to-day."

The message was taken down, and she heard the door close. Lucetta had come to Casterbridge to quicken Henchard's feelings with regard to her. She had quickened them, and now she was indifferent to the achievement.

Her morning view of Elizabeth-Jane as a disturbing element hanged, and she no longer felt strongly the necessity of getting rid of the girl for her stepfather's sake. When the young woman came in, sweetly unconscious of the turn in the tide, Lucetta went up to her, and said quite sincerely—

"I'm so glad you've come. You'll live with me a long time, won't you?"

Elizabeth as a watch-dog to keep her father off—what a new idea. Yet it was not unpleasing. Henchard had neglected her all these days, after compromising her indescribably in the past. The least he could have done when he found himself free, and herself affluent, would have been to respond heartily and promptly to her invitation.

Her emotions rose, fell, undulated, filled her with wild surmise at their suddenness; and so passed Lucetta's experiences of that day.

XXIV

POOR ELIZABETH-JANE, LITTLE thinking what her malignant star had done to blast the budding attentions she had won from Donald Farfrae, was glad to hear Lucetta's words about remaining.

For in addition to Lucetta's house being a home, that raking view of the market-place which it afforded had as much attraction for her as for Lucetta. The *carrefour* was like the regulation Open Place in spectacular dramas, where the incidents that occur always happen to bear on the lives of the adjoining residents. Farmers, merchants, dairymen, quacks, hawkers, appeared there from week to week, and disappeared as the afternoon wasted away. It was the node of all orbits.

From Saturday to Saturday was as from day to day with the two young women now. In an emotional sense they did not live at all during the intervals. Wherever they might go wandering on other days, on market-day they were sure to be at home. Both stole sly glances out of the window at Farfrae's shoulders and poll. His face they sel-

dom saw, for, either through shyness, or not to disturb his mercantile mood, he avoided looking towards their quarters.

Thus things went on, till a certain market-morning brought a
new sensation. Elizabeth and Lucetta were sitting at breakfast when a
parcel containing two dresses arrived for the latter from London. She
called Elizabeth from her breakfast, and entering her friend's bedroom Elizabeth saw the gowns spread out on the bed, one of a deep
cherry colour, the other lighter—a glove lying at the end of each
sleeve, a bonnet at the top of each neck, and parasols across the
gloves, Lucetta standing beside the suggested human figure in an attitude of contemplation.

"I wouldn't think so hard about it," said Elizabeth, marking the
intensity with which Lucetta was alternating the question whether
this or that would suit best.

"But settling upon new clothes is so trying," said Lucetta. "You
are that person" (pointing to one of the arrangements), "or you are
that totally different person" (pointing to the other), "for the whole
of the coming spring: and one of the two, you don't know which,
may turn out to be very objectionable."

It was finally decided by Miss Templeman that she would be the
cherry-coloured person at all hazards. The dress was pronounced to
be a fit, and Lucetta walked with it into the front room, Elizabeth following her.

The morning was exceptionally bright for the time of year. The
sun fell so flat on the houses and pavement opposite Lucetta's residence that they poured their brightness into her rooms. Suddenly,
after a rumbling of wheels, there were added to this steady light a
fantastic series of circling irradiations upon the ceiling, and the companions turned to the window. Immediately opposite a vehicle of
strange description had come to a standstill, as if it had been placed
there for exhibition.

It was the new-fashioned agricultural implement called a horse-
drill, till then unknown, in its modern shape, in this part of the country, where the venerable seed-lip* was still used for sowing as in the
days of the Heptarchy.† Its arrival created about as much sensation in

---

*Basket used to carry seed.
†The seven kingdoms of seventh-century Anglo-Saxon Britain.

the corn-market as a flying machine would create at Charing Cross. The farmers crowded round it, women drew near it, children crept under and into it. The machine was painted in bright hues of green, yellow, and red, and it resembled as a whole a compound of hornet, grasshopper, and shrimp, magnified enormously. Or it might have been likened to an upright musical instrument with the front gone. That was how it struck Lucetta. "Why, it is a sort of agricultural piano," she said.

"It has something to do with corn," said Elizabeth.

"I wonder who thought of introducing it here?"

Donald Farfrae was in the minds of both as the innovator, for though not a farmer he was closely leagued with farming operations. And as if in response to their thought he came up at that moment, looked at the machine, walked round it, and handled it as if he knew something about its make. The two watchers had inwardly started at his coming, and Elizabeth left the window, went to the back of the room, and stood as if absorbed in the panelling of the wall. She hardly knew that she had done this till Lucetta, animated by the conjunction of her new attire with the sight of Farfrae, spoke out: "Let us go and look at the instrument, whatever it is."

Elizabeth-Jane's bonnet and shawl were pitchforked on in a moment, and they went out. Among all the agriculturists gathering round the only appropriate possessor of the new machine seemed to be Lucetta, because she alone rivalled it in colour.

They examined it curiously; observing the rows of trumpet-shaped tubes one within the other, the little scoops, like revolving salt-spoons, which tossed the seed into the upper ends of the tubes that conducted it to the ground; till somebody said, "Good morning, Elizabeth-Jane." She looked up, and there was her stepfather.

His greeting had been somewhat dry and thunderous, and Elizabeth-Jane, embarrassed out of her equanimity, stammered at random. "This is the lady I live with, father—Miss Templeman."

Henchard put his hand to his hat, which he brought down with a great wave till it met his body at the knee. Miss Templeman bowed. "I am happy to become acquainted with you, Mr. Henchard," she said. "This is a curious machine."

"Yes," Henchard replied; and he proceeded to explain it, and still more forcibly to ridicule it.

"Who brought it here?" said Lucetta.

"Oh, don't ask me, ma'am!" said Henchard. "The thing—why 'tis impossible it should act. 'Twas brought here by one of our machinists on the recommendation of a jumped-up jackanapes of a fellow who thinks——" His eye caught Elizabeth-Jane's imploring face, and he stopped, probably thinking that the suit might be progressing.

He turned to go away. Then something seemed to occur which his stepdaughter fancied must really be a hallucination of hers. A murmur apparently came from Henchard's lips in which she detected the words, "You refused to see me!" reproachfully addressed to Lucetta. She could not believe that they had been uttered by her stepfather; unless, indeed, they might have been spoken to one of the yellow-gaitered farmers near them. Yet Lucetta seemed silent; and then all thought of the incident was dissipated by the humming of a song, which sounded as though from the interior of the machine. Henchard had by this time vanished into the market-house, and both the women glanced towards the corn-drill. They could see behind it the bent back of a man who was pushing his head into the internal works to master their simple secrets. The hummed song went on—

> " 'Tw—s on a s—m—r aftern—n,
> A wee be—re the s—n w—nt d—n,
> When Kitty wi' a brave n—w g—wn
> C—me ow're the h—lls to Gowrie."*

Elizabeth-Jane had apprehended the singer in a moment, and looked guilty of she did not know what. Lucetta next recognized him, and more mistress of herself said archly, "The 'Lass of Gowrie' from the inside of a seed-drill—what a phenomenon!"

Satisfied at last with his investigation the young man stood upright, and met their eyes across the summit.

"We are looking at the wonderful new drill," Miss Templeman said. "But practically it is a stupid thing—is it not?" she added, on the strength of Henchard's information.

"Stupid? O no!" said Farfrae gravely. "It will revolutionize sowing heerabout! No more sowers flinging their seed about broadcast,

---

*Popular Scots ballad with words by Carolina Nairne (1766–1845).

so that some falls by the wayside and some among thorns* and all that. Each grain will go straight to its intended place, and nowhere else whatever!"

"Then the romance of the sower is gone for good," observed Elizabeth-Jane, who felt herself at one with Farfrae in Bible-reading at least. " 'He that observeth the wind shall not sow,'† so the Preacher said; but his words will not be to the point any more. How things change!"

"Ay; ay . . . It must be so!" Donald admitted, his gaze fixing itself on a blank point far away. "But the machines are already very common in the East and North of England," he added apologetically.

Lucetta seemed to be outside this train of sentiment, her acquaintance with the Scriptures being somewhat limited. "Is the machine yours?" she asked of Farfrae.

"O no, madam," said he, becoming embarrassed and deferential at the sound of her voice, though with Elizabeth-Jane he was quite at his ease. "No, no—I merely recommended that it should be got."

In the silence which followed Farfrae appeared only conscious of her; to have passed from perception of Elizabeth into a brighter sphere of existence than she appertained to. Lucetta, discerning that he was much mixed that day, partly in his mercantile mood and partly in his romantic one, said gaily to him—

"Well, don't forsake the machine for us," and went indoors with her companion.

The latter felt that she had been in the way, though why was unaccountable to her. Lucetta explained the matter somewhat by saying when they were again in the sitting-room—

"I had occasion to speak to Mr. Farfrae the other day, and so I knew him this morning."

Lucetta was very kind towards Elizabeth that day. Together they saw the market thicken, and in course of time thin away with the slow decline of the sun towards the upper end of the town, its rays taking the street endways and enfilading the long thoroughfare from top to bottom. The gigs and vans disappeared one by one till there was not a vehicle in the street. The time of the riding world was over; the pedes-

*Biblical reference to Christ's parable of the sower (Matthew 13:3–9).
†Paraphrase of Ecclesiastes 11:4.

trian world held sway. Field labourers and their wives and children trooped in from the villages for their weekly shopping, and instead of a rattle of wheels and a tramp of horses ruling the sound as earlier, there was nothing but the shuffle of many feet. All the implements were gone; all the farmers; all the moneyed class. The character of the town's trading had changed from bulk to multiplicity, and pence were handled now as pounds had been handled earlier in the day.

Lucetta and Elizabeth looked out upon this, for though it was night and the street lamps were lighted, they had kept their shutters unclosed. In the faint blink of the fire they spoke more freely.

"Your father was distant with you," said Lucetta.

"Yes." And having forgotten the momentary mystery of Henchard's seeming speech to Lucetta she continued, "It is because he does not think I am respectable. I have tried to be so more than you can imagine, but in vain! My mother's separation from my father was unfortunate for me. You don't know what it is to have shadows like that upon your life."

Lucetta seemed to wince. "I do not—of that kind precisely," she said, "but you may feel a—sense of disgrace—shame—in other ways."

"Have you ever had any such feeling?" said the younger innocently.

"O no," said Lucetta quickly. "I was thinking of—what happens sometimes when women get themselves in strange positions in the eyes of the world from no fault of their own."

"It must make them very unhappy afterwards."

"It makes them anxious; for might not other women despise them?"

"Not altogether despise them. Yet not quite like or respect them."

Lucetta winced again. Her past was by no means secure from investigation, even in Casterbridge. For one thing Henchard had never returned to her the cloud of letters she had written and sent him in her first excitement. Possibly they were destroyed; but she could have wished that they had never been written.

The rencounter with Farfrae and his bearing towards Lucetta had made the reflective Elizabeth more observant of her brilliant and amiable companion. A few days afterwards, when her eyes met Lucetta's as the latter was going out, she somehow knew that Miss Templeman was nourishing a hope of seeing the attractive Scotchman. The fact was printed large all over Lucetta's cheeks and eyes to any one who could read her as Elizabeth-Jane was beginning to do. Lucetta passed on and closed the street door.

A seer's spirit took possession of Elizabeth, impelling her to sit down by the fire and divine events so surely from data already her own that they could be held as witnessed. She followed Lucetta thus mentally—saw her encounter Donald somewhere as if by chance—saw him wear his special look when meeting women, with an added intensity because this one was Lucetta. She depicted his impassioned manner; beheld the indecision of both between their lothness to separate and their desire not to be observed; depicted their shaking of hands; how they probably parted with frigidity in their general contour and movements, only in the smaller features showing the spark of passion, thus invisible to all but themselves. This discerning silent witch had not done thinking of these things when Lucetta came noiselessly behind her and made her start.

It was all true as she had pictured—she could have sworn it. Lucetta had a heightened luminousness in her eye over and above the advanced colour of her cheeks.

"You've seen Mr. Farfrae," said Elizabeth demurely.

"Yes," said Lucetta. "How did you know?"

She knelt down on the hearth and took her friend's hands excitedly in her own. But after all she did not say when or how she had seen him or what he had said.

That night she became restless; in the morning she was feverish; and at breakfast-time she told her companion that she had something on her mind—something which concerned a person in whom she was interested much. Elizabeth was earnest to listen and sympathize.

"This person—a lady—once admired a man much—very much," she said tentatively.

"Ah," said Elizabeth-Jane.

"They were intimate—rather. He did not think so deeply of her as she did of him. But in an impulsive moment, purely out of reparation, he proposed to make her his wife. She agreed. But there was an unexpected hitch in the proceedings; though she had been so far compromised with him that she felt she could never belong to another man, as a pure matter of conscience, even if she should wish to.

After that they were much apart, heard nothing of each other for a long time, and she felt her life quite closed up for her."

"Ah—poor girl!"

"She suffered much on account of him; though I should add that he could not altogether be blamed for what had happened. At last the obstacle which separated them was providentially removed; and he came to marry her."

"How delightful!"

"But in the interval she—my poor friend—had seen a man she liked better than him. Now comes the point: Could she in honour dismiss the first?"

"A new man she liked better—that's bad!"

"Yes," said Lucetta, looking pained at a boy who was swinging the town pump-handle. "It is bad! Though you must remember that she was forced into an equivocal position with the first man by an accident—that he was not so well educated or refined as the second, and that she had discovered some qualities in the first that rendered him less desirable as a husband than she had at first thought him to be."

"I cannot answer," said Elizabeth-Jane thoughtfully. "It is so difficult. It wants a Pope to settle that!"

"You prefer not to, perhaps?" Lucetta showed in her appealing tone how much she leant on Elizabeth's judgment.

"Yes, Miss Templeman," admitted Elizabeth. "I would rather not say."

Nevertheless, Lucetta seemed relieved by the simple fact of having opened out the situation a little, and was slowly convalescent of her headache. "Bring me a looking-glass. How do I appear to people?" she said languidly.

"Well—a little worn," answered Elizabeth, eyeing her as a critic eyes a doubtful painting; fetching the glass she enabled Lucetta to survey herself in it, which Lucetta anxiously did.

"I wonder if I wear well, as times go!" she observed after a while.

"Yes—fairly."

"Where am I worst?"

"Under your eyes—I notice a little brownness there."

"Yes. That is my worst place, I know. How many years more do you think I shall last before I get hopelessly plain?"

There was something curious in the way in which Elizabeth,

though the younger, had come to play the part of experienced sage in these discussions. "It may be five years," she said judicially. "Or, with a quiet life, as many as ten. With no love you might calculate on ten."

Lucetta seemed to reflect on this as on an unalterable, impartial verdict. She told Elizabeth-Jane no more of the past attachment she had roughly adumbrated as the experiences of a third person; and Elizabeth, who in spite of her philosophy was very tender-hearted, sighed that night in bed at the thought that her pretty, rich Lucetta did not treat her to the full confidence of names and dates in her confessions. For by the "she" of Lucetta's story Elizabeth had not been beguiled.

XXV

THE NEXT PHASE OF the supersession of Henchard in Lucetta's heart was an experiment in calling on her performed by Farfrae with some apparent trepidation. Conventionally speaking he conversed with both Miss Templeman and her companion; but in fact it was rather that Elizabeth sat invisible in the room. Donald appeared not to see her at all, and answered her wise little remarks with curtly indifferent monosyllables, his looks and faculties hanging on the woman who could boast of a more Protean* variety in her phases, moods, opinions, and also principles, than could Elizabeth. Lucetta had persisted in dragging her into the circle; but she had remained like an awkward third point which that circle would not touch.

Susan Henchard's daughter bore up against the frosty ache of the treatment, as she had borne up under worse things, and contrived as soon as possible to get out of the inharmonious room without being missed. The Scotchman seemed hardly the same Farfrae who had danced with her and walked with her in a delicate poise between love and friendship—that period in the history of a love when alone it can be said to be unalloyed with pain.

She stoically looked from her bedroom window, and contemplated her fate as if it were written on the top of the church-tower

---

*Always changing (a reference to Proteus, the shape-shifting god of the sea).

hard by. "Yes," she said at last, bringing down her palm upon the sill with a pat: He is the second man of that story she told me!"

All this time Henchard's smouldering sentiments towards Lucetta had been fanned into higher and higher inflammation by the circumstances of the case. He was discovering that the young woman for whom he once felt a pitying warmth which had been almost chilled out of him by reflection, was, when now qualified with a slight inaccessibility and a more matured beauty, the very being to make him satisfied with life. Day after day proved to him, by her silence, that it was no use to think of bringing her round by holding aloof; so he gave in, and called upon her again, Elizabeth-Jane being absent.

He crossed the room to her with a heavy tread of some awkwardness, his strong, warm gaze upon her—like the sun beside the moon in comparison with Farfrae's modest look—and with something of a hail-fellow bearing, as, indeed, was not unnatural. But she seemed so transubstantiated by her change of position, and held out her hand to him in such cool friendship, that he became deferential, and sat down with a perceptible loss of power. He understood but little of fashion in dress, yet enough to feel himself inadequate in appearance beside her whom he had hitherto been dreaming of as almost his property. She said something very polite about his being good enough to call. This caused him to recover balance. He looked her oddly in the face, losing his awe.

"Why, of course I have called, Lucetta," he said. "What does that nonsense mean? You know I couldn't have helped myself if I had wished—that is, if I had any kindness at all. I've called to say that I am ready, as soon as custom will permit, to give you my name in return for your devotion, and what you lost by it in thinking too little of yourself and too much of me; to say that you can fix the day or month, with my full consent, whenever in your opinion it would be seemly: you know more of these things than I."

"It is full early yet," she said evasively.

"Yes, yes; I suppose it is. But you know, Lucetta, I felt directly my poor ill-used Susan died, and when I could not bear the idea of marrying again, that after what had happened between us it was my duty not to let any unnecessary delay occur before putting things to rights. Still, I wouldn't call in a hurry, because—well, you can guess how this money you've come into made me feel." His voice slowly fell; he was conscious that in this room his accents and manner wore a roughness not observable in the street. He looked about the room at the novel hangings and ingenious furniture with which she had surrounded herself.

"Upon my life I didn't know such furniture as this could be bought in Casterbridge," he said.

"Nor can it be," said she. "Nor will it till fifty years more of civilization have passed over the town. It took a waggon and four horses to get it here."

"H'm. It looks as if you were living on capital."

"O no, I am not."

"So much the better. But the fact is, your setting up like this makes my bearing towards you rather awkward."

"Why?"

An answer was not really needed, and he did not furnish one. "Well," he went on, "there's nobody in the world I would have wished to see enter into this wealth before you, Lucetta, and nobody, I am sure, who will become it more." He turned to her with congratulatory admiration so fervid that she shrank somewhat, notwithstanding that she knew him so well.

"I am greatly obliged to you for all that," said she, rather with an air of speaking ritual. The stint of reciprocal feeling was perceived, and Henchard showed chagrin at once—nobody was more quick to show that than he.

"You may be obliged or not for't. Though the things I say may not have the polish of what you've lately learnt to expect for the first time in your life, they are real, my lady Lucetta."

"That's rather a rude way of speaking to me," pouted Lucetta, with stormy eyes.

"Not at all!" replied Henchard hotly. "But there, there, I don't wish to quarrel with 'ee. I come with an honest proposal for silencing your Jersey enemies, and you ought to be thankful."

"How can you speak so!" she answered, firing quickly. "Knowing that my only crime was the indulging in a foolish girl's passion for you with too little regard for correctness, and that I was what I call innocent all the time they called me guilty, you ought not to be so cutting! I suffered enough at that worrying time, when you wrote to tell me of your wife's return and my consequent dismissal, and if I am a little independent now, surely the privilege is due to me!"

"Yes, it is," he said. "But it is not by what is, in this life, but by what appears, that you are judged; and I therefore think you ought to accept me—for your own good name's sake. What is known in your native Jersey may get known here."

"How you keep on about Jersey! I am English!"

"Yes, yes. Well, what do you say to my proposal?"

For the first time in their acquaintance Lucetta had the move; and yet she was backward. "For the present let things be," she said with some embarrassment. "Treat me as an acquaintance; and I'll treat you as one. Time will——" she stopped; and he said nothing to fill the gap for awhile, there being no pressure of half acquaintance to drive them into speech if they were not minded for it.

"That's the way the wind blows, is it?" he said at last grimly, nodding an affirmative to his own thoughts.

A yellow flood of reflected sunlight filled the room for a few instants. It was produced by the passing of a load of newly trussed hay from the country, in a waggon marked with Farfrae's name. Beside it rode Farfrae himself on horseback. Lucetta's face became—as a woman's face becomes when the man she loves rises upon her gaze like an apparition.

A turn of the eye by Henchard, a glance from the window; and the secret of her inaccessibility would have been revealed. But Henchard in estimating her tone was looking down so plumb-straight that he did not note the warm consciousness upon Lucetta's face.

"I shouldn't have thought it—I shouldn't have thought it of women!" he said emphatically by-and-by, rising and shaking himself into activity; while Lucetta was so anxious to divert him from any suspicion of the truth that she asked him to be in no hurry. Bringing him some apples she insisted upon paring one for him.

He would not take it. "No, no; such is not for me," he said drily, and moved to the door. At going out he turned his eye upon her.

"You came to live in Casterbridge entirely on my account," he said. "Yet now you are here you won't have anything to say to my offer!"

He had hardly gone down the staircase when she dropped upon the sofa and jumped up again in a fit of desperation. "I will love him!"

she cried passionately; "as for him—he's hot-tempered and stern, and it would be madness to bind myself to him knowing that. I won't be a slave to the past—I'll love where I choose!"

Yet having decided to break away from Henchard one might have supposed her capable of aiming higher than Farfrae. But Lucetta reasoned nothing: she feared hard words from the people with whom she had been earlier associated; she had no relatives left; and with native lightness of heart took kindly to what fate offered.

Elizabeth-Jane, surveying the position of Lucetta between her two lovers from the crystalline sphere of a straightforward mind, did not fail to perceive that her father, as she called him, and Donald Farfrae became more desperately enamoured of her friend every day. On Farfrae's side it was the unforced passion of youth. On Henchard's the artificially stimulated coveting of maturer age.

The pain she experienced from the almost absolute obliviousness to her existence that was shown by the pair of them became at times half dissipated by her sense of its humorousness. When Lucetta had pricked her finger they were as deeply concerned as if she were dying; when she herself had been seriously sick or in danger they uttered a conventional word of sympathy at the news, and forgot all about it immediately. But, as regarded Henchard, this perception of hers also caused her some filial grief, she could not help asking what she had done to be neglected so, after the professions of solicitude he had made. As regarded Farfrae, she thought, after honest reflection, that it was quite natural. What was she beside Lucetta?—as one of the "meaner beauties of the night,"[18] when the moon had risen in the skies.

She had learnt the lesson of renunciation, and was as familiar with the wreck of each day's wishes as with the diurnal setting of the sun. If her earthly career had taught her few book philosophies it had at least well practised her in this. Yet her experience had consisted less in a series of pure disappointments than in a series of substitutions. Continually it had happened that what she had desired had not been granted her, and that what had been granted her she had not desired. So she viewed with an approach to equanimity the now cancelled days when Donald had been her undeclared lover, and wondered what unwished-for thing Heaven might send her in place of him.

XXVI

IT CHANCED THAT ON a fine spring morning Henchard and Farfrae met in the chestnut-walk which ran along the south wall of the town. Each had just come out from his early breakfast, and there was not another soul near. Henchard was reading a letter from Lucetta, sent in answer to a note from him, in which she made some excuse for not immediately granting him a second interview that he had desired.

Donald had no wish to enter into conversation with his former friend on their present constrained terms; neither would he pass him in scowling silence. He nodded, and Henchard did the same. They had receded from each other several paces when a voice cried "Farfrae!" It was Henchard's, who stood regarding him.

"Do you remember," said Henchard, as if it were the presence of the thought and not of the man which made him speak, "do you remember my story of that second woman—who suffered for her thoughtless intimacy with me?"

"I do," said Farfrae.

"Do you remember my telling 'ee how it all began and how it ended?"

"Yes."

"Well, I have offered to marry her now that I can; but she won't marry me. Now what would you think of her—I put it to you?"

"Well, ye owe her nothing more now," said Farfrae heartily.

"It is true," said Henchard, and went on.

That he had looked up from a letter to ask his questions completely shut out from Farfrae's mind all vision of Lucetta as the culprit. Indeed, her present position was so different from that of the young woman of Henchard's story as of itself to be sufficient to blind him absolutely to her identity. As for Henchard, he was reassured by Farfrae's words and manner against a suspicion which had crossed his mind. They were not those of a conscious rival.

Yet that there was rivalry by some one he was firmly persuaded. He could feel it in the air around Lucetta, see it in the turn of her pen. There was an antagonistic force in exercise, so that when he had tried to hang near her he seemed standing in a refluent current. That it was not innate caprice he was more and more certain. Her windows gleamed as if they did not want him; her curtains seemed to hang slily, as if they screened an ousting presence. To discover whose presence that was—whether really Farfrae's after all, or another's—he exerted himself to the utmost to see her again; and at length succeeded.

At the interview, when she offered him tea, he made it a point to launch a cautious inquiry if she knew Mr. Farfrae.

O yes, she knew him, she declared; she could not help knowing almost everybody in Casterbridge, living in such a gazebo* over the centre and arena of the town.

"Pleasant young fellow," said Henchard.

"Yes," said Lucetta.

"We both know him," said kind Elizabeth-Jane, to relieve her companion's divined embarrassment.

There was a knock at the door; literally, three full knocks and a little one at the end.

"That kind of knock means half-and-half-somebody between gentle and simple,"† said the corn-merchant to himself. "I shouldn't wonder therefore if it is he." In a few seconds surely enough Donald walked in.

Lucetta was full of little fidgets and flutters, which increased Henchard's suspicions without affording any special proof of their correctness. He was well-nigh ferocious at the sense of the queer situation in which he stood towards this woman. One who had reproached him for deserting her when calumniated, who had urged claims upon his consideration on that account, who had lived waiting for him, who at the first decent moment had come to ask him to rectify, by making her his, the false position into which she had placed herself for his sake; such she had been. And now he sat at her tea-table eager to gain her attention, and in his amatory rage feeling the other man present to be a villain, just as any young fool of a lover might feel.

They sat stiffly side by side at the darkening table, like some Tuscan painting of the two disciples supping at Emmaus.‡ Lucetta, forming the third and haloed figure, was opposite them; Elizabeth-Jane, being out of

---

*Structure that affords a view.

†Social station between the gentry and the laboring class.

‡Village at which Christ appeared to two disciples after his resurrection (Luke 24:13–31).

the game, and out of the group, could observe all from afar, like the evangelist who had to write it down: that there were long spaces of tac- iturnity, when all exterior circumstance was subdued to the touch of spoons and china, the click of a heel on the pavement under the win- dow, the passing of a wheelbarrow or cart, the whistling of the carter, the gush of water into householders' buckets at the town-pump oppo- site; the exchange of greetings among their neighbours, and the rattle of the yokes by which they carried off their evening supply.

"More bread-and-butter?" said Lucetta to Henchard and Farfrae equally, holding out between them a plateful of long slices. Henchard took a slice by one end and Donald by the other; each feeling certain he was the man meant; neither let go, and the slice came in two.

"Oh—I am so sorry!" cried Lucetta, with a nervous titter. Farfrae tried to laugh; but he was too much in love to see the incident in any but a tragic light.

"How ridiculous of all three of them!" said Elizabeth to herself.

Henchard left the house with a ton of conjecture, though without a grain of proof, that the counter-attraction was Farfrae; and therefore he would not make up his mind. Yet to Elizabeth- Jane it was plain as the town-pump that Donald and Lucetta were incipient lovers. More than once, in spite of her care, Lucetta had been unable to restrain her glance from flitting across into Far- frae's eyes like a bird to its nest. But Henchard was constructed upon too large a scale to discern such minutia as these by an evening light, which to him were as the notes of an insect that lie above the compass of the human ear.

But he was disturbed. And the sense of occult rivalry in suitorship was so much superadded to the palpable rivalry of their business lives. To the coarse materiality of that rivalry it added an inflaming soul.

The thus vitalized antagonism took the form of action by Hen- chard sending for Jopp, the manager originally displaced by Farfrae's arrival. Henchard had frequently met this man about the streets, ob- served that his clothing spoke of neediness, heard that he lived in Mixen Lane—a back slum of the town, the *pis aller** of Casterbridge domiciliation—itself almost a proof that a man had reached a stage when he would not stick at trifles.

---

*Last resort (French).

Jopp came after dark, by the gates of the storeyard, and felt his way through the hay and straw to the office where Henchard sat in solitude awaiting him.

"I am again out of a foreman," said the corn-factor. "Are you in a place?"

"Not so much as a beggar's, sir."

"How much do you ask?"

Jopp named his price, which was very moderate.

"When can you come?"

"At this hour and moment, sir," said Jopp, who, standing hands-pocketed at the street corner till the sun had faded the shoulders of his coat to scarecrow green, had regularly watched Henchard in the market-place, measured him, and learnt him, by virtue of the power which the still man has in his stillness of knowing the busy one better than he knows himself. Jopp, too, had had a convenient experience; he was the only one in Casterbridge besides Henchard and the close-lipped Elizabeth who knew that Lucetta came truly from Jersey, and but proximately from Bath. "I know Jersey, too, sir," he said. "Was living there when you used to do business that way. O yes—have often seen ye there."

"Indeed! Very good. Then the thing is settled. The testimonials you showed me when you first tried for't are sufficient."

That characters deteriorate in time of need possibly did not occur to Henchard. Jopp said, "Thank you," and stood more firmly, in the consciousness that at last he officially belonged to that spot.

"Now," said Henchard, digging his strong eyes into Jopp's face, "one thing is necessary to me, as the biggest corn-and-hay-dealer in these parts. The Scotchman, who's taking the town trade so bold into his hands, must be cut out. D'ye hear? We two can't live side by side—that's clear and certain."

"I've seen it all," said Jopp.

"By fair competition I mean, of course," Henchard continued. "But as hard, keen, and unflinching as fair—rather more so. By such a desperate bid against him for the farmers' custom as will grind him into the ground—starve him out. I've capital, mind ye, and I can do it."

"I'm all that way of thinking," said the new foreman. Jopp's dislike of Farfrae as the man who had once usurped his place, while it made him a willing tool, made him, at the same time, commercially as unsafe a colleague as Henchard could have chosen.

"I sometimes think," he added, "that he must have some glass that he sees next year in. He has such a knack of making everything bring him fortune."

"He's deep beyond all honest men's discerning; but we must make him shallower. We'll under-sell him, and over-buy him, and so snuff him out."

They then entered into specific details of the process by which this would be accomplished, and parted at a late hour.

Elizabeth-Jane heard by accident that Jopp had been engaged by her stepfather. She was so fully convinced that he was not the right man for the place that, at the risk of making Henchard angry, she expressed her apprehension to him when they met. But it was done to no purpose. Henchard shut up her argument with a sharp rebuff.

The season's weather seemed to favour their scheme. The time was in the years immediately before foreign competition had revolutionized the trade in grain, when still, as from the earliest ages, the wheat quotations from month to month depended entirely upon the home harvest. A bad harvest, or the prospect of one, would double the price of corn in a few weeks; and the promise of a good yield would lower it as rapidly. Prices were like the roads of the period, steep in gradient, reflecting in their phases the local conditions, without engineering, levellings, or averages.

The farmer's income was ruled by the wheat-crop within his own horizon, and the wheat-crop by the weather. Thus, in person, he became a sort of flesh-barometer, with feelers always directed to the sky and wind around him. The local atmosphere was everything to him; the atmospheres of other countries a matter of indifference. The people, too, who were not farmers, the rural multitude, saw in the god of the weather a more important personage than they do now. Indeed, the feeling of the peasantry in this matter was so intense as to be almost unrealizable in these equable days. Their impulse was well-nigh to prostrate themselves in lamentation before untimely rains and tempests, which came as the Alastor* of those households whose crime it was to be poor.

---

*Avenging spirit.

After midsummer they watched the weathercocks as men waiting in antechambers watch the lackey. Sun elated them; quiet rain sobered them; weeks of watery tempest stupefied them. That aspect of the sky which they now regard as disagreeable they then beheld as maleficent.

It was June, and the weather was very unfavourable. Casterbridge, being as it were the bell-board on which all the adjacent hamlets and villages sounded their notes, was decidedly dull. Instead of new articles in the shop-windows those that had been rejected in the foregoing summer were brought out again; superseded reap-hooks, badly-shaped rakes, shop-worn leggings, and time-stiffened water-tights reappeared, furbished up as near to new as possible.

Henchard, backed by Jopp, read a disastrous garnering, and resolved to base his strategy against Farfrae upon that reading. But before acting he wished—what so many have wished—that he could know for certain what was at present only strong probability. He was superstitious—as such headstrong natures often are—and he nourished in his mind an idea bearing on the matter; an idea he shrank from disclosing even to Jopp.

In a lonely hamlet a few miles from the town—so lonely that what are called lonely villages were teeming by comparison—there lived a man of curious repute as a forecaster or weather-prophet. The way to his house was crooked and miry—even difficult in the present unpropitious season. One evening when it was raining so heavily that ivy and laurel resounded like distant musketry, and an out-door man could be excused for shrouding himself to his ears and eyes, such a shrouded figure on foot might have been perceived travelling in the direction of the hazel-copse which dripped over the prophet's cot. The turnpike-road became a lane, the lane a cart-track, the cart-track a bridle-path, the bridle-path a foot-way, the foot-way overgrown. The solitary walker slipped here and there, and stumbled over the natural springes* formed by the brambles, till at length he reached the house, which, with its garden, was surrounded with a high, dense hedge. The cottage, comparatively a large one, had been built of mud by the occupier's own hands, and thatched also by himself. Here he had always lived, and here it was assumed he would die.

---

*Snares for catching small game.

He existed on unseen supplies; for it was an anomalous thing that while there was hardly a soul in the neighbourhood but affected to laugh at this man's assertions, uttering the formula, "There's nothing in 'em," with full assurance on the surface of their faces, very few of them were unbelievers in their secret hearts. Whenever they consulted him they did it "for a fancy." When they paid him they said, "Just a trifle for Christmas," or "Candlemas," as the case might be.

He would have preferred more honesty in his clients, and less sham ridicule; but fundamental belief consoled him for superficial irony. As stated, he was enabled to live; people supported him with their backs turned. He was sometimes astonished that men could profess so little and believe so much at his house, when at church they professed so much and believed so little.

Behind his back he was called "Wide-oh," on account of his reputation; to his face "Mr." Fall.

The hedge of his garden formed an arch over the entrance, and a door was inserted as in a wall. Outside the door the tall traveller stopped, bandaged his face with a handkerchief as if he were suffering from toothache, and went up the path. The window shutters were not closed, and he could see the prophet within, preparing his supper.

In answer to the knock Fall came to the door, candle in hand. The visitor stepped back a little from the light, and said, "Can I speak to 'ee?" in significant tones. The other's invitation to come in was responded to by the country formula, "This will do, thank 'ee," after which the householder has no alternative but to come out. He placed the candle on the corner of the dresser, took his hat from a nail, and joined the stranger in the porch, shutting the door behind him.

"I've long heard that you can—do things of a sort?" began the other, repressing his individuality as much as he could.

"Maybe so, Mr. Henchard," said the weather-caster.

"Ah—why do you call me that?" asked the visitor with a start.

"Because it's your name. Feeling you'd come I've waited for 'ee; and thinking you might be leery from your walk I laid two supper plates—look ye here." He threw open the door and disclosed the supper-table, at which appeared a second chair, knife and fork, plate and mug, as he had declared.

Henchard felt like Saul at his reception by Samuel;* he remained in silence for a few moments, then throwing off the disguise of frigidity which he had hitherto preserved he said, "Then I have not come in vain. . . . Now, for instance, can ye charm away warts?"

"Without trouble."

"Cure the evil?"†

"That I've done—with consideration—if they will wear the toad-bag‡ by night as well as by day."

"Forecast the weather?"

"With labour and time."

"Then take this," said Henchard. " 'Tis a crown-piece. Now, what is the harvest fortnight to be? When can I know?"

"I've worked it out already, and you can know at once." (The fact was that five farmers had already been there on the same errand from different parts of the country.) "By the sun, moon, and stars, by the clouds, the winds, the trees, and grass, the candle-flame and swallows, the smell of the herbs; likewise by the cats' eyes, the ravens, the leeches, the spiders, and the dungmixen, the last fortnight in August will be—rain and tempest."

"You are not certain, of course?"

"As one can be in a world where all's unsure. 'Twill be more like living in Revelations this autumn than in England. Shall I sketch it out for 'ee in a scheme?"

"O no, no," said Henchard. "I don't altogether believe in forecasts, come to second thoughts on such. But I——"

"You don't—you don't—'tis quite understood," said Wide-oh, without a sound of scorn. "You have given me a crown because you've one too many. But won't you join me at supper, now 'tis waiting and all?"

Henchard would gladly have joined; for the savour of the stew had floated from the cottage into the porch with such appetizing distinctness that the meat, the onions, the pepper, and the herbs could be severally recognized by his nose. But as sitting down to hob-and-

---

*Saul is made the special guest of the seer Samuel, whom he has come to consult (1 Samuel 9:14–24).
†Scrofula, a degeneration of the lymph glands.
‡Bag filled with toads' legs, intended to cure scrofula.

nob* there would have seemed to mark him too implicitly as the weathercaster's apostle, he declined, and went his way.

The next Saturday Henchard bought grain to such an enormous extent that there was quite a talk about his purchases among his neighbours the lawyer, the wine merchant, and the doctor; also on the next, and on all available days. When his granaries were full to choking, all the weathercocks of Casterbridge creaked and set their faces in another direction, as if tired of the south-west. The weather changed; the sunlight, which had been like tin for weeks, assumed the hues of topaz. The temperament of the welkin† passed from the phlegmatic to the sanguine; an excellent harvest was almost a certainty; and as a consequence prices rushed down.

All these transformations, lovely to the outsider, to the wrong-headed corn-dealer were terrible. He was reminded of what he had well known before, that a man might gamble upon the square green areas of fields as readily as upon those of a card-room.

Henchard had backed bad weather, and apparently lost. He had mistaken the turn of the flood for the turn of the ebb. His dealings had been so extensive that settlement could not long be postponed, and to settle he was obliged to sell off corn that he had bought only a few weeks before at figures higher by many shillings a quarter. Much of the corn he had never seen; it had not even been moved from the ricks in which it lay stacked miles away. Thus he lost heavily.

In the blaze of an early August day he met Farfrae in the market-place. Farfrae knew of his dealings (though he did not guess their intended bearing on himself) and commiserated him; for since their exchange of words in the South Walk they had been on stiffly speaking terms. Henchard for the moment appeared to resent the sympathy; but he suddenly took a careless turn.

"Ho, no, no!—nothing serious, man!" he cried with fierce gaiety. "These things always happen, don't they? I know it has been said that figures have touched me tight lately; but is that anything rare? The case is not so bad as folk make out perhaps. And dammy, a man must be a fool to mind the common hazards of trade!"

But he had to enter the Casterbridge Bank that day for reasons

---

*Chat.
†Sky.

which had never before sent him there—and to sit a long time in the partners' room with a constrained bearing: It was rumoured soon after that much real property as well as vast stores of produce, which had stood in Henchard's name in the town and neighbourhood, was actually the possession of his bankers.

Coming down the steps of the bank he encountered Jopp. The gloomy transactions just completed within had added fever to the original sting of Farfrae's sympathy that morning, which Henchard fancied might be satire disguised, so that Jopp met with anything but a bland reception. The latter was in the act of taking off his hat to wipe his forehead, and saying, "A fine hot day," to an acquaintance.

"You can wipe and wipe, and say, 'A fine hot day,' can ye!" cried Henchard in a savage undertone, imprisoning Jopp between himself and the bank wall. "If it hadn't been for your blasted advice it might have been a fine day enough! Why did ye let me go on, hey?—when a word of doubt from you or anybody would have made me think twice! For you can never be sure of weather till 'tis past."

"My advice, sir, was to do what you thought best."

"A useful fellow! And the sooner you help somebody else in that way the better!" Henchard continued his address to Jopp in similar terms till it ended in Jopp's dismissal there and then, Henchard turning upon his heel and leaving him.

"You shall be sorry for this, sir; sorry as a man can be!" said Jopp, standing pale, and looking after the corn-merchant as he disappeared in the crowd of market-men hard by.

XXVII

IT WAS THE EVE of harvest. Prices being low Farfrae was buying. As was usual, after reckoning too surely on famine weather the local farmers had flown to the other extreme, and (in Farfrae's opinion) were selling off too recklessly—calculating with just a trifle too much certainty upon an abundant yield. So he went on buying old corn at its comparatively ridiculous price: for the produce of the previous year, though not large, had been of excellent quality.

When Henchard had squared his affairs in a disastrous way, and got rid of his burdensome purchases at a monstrous loss, the harvest began. There were three days of excellent weather, and then—"What if that curst conjuror should be right after all!" said Henchard.

The fact was, that no sooner had the sickles begun to play than the atmosphere suddenly felt as if cress would grow in it without other nourishment. It rubbed people's cheeks like damp flannel when they walked abroad. There was a gusty, high, warm wind; isolated raindrops starred the window-panes at remote distances: the sunlight would flap out like a quickly opened fan, throw the pattern of the window upon the floor of the room in a milky, colourless shine, and withdraw as suddenly as it had appeared.

From that day and hour it was clear that there was not to be so successful an ingathering after all. If Henchard had only waited long enough he might at least have avoided loss though he had not made a profit. But the momentum of his character knew no patience. At this turn of the scales he remained silent. The movements of his mind seemed to tend to the thought that some power was working against him.

"I wonder," he asked himself with eerie misgiving; "I wonder if it can be that somebody has been roasting a waxen image of me, or stirring an unholy brew to confound me! I don't believe in such power; and yet—what if they should ha' been doing it!" Even he could not admit that the perpetrator, if any, might be Farfrae. These isolated hours of superstition came to Henchard in time of moody depression, when all his practical largeness of view had oozed out of him.

Meanwhile Donald Farfrae prospered. He had purchased in so depressed a market that the present moderate stiffness of prices was sufficient to pile for him a large heap of gold where a little one had been.

"Why, he'll soon be Mayor!" said Henchard. It was indeed hard that the speaker should, of all others, have to follow the triumphal chariot of this man to the Capitol.[19]

The rivalry of the masters was taken up by the men.

September-night shades had fallen upon Casterbridge; the clocks had struck half-past eight, and the moon had risen. The streets of the town were curiously silent for such a comparatively early hour. A sound of jangling horse-bells and heavy wheels passed up the street. These were followed by angry voices outside Lucetta's house, which led her and Elizabeth-Jane to run to the windows, and pull up the blinds.

The neighbouring Market House and Town Hall abutted against its next neighbour the Church except in the lower storey, where an arched thoroughfare gave admittance to a large square called Bull Stake. A stone post rose in the midst, to which the oxen had formerly been tied for baiting with dogs to make them tender before they were killed in the adjoining shambles. In a corner stood the stocks.

The thoroughfare leading to this spot was now blocked by two four-horse waggons and horses, one laden with hay-trusses, the leaders having already passed each other, and become entangled head to tail. The passage of the vehicles might have been practicable if empty; but built up with hay to the bedroom windows as one was, it was impossible.

"You must have done it a' purpose!" said Farfrae's waggoner. "You can hear my horses' bells half-a-mile such a night as this!"

"If ye'd been minding your business instead of zwailing* along in such a gawk-hammer† way, you would have zeed me!" retorted the wroth representative of Henchard.

However, according to the strict rule of the road it appeared that Henchard's man was most in the wrong; he therefore attempted to back into the High Street. In doing this the near hind-wheel rose against the churchyard wall, and the whole mountainous load went over, two of the four wheels rising in the air, and the legs of the thill horse.‡

Instead of considering how to gather up the load the two men closed in a fight with their fists. Before the first round was quite over Henchard came upon the spot, somebody having run for him.

Henchard sent the two men staggering in contrary directions by collaring one with each hand, turned to the horse that was down, and extricated him after some trouble. He then inquired into the circumstances; and seeing the state of his waggon and its load began hotly rating Farfrae's man.

Lucetta and Elizabeth-Jane had by this time run down to the street corner, whence they watched the bright heap of new hay lying

*Swaying.
†Idiotic.
‡Last horse in a team pulling a carriage.

in the moon's rays, and passed and re-passed by the forms of Henchard and the waggoners. The women had witnessed what nobody else had seen—the origin of the mishap; and Lucetta spoke.

"I saw it all, Mr. Henchard," she cried; "and your man was most in the wrong!"

Henchard paused in his harangue and turned. "Oh, I didn't notice you, Miss Templeman," said he. "My man in the wrong? Ah, to be sure; to be sure! But I beg your pardon notwithstanding. The other's is the empty waggon, and he must have been most to blame for coming on."

"No; I saw it, too," said Elizabeth-Jane. "And I can assure you he couldn't help it."

"You can't trust their senses!" murmured Henchard's man.

"Why not?" asked Henchard sharply.

"Why, you see, sir, all the women side with Farfrae—being a damn young dand—of the sort that he is—one that creeps into a maid's heart like the giddying worm into a sheep's brain*—making crooked seem straight to their eyes!"

"But do you know who that lady is you talk about in such a fashion? Do you know that I pay my attentions to her, and have for some time? Just be careful!"

"Not I. I know nothing, sir, outside eight shillings a week."

"And that Mr. Farfrae is well aware of it? He's sharp in trade, but he wouldn't do anything so underhand as what you hint at."

Whether because Lucetta heard this low dialogue, or not, her white figure disappeared from her doorway inward, and the door was shut before Henchard could reach it to converse with her further. This disappointed him, for he had been sufficiently disturbed by what the man had said to wish to speak to her more closely. While pausing the old constable came up.

"Just see that nobody drives against that hay and waggon to-night, Stubberd," said the corn-merchant. "It must bide till the morning, for all hands are in the fields still. And if any coach or road-waggon wants to come along, tell 'em they must go round by the back street, and be hanged to 'em. . . . Any case tomorrow up in Hall?"

"Yes, sir. One in number, sir."

---

*Worm that infiltrates the brain of a sheep, making the animal "giddy" before killing it.

"Oh, what's that?"

"An old flagrant* female, sir, swearing and committing a nuisance in a horrible profane manner against the church wall, sir, as if 'twere no more than a pot-house!† That's all, sir."

"Oh. The Mayor's out o' town, isn't he?"

"He is, sir."

"Very well, then I'll be there. Don't forget to keep an eye on that hay. Good night t' 'ee."

During those moments Henchard had determined to follow up Lucetta notwithstanding her elusiveness, and he knocked for admission.

The answer he received was an expression of Miss Templeman's sorrow at being unable to see him again that evening because she had an engagement to go out.

Henchard walked away from the door to the opposite side of the street, and stood by his hay in a lonely reverie, the constable having strolled elsewhere, and the horses being removed. Though the moon was not bright as yet there were no lamps lighted, and he entered the shadow of one of the projecting jambs which formed the thoroughfare to Bull Stake; here he watched Lucetta's door.

Candle-lights were flitting in and out of her bedroom, and it was obvious that she was dressing for the appointment, whatever the nature of that might be at such an hour. The lights disappeared, the clock struck nine, and almost at the moment Farfrae came round the opposite corner and knocked. That she had been waiting just inside for him was certain, for she instantly opened the door herself. They went together by the way of a back lane westward, avoiding the front street; guessing where they were going he determined to follow.

The harvest had been so delayed by the capricious weather that whenever a fine day occurred all sinews were strained to save what could be saved of the damaged crops. On account of the rapid shortening of the days the harvesters worked by moonlight. Hence to-night the wheat-fields abutting on the two sides of the square formed by Casterbridge town were animated by the gathering hands. Their shouts and laughter had reached Henchard at the Market House, while

---

*Malaproprism for "vagrant."

†Tavern.

he stood there waiting, and he had little doubt from the turn which Farfrae and Lucetta had taken that they were bound for the spot.

Nearly the whole town had gone into the fields. The Casterbridge populace still retained the primitive habit of helping one another in time of need; and thus, though the corn belonged to the farming section of the little community—that inhabiting the Durnover quarter—the remainder was no less interested in the labour of getting it home.

Reaching the top of the lane Henchard crossed the shaded avenue on the walls, slid down the green rampart, and stood amongst the stubble. The "stitches" or shocks* rose like tents about the yellow expanse, those in the distance becoming lost in the moonlit hazes.

He had entered at a point removed from the scene of immediate operations; but two others had entered at that place, and he could see them winding among the shocks. They were paying no regard to the direction of their walk, whose vague serpentining soon began to bear down towards Henchard. A meeting promised to be awkward, and he therefore stepped into the hollow of the nearest shock, and sat down.

"You have my leave," Lucetta was saying gaily. "Speak what you like."

"Well, then," replied Farfrae, with the unmistakable inflection of the lover pure, which Henchard had never heard in full resonance on his lips before, "you are sure to be much sought after for your position, wealth, talents, and beauty. But will ye resist the temptation to be one of those ladies with lots of admirers—ay—and be content to have only a homely one?"

"And he the speaker?" said she, laughing. "Very well, sir, what next?"

"Ah! I'm afraid that what I feel will make me forget my manners!"

"Then I hope you'll never have any, if you lack them only for that cause." After some broken words which Henchard lost she added, "Are you sure you won't be jealous?"

Farfrae seemed to assure her that he would not, by taking her hand.

"You are convinced, Donald, that I love nobody else," she presently said. "But I should wish to have my own way in some things."

"In everything! What special thing did you mean?"

---

*Piles of drying grain sheaves.

"If I wished not to live always in Casterbridge, for instance, upon finding that I should not be happy here?"

Henchard did not hear the reply; he might have done so and much more, but he did not care to play the eavesdropper. They went on towards the scene of activity, where the sheaves were being handed, a dozen a minute, upon the carts and waggons which carried them away.

Lucetta insisted on parting from Farfrae when they drew near the workpeople. He had some business with them and, though he entreated her to wait a few minutes, she was inexorable, and tripped off homeward alone.

Henchard thereupon left the field and followed her. His state of mind was such that on reaching Lucetta's door he did not knock but opened it, and walked straight up to her sitting-room, expecting to find her there. But the room was empty, and he perceived that in his haste he had somehow passed her on the way hither. He had not to wait many minutes, however, for he soon heard her dress rustling in the hall, followed by a soft closing of the door. In a moment she appeared.

The light was so low that she did not notice Henchard at first. As soon as she saw him she uttered a little cry, almost of terror.

"How can you frighten me so?" she exclaimed, with a flushed face. "It is past ten o'clock, and you have no right to surprise me here at such a time."

"I don't know that I've not the right. At any rate I have the excuse. Is it so necessary that I should stop to think of manners and customs?"

"It is too late for propriety, and might injure me."

"I called an hour ago, and you would not see me, and I thought you were in when I called now. It is you, Lucetta, who are doing wrong. It is not proper in 'ee to throw me over like this. I have a little matter to remind you of, which you seem to forget."

She sank into a chair, and turned pale.

"I don't want to hear it—I don't want to hear it!" she said through her hands, as he, standing close to the edge of her gown, began to allude to the Jersey days.

"But you ought to hear it," said he.

"It came to nothing; and through you. Then why not leave me the freedom that I gained with such sorrow! Had I found that you proposed to marry me for pure love I might have felt bound now. But

I soon learnt that you had planned it out of mere charity—almost as an unpleasant duty—because I had nursed you, and compromised myself, and you thought you must repay me. After that I did not care for you so deeply as before."

"Why did you come here to find me, then?"

"I thought I ought to marry you for conscience' sake, since you were free, even though I—did not like you so well."

"And why then don't you think so now?"

She was silent. It was only too obvious that conscience had ruled well enough till new love had intervened and usurped that rule. In feeling this she herself forgot for the moment her partially justifying argument—that having discovered Henchard's infirmities of temper, she had some excuse for not risking her happiness in his hands after once escaping them. The only thing she could say was, "I was a poor girl then; and now my circumstances have altered, so I am hardly the same person."

"That's true. And it makes the case awkward for me. But I don't want to touch your money. I am quite willing that every penny of your property shall remain to your personal use. Besides, that argument has nothing in it. The man you are thinking of is not better than I."

"If you were as good as he you would leave me!" she cried passionately.

This unluckily aroused Henchard. "You cannot in honour refuse me," he said. "And unless you give me your promise this very night to be my wife, before a witness, I'll reveal our intimacy—in common fairness to other men!"

A look of resignation settled upon her. Henchard saw its bitterness; and had Lucetta's heart been given to any other man in the world than Farfrae he would probably have had pity upon her at that moment. But the supplanter was the upstart (as Henchard called him) who had mounted into prominence upon his shoulders, and he could bring himself to show no mercy.

Without another word she rang the bell, and directed that Elizabeth-Jane should be fetched from her room. The latter appeared, surprised in the midst of her lucubrations. As soon as she saw Henchard she went across to him dutifully.

"Elizabeth-Jane," he said, taking her hand, "I want you to hear this." And turning to Lucetta: "Will you, or will you not, marry me?"

"If you—wish it, I must agree!"

"You say yes?"

"I do."

No sooner had she given the promise than she fell back in a fainting state.

"What dreadful thing drives her to say this, father, when it is such a pain to her?" asked Elizabeth, kneeling down by Lucetta. "Don't compel her to do anything against her will! I have lived with her, and know that she cannot bear much."

"Don't be a no'thern simpleton!" said Henchard drily. "This promise will leave him free for you, if you want him, won't it?"

At this Lucetta seemed to wake from her swoon with a start.

"Him? Who are you talking about?" she said wildly.

"Nobody, as far as I am concerned," said Elizabeth firmly.

"Oh—well. Then it is my mistake," said Henchard. "But the business is between me and Miss Templeman. She agrees to be my wife."

"But don't dwell on it just now," entreated Elizabeth, holding Lucetta's hand.

"I don't wish to, if she promises," said Henchard.

"I have, I have," groaned Lucetta, her limbs hanging like flails, from very misery and faintness. "Michael, please don't argue it any more!"

"I will not," he said. And taking up his hat he went away.

Elizabeth-Jane continued to kneel by Lucetta. "What is this?" she said. "You called my father 'Michael' as if you knew him well? And how is it he has got this power over you, that you promise to marry him against your will? Ah—you have many many secrets from me!"

"Perhaps you have some from me," Lucetta murmured with closed eyes, little thinking, however, so unsuspicious was she, that the secret of Elizabeth's heart concerned the young man who had caused this damage to her own.

"I would not do anything against you at all!" stammered Elizabeth, keeping in all signs of emotion till she was ready to burst. "I cannot understand how my father can command you so; I don't sympathize with him in it at all. I'll go to him and ask him to release you."

"No, no," said Lucetta. "Let it all be."

XXVIII

THE NEXT MORNING HENCHARD went to the Town Hall below Lucetta's house, to attend Petty Sessions,* being still a magistrate for the year by virtue of his late position as Mayor. In passing he looked up at her windows, but nothing of her was to be seen.

Henchard as a Justice of the Peace may at first seem to be an even greater incongruity than Shallow and Silence† themselves. But his rough and ready perceptions, his sledge-hammer directness, had often served him better than nice legal knowledge in despatching such simple business as fell to his hands in this Court. To-day Dr. Chalkfield, the Mayor for the year, being absent, the corn-merchant took the big chair, his eyes still abstractedly stretching out of the window to the ashlar‡ front of High-Place Hall.

There was one case only; and the offender stood before him. She was an old woman of mottled countenance, attired in a shawl of that nameless tertiary hue which comes, but cannot be made—a hue neither tawny, russet, hazel, nor ash; a sticky black bonnet that seemed to have been worn in the country of the Psalmist where the clouds drop fatness[20] and an apron that had been white in times so comparatively recent as still to contrast visibly with the rest of her clothes. The steeped aspect of the woman as a whole showed her to be no native of the country-side or even of a country-town.

She looked cursorily at Henchard and the second magistrate, and Henchard looked at her, with a momentary pause, as if she had reminded him indistinctly of somebody or something which passed from his mind as quickly as it had come. "Well, and what has she been doing?" he said, looking down at the charge-sheet.

"She is charged, sir, with the offence of disorderly female and nuisance," whispered Stubberd.

"Where did she do that?" said the other magistrate.

"By the church, sir, of all the horrible places in the world!—I caught her in the act, your worship."

---

*Courts for handling local disputes or offenses.
†Buffoonish country magistrates in Shakespeare's *Henry IV, Part II*.
‡Square-hewn stone.

"Stand back then," said Henchard, "and let's hear what you've got to say."

Stubberd was sworn, the magistrate's clerk dipped his pen, Henchard being no note-taker himself, and the constable began—

"Hearing a' illegal noise I went down the street at twenty-five minutes past eleven P.M. on the night of the fifth instinct, Hannah Dominy.* When I had———"

"Don't go on so fast, Stubberd," said the clerk.

The constable waited, with his eyes on the clerk's pen, till the latter stopped scratching and said, "yes." Stubberd continued: "When I had proceeded to the spot I saw defendant at another spot, namely, the gutter." He paused, watching the point of the clerk's pen again.

"Gutter, yes, Stubberd."

"Spot measuring twelve feet nine inches or thereabouts, from where I———" Still careful not to outrun the clerk's penmanship Stubberd pulled up again; for having got his evidence by heart it was immaterial to him whereabouts he broke off.

"I object to that," spoke up the old woman, " 'spot measuring twelve feet nine or thereabouts from where I,' is not sound testimony!"

The magistrates consulted, and the second one said that the bench was of opinion that twelve feet nine inches from a man on his oath was admissible.

Stubberd, with a suppressed gaze of victorious rectitude at the old woman, continued: "Was standing myself. She was wambling† about quite dangerous to the thoroughfare, and when I approached to draw near she committed the nuisance, and insulted me."

" 'Insulted me.' . . . Yes, what did she say?"

"She said, 'Put away that dee‡ lantern,' she says."

"Yes."

"Says she, 'Dost hear, old turmit-head?§ Put away that dee lantern. I have floored fellows a dee sight finer-looking than a dee fool like thee, you son of a bee,|| dee me if I haint,' she says."

---

*Malaproprisms: "instinct" for "instant" (here meaning "month"), and "Hannah Dominy" for *Anno Domini* ("year of the lord").
†Stumbling.
‡Damned.
§Turnip-head; that is, idiot.
| |Son of a bitch.

"I object to that conversation!" interposed the old woman. "I was not capable enough to hear what I said, and what is said out of my hearing is not evidence."

There was another stoppage for consultation, a book was referred to, and finally Stubberd was allowed to go on again. The truth was that the old woman had appeared in court so many more times than the magistrates themselves, that they were obliged to keep a sharp lookout upon their procedure. However, when Stubberd had rambled on a little further Henchard broke out impatiently, "Come— we don't want to hear any more of them cust dees and bees! Say the words out like a man, and don't be so modest, Stubberd; or else leave it alone!" Turning to the woman, "Now then, have you any questions to ask him, or anything to say?"

"Yes," she replied with a twinkle in her eye; and the clerk dipped his pen.

"Twenty years ago or thereabout I was selling of furmity in a tent at Weydon Fair——"

" 'Twenty years ago'—well, that's beginning at the beginning; suppose you go back to the Creation!" said the clerk, not without satire.

But Henchard stared, and quite forgot what was evidence and what was not.

"A man and a woman with a little child came into my tent," the woman continued. "They sat down and had a basin apiece. Ah, Lord's my life! I was of a more respectable station in the world then than I am now, being a land smuggler* in a large way of business; and I used to season my furmity with rum for them who asked for't. I did it for the man; and then he had more and more; till at last he quarrelled with his wife, and offered to sell her to the highest bidder. A sailor came in and bid five guineas, and paid the money, and led her away. And the man who sold his wife in that fashion is the man sitting there in the great big chair." The speaker concluded by nodding her head at Henchard and folding her arms.

Everybody looked at Henchard. His face seemed strange, and in tint as if it had been powdered over with ashes. "We don't want to hear your life and adventures," said the second magistrate sharply,

---

*Receiver and distributor of smuggled goods.

filling the pause which followed. "You've been asked if you've any-thing to say bearing on the case."

"That bears on the case. It proves that he's no better than I, and has no right to sit there in judgment upon me."

" 'Tis a concocted story," said the clerk. "So hold your tongue!"

"No—'tis true." The words came from Henchard. " 'Tis as true as the light," he said slowly. "And upon my soul it does prove that I'm no better than she! And to keep out of any temptation to treat her hard for her revenge, I'll leave her to you."

The sensation in the court was indescribably great. Henchard left the chair, and came out, passing through a group of people on the steps and outside that was much larger than usual; for it seemed that the old furmity dealer had mysteriously hinted to the denizens of the lane in which she had been lodging since her arrival, that she knew a queer thing or two about their great local man Mr. Henchard, if she chose to tell it. This had brought them hither.

"Why are there so many idlers round the Town Hall to-day?" said Lucetta to her servant when the case was over. She had risen late, and had just looked out of the window.

"Oh, please, ma'am, 'tis this larry* about Mr. Henchard. A woman has proved that before he became a gentleman he sold his wife for five guineas in a booth at a fair."

In all the accounts which Henchard had given her of the separa-tion from his wife Susan for so many years, of his belief in her death, and so on, he had never clearly explained the actual and immediate cause of that separation. The story she now heard for the first time.

A gradual misery overspread Lucetta's face as she dwelt upon the promise wrung from her the night before. At bottom, then, Hen-chard was this. How terrible a contingency for a woman who should commit herself to his care.

During the day she went out to the Ring and to other places, not coming in till nearly dusk. As soon as she saw Elizabeth-Jane after her return indoors she told her that she had resolved to go away from home to the seaside for a few days—to Port-Bredy; Casterbridge was so gloomy.

Elizabeth, seeing that she looked wan and disturbed, encouraged

---

*Confusion, excitement.

her in the idea, thinking a change would afford her relief. She could not help suspecting that the gloom which seemed to have come over Casterbridge in Lucetta's eyes might be partially owing to the fact that Farfrae was away from home.

Elizabeth saw her friend depart for Port-Bredy, and took charge of High-Place Hall till her return. After two or three days of solitude and incessant rain Henchard called at the house. He seemed disappointed to hear of Lucetta's absence, and though he nodded with outward indifference he went away handling his beard with a nettled mien.

The next day he called again. "Is she come now?" he asked.

"Yes. She returned this morning," replied his stepdaughter. "But she is not indoors. She has gone for a walk along the turnpike-road to Port-Bredy. She will be home by dusk."

After a few words, which only served to reveal his restless impatience, he left the house again.

XXIX

AT THIS HOUR LUCETTA was bounding along the road to Port-Bredy just as Elizabeth had announced. That she had chosen for her afternoon walk the road along which she had returned to Casterbridge three hours earlier in a carriage was curious—if anything should be called curious in concatenations of phenomena wherein each is known to have its accounting cause. It was the day of the chief market—Saturday—and Farfrae for once had been missed from his corn-stand in the dealers' room. Nevertheless, it was known that he would be home that night—"for Sunday," as Casterbridge expressed it.

Lucetta, in continuing her walk, had at length reached the end of the ranked trees which bordered the highway in this and other directions out of the town. This end marked a mile; and here she stopped.

The spot was a vale between two gentle acclivities, and the road, still adhering to its Roman foundation, stretched onward straight as a surveyor's line till lost to sight on the most distant ridge. There was neither hedge nor tree in the prospect now, the road clinging to the stubbly expanse of corn-land like a stripe to an undulating garment. Near her was a barn—the single building of any kind within her horizon.

She strained her eyes up the lessening road, but nothing appeared thereon—not so much as a speck. She sighed one word—"Donald!" and turned her face to the town for retreat.

Here the case was different. A single figure was approaching her—Elizabeth-Jane's.

Lucetta, in spite of her loneliness, seemed a little vexed. Elizabeth's face, as soon as she recognized her friend, shaped itself into affectionate lines while yet beyond speaking distance. "I suddenly thought I would come and meet you," she said, smiling.

Lucetta's reply was taken from her lips by an unexpected diversion. A by-road on her right hand descended from the fields into the highway at the point where she stood, and down the track a bull was rambling uncertainly towards her and Elizabeth, who, facing the other way, did not observe him.

In the latter quarter of each year cattle were at once the mainstay and the terror of families about Casterbridge and its neighbourhood, where breeding was carried on with Abrahamic success.* The head of stock driven into and out of the town at this season to be sold by the local auctioneer was very large; and all these horned beasts, in travelling to and fro, sent women and children to shelter as nothing else could do. In the main the animals would have walked along quietly enough; but the Casterbridge tradition was that to drive stock it was indispensable that hideous cries, coupled with Yahoo† antics and gestures, should be used, large sticks flourished, stray dogs called in, and in general everything done that was likely to infuriate the viciously disposed and terrify the mild. Nothing was commoner than for a householder on going out of his parlour to find his hall or passage full of little children, nursemaids, aged women, or a ladies' school, who apologized for their presence by saying, "A bull passing down street from the sale."

Lucetta and Elizabeth regarded the animal in doubt, he meanwhile drawing vaguely towards them. It was a large specimen of the

*Reference to the many descendants of the biblical patriarch Abraham.
†In Jonathan Swift's *Gulliver's Travels* (1726), the hero encounters the Yahoos, an ugly and wildly uncouth race that Gulliver finally recognizes as human beings.

breed, in colour rich dun, though disfigured at present by splotches of mud about his seamy sides. His horns were thick and tipped with brass; his two nostrils like the Thames Tunnel as seen in the perspective toys of yore.* Between them, through the gristle of his nose, was a stout copper ring, welded on, and irremovable as Gurth's collar of brass.† To the ring was attached an ash staff about a yard long, which the bull with the motions of his head flung about like a flail.

It was not till they observed this dangling stick that the young women were really alarmed; for it revealed to them that the bull was an old one, too savage to be driven, which had in some way escaped, the staff being the means by which the drover controlled him and kept his horns at arms' length.

They looked round for some shelter or hiding-place, and thought of the barn hard by. As long as they had kept their eyes on the bull he had shown some deference in his manner of approach; but no sooner did they turn their backs to seek the barn than he tossed his head and decided to thoroughly terrify them. This caused the two helpless girls to run wildly, whereupon the bull advanced in a deliberate charge.

The barn stood behind a green slimy pond, and it was closed save as to one of the usual pair of doors facing them, which had been propped open by a hurdle-stake, and for this opening they made. The interior had been cleared by a recent bout of threshing except at one end, where there was a stack of dry clover. Elizabeth-Jane took in the situation. "We must climb up there," she said.

But before they had even approached it they heard the bull scampering through the pond without, and in a second he dashed into the barn, knocking down the hurdle-stake in passing; the heavy door slammed behind him; and all three were imprisoned in the barn together. The mistaken creature saw them, and stalked towards the end of the barn into which they had fled. The girls doubled so adroitly that their pursuer was against the wall when the fugitives were already half way to the other end. By the time that his length would allow him to turn and follow them thither they had crossed over; thus the pursuit went on, the hot air from his nostrils blowing over

---

*Peep-show toys with three-dimensional views of noted buildings or landscapes.
†In Sir Walter Scott's *Ivanhoe* (1820), the serf Gurth wears a collar inscribed with his owner's name.

them like a sirocco,* and not a moment being attainable by Elizabeth or Lucetta in which to open the door. What might have happened had their situation continued cannot be said; but in a few moments a rattling of the door distracted their adversary's attention, and a man appeared. He ran forward towards the leading-staff, seized it, and wrenched the animal's head as if he would snap it off. The wrench was in reality so violent that the thick neck seemed to have lost its stiffness and to become half-paralysed, whilst the nose dropped blood. The premeditated human contrivance of the nose-ring was too cunning for impulsive brute force, and the creature flinched.

The man was seen in the partial gloom to be large-framed and unhesitating. He led the bull to the door, and the light revealed Henchard. He made the bull fast without, and re-entered to the succour of Lucetta; for he had not perceived Elizabeth, who had climbed on to the clover-heap. Lucetta was hysterical, and Henchard took her in his arms and carried her to the door.

"You—have saved me!" she cried, as soon as she could speak.

"I have returned your kindness," he responded tenderly. "You once saved me."

"How—comes it to be you—you?" she asked, not heeding his reply.

"I came out here to look for you. I have been wanting to tell you something these two or three days; but you have been away, and I could not. Perhaps you cannot talk now?"

"Oh—no! Where is Elizabeth?"

"Here am I!" cried the missing one cheerfully; and without waiting for the ladder to be placed she slid down the face of the clover-stack to the floor.

Henchard supporting Lucetta on one side, and Elizabeth-Jane on the other, they went slowly along the rising road. They had reached the top and were descending again when Lucetta, now much recovered, recollected that she had dropped her muff in the barn.

"I'll run back," said Elizabeth-Jane. "I don't mind it at all, as I am not tired as you are." She thereupon hastened down again to the barn, the others pursuing their way.

Elizabeth soon found the muff, such an article being by no means

---

*Hot wind blowing from northern Africa to southern Europe.

small at that time. Coming out she paused to look for a moment at the bull, now rather to be pitied with his bleeding nose, having perhaps rather intended a practical joke than a murder. Henchard had secured him by jamming the staff into the hinge of the barn-door, and wedg-ing it there with a stake. At length she turned to hasten onward after her contemplation, when she saw a green-and-black gig approaching from the contrary direction, the vehicle being driven by Farfrae.

His presence here seemed to explain Lucetta's walk that way. Donald saw her, drew up, and was hastily made acquainted with what had occurred. At Elizabeth-Jane mentioning how greatly Lucetta had been jeopardized, he exhibited an agitation different in kind no less than in intensity from any she had seen in him before. He became so absorbed in the circumstance that he scarcely had sufficient knowl-edge of what he was doing to think of helping her up beside him.

"She has gone on with Mr. Henchard, you say?" he inquired at last.

"Yes. He is taking her home. They are almost there by this time."

"And you are sure she can get home?"

Elizabeth-Jane was quite sure.

"Your stepfather saved her?"

"Entirely."

Farfrae checked his horse's pace; she guessed why. He was think-ing that it would be best not to intrude on the other two just now. Henchard had saved Lucetta, and to provoke a possible exhibition of her deeper affection for himself was as ungenerous as it was unwise.

The immediate subject of their talk being exhausted she felt more embarrassed at sitting thus beside her past lover; but soon the two figures of the others were visible at the entrance to the town. The face of the woman was frequently turned back, but Farfrae did not whip on the horse. When these reached the town walls Henchard and his companion had disappeared down the street; Farfrae set down Elizabeth-Jane on her expressing a particular wish to alight there, and drove round to the stables at the back of his lodgings.

On this account he entered the house through his garden, and going up to his apartments found them in a particularly disturbed state, his boxes being hauled out upon the landing, and his bookcase standing in three pieces. These phenomena, however, seemed to cause him not the least surprise. "When will everything be sent up?" he said to the mistress of the house, who was superintending.

"I am afraid not before eight, sir," said she. "You see we wasn't aware till this morning that you were going to move, or we could have been forwarder."

"A—well, never mind, never mind!" said Farfrae cheerily. "Eight o'clock will do well enough if it be not later. Now, don't ye be standing here talking, or it will be twelve, I doubt." Thus speaking he went out by the front door and up the street.

During this interval Henchard and Lucetta had had experiences of a different kind. After Elizabeth's departure for the muff the corn-merchant opened himself frankly, holding her hand within his arm, though she would fain have withdrawn it. "Dear Lucetta, I have been very, very anxious to see you these two or three days," he said; "ever since I saw you last! I have thought over the way I got your promise that night. You said to me, 'If I were a man I should not insist.' That cut me deep. I felt that there was some truth in it. I don't want to make you wretched; and to marry me just now would do that as nothing else could—it is but too plain. Therefore I agree to an indefinite engagement—to put off all thought of marriage for a year or two."

"But—but—can I do nothing of a different kind?" said Lucetta. "I am full of gratitude to you—you have saved my life. And your care of me is like coals of fire on my head! I am a monied person now. Surely I can do something in return for your goodness—something practical?"

Henchard remained in thought. He had evidently not expected this. "There is one thing you might do, Lucetta," he said. "But not exactly of that kind."

"Then of what kind is it?" she asked with renewed misgiving.

"I must tell you a secret to ask it.——You may have heard that I have been unlucky this year? I did what I have never done before—speculated rashly; and I lost. That's just put me in a strait."

"And you would wish me to advance some money?"

"No, no!" said Henchard, almost in anger. "I'm not the man to sponge on a woman, even though she may be so nearly my own as you. No, Lucetta; what you can do is this; and it would save me. My great creditor is Grower, and it is at his hands I shall suffer if at anybody's; while a fortnight's forbearance on his part would be enough to allow me to pull through. This may be got out of him in one way—that you would let it be known to him that you are my intended—that we are to be quietly married in the next fortnight.——

Now stop, you haven't heard all! Let him have this story, without, of course, any prejudice to the fact that the actual engagement between us is to be a long one. Nobody else need know: you could go with me to Mr. Grower and just let me speak to 'ee before him as if we were on such terms. We'll ask him to keep it secret. He will willingly wait then. At the fortnight's end I shall be able to face him; and I can coolly tell him all is postponed between us for a year or two. Not a soul in the town need know how you've helped me. Since you wish to be of use, there's your way."

It being now what the people called the "pinking in" of the day, that is, the quarter-hour just before dusk, he did not at first observe the result of his own words upon her.

"If it were anything else," she began, and the dryness of her lips was represented in her voice.

"But it is such a little thing!" he said, with a deep reproach. "Less than you have offered—just the beginning of what you have so lately promised! I could have told him as much myself, but he would not have believed me."

"It is not because I won't—it is because I absolutely can't," she said, with rising distress.

"You are provoking!" he burst out. "It is enough to make me force you to carry out at once what you have promised."

"I cannot!" she insisted desperately.

"Why? When I have only within these few minutes released you from your promise to do the thing offhand."

"Because—he was a witness!"

"Witness? Of what?"

"If I must tell you——. Don't, don't upbraid me!"

"Well! Let's hear what you mean?"

"Witness of my marriage—Mr. Grower was!"

"Marriage?"

"Yes. With Mr. Farfrae. O Michael! I am already his wife. We were married this week at Port-Bredy. There were reasons against our doing it here. Mr. Grower was a witness because he happened to be at Port-Bredy at the time."

Henchard stood as if idiotized. She was so alarmed at his silence that she murmured something about lending him sufficient money to tide over the perilous fortnight.

"Married him?" said Henchard at length. "My good—what, married him whilst—bound to marry me?"

"It was like this," she explained, with tears in her eyes and quavers in her voice; "don't—don't be cruel! I loved him so much, and I thought you might tell him of the past—and that grieved me! And then, when I had promised you, I learnt of the rumour that you had—sold your first wife at a fair like a horse or cow! How could I keep my promise after hearing that? I could not risk myself in your hands; it would have been letting myself down to take your name after such a scandal. But I knew I should lose Donald if I did not secure him at once—for you would carry out your threat of telling him of our former acquaintance, as long as there was a chance of keeping me for yourself by doing so. But you will not do so now, will you, Michael? for it is too late to separate us."

The notes of St. Peter's bells in full peal had been wafted to them while he spoke; and now the genial thumping of the town band, renowned for its unstinted use of the drum-stick, throbbed down the street.

"Then this racket they are making is on account of it, I suppose?" said he.

"Yes—I think he has told them, or else Mr. Grower has. . . . May I leave you now? My—he was detained at Port-Bredy to-day, and sent me on a few hours before him."

"Then it is *his wife's* life I have saved this afternoon."

"Yes—and he will be for ever grateful to you."

"I am much obliged to him. . . . O you false woman!" burst from Henchard. "You promised me!"

"Yes, yes! But it was under compulsion, and I did not know all your past——"

"And now I've a mind to punish you as you deserve! One word to this bran-new husband of how you courted me, and your precious happiness is blown to atoms!"

"Michael—pity me, and be generous!"

"You don't deserve pity! You did; but you don't now."

"I'll help you to pay off your debt."

"A pensioner of Farfrae's wife—not I! Don't stay with me longer—I shall say something worse. Go home!"

She disappeared under the trees of the south walk as the band came round the corner, awaking the echoes of every stock and stone in celebration of her happiness. Lucetta took no heed, but ran up the back street and reached her own home unperceived.

XXX

FARFRAE'S WORDS TO HIS landlady had referred to the removal of his boxes and other effects from his late lodgings to Lucetta's house. The work was not heavy, but it had been much hindered on account of the frequent pauses necessitated by exclamations of surprise at the event, of which the good woman had been briefly informed by letter a few hours earlier.

At the last moment of leaving Port-Bredy, Farfrae, like John Gilpin,[21] had been detained by important customers, whom, even in the exceptional circumstances, he was not the man to neglect. Moreover, there was a convenience in Lucetta arriving first at her house. Nobody there as yet knew what had happened; and she was best in a position to break the news to the inmates, and give directions for her husband's accommodation. He had, therefore, sent on his two-days' bride in a hired brougham, whilst he went across the country to a certain group of wheat and barley ricks a few miles off, telling her the hour at which he might be expected the same evening. This accounted for her trotting out to meet him after their separation of four hours.

By a strenuous effort, after leaving Henchard she calmed herself in readiness to receive Donald at High-Place Hall when he came on from his lodgings. One supreme fact empowered her to this, the sense that, come what would, she had secured him. Half-an-hour after her arrival he walked in, and she met him with a relieved gladness, which a month's perilous absence could not have intensified.

"There is one thing I have not done; and yet it is important," she said earnestly, when she had finished talking about the adventure with the bull. "That is, broken the news of our marriage to my dear Elizabeth-Jane."

"Ah, and you have not?" he said thoughtfully. "I gave her a lift from the barn homewards; but I did not tell her either; for I thought she might have heard of it in the town, and was keeping back her congratulations from shyness, and all that."

"She can hardly have heard of it. But I'll find out; I'll go to her now. And, Donald, you don't mind her living on with me just the same as before? She is so quiet and unassuming."

"O no, indeed I don't," Farfrae answered with, perhaps, a faint awkwardness. "But I wonder if she would care to?"

"O yes!" said Lucetta eagerly. "I am sure she would like to. Besides, poor thing, she has no other home."

Farfrae looked at her and saw that she did not suspect the secret of her more reserved friend. He liked her all the better for the blindness. "Arrange as you like with her by all means," he said. "It is I who have come to your house, not you to mine."

"I'll run and speak to her," said Lucetta.

When she got upstairs to Elizabeth-Jane's room the latter had taken off her out-door things, and was resting over a book. Lucetta found in a moment that she had not yet learnt the news.

"I did not come down to you, Miss Templeman," she said simply. "I was coming to ask if you had quite recovered from your fright, but I found you had a visitor. What are the bells ringing for, I wonder? And the band, too, is playing. Somebody must be married; or else they are practising for Christmas."

Lucetta uttered a vague "Yes," and seating herself by the other young woman looked musingly at her. "What a lonely creature you are," she presently said; "never knowing what's going on, or what people are talking about everywhere with keen interest. You should get out, and gossip about as other women do, and then you wouldn't be obliged to ask me a question of that kind. Well, now, I have something to tell you."

Elizabeth-Jane said she was so glad, and made herself receptive.

"I must go rather a long way back," said Lucetta, the difficulty of explaining herself satisfactorily to the pondering one beside her growing more apparent at each syllable. "You remember that trying case of conscience I told you of some time ago—about the first lover and the second lover?" She let out in jerky phrases a leading word or two of the story she had told.

"O yes—I remember; the story of *your friend*," said Elizabeth drily, regarding the irises of Lucetta's eyes as though to catch their exact shade. "The two lovers—the old and the new: how she wanted to marry the second, but felt she ought to marry the first; so that she neglected the better course to follow the evil, like the poet Ovid I've just been construing: 'Video meliora proboque, deteriora sequor.' "[22]

"O no; she didn't follow evil exactly!" said Lucetta hastily.

"But you said that she—or as I may say *you*"—answered Elizabeth, dropping the mask, "were in honour and conscience bound to marry the first?"

Lucetta's blush at being seen through came and went again before she replied anxiously. "You will never breathe this, will you, Elizabeth-Jane?"

"Certainly not, if you say not."

"Then I will tell you that the case is more complicated—worse, in fact—than it seemed in my story. I and the first man were thrown together in a strange way, and felt that we ought to be united, as the world had talked of us. He was a widower, as he supposed. He had not heard of his first wife for many years. But the wife returned, and we parted. She is now dead; and the husband comes paying me addresses again, saying, 'Now we'll complete our purpose.' But, Elizabeth-Jane, all this amounts to a new courtship of me by him; I was absolved from all vows by the return of the other woman."

"Have you not lately renewed your promise?" said the younger with quiet surmise. She had divined Man Number One.

"That was wrung from me by a threat."

"Yes, it was. But I think when any one gets coupled up with a man in the past so unfortunately as you have done, she ought to become his wife if she can, even if she were not the sinning party."

Lucetta's countenance lost its sparkle. "He turned out to be a man I should be afraid to marry," she pleaded. "Really afraid! And it was not till after my renewed promise that I knew it."

"Then there is only one course left to honesty. You must remain a single woman."

"But think again! Do consider——"

"I am certain," interrupted her companion hardily. "I have guessed very well who the man is. My father; and I say it is him or nobody for you."

Any suspicion of impropriety was to Elizabeth-Jane like a red rag to a bull. Her craving for correctness of procedure was, indeed, almost vicious. Owing to her early troubles with regard to her mother a semblance of irregularity had terrors for her which those whose names are safeguarded from suspicion know nothing of. "You ought to marry Mr. Henchard or nobody—certainly not another man!" she went on with a quivering lip in whose movement two passions shared.

"I don't admit that!" said Lucetta passionately.

"Admit it or not, it is true!"

Lucetta covered her eyes with her right hand, as if she could plead no more, holding out her left to Elizabeth-Jane.

"Why, you *have* married him!" cried the latter, jumping up with pleasure after a glance at Lucetta's fingers. "When did you do it? Why did you not tell me, instead of teasing me like this? How very honourable of you! He did treat my mother badly once, it seems, in a moment of intoxication. And it is true that he is stern sometimes. But you will rule him entirely, I am sure, with your beauty and wealth and accomplishments. You are the woman he will adore, and we shall all three be happy together now!"

"O, my Elizabeth-Jane!" cried Lucetta distressfully. " 'Tis somebody else that I have married! I was so desperate—so afraid of being forced to anything else—so afraid of revelations that would quench his love for me, that I resolved to do it off-hand, come what might, and purchase a week of happiness at any cost!"

"You—have—married Mr. Farfrae!" cried Elizabeth-Jane, in Nathan tones.*

Lucetta bowed. She had recovered herself.

"The bells are ringing on that account," she said. "My husband is downstairs. He will live here till a more suitable house is ready for us; and I have told him that I want you to stay with me just as before."

"Let me think of it alone," the girl quickly replied, corking up the turmoil of her feeling with grand control.

"You shall. I am sure we shall be happy together."

Lucetta departed to join Donald below, a vague uneasiness floating over her joy at seeing him quite at home there. Not on account of her friend Elizabeth did she feel it: for of the bearings of Elizabeth-Jane's emotions she had not the least suspicion; but on Henchard's alone.

Now the instant decision of Susan Henchard's daughter was to

---

*In the Bible (2 Samuel 12:7–12), Nathan chastises King David for engineering the death of Uriah the Hittite so that David can marry Uriah's wife, Bathsheba.

dwell in that house no more. Apart from her estimate of the propriety of Lucetta's conduct, Farfrae had been so nearly her avowed lover
that she felt she could not abide there.

It was still early in the evening when she hastily put on her things
and went out. In a few minutes, knowing the ground, she had found
a suitable lodging, and arranged to enter it that night. Returning and
entering noiselessly she took off her pretty dress and arrayed herself
in a plain one, packing up the other to keep as her best; for she would
have to be very economical now. She wrote a note to leave for Lucetta,
who was closely shut up in the drawing-room with Farfrae; and then
Elizabeth-Jane called a man with a wheelbarrow; and seeing her boxes
put into it she trotted off down the street to her rooms. They were in
the street in which Henchard lived, and almost opposite his door.

Here she sat down and considered the means of subsistence. The
little annual sum settled on her by her stepfather would keep body
and soul together. A wonderful skill in netting of all sorts—acquired
in childhood by making seines in Newson's home—might serve her
in good stead; and her studies, which were pursued unremittingly,
might serve her in still better.

By this time the marriage that had taken place was known
throughout Casterbridge; had been discussed noisily on kerbstones,
confidentially behind counters, and jovially at the Three Mariners.
Whether Farfrae would sell his business and set up for a gentleman
on his wife's money, or whether he would show independence
enough to stick to his trade in spite of his brilliant alliance, was a
great point of interest.

XXXI

THE RETORT OF THE furmity-woman before the magistrates had spread;
and in four-and-twenty hours there was not a person in Casterbridge
who remained unacquainted with the story of Henchard's mad freak
at Weydon-Priors Fair, long years before. The amends he had made in
after life were lost sight of in the dramatic glare of the original act.
Had the incident been well known of old and always, it might by this

time have grown to be lightly regarded as the rather tall wild oat, but well-nigh the single one, of a young man with whom the steady and mature (if somewhat headstrong) burgher of to-day had scarcely a point in common. But the act having lain as dead and buried ever since, the interspace of years was unperceived; and the black spot of his youth wore the aspect of a recent crime.

Small as the police-court incident had been in itself, it formed the edge or turn in the incline of Henchard's fortunes. On that day—almost at that minute—he passed the ridge of prosperity and honour, and began to descend rapidly on the other side. It was strange how soon he sank in esteem. Socially he had received a startling fillip downwards; and, having already lost commercial buoyancy from rash transactions, the velocity of his descent in both aspects became accelerated every hour.

He now gazed more at the pavements and less at the house-fronts when he walked about; more at the feet and leggings of men, and less into the pupils of their eyes with the blazing regard which formerly had made them blink.

New events combined to undo him. It had been a bad year for others besides himself, and the heavy failure of a debtor whom he had trusted generously completed the overthrow of his tottering credit. And now, in his desperation, he failed to preserve that strict correspondence between bulk and sample which is the soul of commerce in grain. For this, one of his men was mainly to blame; that worthy, in his great unwisdom, having picked over the sample of an enormous quantity of second-rate corn which Henchard had in hand, and removed the pinched, blasted, and smutted grains in great numbers. The produce if honestly offered would have created no scandal; but the blunder of misrepresentation, coming at such a moment, dragged Henchard's name into the ditch.

The details of his failure were of the ordinary kind. One day Elizabeth-Jane was passing the King's Arms, when she saw people bustling in and out more than usual when there was no market. A bystander informed her, with some surprise at her ignorance, that it was a meeting of the Commissioners under Mr. Henchard's bankruptcy. She felt quite tearful, and when she heard that he was present in the hotel she wished to go in and see him, but was advised not to intrude that day.

The room in which debtor and creditors had assembled was a front one, and Henchard, looking out of the window, had caught sight of Elizabeth-Jane through the wire blind. His examination had closed, and the creditors were leaving. The appearance of Elizabeth threw him into a reverie; till, turning his face from the window, and towering above all the rest, he called their attention for a moment more. His countenance had somewhat changed from its flush of prosperity; the black hair and whiskers were the same as ever, but a film of ash was over the rest.

"Gentlemen," he said, "over and above the assets that we've been talking about, and that appear on the balance-sheet, there be these. It all belongs to ye, as much as everything else I've got, and I don't wish to keep it from you, not I." Saying this, he took his gold watch from his pocket and laid it on the table; then his purse—the yellow canvas money-bag, such as was carried by all farmers and dealers—untying it, and shaking the money out upon the table beside the watch. The latter he drew back quickly for an instant, to remove the hair-guard* made and given him by Lucetta. "There, now you have all I've got in the world," he said. "And I wish for your sakes 'twas more."

The creditors, farmers almost to a man, looked at the watch, and at the money, and into the street; when Farmer James Everdene of Weatherbury spoke.

"No, no, Henchard," he said warmly. "We don't want that. 'Tis honourable in ye; but keep it. What do you say, neighbours—do ye agree?"

"Ay, sure: we don't wish it at all," said Grower, another creditor.

"Let him keep it, of course," murmured another in the background—a silent, reserved young man named Boldwood; and the rest responded unanimously.

"Well," said the senior Commissioner, addressing Henchard, "though the case is a desperate one, I am bound to admit that I have never met a debtor who behaved more fairly. I've proved the balance sheet to be as honestly made out as it could possibly be; we have had no trouble; there have been no evasions and no concealments. The rashness of dealing which led to this unhappy situation is obvious enough; but as far as I can see every attempt has been made to avoid wronging anybody."

Henchard was more affected by this than he cared to let them per-

*Protective pouch for a watch, woven from hair.

ceive, and he turned aside to the window again. A general murmur of agreement followed the Commissioner's words; and the meeting dispersed. When they were gone Henchard regarded the watch they had returned to him. " 'Tisn't mine by rights," he said to himself. "Why the devil didn't they take it?—I don't want what don't belong to me!" Moved by a recollection he took the watch to the maker's just opposite, sold it there and then for what the tradesman offered, and went with the proceeds to one among the smaller of his creditors, a cottager of Durnover in straitened circumstances, to whom he handed the money.

When everything was ticketed that Henchard had owned, and the auctions were in progress, there was quite a sympathetic reaction in the town, which till then for some time past had done nothing but condemn him. Now that Henchard's whole career was pictured distinctly to his neighbours, and they could see how admirably he had used his one talent of energy to create a position of affluence out of absolutely nothing—which was really all he could show when he came to the town as a journeyman hay-trusser, with his wimble and knife in his basket—they wondered and regretted his fall.

Try as she might, Elizabeth could never meet with him. She believed in him still, though nobody else did; and she wanted to be allowed to forgive him for his roughness to her, and to help him in his trouble.

She wrote to him; he did not reply. She then went to his house— the great house she had lived in so happily for a time—with its front of dun brick, vitrified* here and there, and its heavy sash-bars—but Henchard was to be found there no more. The ex-Mayor had left the home of his prosperity, and gone into Jopp's cottage by the Priory Mill—the sad purlieu to which he had wandered on the night of his discovery that she was not his daughter. Thither she went.

Elizabeth thought it odd that he had fixed on this spot to retire to, but assumed that necessity had no choice. Trees which seemed old enough to have been planted by the friars still stood around, and the back hatch of the original mill yet formed a cascade which had raised its terrific roar for centuries. The cottage itself was built of old stones from the long dismantled Priory, scraps of tracery, moulded window-jambs, and arch-labels,† being mixed in with the rubble of the walls.

---

*Sun-glazed.
†Moldings over windows.

In this cottage he occupied a couple of rooms, Jopp, whom Henchard had employed, abused, cajoled, and dismissed by turns, being the householder. But even here her stepfather could not be seen.

"Not by his daughter?" pleaded Elizabeth.

"By nobody—at present: that's his order," she was informed.

Afterwards she was passing by the corn-stores and hay-barns which had been the headquarters of his business. She knew that he ruled there no longer; but it was with amazement that she regarded the familiar gateway. A smear of decisive lead-coloured paint had been laid on to obliterate Henchard's name, though its letters dimly loomed through like ships in a fog. Over these, in fresh white, spread the name of Farfrae.

Abel Whittle was edging his skeleton in at the wicket, and she said, "Mr. Farfrae is master here?"

"Yaas, Miss Henchet," he said, "Mr. Farfrae have bought the concern and all of we work-folk with it; and 'tis better for us than 'twas—though I shouldn't say that to you as a daughter-law.* We work harder, but we bain't made afeard now. It was fear made my few poor hairs so thin! No busting out, no slamming of doors, no meddling with yer eternal soul and all that; and though 'tis a shilling a week less I'm the richer man; for what's all the world if yer mind is always in a larry, Miss Henchet?"

The intelligence was in a general sense true; and Henchard's stores, which had remained in a paralyzed condition during the settlement of his bankruptcy, were stirred into activity again when the new tenant had possession. Thenceforward the full sacks, looped with the shining chain, went scurrying up and down under the cat-head,† hairy arms were thrust out from the different door-ways, and the grain was hauled in; trusses of hay were tossed anew in and out of the barns, and the wimbles creaked; while the scales and steelyards‡ began to be busy where guess-work had formerly been the rule.

---

*Stepdaughter.
†Beam over which a rope is slung to lift heavy objects.
‡Weighing devices.

XXXII

Two bridges stood near the lower part of Casterbridge town. The first, of weather-stained brick, was immediately at the end of High Street, where a diverging branch from that thoroughfare ran round to the low-lying Durnover lanes; so that the precincts of the bridge formed the merging point of respectability and indigence. The second bridge, of stone, was further out on the highway—in fact, fairly in the meadows, though still within the town boundary.

These bridges had speaking countenances. Every projection in each was worn down to obtuseness, partly by weather, more by friction from generations of loungers, whose toes and heels had from year to year made restless movements against these parapets, as they had stood there meditating on the aspect of affairs. In the case of the more friable bricks and stones even the flat faces were worn into hollows by the same mixed mechanism. The masonry of the top was clamped with iron at each joint; since it had been no uncommon thing for desperate men to wrench the coping off and throw it down the river, in reckless defiance of the magistrates.

For to this pair of bridges gravitated all the failures of the town; those who had failed in business, in love, in sobriety, in crime. Why the unhappy hereabout usually chose the bridges for their meditations in preference to a railing, a gate, or a stile, was not so clear.

There was a marked difference of quality between the personages who haunted the near bridge of brick and the personages who haunted the far one of stone. Those of lowest character preferred the former, adjoining the town; they did not mind the glare of the public eye. They had been of comparatively no account during their successes; and, though they might feel dispirited, they had no particular sense of shame in their ruin. Their hands were mostly kept in their pockets; they wore a leather strap round their hips or knees, and boots that required a great deal of lacing, but seemed never to get any. Instead of sighing at their adversities they spat, and instead of saying the iron had entered into their souls they said they were down on their luck. Jopp in his times of distress had often stood here; so had Mother Cuxsom, Christopher Coney, and poor Abel Whittle.

The misérables who would pause on the remoter bridge were of a politer stamp. They included bankrupts, hypochondriacs, persons

who were what is called "out of a situation" from fault or luckless-
ness, the inefficient of the professional class—shabby-genteel men,
who did not know how to get rid of the weary time between breakfast and dinner, and the yet more weary time between dinner and
dark. The eyes of this species were mostly directed over the parapet
upon the running water below. A man seen there looking thus fixedly
into the river was pretty sure to be one whom the world did not treat
kindly for some reason or other. While one in straits on the town-
ward bridge did not mind who saw him so, and kept his back to the
parapet to survey the passers-by, one in straits on this never faced the
road, never turned his head at coming footsteps, but, sensitive to his
own condition, watched the current whenever a stranger approached, as if some strange fish interested him, though every finned
thing had been poached out of the river years before.

There and thus they would muse; if their grief were the grief of
oppression they would wish themselves kings; if their grief were
poverty, wish themselves millionaires; if sin, they would wish they
were saints or angels; if despised love, that they were some much-
courted Adonis of county fame. Some had been known to stand and
think so long with this fixed gaze downward that eventually they had
allowed their poor carcases to follow that gaze; and they were discovered the next morning out of reach of their troubles, either here
or in the deep pool called Blackwater, a little higher up the river.

To this bridge came Henchard, as other unfortunates had come before him, his way thither being by the riverside path on the chilly edge
of the town. Here he was standing one windy afternoon when
Durnover church clock struck five. While the gusts were bringing the
notes to his ears across the damp intervening flat a man passed behind
him and greeted Henchard by name. Henchard turned slightly and saw
that the comer was Jopp, his old foreman, now employed elsewhere,
to whom, though he hated him, he had gone for lodgings because
Jopp was the one man in Casterbridge whose observation and opinion
the fallen corn-merchant despised to the point of indifference.

Henchard returned him a scarcely perceptible nod, and Jopp
stopped.

"He and she are gone into their new house to-day," said Jopp.

"Oh," said Henchard absently. "Which house is that?"

"Your old one."

"Gone into my house?" And starting up Henchard added, "My house of all others in the town!"

"Well, as somebody was sure to live there, and you couldn't, it can do 'ee no harm that he's the man."

It was quite true: he felt that it was doing him no harm. Farfrae, who had already taken the yards and stores, had acquired possession of the house for the obvious convenience of its contiguity. And yet this act of his taking up residence within those roomy chambers while he, their former tenant, lived in a cottage, galled Henchard indescribably.

Jopp continued: "And you heard of that fellow who bought all the best furniture at your sale? He was bidding for no other than Farfrae all the while! It has never been moved out of the house, as he'd already got the lease."

"My furniture too! Surely he'll buy my body and soul likewise!"

"There's no saying he won't, if you be willing to sell." And having planted these wounds in the heart of his once imperious master Jopp went on his way; while Henchard stared and stared into the racing river till the bridge seemed moving backward with him.

The low land grew blacker, and the sky a deeper grey. When the landscape looked like a picture blotted in with ink, another traveller approached the great stone bridge. He was driving a gig, his direction being also townwards. On the round of the middle of the arch the gig stopped. "Mr. Henchard?" came from it in the voice of Farfrae. Henchard turned his face.

Finding that he had guessed rightly Farfrae told the man who accompanied him to drive home; while he alighted and went up to his former friend.

"I have heard that you think of emigrating, Mr. Henchard," he said. "Is it true? I have a real reason for asking."

Henchard withheld his answer for several instants, and then said, "Yes; it is true. I am going where you were going to a few years ago, when I prevented you and got you to bide here. 'Tis turn and turn about, isn't it! Do ye mind how we stood like this in the Chalk Walk when I persuaded 'ee to stay? You then stood without a chattel to your name, and I was the master of the house in Corn Street. But now I stand without a stick or a rag, and the master of that house is you."

"Yes, yes; that's so! It's the way o' the warrld," said Farfrae.

"Ha, ha, true!" cried Henchard, throwing himself into a mood of jocularity. "Up and down! I'm used to it. What's the odds after all!"

"Now listen to me, if it's no taking up your time," said Farfrae, "just as I listened to you. Don't go. Stay at home."

"But I can do nothing else, man!" said Henchard scornfully. "The little money I have will just keep body and soul together for a few weeks, and no more. I have not felt inclined to go back to journey-work* yet; but I can't stay doing nothing, and my best chance is elsewhere."

"No; but what I propose is this—if ye will listen. Come and live in your old house. We can spare some rooms very well—I am sure my wife would not mind it at all—until there's an opening for ye."

Henchard started. Probably the picture drawn by the unsuspecting Donald of himself under the same roof with Lucetta was too striking to be received with equanimity. "No, no," he said gruffly; "we should quarrel."

"You should hae a part to yourself," said Farfrae; "and nobody to interfere wi' you. It will be a deal healthier than down there by the river where you live now."

Still Henchard refused. "You don't know what you ask," he said. "However, I can do no less than thank 'ee."

They walked into the town together side by side, as they had done when Henchard persuaded the young Scotchman to remain. "Will you come in and have some supper?" said Farfrae when they reached the middle of the town, where their paths diverged right and left.

"No, no."

"By-the-bye, I had nearly forgot. I bought a good deal of your furniture."

"So I have heard."

"Well, it was no that I wanted it so very much for myself; but I wish ye to pick out all that you care to have—such things as may be endeared to ye by associations, or particularly suited to your use. And take them to your own house—it will not be depriving me; we can do with less very well, and I will have plenty of opportunities of getting more."

"What—give it to me for nothing?" said Henchard. "But you paid the creditors for it!"

"Ah, yes; but maybe it's worth more to you than it is to me."

---

*Work performed for daily wages.

Henchard was a little moved. "I—sometimes think I've wronged 'ee!" he said, in tones which showed the disquietude that the night shades hid in his face. He shook Farfrae abruptly by the hand, and hastened away as if unwilling to betray himself further. Farfrae saw him turn through the thoroughfare into Bull Stake and vanish down towards the Priory Mill.

Meanwhile Elizabeth-Jane, in an upper room no larger than the Prophet's chamber* and with the silk attire of her palmy days packed away in a box, was netting with great industry between the hours which she devoted to studying such books as she could get hold of.

Her lodgings being nearly opposite her stepfather's former residence, now Farfrae's, she could see Donald and Lucetta speeding in and out of their door with all the bounding enthusiasm of their situation. She avoided looking that way as much as possible, but it was hardly in human nature to keep the eyes averted when the door slammed.

While living on thus quietly she heard the news that Henchard had caught cold and was confined to his room—possibly a result of standing about the meads in damp weather. She went off to his house at once. This time she was determined not to be denied admittance, and made her way upstairs. He was sitting up in the bed with a greatcoat round him, and at first resented her intrusion. "Go away—go away," he said. "I don't like to see 'ee!"

"But, father—"

"I don't like to see 'ee," he repeated.

However, the ice was broken, and she remained. She made the room more comfortable, gave directions to the people below, and by the time she went away had reconciled her stepfather to her visiting him.

The effect, either of her ministrations or of her mere presence, was a rapid recovery. He soon was well enough to go out; and now things seemed to wear a new colour in his eyes. He no longer thought of emigration, and thought more of Elizabeth. The having nothing to do made him more dreary than any other circumstance; and one day, with better views of Farfrae than he had held for some time, and a sense that honest work was not a thing to be ashamed of, he stoically went down to Farfrae's yard and asked to be taken on as a journeyman hay-trusser. He was engaged at once. This hiring of

---

*Small room inhabited by the prophet Elisha (see the Bible, 2 Kings 4:10).

Henchard was done through a foreman, Farfrae feeling that it was undesirable to come personally in contact with the ex-cornfactor more than was absolutely necessary. While anxious to help him he was well aware by this time of his uncertain temper, and thought reserved relations best. For the same reason his orders to Henchard to proceed to this and that country farm trussing in the usual way were always given through a third person.

For a time these arrangements worked well, it being the custom to truss in the respective stack-yards, before bringing it away, the hay bought at the different farms about the neighbourhood; so that Henchard was often absent at such places the whole week long. When this was all done, and Henchard had become in a measure broken in, he came to work daily on the home premises like the rest. And thus the once flourishing merchant and Mayor and what not stood as a day-labourer in the barns and granaries he formerly had owned.

"I have worked as a journeyman before now, ha'n't I?" he would say in his defiant way; "and why shouldn't I do it again?" But he looked a far different journeyman from the one he had been in his earlier days. Then he had worn clean, suitable clothes, light and cheerful in hue; leggings yellow as marigolds, corduroys immaculate as new flax, and a neckerchief like a flower-garden. Now he wore the remains of an old blue cloth suit of his gentlemanly times, a rusty silk hat, and a once black satin stock, soiled and shabby. Clad thus he went to and fro, still comparatively an active man—for he was not much over forty—and saw with the other men in the yard Donald Farfrae going in and out the green door that led to the garden, and the big house, and Lucetta.

At the beginning of the winter it was rumoured about Casterbridge that Mr. Farfrae, already in the Town Council, was to be proposed for Mayor in a year or two.

"Yes; she was wise, she was wise in her generation!"[23] said Henchard to himself when he heard of this one day on his way to Farfrae's haybarn. He thought it over as he wimbled his bonds, and the piece of news acted as a reviviscent* breath to that old view of his—of Donald Farfrae as his triumphant rival who rode rough-shod over him.

---

*Reviving.

"A fellow of his age going to be Mayor, indeed!" he murmured with a corner-drawn smile on his mouth. "But 'tis her money that floats en upward. Ha-ha—how cust odd it is! Here be I, his former master, working for him as man, and he the man standing as master, with my house and my furniture and my what-you-may-call wife all his own."

He repeated these things a hundred times a day. During the whole period of his acquaintance with Lucetta he had never wished to claim her as his own so desperately as he now regretted her loss. It was no mercenary hankering after her fortune that moved him; though that fortune had been the means of making her so much the more desired by giving her the air of independence and sauciness which attracts men of his composition. It had given her servants, house, and fine clothing—a setting that invested Lucetta with a startling novelty in the eyes of him who had known her in her narrow days.

He accordingly lapsed into moodiness, and at every allusion to the possibility of Farfrae's near election to the municipal chair his former hatred of the Scotchman returned. Concurrently with this he underwent a moral change. It resulted in his significantly saying every now and then, in tones of recklessness, "Only a fortnight more!"—"Only a dozen days!" and so forth, lessening his figures day by day.

"Why d'ye say only a dozen days?" asked Solomon Longways as he worked beside Henchard in the granary weighing oats.

"Because in twelve days I shall be released from my oath."

"What oath?"

"The oath to drink no spirituous liquid. In twelve days it will be twenty-one years since I swore it, and then I mean to enjoy myself, please God!"

Elizabeth-Jane sat at her window one Sunday, and while there she heard in the street below a conversation which introduced Henchard's name. She was wondering what was the matter, when a third person who was passing by asked the question in her mind.

"Michael Henchard have busted out drinking after taking nothing for twenty-one years!"

Elizabeth-Jane jumped up, put on her things, and went out.

XXXIII

AT THIS DATE THERE prevailed in Casterbridge a convivial custom—scarcely recognized as such, yet none the less established. On the afternoon of every Sunday a large contingent of the Casterbridge journeymen—steady church-goers and sedate characters—having attended service, filed from the church doors across the way to the Three Mariners Inn. The rear was usually brought up by the choir, with their bass-viols, fiddles, and flutes under their arms.

The great point, the point of honour, on these sacred occasions was for each man to strictly limit himself to half-a-pint of liquor. This scrupulosity was so well understood by the landlord that the whole company was served in cups of that measure. They were all exactly alike—straight-sided, with two leafless lime-trees done in eel-brown on the sides—one towards the drinker's lips, the other confronting his comrade. To wonder how many of these cups the landlord possessed altogether was a favourite exercise of children in the marvellous. Forty at least might have been seen at these times in the large room, forming a ring round the margin of the great sixteen-legged oak table, like the monolithic circle at Stonehenge in its pristine days. Outside and above the forty cups came a circle of forty smoke-jets from forty clay pipes; outside the pipes the countenances of the forty church-goers, supported at the back by a circle of forty chairs.

The conversation was not the conversation of week-days, but a thing altogether finer in point and higher in tone. They invariably discussed the sermon, dissecting it, weighing it, as above or below the average—the general tendency being to regard it as a scientific feat or performance which had no relation to their own lives, except as between critics and the thing criticized. The bass-viol player and the clerk usually spoke with more authority than the rest on account of their official connection with the preacher.

Now the Three Mariners was the inn chosen by Henchard as the place for closing his long term of dramless years. He had so timed his entry as to be well established in the large room by the time the forty church-goers entered to their customary cups. The flush upon his face proclaimed at once that the vow of twenty-one years had lapsed, and the era of recklessness begun anew. He was seated on a small table, drawn up to the side of the massive oak board reserved for the churchmen, a few of whom nodded to him as they took their places and said, "How be ye, Mr. Henchard? Quite a stranger here."

Henchard did not take the trouble to reply for a few moments, and his eyes rested on his stretched-out legs and boots. "Yes," he said at length; "that's true. I've been down in spirit for weeks; some of ye know the cause. I am better now; but not quite serene. I want you fellows of the choir to strike up a tune; and what with that and this brew of Stannidge's, I am in hopes of getting altogether out of my minor key."

"With all my heart," said the first fiddle. "We've let back our strings, that's true; but we can soon pull 'em up again. Sound A, neighbours, and give the man a stave."

"I don't care a curse what the words be," said Henchard. "Hymns, ballets or rantipole* rubbish; the Rogue's March† or the cherubim's warble‡—all the same to me if 'tis good harmony, and well put out."

"Well—heh, heh—it may be we can do that, and not a man among us that have sat in the gallery less than twenty year," said the leader of the band. "As 'tis Sunday, neighbours, suppose we raise the Fourth Psa'am, to Samuel Wakely's tune,§ as improved by me?"

"Hang Samuel Wakely's tune, as improved by thee!" said Henchard. "Chuck across one of your psalters—old Wiltshire‖is the only tune worth singing—the psalm-tune that would make my blood ebb and flow like the sea when I was a steady chap. I'll find some words to fit en." He took one of the psalters and began turning over the leaves.

Chancing to look out of the window at that moment he saw a flock of people passing by, and perceived them to be the congregation of the upper church, now just dismissed, their sermon having been a longer one than that the lower parish was favoured with. Among the rest of the leading inhabitants walked Mr. Councillor Farfrae with Lucetta upon his arm, the observed and imitated of all the smaller tradesmen's womankind. Henchard's mouth changed a little, and he continued to turn over the leaves.

"Now then," he said, "Psalm the Hundred-and-Ninth, to the tune of Wiltshire: verses ten to fifteen. I gi'e ye the words:

---

*Loud.
†Song played when a disgraced soldier is dismissed from the army.
‡That is, angel's song.
§Wakely was a nineteenth-century composer of popular hymns.
‖Tune by Sir George Smart, a favorite of Hardy's.

'His seed shall orphans be, his wife
     A widow plunged in grief;
His vagrant children beg their bread
     Where none can give relief.

His ill-got riches shall be made
     To usurers a prey;
The fruit of all his toil shall be
     By strangers borne away.

None shall be found that to his wants
     Their mercy will extend,
Or to his helpless orphan seed
     The least assistance lend.

A swift destruction soon shall seize
     On his unhappy race;
And the next age his hated name
     Shall utterly deface.' "

"I know the Psa'am—I know the Psa'am!" said the leader hastily; "but I would as lief not sing it. 'Twasn't made for singing. We chose it once when the gipsy stole the pa'son's mare, thinking to please him, but pa'son were quite upset. Whatever Servant David* were thinking about when he made a Psalm that nobody can sing without disgracing himself, I can't fathom! Now then, the Fourth Psalm, to Samuel Wakely's tune, as improved by me."

" 'Od seize your sauce—I tell ye to sing the Hundred-and-Ninth to Wiltshire, and sing it you shall!" roared Henchard. "Not a single one of all the droning crew of ye goes out of this room till that Psalm is sung!" He slipped off the table, seized the poker, and going to the door placed his back against it. "Now then, go ahead, if you don't wish to have your cust pates broke!"

"Don't 'ee, don't 'ee take on so!—As 'tis the Sabbath-day, and 'tis Servant David's words and not ours, perhaps we don't mind for once,

---

*King David was supposed to have written the Psalms.

hey?" said one of the terrified choir, looking round upon the rest. So the instruments were tuned and the comminatory* verses sung.

"Thank ye, thank ye," said Henchard in a softened voice, his eyes growing downcast, and his manner that of a man much moved by the strains. "Don't you blame David," he went on in low tones, shaking his head without raising his eyes. "He knew what he was about when he wrote that! . . . If I could afford it, be hanged if I wouldn't keep a church choir at my own expense to play and sing to me at these low, dark times of my life. But the bitter thing is, that when I was rich I didn't need what I could have, and now I be poor I can't have what I need!"

While they paused, Lucetta and Farfrae passed again, this time homeward, it being their custom to take, like others, a short walk out on the highway and back, between church and tea-time. "There's the man we've been singing about," said Henchard.

The players and singers turned their heads and saw his meaning. "Heaven forbid!" said the bass-player.

" 'Tis the man," repeated Henchard doggedly.

"Then if I'd known," said the performer on the clarionet solemnly, "that 'twas meant for a living man, nothing should have drawn out of my wynd-pipe the breath for that Psalm, so help me!"

"Nor from mine," said the first singer. "But, thought I, as it was made so long ago perhaps there isn't much in it, so I'll oblige a neighbour; for there's nothing to be said against the tune."

"Ah, my boys, you've sung it," said Henchard triumphantly. "As for him, it was partly by his songs that he got over me, and heaved me out. . . . I could double him up like that—and yet I don't." He laid the poker across his knee, bent it as if it were a twig, flung it down, and came away from the door.

It was at this time that Elizabeth-Jane, having heard where her stepfather was, entered the room with a pale and agonized countenance. The choir and the rest of the company moved off, in accordance with their half-pint regulation. Elizabeth-Jane went up to Henchard, and entreated him to accompany her home.

By this hour the volcanic fires of his nature had burnt down, and having drunk no great quantity as yet he was inclined to acquiesce. She

---

*Threatening, denunciatory.

took his arm, and together they went on. Henchard walked blankly, like a blind man, repeating to himself the last words of the singers—

> "And the next age his hated name
> Shall utterly deface."

At length he said to her, "I am a man to my word. I have kept my oath for twenty-one years; and now I can drink with a good conscience. . . . If I don't do for him—well, I am a fearful practical joker when I choose! He has taken away everything from me, and by heavens, if I meet him I won't answer for my deeds!"

These half-uttered words alarmed Elizabeth—all the more by reason of the still determination of Henchard's mien.

"What will you do?" she asked cautiously, while trembling with disquietude, and guessing Henchard's allusion only too well.

Henchard did not answer, and they went on till they had reached his cottage. "May I come in?" she said.

"No, no; not to-day," said Henchard; and she went away; feeling that to caution Farfrae was almost her duty, as it was certainly her strong desire.

As on the Sunday, so on the week-days, Farfrae and Lucetta might have been seen flitting about the town like two butterflies—or rather like a bee and a butterfly in league for life. She seemed to take no pleasure in going anywhere except in her husband's company; and hence when business would not permit him to waste an afternoon she remained indoors waiting for the time to pass till his return, her face being visible to Elizabeth-Jane from her window aloft. The latter, however, did not say to herself that Farfrae should be thankful for such devotion, but, full of her reading, she cited Rosalind's* exclamation: "Mistress, know yourself; down on your knees and thank Heaven fasting for a good man's love."

She kept her eye upon Henchard also. One day he answered her inquiry for his health by saying that he could not endure Abel Whittle's pitying eyes upon him while they worked together in the yard. "He is such a fool," said Henchard, "that he can never get out of his mind the time when I was master there."

---

*In Shakespeare's *As You Like It* (act 3, scene 5).

"I'll come and wimble for you instead of him, if you will allow me," said she. Her motive on going to the yard was to get an opportunity of observing the general position of affairs on Farfrae's premises now that her stepfather was a workman there. Henchard's threats had alarmed her so much that she wished to see his behaviour when the two were face to face.

For two or three days after her arrival Donald did not make any appearance. Then one afternoon the green door opened, and through came, first Farfrae, and at his heels Lucetta. Donald brought his wife forward without hesitation, it being obvious that he had no suspicion whatever of any antecedents in common between her and the now journeyman hay-trusser.

Henchard did not turn his eyes toward either of the pair, keeping them fixed on the bond he twisted, as if that alone absorbed him. A feeling of delicacy, which ever prompted Farfrae to avoid anything that might seem like triumphing over a fallen rival, led him to keep away from the hay-barn where Henchard and his daughter were working, and to go on to the corn department. Meanwhile Lucetta, never having been informed that Henchard had entered her husband's service, rambled straight on to the barn, where she came suddenly upon Henchard, and gave vent to a little "Oh!" which the happy and busy Donald was too far off to hear. Henchard, with withering humility of demeanour, touched the brim of his hat to her as Whittle and the rest had done, to which she breathed a dead-alive "Good afternoon."

"I beg your pardon, ma'am?" said Henchard, as if he had not heard.

"I said good afternoon," she faltered.

"O yes, good afternoon, ma'am," he replied, touching his hat again. "I am glad to see you, ma'am." Lucetta looked embarrassed, and Henchard continued: "For we humble workmen here feel it a great honour that a lady should look in and take an interest in us."

She glanced at him entreatingly; the sarcasm was too bitter, too unendurable.

"Can you tell me the time, ma'am?" he asked.

"Yes," she said hastily; "half-past four."

"Thank 'ee. An hour and a half longer before we are released from work. Ah, ma'am, we of the lower classes know nothing of the gay leisure that such as you enjoy!"

As soon as she could do so Lucetta left him, nodded and smiled to Elizabeth-Jane, and joined her husband at the other end of the enclosure, where she could be seen leading him away by the outer gates, so as to avoid passing Henchard again. That she had been taken by surprise was obvious. The result of this casual rencounter was that the next morning a note was put into Henchard's hand by the postman. "Will you," said Lucetta, with as much bitterness as she could put into a small communication, "will you kindly undertake not to speak to me in the biting undertones you used to-day, if I walk through the yard at any time? I bear you no ill-will, and I am only too glad that you should have employment of my dear husband; but in common fairness treat me as his wife, and do not try to make me wretched by covert sneers. I have committed no crime, and done you no injury."

"Poor fool!" said Henchard with fond savagery, holding out the note. "To know no better than commit herself in writing like this! Why, if I were to show that to her dear husband—pooh!" He threw the letter into the fire.

Lucetta took care not to come again among the hay and corn. She would rather have died than run the risk of encountering Henchard at such close quarters a second time. The gulf between them was growing wider every day. Farfrae was always considerate to his fallen acquaintance; but it was impossible that he should not, by degrees, cease to regard the ex-corn-merchant as more than one of his other workmen. Henchard saw this, and concealed his feelings under a cover of stolidity, fortifying his heart by drinking more freely at the Three Mariners every evening.

Often did Elizabeth-Jane, in her endeavours to prevent his taking other liquor, carry tea to him in a little basket at five o'clock. Arriving one day on this errand she found her stepfather was measuring up clover-seed and rape-seed in the corn-stores on the top floor, and she ascended to him. Each floor had a door opening into the air under a cat-head, from which a chain dangled for hoisting the sacks.

When Elizabeth's head rose through the trap she perceived that the upper door was open, and that her stepfather and Farfrae stood just within it in conversation, Farfrae being nearest the dizzy edge, and Henchard a little way behind. Not to interrupt them she re-

mained on the steps without raising her head any higher. While waiting thus she saw—or fancied she saw, for she had a terror of feeling
certain—her stepfather slowly raise his hand to a level behind Farfrae's shoulders, a curious expression taking possession of his face.
The young man was quite unconscious of the action, which was so
indirect that, if Farfrae had observed it, he might almost have regarded it as an idle outstretching of the arm. But it would have been
possible, by a comparatively light touch, to push Farfrae off his balance, and send him head over heels into the air.

Elizabeth felt quite sick at heart on thinking of what this might
have meant. As soon as they turned she mechanically took the tea to
Henchard, left it, and went away. Reflecting, she endeavoured to assure herself that the movement was an idle eccentricity, and no more.
Yet, on the other hand, his subordinate position in an establishment
where he once had been master might be acting on him like an irri-
tant poison; and she finally resolved to caution Donald.

XXXIV

NEXT MORNING, ACCORDINGLY, SHE rose at five o'clock and went into the
street. It was not yet light; a dense fog prevailed, and the town was as
silent as it was dark, except that from the rectangular avenues which
framed in the borough there came a chorus of tiny rappings, caused
by the fall of water-drops condensed on the boughs; now it was
wafted from the West Walk, now from the South Walk; and then from
both quarters simultaneously. She moved on to the bottom of Corn
Street, and, knowing his time well, waited only a few minutes before
she heard the familiar bang of his door, and then his quick walk towards her. She met him at the point where the last tree of the en-
girding avenue flanked the last house in the street.

He could hardly discern her till, glancing inquiringly, he said,
"What—Miss Henchard—and are ye up so airly?"

She asked him to pardon her for waylaying him at such an un-
seemly time. "But I am anxious to mention something," she said.
"And I wished not to alarm Mrs. Farfrae by calling."

"Yes?" said he, with the cheeriness of a superior. "And what may it be? It's very kind of ye, I'm sure."

She now felt the difficulty of conveying to his mind the exact aspect of possibilities in her own. But she somehow began, and introduced Henchard's name. "I sometimes fear," she said with an effort, "that he may be betrayed into some attempt to—insult you, sir."

"But we are the best of friends?"

"Or to play some practical joke upon you, sir. Remember that he has been hardly used."

"But we are quite friendly?"

"Or to do something—that would injure you—hurt you—wound you." Every word cost her twice its length of pain. And she could see that Farfrae was still incredulous. Henchard, a poor man in his employ, was not to Farfrae's view the Henchard who had ruled him. Yet he was not only the same man, but that man with his sinister qualities, formerly latent, quickened into life by his buffetings.

Farfrae, happy, and thinking no evil, persisted in making light of her fears. Thus they parted, and she went homeward, journeymen now being in the street, waggoners going to the harness-makers for articles left to be repaired, farm-horses going to the shoeing smiths, and the sons of labour showing themselves generally on the move. Elizabeth entered her lodging unhappily, thinking she had done no good, and only made herself appear foolish by her weak note of warning.

But Donald Farfrae was one of those men upon whom an incident is never absolutely lost. He revised impressions from a subsequent point of view, and the impulsive judgment of the moment was not always his permanent one. The vision of Elizabeth's earnest face in the rimy* dawn came back to him several times during the day. Knowing the solidity of her character he did not treat her hints altogether as idle-sounds.

But he did not desist from a kindly scheme on Henchard's account that engaged him just then; and when he met Lawyer Joyce, the town-clerk, later in the day, he spoke of it as if nothing had occurred to damp it.

"About that little seedsman's shop," he said; "the shop overlooking the churchyard, which is to let. It is not for myself I want it, but for

---

*Frosty.

our unlucky fellow-townsman Henchard. It would be a new beginning for him, if a small one; and I have told the Council that I would head a private subscription among them to set him up in it—that I would be fifty pounds, if they would make up the other fifty among them."

"Yes, yes; so I've heard; and there's nothing to say against it for that matter," the town-clerk replied, in his plain, frank way. "But, Farfrae, others see what you don't. Henchard hates 'ee—ay, hates 'ee; and 'tis right that you should know it. To my knowledge he was at the Three Mariners last night, saying in public that about you which a man ought not to say about another."

"Is that so—ah, is that so?" said Farfrae, looking down. "Why should he do it?" added the young man bitterly; "what harm have I done him that he should try to wrong me?"

"God only knows," said Joyce, lifting his eyebrows. "It shows much long-suffering in you to put up with him, and keep him in your employ."

"But I cannet discharge a man who was once a good friend to me? How can I forget that when I came here 'twas he enabled me to make a footing for mysel'? No, no. As long as I've a day's wark to offer he shall do it if he chooses. 'Tis not I who will deny him such a little as that. But I'll drop the idea of establishing him in a shop till I can think more about it."

It grieved Farfrae much to give up this scheme. But a damp having been thrown over it by these and other voices in the air, he went and countermanded his orders. The then occupier of the shop was in it when Farfrae spoke to him, and feeling it necessary to give some explanation of his withdrawal from the negotiation Donald mentioned Henchard's name, and stated that the intentions of the Council had been changed.

The occupier was much disappointed, and straightway informed Henchard, as soon as he saw him, that a scheme of the Council for setting him up in a shop had been knocked on the head by Farfrae. And thus out of error enmity grew.

When Farfrae got indoors that evening the teakettle was singing on the high hob of the semi-egg-shaped grate. Lucetta, light as a sylph, ran forward and seized his hands, whereupon Farfrae duly kissed her.

"Oh!" she cried playfully, turning to the window. "See—the blinds are not drawn down, and the people can look in—what a scandal!"

When the candles were lighted, the curtains drawn, and the twain sat at tea, she noticed that he looked serious. Without directly inquiring why she let her eyes linger solicitously on his face.

"Who has called?" he absently asked. "Any folk for me?"

"No," said Lucetta. "What's the matter, Donald?"

"Well—nothing worth talking of," he responded sadly.

"Then, never mind it. You will get through it. Scotchmen are always lucky."

"No—not always!" he said, shaking his head gloomily as he contemplated a crumb on the table. "I know many who have not been so! There was Sandy Macfarlane, who started to America to try his fortune, and he was drowned; and Archibald Leith, he was murdered! And poor Willie Dunbleeze and Maitland Macfreeze—they fell into bad courses, and went the way of all such!"

"Why—you old goosey—I was only speaking in a general sense, of course! You are always so literal. Now when we have finished tea, sing me that funny song about high-heeled shoon and siller tags, and the one-and-forty wooers."

"No, no. I couldna sing to-night! It's Henchard—he hates me; so that I may not be his friend if I would. I would understand why there should be a wee bit envy; but I cannet see a reason for the whole intensity of what he feels. Now, can you, Lucetta? It is more like old-fashioned rivalry in love than just a bit of rivalry in trade."

Lucetta had grown somewhat wan. "No," she replied.

"I give him employment—I cannet refuse it. But neither can I blind myself to the fact that with a man of passions such as his, there is no safeguard for conduct!"

"What have you heard—O Donald, dearest?" said Lucetta in alarm. The words on her lips were "anything about me?"—but she did not utter them. She could not, however, suppress her agitation, and her eyes filled with tears.

"No, no—it is not so serious as ye fancy," declared Farfrae soothingly; though he did not know its seriousness so well as she.

"I wish you would do what we have talked of," mournfully remarked Lucetta. "Give up business, and go away from here. We have plenty of money, and why should we stay?"

Farfrae seemed seriously disposed to discuss this move, and they talked thereon till a visitor was announced. Their neighbour Alderman Vatt came in.

"You've heard, I suppose, of poor Doctor Chalkfield's death? Yes—died this afternoon at five," said Mr. Vatt. Chalkfield was the Councilman who had succeeded to the Mayoralty in the preceding November.

Farfrae was sorry at the intelligence, and Mr. Vatt continued: "Well, we know he's been going some days, and as his family is well provided for we must take it all as it is. Now I have called to ask 'ee this—quite privately. If I should nominate 'ee to succeed him, and there should be no particular opposition, will 'ee accept the chair?"

"But there are folk whose turn is before mine; and I'm over young, and may be thought pushing!" said Farfrae after a pause.

"Not at all. I don't speak for myself only, several have named it. You won't refuse?"

"We thought of going away," interposed Lucetta, looking at Farfrae anxiously.

"It was only a fancy," Farfrae murmured. "I wouldna refuse if it is the wish of a respectable majority in the Council."

"Very well, then, look upon yourself as elected. We have had older men long enough."

When he was gone Farfrae said musingly, "See now how it's ourselves that are ruled by the Powers above us! We plan this, but we do that. If they want to make me Mayor I will stay, and Henchard must rave as he will."

From this evening onward Lucetta was very uneasy. If she had not been imprudence incarnate she would not have acted as she did when she met Henchard by accident a day or two later. It was in the bustle of the market, when no one could readily notice their discourse.

"Michael," said she, "I must again ask you what I asked you months ago—to return me any letters or papers of mine that you may have—unless you have destroyed them? You must see how desirable it is that the time at Jersey should be blotted out, for the good of all parties."

"Why, bless the woman!—I packed up every scrap of your handwriting to give you in the coach—but you never appeared."

She explained how the death of her aunt had prevented her taking the journey on that day. "And what became of the parcel then?" she asked.

He could not say—he would consider. When she was gone he recollected that he had left a heap of useless papers in his former dining-room safe—built up in the wall of his old house—now occupied by Farfrae. The letters might have been amongst them.

A grotesque grin shaped itself on Henchard's face. Had that safe been opened?

On the very evening which followed this there was a great ringing of bells in Casterbridge, and the combined brass, wood, catgut, and leather bands played round the town with more prodigality of percussion-notes than ever. Farfrae was Mayor—the two-hundredth odd of a series forming an elective dynasty dating back to the days of Charles I—and the fair Lucetta was the courted of the town. . . . But, ah! that worm i' the bud*—Henchard; what he could tell!

He, in the meantime, festering with indignation at some erroneous intelligence of Farfrae's opposition to the scheme for installing him in the little seed-shop, was greeted with the news of the municipal election (which, by reason of Farfrae's comparative youth and his Scottish nativity—a thing unprecedented in the case—had an interest far beyond the ordinary). The bell-ringing and the band-playing, loud as Tamerlane's trumpet,† goaded the downfallen Henchard indescribably: the ousting now seemed to him to be complete.

The next morning he went to the corn-yard as usual, and about eleven o'clock Donald entered through the green door, with no trace of the worshipful about him. The yet more emphatic change of places between him and Henchard which this election had established renewed a slight embarrassment in the manner of the modest younger man; but Henchard showed the front of one who had overlooked all this; and Farfrae met his amenities half-way at once.

"I was going to ask you," said Henchard, "about a packet that I may possibly have left in my old safe in the dining-room." He added particulars.

"If so, it is there now," said Farfrae. "I have never opened the safe at all as yet; for I keep ma papers at the bank, to sleep easy o' nights."

---

*The phrase is from Shakespeare's *Twelfth Night* (act 2, scene 4).

†Reference to the central European warrior king Timur Lenk, also known as Tamburlaine or Tamerlane (1336–1405), whose army was famous for carrying large trumpets.

"It was not of much consequence—to me," said Henchard. "But I'll call for it this evening, if you don't mind?"

It was quite late when he fulfilled his promise. He had primed himself with grog, as he did very frequently now, and a curl of sardonic humour hung on his lip as he approached the house, as though he were contemplating some terrible form of amusement. Whatever it was, the incident of his entry did not diminish its force, this being his first visit to the house since he had lived there as owner. The ring of the bell spoke to him like the voice of a familiar drudge who had been bribed to forsake him; the movements of the doors were revivals of dead days.

Farfrae invited him into the dining-room, where he at once unlocked the iron safe built into the wall, *his*, Henchard's safe, made by an ingenious locksmith under his direction. Farfrae drew thence the parcel, and other papers, with apologies for not having returned them.

"Never mind," said Henchard drily. "The fact is they are letters mostly. . . . Yes," he went on, sitting down and unfolding Lucetta's passionate bundle, "here they be. That ever I should see 'em again! I hope Mrs. Farfrae is well after her exertions of yesterday?"

"She has felt a bit weary; and has gone to bed airly on that account."

Henchard returned to the letters, sorting them over with interest, Farfrae being seated at the other end of the dining-table. "You don't forget, of course," he resumed, "that curious chapter in the history of my past which I told you of, and that you gave me some assistance in? These letters are, in fact, related to that unhappy business. Though, thank God, it is all over now."

"What became of the poor woman?" asked Farfrae.

"Luckily she married, and married well," said Henchard. "So that these reproaches she poured out on me do not now cause me any twinges, as they might otherwise have done. . . . Just listen to what an angry woman will say!"

Farfrae, willing to humour Henchard, though quite uninterested, and bursting with yawns, gave well-mannered attention.

" 'For me,' " Henchard read, " 'there is practically no future. A creature too unconventionally devoted to you—who feels it impossible that she can be wife of any other man; and who is yet no more to you than the first woman you meet in the street—such am I. I quite acquit you of any intention to wrong me, yet you are the door through which wrong has come to me. That in the event of your present wife's death you will place me in her position is a consolation so far as it goes—but how far does it go? Thus I sit here, forsaken by my few acquaintance, and forsaken by you!' "

"That's how she went on to me," said Henchard, "acres of words like that, when what had happened was what I could not cure."

"Yes," said Farfrae absently, "it is the way wi' women." But the fact was that he knew very little of the sex; yet detecting a sort of resemblance in style between the effusions of the woman he worshipped and those of the supposed stranger, he concluded that Aphrodite* ever spoke thus, whosesoever the personality she assumed.

Henchard unfolded another letter, and read it through likewise, stopping at the subscription as before. "Her name I don't give," he said blandly. "As I didn't marry her, and another man did, I can scarcely do that in fairness to her."

"Tr-rue, tr-rue," said Farfrae. "But why didn't you marry her when your wife Susan died?" Farfrae asked this and the other questions in the comfortably indifferent tone of one whom the matter very remotely concerned.

"Ah—well you may ask that!" said Henchard, the new-moon-shaped grin adumbrating itself again upon his mouth. "In spite of all her protestations, when I came forward to do so, as in generosity bound, she was not the woman for me."

"She had already married another—maybe?"

Henchard seemed to think it would be sailing too near the wind to descend further into particulars, and he answered "Yes."

"The young lady must have had a heart that bore transplanting very readily!"

"She had, she had," said Henchard emphatically.

He opened a third and fourth letter, and read. This time he approached the conclusion as if the signature were indeed coming with the rest. But again he stopped short. The truth was that, as may be divined, he had quite intended to effect a grand catastrophe at the end of this drama by reading out the name; he had come to the house with no other thought. But sitting here in cold blood he could not do it.

*Greek goddess of love.

Such a wrecking of hearts appalled even him. His quality was such that he could have annihilated them both in the heat of action; but to accomplish the deed by oral poison was beyond the nerve of his enmity.

XXXV

As DONALD STATED, LUCETTA had retired early to her room because of fatigue. She had, however, not gone to rest, but sat in the bedside chair reading and thinking over the events of the day. At the ringing of the door-bell by Henchard she wondered who it should be that would call at that comparatively late hour. The dining-room was almost under her bedroom; she could hear that somebody was admitted there, and presently the indistinct murmur of a person reading became audible.

The usual time for Donald's arrival upstairs came and passed, yet still the reading and conversation went on. This was very singular. She could think of nothing but that some extraordinary crime had been committed, and that the visitor, whoever he might be, was reading an account of it from a special edition of the *Casterbridge Chronicle*. At last she left the room, and descended the stairs. The dining-room door was ajar, and in the silence of the resting household the voice and the words were recognizable before she reached the lower flight. She stood transfixed. Her own words greeted her in Henchard's voice, like spirits from the grave.

Lucetta leant upon the banister with her cheek against the smooth hand-rail, as if she would make a friend of it in her misery. Rigid in this position, more and more words fell successively upon her ear. But what amazed her most was the tone of her husband. He spoke merely in the accents of a man who made a present of his time.

"One word," he was saying, as the crackling of paper denoted that Henchard was unfolding yet another sheet. "Is it quite fair to this young woman's memory to read at such length to a stranger what was intended for your eye alone?"

"Well, yes," said Henchard. "By not giving her name I make it an example of all womankind, and not a scandal to one."

"If I were you I would destroy them," said Farfrae, giving more thought to the letters than he had hitherto done. "As another man's wife it would injure the woman if it were known."

"No, I shall not destroy them," murmured Henchard, putting the letters away. Then he arose, and Lucetta heard no more.

She went back to her bedroom in a semi-paralyzed state. For very fear she could not undress, but sat on the edge of the bed, waiting. Would Henchard let out the secret in his parting words? Her suspense was terrible. Had she confessed all to Donald in their early acquaintance he might possibly have got over it, and married her just the same—unlikely as it had once seemed; but for her or any one else to tell him now would be fatal.

The door slammed; she could hear her husband bolting it. After looking round in his customary way he came leisurely up the stairs. The spark in her eyes well-nigh went out when he appeared round the bedroom door. Her gaze hung doubtful for a moment, then to her joyous amazement she saw that he looked at her with the rallying smile of one who had just been relieved of a scene that was irksome. She could hold out no longer, and sobbed hysterically.

When he had restored her Farfrae naturally enough spoke of Henchard. "Of all men he was the least desirable as a visitor," he said; "but it is my belief that he's just a bit crazed. He has been reading to me a long lot of letters relating to his past life; and I could do no less than indulge him by listening."

This was sufficient. Henchard, then, had not told. Henchard's last words to Farfrae, in short, as he stood on the door-step, had been these:

"Well—I'm much obliged to 'ee for listening. I may tell more about her some day."

Finding this, she was much perplexed as to Henchard's motives in opening the matter at all; for in such cases we attribute to an enemy a power of consistent action which we never find in ourselves or in our friends; and forget that abortive efforts from want of heart are as possible to revenge as to generosity.

Next morning Lucetta remained in bed, meditating how to parry this incipient attack. The bold stroke of telling Donald the truth, dimly conceived, was yet too bold; for she dreaded lest in doing so he, like the rest of the world, should believe that the episode was rather her fault than her misfortune. She decided to employ persuasion—not with Donald, but with the enemy himself. It seemed the only practicable weapon left her as a woman. Having laid her plan she rose, and wrote to him who kept her on these tenterhooks:—

"I overheard your interview with my husband last night, and saw the drift of your revenge. The very thought of it crushes me! Have pity on a distressed woman! If you could see me you would relent. You do not know how anxiety has told upon me lately. I will be at the Ring at the time you leave work—just before the sun goes down. Please come that way. I cannot rest till I have seen you face to face, and heard from your mouth that you will carry this horse-play no further."

To herself she said, on closing up this appeal: "If ever tears and pleadings have served the weak to fight the strong, let them do so now!"

With this view she made a toilette which differed from all she had ever attempted before. To heighten her natural attractions had hitherto been the unvarying endeavour of her adult life, and one in which she was no novice. But now she neglected this, and even proceeded to impair the natural presentation. Beyond a natural reason for her slightly drawn look, she had not slept all the previous night, and this had produced upon her pretty though slightly worn features the aspect of a countenance ageing prematurely from extreme sorrow. She selected—as much from want of spirit as design—her poorest, plainest, and longest discarded attire.

To avoid the contingency of being recognized she veiled herself, and slipped out of the house quickly. The sun was resting on the hill like a drop of blood on an eyelid by the time she had got up the road opposite the amphitheatre, which she speedily entered. The interior was shadowy, and emphatic of the absence of every living thing.

She was not disappointed in the fearful hope with which she awaited him. Henchard came over the top, descended, and Lucetta waited breathlessly. But having reached the arena she saw a change in his bearing: he stood still at a little distance from her; she could not think why.

Nor could any one else have known. The truth was that in appointing this spot, and this hour, for the rendezvous, Lucetta had unwittingly backed up her entreaty by the strongest argument she could have used outside words, with this man of moods, glooms, and superstitions. Her figure in the midst of the huge enclosure, the unusual plainness of her dress, her attitude of hope and appeal, so strongly revived in his soul the memory of another ill-used woman who had stood there and thus in bygone days, and had now passed away into her rest, that he was unmanned, and his heart smote him for having attempted reprisals on one of a sex so weak. When he approached her, and before she had spoken a word, her point was half gained.

His manner as he had come down had been one of cynical carelessness; but he now put away his grim half-smile, and said in a kindly subdued tone, "Good-night t'ye. Of course I'm glad to come if you want me."

"O, thank you," she said apprehensively.

"I am sorry to see 'ee looking so ill," he stammered with unconcealed compunction.

She shook her head. "How can you be sorry," she asked, "when you deliberately cause it?"

"What!" said Henchard uneasily. "Is it anything I have done that has pulled you down like that?"

"It is all your doing," said she. "I have no other grief. My happiness would be secure enough but for your threats. O Michael! don't wreck me like this! You might think that you have done enough! When I came here I was a young woman; now I am rapidly becoming an old one. Neither my husband nor any other man will regard me with interest long."

Henchard was disarmed. His old feeling of supercilious pity for womankind in general was intensified by this suppliant appearing here as the double of the first. Moreover, that thoughtless want of foresight which had led to all her trouble remained with poor Lucetta still; she had come to meet him here in this compromising way without perceiving the risk. Such a woman was very small deer to hunt; he felt ashamed, lost all zest and desire to humiliate Lucetta there and then, and no longer envied Farfrae his bargain. He had married money, but nothing more. Henchard was anxious to wash his hands of the game.

"Well, what do you want me to do?" he said gently. "I am sure I shall be very willing. My reading of those letters was only a sort of practical joke, and I revealed nothing."

"To give me back the letters and any papers you may have that breathe of matrimony or worse."

"So be it. Every scrap shall be yours. . . . But, between you and me, Lucetta, he is sure to find out something of the matter, sooner or later."

"Ah!" she said with eager tremulousness; "but not till I have proved myself a faithful and deserving wife to him, and then he may forgive me everything!"

Henchard silently looked at her: he almost envied Farfrae such love as that, even now. "H'm—I hope so," he said. "But you shall have the letters without fail. And your secret shall be kept. I swear it."

"How good you are!—how shall I get them?"

He reflected, and said he would send them the next morning. "Now don't doubt me," he added. "I can keep my word."

XXXVI

RETURNING FROM HER APPOINTMENT Lucetta saw a man waiting by the lamp nearest to her own door. When she stopped to go in he came and spoke to her. It was Jopp.

He begged her pardon for addressing her. But he had heard that Mr. Farfrae had been applied to by a neighbouring corn-merchant to recommend a working partner; if so, he wished to offer himself. He could give good security, and had stated as much to Mr. Farfrae in a letter; but he would feel much obliged if Lucetta would say a word in his favour to her husband.

"It is a thing I know nothing about," said Lucetta coldly.

"But you can testify to my trustworthiness better than anybody, ma'am," said Jopp. "I was in Jersey several years, and knew you there by sight."

"Indeed," she replied. "But I knew nothing of you."

"I think, ma'am, that a word or two from you would secure for me what I covet very much," he persisted.

She steadily refused to have anything to do with the affair, and cutting him short, because of her anxiety to get indoors before her husband should miss her, left him on the pavement.

He watched her till she had vanished, and then went home. When he got there he sat down in the fireless chimney corner look-

ing at the iron dogs,* and the wood laid across them for heating the
morning kettle. A movement upstairs disturbed him, and Henchard
came down from his bedroom, where he seemed to have been rum-
maging boxes.

"I wish," said Henchard, "you would do me a service, Jopp,
now—to-night, I mean, if you can. Leave this at Mrs. Farfrae's for her.
I should take it myself, of course, but I don't wish to be seen there."

He handed a package in brown paper, sealed. Henchard had been
as good as his word. Immediately on coming indoors he had
searched over his few belongings; and every scrap of Lucetta's writing that he possessed was here. Jopp indifferently expressed his willingness.

"Well, how have ye got on to-day?" his lodger asked. "Any
prospect of an opening?"

"I am afraid not," said Jopp, who had not told the other of his
application to Farfrae.

"There never will be in Casterbridge," declared Henchard deci-
sively. "You must roam further afield." He said good-night to Jopp,
and returned to his own part of the house.

Jopp sat on till his eyes were attracted by the shadow of the can-
dlesnuff on the wall, and looking at the original he found that it had
formed itself into a head like a red-hot cauliflower. Henchard's packet
next met his gaze. He knew there had been something of the nature
of wooing between Henchard and the now Mrs. Farfrae; and his
vague ideas on the subject narrowed themselves down to these: Henchard had a parcel belonging to Mrs. Farfrae, and he had reasons for
not returning that parcel to her in person. What could be inside it?
So he went on and on till, animated by resentment at Lucetta's haugh-
tiness, as he thought it, and curiosity to learn if there were any weak
sides to this transaction with Henchard, he examined the package.
The pen and all its relations being awkward tools in Henchard's
hands he had affixed the seals without an impression, it never occur-
ring to him that the efficacy of such a fastening depended on this.
Jopp was far less of a tyro;† he lifted one of the seals with his
penknife, peeped in at the end thus opened, saw that the bundle con-

---

*Irons to hold burning wood.
†Novice.

sisted of letters; and, having satisfied himself thus far, sealed up the end again by simply softening the wax with the candle, and went off with the parcel as requested.

His path was by the river-side at the foot of the town. Coming into the light at the bridge which stood at the end of High Street he beheld lounging thereon Mother Cuxsom and Nance Mockridge.

"We be just going down Mixen Lane way, to look into Peter's Finger afore creeping to bed," said Mrs. Cuxsom. "There's a fiddle and tambourine going on there. Lord, what's all the world—do ye come along too, Jopp—'twon't hinder ye five minutes."

Jopp had mostly kept himself out of this company, but present circumstances made him somewhat more reckless than usual, and without many words he decided to go to his destination that way.

Though the upper part of Durnover was mainly composed of a curious congeries of barns and farmsteads, there was a less picturesque side to the parish. This was Mixen Lane, now in great part pulled down.

Mixen Lane was the Adullam* of all the surrounding villages. It was the hiding-place of those who were in distress, and in debt, and in trouble of every kind. Farm-labourers and other peasants, who combined a little poaching with their farming, and a little brawling and bibbing† with their poaching, found themselves sooner or later in Mixen Lane. Rural mechanics too idle to mechanize, rural servants too rebellious to serve, drifted or were forced into Mixen Lane.

The lane and its surrounding thicket of thatched cottages stretched out like a spit into the moist and misty lowland. Much that was sad, much that was low, some things that were baneful, could be seen in Mixen Lane. Vice ran freely in and out certain of the doors of the neighbourhood; recklessness dwelt under the roof with the crooked chimney; shame in some bow-windows; theft (in times of privation) in the thatched and mud-walled houses by the sallows.‡ Even slaughter had not been altogether unknown here. In a block of cottages up an alley there might have been erected an altar to disease

---

*The cave to which David flees to escape Saul's wrath (1 Samuel 22:1–2).
†Drinking.
‡Willows.

in years gone by. Such was Mixen Lane in the times when Henchard and Farfrae were Mayors.

Yet this mildewed leaf in the sturdy and flourishing Casterbridge plant lay close to the open country; not a hundred yards from a row of noble elms, and commanding a view across the moor of airy uplands and corn-fields, and mansions of the great. A brook divided the moor from the tenements, and to outward view there was no way across it—no way to the houses but round about by the road. But under every householder's stairs there was kept a mysterious plank nine inches wide; which plank was a secret bridge.

If you, as one of those refugee householders, came in from business after dark—and this was the business time here—you stealthily crossed the moor, approached the border of the aforesaid brook, and whistled opposite the house to which you belonged. A shape thereupon made its appearance on the other side bearing the bridge on end against the sky; it was lowered; you crossed, and a hand helped you to land yourself, together with the pheasants and hares gathered from neighbouring manors. You sold them slily the next morning, and the day after you stood before the magistrates with the eyes of all your sympathizing neighbours concentrated on your back. You disappeared for a time then you were again found quietly living in Mixen Lane.

Walking along the lane at dusk the stranger was struck by two or three peculiar features therein. One was an intermittent rumbling from the back premises of the inn half-way up; this meant a skittle alley. Another was the extensive prevalence of whistling in the various domiciles—a piped note of some kind coming from nearly every open door. Another was the frequency of white aprons over dingy gowns among the women around the doorways. A white apron is a suspicious vesture in situations where spotlessness is difficult; moreover, the industry and cleanliness which the white apron expressed were belied by the postures and gaits of the women who wore it— their knuckles being mostly on their hips (an attitude which lent them the aspect of two-handled mugs), and their shoulders against door-posts; while there was a curious alacrity in the turn of each honest woman's head upon her neck and in the twirl of her honest eyes, at any noise resembling a masculine footfall along the lane.

Yet amid so much that was bad needy respectability also found a home. Under some of the roofs abode pure and virtuous souls whose presence there was due to the iron hand of necessity, and to that alone. Families from decayed villages—families of that once bulky, but now nearly extinct, section of village society called "liviers," or lifeholders—copy-holders* and others, whose roof-trees† had fallen for some reason or other, compelling them to quit the rural spot that had been their home for generations—came here, unless they chose to lie under a hedge by the wayside.

The inn called Peter's Finger was the church of Mixen Lane.

It was centrally situate, as such places should be, and bore about the same social relation to the Three Mariners as the latter bore to the King's Arms. At first sight the inn was so respectable as to be puzzling. The front door was kept shut, and the step was so clean that evidently but few persons entered over its sanded surface. But at the corner of the public-house was an alley, a mere slit, dividing it from the next building. Half-way up the alley was a narrow door, shiny and paint-less from the rub of infinite hands and shoulders. This was the actual entrance to the inn.

A pedestrian would be seen abstractedly passing along Mixen Lane; and then, in a moment, he would vanish, causing the gazer to blink like Ashton at the disappearance of Ravenswood.‡ That abstracted pedestrian had edged into the slit by the adroit fillip of his person sideways; from the slit he edged into the tavern by a similar exercise of skill.

The company at the Three Mariners were persons of quality in comparison with the company which gathered here; though it must be admitted that the lowest fringe of the Mariner's party touched the crest of Peter's at points. Waifs and strays of all sorts loitered about here. The landlady was a virtuous woman who years ago had been unjustly sent to gaol as an accessary to something or other after the fact. She underwent her twelvemonth, and had worn a martyr's coun-tenance ever since, except at times of meeting the constable who ap-prehended her, when she winked her eye.

To this house Jopp and his acquaintances had arrived. The settles on which they sat down were thin and tall, their tops being guyed by

---

*Lifeholders: tenants holding leases extending until the death of a specific family mem-ber; copy-holders: tenants whose leases were recorded in the court-roll.

†Support beams in a roof; the tenants have lost their homes.

‡In Sir Walter Scott's The Bride of Lamermoor (1819), Ashton watches as his rival Ravenswood is swallowed alive by quicksand.

pieces of twine to hooks in the ceiling; for when the guests grew boisterous the settles would rock and overturn without some such security. The thunder of bowls echoed from the backyard; swingels* hung behind the blower† of the chimney; and ex-poachers and ex-gamekeepers, whom squires had persecuted without a cause, sat elbowing each other—men who in past times had met in fights under the moon, till lapse of sentences on the one part, and loss of favour and expulsion from service on the other, brought them here together to a common level, where they sat calmly discussing old times.

"Dos't mind how you could jerk a trout ashore with a bramble, and not ruffle the stream, Charl?" a deposed keeper was saying. " 'Twas at that I caught 'ee once, if you can mind?"

"That can I. But the worst larry for me was that pheasant business at Yalbury Wood. Your wife swore false that time, Joe—O, by Gad, she did—there's no denying it."

"How was that?" asked Jopp.

"Why—Joe closed wi' me, and we rolled down together, close to his garden hedge. Hearing the noise, out ran his wife with the oven pyle,‡ and it being dark under the trees she couldn't see which was uppermost. 'Where beest thee, Joe, under or top?' she screeched. 'O—under, by Gad!' says he. She then began to rap down upon my skull, back, and ribs with the pyle till we'd roll over again. 'Where beest now, dear Joe, under or top?' she'd scream again. By George, 'twas through her I was took! And then when we got up in hall she sware that the cock pheasant was one of her rearing, when 'twas not your bird at all, Joe; 'twas Squire Brown's bird—that's whose 'twas—one that we'd picked off as we passed his wood, an hour afore. It did hurt my feelings to be so wronged! . . . . Ah well—'tis over now."

"I might have had 'ee days afore that," said the keeper. "I was within a few yards of 'ee dozens of times, with a sight more of birds than that poor one."

"Yes—'tis not our greatest doings that the world gets wind of," said the furmity-woman, who, lately settled in this purlieu, sat among the rest. Having travelled a great deal in her time she spoke

---

*Cudgels.
†Plate of metal fixed before a fire to increase the draught.
‡Large, wooden, spatula-shaped tool for placing loaves in an oven.

with cosmopolitan largeness of idea. It was she who presently asked Jopp what was the parcel he kept so snugly under his arm.

"Ah, therein lies a grand secret," said Jopp. "It is the passion of love. To think that a woman should love one man so well, and hate another so unmercifully."

"Who's the object of your meditation, sir?"

"One that stands high in this town. I'd like to shame her! Upon my life, 'twould be as good as a play to read her love-letters, the proud piece of silk and wax-work! For 'tis her love-letters that I've got here."

"Love-letters? then let's hear'em, good soul," said Mother Cuxsom. "Lord, do ye mind, Richard, what fools we used to be when we were younger? Getting a schoolboy to write ours for us; and giving him a penny, do ye mind, not to tell other folks what he'd put inside, do ye mind?"

By this time Jopp had pushed his finger under the seals, and unfastened the letters, tumbling them over and picking up one here and there at random, which he read aloud. These passages soon began to uncover the secret which Lucetta had so earnestly hoped to keep buried, though the epistles, being allusive only, did not make it altogether plain.

"Mrs. Farfrae wrote that!" said Nance Mockridge. " 'Tis a humbling thing for us, as respectable women, that one of the same sex could do it. And now she's vowed herself to another man!"

"So much the better for her," said the aged furmity-woman. "Ah, I saved her from a real bad marriage, and she's never been the one to thank me."

"I say, what a good foundation for a skimmity-ride,"* said Nance.

"True," said Mrs. Cuxsom, reflecting. " 'Tis as good a ground for a skimmity-ride as ever I knowed; and it ought not to be wasted. The last one seen in Casterbridge must have been ten years ago, if a day."

At this moment there was a shrill whistle, and the landlady said to the man who had been called Charl, " 'Tis Jim coming in. Would ye go and let down the bridge for me?"

Without replying Charl and his comrade Joe rose, and receiving a lantern from her went out at the back door and down the garden-path, which ended abruptly at the edge of the stream already men-

---

*Raucous folk custom in which effigies representing an adulterous or bickering couple are paraded through the town (also known as "skimmington").

tioned. Beyond the stream was the open moor, from which a clammy breeze smote upon their faces as they advanced. Taking up the board that had lain in readiness one of them lowered it across the water, and the instant its further end touched the ground footsteps entered upon it, and there appeared from the shade a stalwart man with straps round his knees, a double-barrelled gun under his arm and some birds slung up behind him. They asked him if he had had much luck.

"Not, much," he said indifferently. "All safe inside?"

Receiving a reply in the affirmative he went on inwards, the others withdrawing the bridge and beginning to retreat in his rear. Before, however, they had entered the house a cry of "Ahoy" from the moor led them to pause.

The cry was repeated. They pushed the lantern into an outhouse, and went back to the brink of the stream.

"Ahoy—is this the way to Casterbridge?" said some one from the other side.

"Not in particular," said Charl. "There's a river afore 'ee."

"I don't care—here's for through it!" said the man in the moor. "I've had travelling enough for to-day."

"Stop a minute, then," said Charl, finding that the man was no enemy. "Joe, bring the plank and lantern; here's somebody that's lost his way. You should have kept along the turnpike road, friend, and not have strook across here."

"I should—as I see now. But I saw a light here, and says I to myself, that's an outlying house, depend on't."

The plank was now lowered; and the stranger's form shaped itself from the darkness. He was a middle-aged man, with hair and whiskers prematurely grey, and a broad and genial face. He had crossed on the plank without hesitation, and seemed to see nothing odd in the transit. He thanked them, and walked between them up the garden. "What place is this?" he asked, when they reached the door.

"A public-house."

"Ah. Perhaps it will suit me to put up at. Now then, come in and wet your whistle at my expense for the lift over you have given me."

They followed him into the inn, where the increased light exhibited him as one who would stand higher in an estimate by the eye than in one by the ear. He was dressed with a certain clumsy richness—his coat being furred, and his head covered by a cap of sealskin, which, though the nights were chilly, must have been warm for the daytime, spring being somewhat advanced. In his hand he carried a small mahogany case, strapped, and clamped with brass.

Apparently surprised at the kind of company which confronted him through the kitchen door, he at once abandoned his idea of putting up at the house; but taking the situation lightly, he called for glasses of the best, paid for them as he stood in the passage, and turned to proceed on his way by the front door. This was barred, and while the landlady was unfastening it the conversation about the skimmington was continued in the sitting-room, and reached his ears.

"What do they mean by a 'skimmity-ride'?" he asked.

"O, sir!" said the landlady, swinging her long earrings with deprecating modesty; " 'tis a' old foolish thing they do in these parts when a man's wife is—well, not too particularly his own. But as a respectable householder I don't encourage it."

"Still, are they going to do it shortly? It is a good sight to see, I suppose?"

"Well, sir!" she simpered. And then, bursting into naturalness, and glancing from the corner of her eye, " 'Tis the funniest thing under the sun! And it costs money."

"Ah! I remember hearing of some such thing. Now I shall be in Casterbridge for two or three weeks to come, and should not mind seeing the performance. Wait a moment." He turned back, entered the sitting-room, and said, "Here, good folks; I should like to see the old custom you are talking of, and I don't mind being something towards it—take that." He threw a sovereign on the table and returned to the landlady at the door, of whom, having inquired the way into the town, he took his leave.

"There were more where that one came from," said Charl, when the sovereign had been taken up and handed to the landlady for safe keeping. "By George! we ought to have got a few more while we had him here."

"No, no," answered the landlady. "This is a respectable house, thank God! And I'll have nothing done but what's honourable."

"Well," said Jopp; "now we'll consider the business begun, and will soon get it in train."

"We will!" said Nance. "A good laugh warms my heart more than a cordial, and that's the truth on't."

Jopp gathered up the letters, and it being now somewhat late he did not attempt to call at Farfrae's with them that night. He reached home, sealed them up as before, and delivered the parcel at its address next morning. Within an hour its contents were reduced to ashes by Lucetta, who, poor soul! was inclined to fall down on her knees in thankfulness that at last no evidence remained of the unlucky episode with Henchard in her past. For though hers had been rather the laxity of inadvertence than of intention, that episode, if known, was not the less likely to operate fatally between herself and her husband.

XXXVII

SUCH WAS THE STATE of things when the current affairs of Casterbridge were interrupted by an event of such magnitude that its influence reached to the lowest social stratum there, stirring the depths of its society simultaneously with the preparations for the skimmington. It was one of those excitements which, when they move a country town, leave a permanent mark upon its chronicles, as a warm summer permanently marks the ring in the tree-trunk corresponding to its date.

A Royal Personage was about to pass through the borough on his course further west,* to inaugurate an immense engineering work out that way. He had consented to halt half-an-hour or so in the town, and to receive an address from the corporation of Casterbridge, which, as a representative centre of husbandry, wished thus to express its sense of the great services he had rendered to agricultural science and economics, by his zealous promotion of designs for placing the art of farming on a more scientific footing.

Royalty had not been seen in Casterbridge since the days of the third King George,† and then only by candlelight for a few minutes, when that monarch, on a night-journey, had stopped to change horses at the King's Arms. The inhabitants therefore decided to make

---

*Prince Albert passed through the region in which the novel is set in July 1849.
†George III reigned from 1760 to 1820.

a thorough *fête carillonnée** of the unwonted occasion. Half-an-hour's pause was not long, it is true; but much might be done in it by a judicious grouping of incidents, above all, if the weather were fine.

The address was prepared on parchment by an artist who was handy at ornamental lettering, and was laid on with the best gold-leaf and colours that the sign-painter had in his shop. The Council met on the Tuesday before the appointed day, to arrange the details of the procedure. While they were sitting, the door of the Council Chamber standing open, they heard a heavy footstep coming up the stairs. It advanced along the passage, and Henchard entered the room, in clothes of frayed and threadbare shabbiness, the very clothes which he had used to wear in the primal days when he had sat among them.

"I have a feeling," he said, advancing to the table and laying his hand upon the green cloth, "that I should like to join ye in this reception of our illustrious visitor. I suppose I could walk with the rest?"

Embarrassed glances were exchanged by the Council, and Grower nearly ate the end of his quill-pen off, so gnawed he it during the silence. Farfrae the young Mayor, who by virtue of his office sat in the large chair, intuitively caught the sense of the meeting, and as spokesman was obliged to utter it, glad as he would have been that the duty should have fallen to another tongue.

"I hardly see that it would be proper, Mr. Henchard," said he. "The Council are the Council, and as ye are no longer one of the body, there would be an irregularity in the proceeding. If ye were included, why not others?"

"I have a particular reason for wishing to assist at the ceremony."

Farfrae looked round. "I think I have expressed the feeling of the Council," he said.

"Yes, yes," from Dr. Bath, Lawyer Long, Alderman Tubber, and several more.

"Then I am not to be allowed to have anything to do with it officially?"

"I am afraid so; it is out of the question, indeed. But of course you can see the doings full well, such as they are to be, like the rest of the spectators."

---

*Festival of chimes (French).

Henchard did not reply to that very obvious suggestion, and, turning on his heel, went away.

It had been only a passing fancy of his, but opposition crystallized it into a determination. "I'll welcome his Royal Highness, or nobody shall!" he went about saying. "I am not going to be sat upon by Farfrae, or any of the rest of the paltry crew! You shall see."

The eventful morning was bright, a full-faced sun confronting early window-gazers eastward, and all perceived (for they were practised in weather-lore) that there was permanence in the glow. Visitors soon began to flock in from county houses, villages, remote copses, and lonely uplands, the latter in oiled boots and tilt bonnets, to see the reception, or if not to see it, at any rate to be near it. There was hardly a workman in the town who did not put a clean shirt on. Solomon Longways, Christopher Coney, Buzzford, and the rest of that fraternity, showed their sense of the occasion by advancing their customary eleven o'clock pint to half-past ten; from which they found a difficulty in getting back to the proper hour for several days.

Henchard had determined to do no work that day. He primed himself in the morning with a glass of rum, and walking down the street met Elizabeth-Jane, whom he had not seen for a week. "It was lucky," he said to her, "my twenty-one years had expired before this came on, or I should never have had the nerve to carry it out."

"Carry out what?" said she, alarmed.

"This welcome I am going to give our Royal visitor."

She was perplexed. "Shall we go and see it together?" she said.

"See it! I have other fish to fry. You see it. It will be worth seeing!"

She could do nothing to elucidate this, and decked herself out with a heavy heart. As the appointed time drew near she got sight again of her stepfather. She thought he was going to the Three Mariners; but no, he elbowed his way through the gay throng to the shop of Woolfrey, the draper. She waited in the crowd without.

In a few minutes he emerged, wearing, to her surprise, a brilliant rosette, while more surprising still, in his hand he carried a flag of somewhat homely construction, formed by tacking one of the small Union Jacks, which abounded in the town to-day, to the end of a deal wand—probably the roller from a piece of calico. Henchard rolled up his flag on the doorstep, put it under his arm, and went down the street.

Suddenly the taller members of the crowd turned their heads, and the shorter stood on tiptoe. It was said that the Royal *cortège* approached. The railway had stretched out an arm towards Casterbridge at this time, but had not reached it by several miles as yet;* so that the intervening distance, as well as the remainder of the journey, was to be traversed by road in the old fashion. People thus waited—the county families in their carriages, the masses on foot—and watched the far-stretching London highway to the ringing of bells and chatter of tongues.

From the background Elizabeth-Jane watched the scene. Some seats had been arranged from which ladies could witness the spectacle, and the front seat was occupied by Lucetta, the Mayor's wife, just at present. In the road under her eyes stood Henchard. She appeared so bright and pretty that, as it seemed, he was experiencing the momentary weakness of wishing for her notice. But he was far from attractive to a woman's eye, ruled as that is so largely by the superficies of things. He was not only a journeyman, unable to appear as he formerly had appeared, but he disdained to appear as well as he might. Everybody else, from the Mayor to the washerwoman, shone in new vesture according to means; but Henchard had doggedly retained the fretted and weather-beaten garments of bygone years.

Hence, alas, this occurred: Lucetta's eyes slid over him to this side and to that without anchoring on his features—as gaily dressed women's eyes will too often do on such occasions. Her manner signified quite plainly that she meant to know him in public no more.

But she was never tired of watching Donald, as he stood in animated converse with his friends a few yards off, wearing round his young neck the official gold chain with great square links, like that round the Royal unicorn.† Every trilling emotion that her husband showed as he talked had its reflex on her face and lips, which moved in little duplicates to his. She was living his part rather than her own, and cared for no one's situation but Farfrae's that day.

At length a man stationed at the furthest turn of the high road, namely, on the second bridge of which mention has been made, gave a signal; and the Corporation in their robes proceeded from the front of the Town Hall to the archway erected at the entrance to the town.

---

*The railroad arrived in Dorchester in 1847 (two years before the actual visit of Prince Albert).

†Figure on the royal coat of arms.

The carriages containing the Royal visitor and his suite arrived at the spot in a cloud of dust, a procession was formed, and the whole came on to the Town Hall at a walking pace.

This spot was the centre of interest. There were a few clear yards in front of the Royal carriage, sanded; and into this space a man stepped before any one could prevent him. It was Henchard. He had unrolled his private flag, and removing his hat he staggered to the side of the slowing vehicle, waving the Union Jack to and fro with his left hand, while he blandly held out his right to the Illustrious Personage.

All the ladies said with bated breath, "O, look there!" and Lucetta was ready to faint. Elizabeth-Jane peeped through the shoulders of those in front, saw what it was, and was terrified; and then her interest in the spectacle as a strange phenomenon got the better of her fear.

Farfrae, with Mayoral authority, immediately rose to the occasion. He seized Henchard by the shoulder, dragged him back, and told him roughly to be off. Henchard's eyes met his, and Farfrae observed the fierce light in them despite his excitement and irritation. For a moment Henchard stood his ground rigidly; then by an unaccountable impulse gave way and retired. Farfrae glanced to the ladies' gallery, and saw that his Calphurnia's* cheek was pale.

"Why—it is your husband's old patron!" said Mrs. Blowbody, a lady of the neighbourhood who sat beside Lucetta.

"Patron!" said Donald's wife with quick indignation.

"Do you say the man is an acquaintance of Mr. Farfrae's?" observed Mrs. Bath, the physician's wife, a new-comer to the town through her recent marriage with the doctor.

"He works for my husband," said Lucetta.

"Oh—is that all? They have been saying to me that it was through him your husband first got a footing in Casterbridge. What stories people will tell!"

"They will indeed. It was not so at all. Donald's genius would have enabled him to get a footing anywhere, without anybody's help! He would have been just the same if there had been no Henchard in the world!"

It was partly Lucetta's ignorance of the circumstances of Donald's

---

*Calpurnia is the worried wife of the soon-to-be-murdered Caesar in Shakespeare's *Julius Caesar* (act 2, scene 2).

arrival which led her to speak thus; partly the sensation that every-body seemed bent on snubbing her at this triumphant time. The in-cident had occupied but a few moments, but it was necessarily witnessed by the Royal Personage, who, however, with practised tact, affected not to have noticed anything unusual. He alighted, the Mayor advanced, the address was read; the Illustrious Personage replied, then said a few words to Farfrae, and shook hands with Lucetta as the Mayor's wife. The ceremony occupied but a few minutes, and the car-riages rattled heavily as Pharaoh's chariots* down Corn Street and out upon the Budmouth Road, in continuation of the journey coastward.

In the crowd stood Coney, Buzzford, and Longways. "Some dif-ference between him now and when he zung at the Dree Mariners," said the first. " 'Tis wonderful how he could get a lady of her quality to go snacks wi' en† en such quick time."

"True. Yet how folk do worship fine clothes! Now there's a bet-ter-looking woman than she that nobody notices at all, because she's akin to that hontish‡ fellow Henchard."

"I could worship ye, Buzz, for saying that," remarked Nance Mockridge. "I do like to see the trimming pulled off such Christmas candles. I am quite unequal to the part of villain myself, or I'd gi'e all my small silver to see that lady toppered.§ . . . And perhaps I shall soon," she added significantly.

"That's not a noble passiont for a 'oman to keep up," said Long-ways.

Nance did not reply, but every one knew what she meant. The ideas diffused by the reading of Lucetta's letters at Peter's Finger had condensed into a scandal, which was spreading like a miasmatic fog through Mixen Lane, and thence up the back streets of Casterbridge.

This mixed assemblage of idlers known to each other presently fell apart into two bands by a process of natural selection, the fre-quenters of Peter's Finger going off Mixen Lane-wards, where most of them lived, while Coney, Buzzford, Longways, and that connection remained in the street.

---

*The Egyptians pursued the fleeing Israelites in heavy chariots (Exodus 14:7–25).
†Marry him.
‡Haughty.
§Humbled.

"You know what's brewing down there, I suppose?" said Buzz-ford mysteriously to the others.

Coney looked at him. "Not the skimmity-ride?"

Buzzford nodded.

"I have my doubts if it will be carried out," said Longways. "If they are getting it up they are keeping it mighty close."

"I heard they were thinking of it a fortnight ago, at all events."

"If I were sure o't I'd lay information," said Longways emphatically. " 'Tis too rough a joke, and apt to wake riots in towns. We know that the Scotchman is a right enough man, and that his lady has been a right enough 'oman since she came here, and if there was anything wrong about her afore, that's their business, not ours."

Coney reflected. Farfrae was still liked in the community; but it must be owned that, as the Mayor and man of money, engrossed with affairs and ambitions, he had lost in the eyes of the poorer inhabitants something of that wondrous charm which he had had for them as a light-hearted penniless young man, who sang ditties as readily as the birds in the trees. Hence the anxiety to keep him from annoyance showed not quite the ardour that would have animated it in former days.

"Suppose we make inquiration into it, Christopher," continued Longways; "and if we find there's really anything in it, drop a letter to them most concerned, and advise 'em to keep out of the way?"

This course was decided on, and the group separated, Buzzford saying to Coney, "Come, my ancient friend; let's move on. There's nothing more to see here."

These well-intentioned ones would have been surprised had they known how ripe the great jocular plot really was. "Yes, to-night," Jopp had said to the Peter's party at the corner of Mixen Lane. "As a wind-up to the Royal visit the hit will be all the more pat by reason of their great elevation to-day."

To him, at least, it was not a joke, but a retaliation.

XXXVIII

THE PROCEEDINGS HAD BEEN brief—too brief—to Lucetta, whom an intoxicating *Weltlust** had fairly mastered; but they had brought her a great triumph nevertheless. The shake of the Royal hand still lingered in her fingers; and the chit-chat she had overheard, that her husband might possibly receive the honour of knighthood, though idle to a degree, seemed not the wildest vision; stranger things had occurred to men so good and captivating as her Scotchman was.

After the collision with the Mayor, Henchard had withdrawn behind the ladies' stand; and there he stood, regarding with a stare of abstraction the spot on the lapel of his coat where Farfrae's hand had seized it. He put his own hand there, as if he could hardly realize such an outrage from one whom it had once been his wont to treat with ardent generosity. While pausing in this half-stupefied state the conversation of Lucetta with the other ladies reached his ears; and he distinctly heard her deny him—deny that he had assisted Donald, that he was anything more than a common journeyman.

He moved on homeward, and met Jopp in the archway to the Bull Stake. "So you've had a snub," said Jopp.

"And what if I have?" answered Henchard sternly.

"Why, I've had one too, so we are both under the same cold shade." He briefly related his attempt to win Lucetta's intercession.

Henchard merely heard his story, without taking it deeply in. His own relation to Farfrae and Lucetta overshadowed all kindred ones. He went on saying brokenly to himself, "She has supplicated to me in her time; and now her tongue won't own me nor her eyes see me! . . . And he—how angry he looked. He drove me back as if I were a bull breaking fence. . . . I took it like a lamb, for I saw it could not be settled there. He can rub brine on a green wound!† . . . But he shall pay for it, and she shall be sorry. It must come to a tussle—face to face; and then we'll see how a coxcomb can front a man!"

Without further reflection the fallen merchant, bent on some wild purpose, ate a hasty dinner and went forth to find Farfrae. After being injured by him as a rival, and snubbed by him as a journey-

---

*Worldly pleasure (German).
†Fresh wound.

man, the crowning degradation had been reserved for this day—that he should be shaken at the collar by him as a vagabond in the face of the whole town.

The crowds had dispersed. But for the green arches which still stood as they were erected Casterbridge life had resumed its ordinary shape. Henchard went down Corn Street till he came to Farfrae's house, where he knocked, and left a message that he would be glad to see his employer at the granaries as soon as he conveniently could come there. Having done this he proceeded round to the back and entered the yard.

Nobody was present, for, as he had been aware, the labourers and carters were enjoying a half-holiday on account of the events of the morning—though the carters would have to return for a short time later on, to feed and litter down the horses. He had reached the granary steps and was about to ascend, when he said to himself aloud, "I'm stronger than he."

Henchard returned to a shed, where he selected a short piece of rope from several pieces that were lying about; hitching one end of this to a nail, he took the other in his right hand and turned himself bodily round, while keeping his arm against his side; by this contrivance he pinioned the arm effectively. He now went up the ladders to the top floor of the corn-stores.

It was empty except of a few sacks, and at the further end was the door often mentioned, opening under the cathead and chain that hoisted the sacks. He fixed the door open and looked over the sill. There was a depth of thirty or forty feet to the ground; here was the spot on which he had been standing with Farfrae when Elizabeth-Jane had seen him lift his arm, with many misgivings as to what the movement portended.

He retired a few steps into the loft and waited. From this elevated perch his eye could sweep the roofs round about, the upper parts of the luxurious chestnut trees, now delicate in leaves of a week's age, and the drooping boughs of the limes; Farfrae's garden and the green door leading therefrom. In course of time—he could not say how long—that green door opened and Farfrae came through. He was dressed as if for a journey. The low light of the nearing evening caught his head and face when he emerged from the shadow of the wall, warming them to a complexion of flame-colour. Henchard watched him with his mouth firmly set, the squareness of his jaw and the verticality of his profile being unduly marked.

Farfrae came on with one hand in his pocket, and humming a tune in a way which told that the words were most in his mind. They were those of the song he had sung when he arrived years before at the Three Mariners, a poor young man, adventuring for life and fortune, and scarcely knowing whitherward:—

> "And here's a hand, my trusty fiere,
> And gie's a hand o' thine."*

Nothing moved Henchard like an old melody. He sank back. "No; I can't do it!" he, gasped. "Why does the infernal fool begin that now!"

At length Farfrae was silent, and Henchard looked out of the loft door. "Will ye come up here?" he said.

"Ay, man," said Farfrae. "I couldn't see ye. What's wrang?"

A minute later Henchard heard his feet on the lowest ladder. He heard him land on the first floor, ascend and land on the second, begin the ascent to the third. And then his head rose through the trap behind.

"What are you doing up here at this time?" he asked, coming forward. "Why didn't ye take your holiday like the rest of the men?" He spoke in a tone which had just severity enough in it to show that he remembered the untoward event of the forenoon, and his conviction that Henchard had been drinking.

Henchard said nothing; but going back he closed the stair hatchway, and stamped upon it so that it went tight into its frame; he next turned to the wondering young man, who by this time observed that one of Henchard's arms was bound to his side.

"Now," said Henchard quietly, "we stand face to face—man and man: Your money and your fine wife no longer lift 'ee above me as they did but now, and my poverty does not press me down."

"What does it all mean?" asked Farfrae simply.

"Wait a bit, my lad. You should ha' thought twice before you affronted to extremes a man who had nothing to lose. I've stood your rivalry, which ruined me, and your snubbing, which humbled me; but your hustling, that disgraced me, I won't stand!"

---

*From Robert Burns's "Auld Lang Syne" (*fiere* means "friend").

Farfrae warmed a little at this. "Ye'd no business there," he said.

"As much as any one among ye! What, you forward stripling, tell a man of my age he'd no business there!" The anger-vein swelled in his forehead as he spoke.

"You insulted Royalty, Henchard; and 'twas my duty, as the chief magistrate, to stop you."

"Royalty be damned," said Henchard. "I am as loyal as you, come to that!"

"I am not here to argue. Wait till you cool doon, wait till you cool; and you will see things the same way as I do."

"You may be the one to cool first," said Henchard grimly. "Now this is the case. Here be we, in this four-square loft, to finish out that little wrestle you began this morning. There's the door, forty foot above ground. One of us two puts the other out by that door—the master stays inside. If he likes he may go down afterwards and give the alarm that the other has fallen out by accident—or he may tell the truth—that's his business. As the strongest man I've tied one arm to take no advantage of 'ee. D'ye understand? Then here's at 'ee!"

There was no time for Farfrae to do aught but one thing, to close with Henchard, for the latter had come on at once. It was a wrestling match, the object of each being to give his antagonist a back fall; and on Henchard's part, unquestionably, that it should be through the door.

At the outset Henchard's hold by his only free hand, the right, was on the left side of Farfrae's collar, which he firmly grappled, the latter holding Henchard by his collar with the contrary hand. With his right he endeavoured to get hold of his antagonist's left arm, which, however, he could not do, so adroitly did Henchard keep it in the rear as he gazed upon the lowered eyes of his fair and slim antagonist.

Henchard planted the first toe forward, Farfrae crossing him with his; and thus far the struggle had very much the appearance of the ordinary wrestling of those parts. Several minutes were passed by them in this attitude, the pair rocking and writhing like trees in a gale, both preserving an absolute silence. By this time their breathing could be heard. Then Farfrae tried to get hold of the other side of Henchard's collar, which was resisted by the larger man exerting all his force in a wrenching movement, and this part of the struggle ended by his forcing Farfrae down on his knees by sheer pressure of one of his muscular arms. Hampered as he was, however, he could not keep him there, and Farfrae finding his feet again the struggle proceeded as before.

By a whirl Henchard brought Donald dangerously near the precipice; seeing his position the Scotchman for the first time locked himself to his adversary, and all the efforts of that infuriated Prince of Darkness—as he might have been called from his appearance just now—were inadequate to lift or loosen Farfrae for a time. By an extraordinary effort he succeeded at last, though not until they had got far back again from the fatal door. In doing so Henchard contrived to turn Farfrae a complete somersault. Had Henchard's other arm been free it would have been all over with Farfrae then. But again he regained his feet, wrenching Henchard's arm considerably, and causing him sharp pain, as could be seen from the twitching of his face. He instantly delivered the younger man an annihilating turn by the left fore-hip, as it used to be expressed, and following up his advantage thrust him towards the door, never loosening his hold till Farfrae's fair head was hanging over the window-sill, and his arm dangling down outside the wall.

"Now," said Henchard between his gasps, "this is the end of what you began this morning. Your life is in my hands."

"Then take it, take it!" said Farfrae. "Ye've wished to long enough!"

Henchard looked down upon him in silence, and their eyes met. "O Farfrae!—that's not true!" he said bitterly. "God is my witness that no man ever loved another as I did thee at one time. . . . And now—though I came here to kill 'ee, I cannot hurt thee! Go and give me in charge—do what you will—I care nothing for what comes of me!"

He withdrew to the back part of the loft, loosened his arm, and flung himself into a corner upon some sacks, in the abandonment of remorse. Farfrae regarded him in silence; then went to the hatch and descended through it. Henchard would fain have recalled him; but his tongue failed in its task, and the young man's steps died on his ear.

Henchard took his full measure of shame and self-reproach. The scenes of his first acquaintance with Farfrae rushed back upon him—that time when the curious mixture of romance and thrift in the young man's composition so commanded his heart that Farfrae could play upon him as on an instrument. So thoroughly subdued was he that he remained on the sacks in a crouching attitude, unusual for a man, and for such a man. Its womanliness sat tragically on the figure of so stern a piece of virility. He heard a conversation below, the opening of the coach-house door, and the putting in of a horse, but took no notice.

Here he stayed till the thin shades thickened to opaque obscurity, and the loft-door became an oblong of gray light—the only visible shape around. At length he arose, shook the dust from his clothes wearily, felt his way to the hatch, and gropingly descended the steps till he stood in the yard.

"He thought highly of me once," he murmured. "Now he'll hate me and despise me for ever!"

He became possessed by an overpowering wish to see Farfrae again that night, and by some desperate pleading to attempt the well-nigh impossible task of winning pardon for his late mad attack. But as he walked towards Farfrae's door he recalled the unheeded doings in the yard while he had lain above in a sort of stupor. Farfrae he remembered had gone to the stable and put the horse into the gig; while doing so Whittle had brought him a letter; Farfrae had then said that he would not go towards Budmouth as he had intended—that he was unexpectedly summoned to Weatherbury, and meant to call at Mellstock on his way thither, that place lying but one or two miles out of his course.

He must have come prepared for a journey when he first arrived in the yard, unsuspecting enmity; and he must have driven off (though in a changed direction) without saying a word to any one on what had occurred between themselves.

It would therefore be useless to call at Farfrae's house till very late. There was no help for it but to wait till his return, though waiting was almost torture to his restless and self-accusing soul. He walked about the streets and outskirts of the town, lingering here and there till he reached the stone bridge of which mention has been made, an accustomed halting-place with him now. Here he spent a long time, the purl* of waters through the weirs meeting his ear, and the Casterbridge lights glimmering at no great distance off.

While leaning thus upon the parapet his listless attention was awakened by sounds of an unaccustomed kind from the town quarter. They were a confusion of rhythmical noises, to which the streets added yet more confusion by encumbering them with echoes. His first incurious thought that the clangour arose from the town band,

---

*The sound of running water.

engaged in an attempt to round off a memorable day by a burst of evening harmony, was contradicted by certain peculiarities of reverberation. But inexplicability did not rouse him to more than a cursory heed; his sense of degradation was too strong for the admission of foreign ideas; and he leant against the parapet as before.

XXXIX

WHEN FARFRAE DESCENDED OUT of the loft breathless from his encounter with Henchard, he paused at the bottom to recover himself. He arrived at the yard with the intention of putting the horse into the gig himself (all the men having a holiday), and driving to a village on the Budmouth Road. Despite the fearful struggle he decided still to persevere in his journey, so as to recover himself before going indoors and meeting the eyes of Lucetta. He wished to consider his course in a case so serious.

When he was just on the point of driving off Whittle arrived with a note badly addressed, and bearing the word "immediate" upon the outside. On opening it he was surprised to see that it was unsigned. It contained a brief request that he would go to Weatherbury that evening about some business which he was conducting there. Farfrae knew nothing that could make it pressing; but as he was bent upon going out he yielded to the anonymous request, particularly as he had a call to make at Mellstock which could be included in the same tour. Thereupon he told Whittle of his change of direction, in words which Henchard had overheard; and set out on his way. Farfrae had not directed his man to take the message indoors, and Whittle had not been supposed to do so on his own responsibility.

Now the anonymous letter was a well-intentioned but clumsy contrivance of Longways and other of Farfrae's men to get him out of the way for the evening, in order that the satirical mummery* should fall flat, if it were attempted. By giving open information they would have brought down upon their heads the vengeance of those among

---

*Mocking pantomime.

their comrades who enjoyed these boisterous old games; and therefore
the plan of sending a letter recommended itself by its indirectness.

For poor Lucetta they took no protective measure, believing with
the majority there was some truth in the scandal, which she would
have to bear as she best might.

It was about eight o'clock, and Lucetta was sitting in the drawing-
room alone. Night had set in for more than half an hour, but she had
not had the candles lighted, for when Farfrae was away she preferred
waiting for him by the firelight, and, if it were not too cold, keeping one
of the window-sashes a little way open that the sound of his wheels
might reach her ears early. She was leaning back in her chair, in a more
hopeful mood than she had enjoyed since her marriage. The day had
been such a success; and the temporary uneasiness which Henchard's
show of effrontery had wrought in her disappeared with the quiet disappearance of Henchard himself under her husband's reproof. The floating evidences of her absurd passion for him, and its consequences, had
been destroyed, and she really seemed to have no cause for fear.

The reverie in which these and other subjects mingled was disturbed by a hubbub in the distance, that increased moment by moment. It did not greatly surprise her, the afternoon having been given
up to recreation by a majority of the populace since the passage of the
Royal equipages. But her attention was at once riveted to the matter by
the voice of a maid-servant next door, who spoke from an upper window across the street to some other maid even more elevated than she.
"Which way be they going now?" inquired the first with interest.

"I can't be sure for a moment," said the second, "because of the
malter's chimbley.* O yes—I can see 'em. Well, I declare, I declare!"

"What, what?" from the first, more enthusiastically.

"They are coming up Corn Street after all! They sit back to back!"

"What—two of 'em—are there two figures?"

"Yes. Two images on a donkey, back to back, their elbows tied to
one another's! She's facing the head, and he's facing the tail."

"Is it meant for anybody particular?"

"Well—it mid be. The man has got on a blue coat and kerseymere leggings; he has black whiskers, and a reddish face. 'Tis a
stuffed figure, with a falseface."

---

*Chimney.

The din was increasing now—then it lessened a little.

"There—I shan't see, after all!" cried the disappointed first maid.

"They have gone into a back street—that's all," said the one who occupied the enviable position in the attic. "There—now I have got 'em all endways nicely!"

"What's the woman like? Just say, and I can tell in a moment if 'tis meant for one I've in mind."

"My—why—'tis dressed just as *she* was dressed when she sat in the front seat at the time the play-actors came to the Town Hall!"

Lucetta started to her feet; and almost at the instant the door of the room was quickly and softly opened. Elizabeth-Jane advanced into the firelight.

"I have come to see you," she said breathlessly. "I did not stop to knock—forgive me! I see you have not shut your shutters, and the window is open."

Without waiting for Lucetta's reply she crossed quickly to the window and pulled out one of the shutters. Lucetta glided to her side. "Let it be—hush!" she said peremptorily, in a dry voice, while she seized Elizabeth-Jane by the hand, and held up her finger. Their intercourse had been so low and hurried that not a word had been lost of the conversation without; which had thus proceeded:—

"Her neck is uncovered, and her hair in bands, and her back-comb in place; she's got on a puce silk, and white stockings, and coloured shoes."

Again Elizabeth-Jane attempted to close the window, but Lucetta held her by main force.

" 'Tis me!" she said, with a face pale as death. "A procession—a scandal—an effigy of me, and him!"

The look of Elizabeth betrayed that the latter knew it already.

"Let us shut it out!" coaxed Elizabeth-Jane, noting that the rigid wildness of Lucetta's features were growing yet more rigid and wild with the nearing of the noise and laughter. "Let us shut it out!"

"It is of no use!" she shrieked out. "He will see it, won't he? Donald will see it! He is just coming home—and it will break his heart—he will never love me any more—and O, it will kill me—kill me!"

Elizabeth-Jane was frantic now. "O, can't something be done to stop it?" she cried. "Is there nobody to do it—not one?"

She relinquished Lucetta's hands, and ran to the door. Lucetta herself, saying recklessly "I will see it!" turned to the window, threw up the sash, and went out upon the balcony. Elizabeth immediately followed her, and put her arm round her to pull her in. Lucetta's eyes were straight upon the spectacle of the uncanny revel, now advancing rapidly. The numerous lights around the two effigies threw them up into lurid distinctness; it was impossible to mistake the pair for other than the intended victims.

"Come in, come in," implored Elizabeth; "and let me shut the window!"

"She's me—she's me—even to the parasol—my green parasol!" cried Lucetta with a wild laugh as she stepped in. She stood motionless for one second—then fell heavily to the floor.

Almost at the instant of her fall the rude music of the skimmington ceased. The roars of sarcastic laughter went off in ripples, and the trampling died out like the rustle of a spent wind. Elizabeth was only indirectly conscious of this; she had rung the bell, and was bending over Lucetta, who remained convulsed on the carpet in the paroxysms of an epileptic seizure. She rang again and again, in vain; the probability being that the servants had all run out of the house to see more of the Dæmonic Sabbath than they could see within.

At last Farfrae's man, who had been agape on the door-step, came up; then the cook. The shutters, hastily pushed to by Elizabeth, were quite closed, a light was obtained, Lucetta carried to her room, and the man sent off for a doctor. While Elizabeth was undressing her she recovered consciousness; but as soon as she remembered what had passed the fit returned.

The doctor arrived with unhoped-for promptitude; he had been standing at his door, like others, wondering what the uproar meant. As soon as he saw the unhappy sufferer he said, in answer to Elizabeth's mute appeal, "This is serious."

"It is a fit," Elizabeth said.

"Yes. But a fit in the present state of her health means mischief. You must send at once for Mr. Farfrae. Where is he?"

"He has driven into the country, sir," said the parlour-maid; "to some place on the Budmouth Road. He's likely to be back soon."

"Never mind; he must be sent for, in case he should not hurry." The doctor returned to the bedside again. The man was despatched, and they soon heard him clattering out of the yard at the back.

Meanwhile Mr. Benjamin Grower, that prominent burgess of whom mention has been already made, hearing the din of cleavers, tongs, tambourines, kits, crouds, humstrums, serpents,* rams'-horns, and other historical kinds of music as he sat indoors in the High Street, had put on his hat and gone out to learn the cause. He came to the corner above Farfrae's, and soon guessed the nature of the proceedings; for being a native of the town he had witnessed such rough jests before. His first move was to search hither and thither for the constables; there were two in the town, shrivelled men whom he ultimately found in hiding up an alley yet more shrivelled than usual, having some not ungrounded fears that they might be roughly handled if seen.

"What can we two poor lammigers do against such a multitude!" expostulated Stubberd, in answer to Mr. Grower's chiding. " 'Tis tempting 'em to commit *felo de se*† upon us, and that would be the death of the perpetrator; and we wouldn't be the cause of a fellow-creature's death on no account, not we!"

"Get some help, then! Here, I'll come with you. We'll see what a few words of authority can do. Quick now; have you got your staves?"‡

"We didn't want the folk to notice us as law officers, being so short-handed, sir; so we pushed our Gover'ment staves up this water-pipe."

"Out with 'em, and come along, for Heaven's sake! Ah, here's Mr. Blowbody; that's lucky." (Blowbody was the third of the three borough magistrates.

"Well, what's the row?" said Blowbody. "Got their names—hey?"

"No. Now," said Grower to one of the constables, "you go with Mr. Blowbody round by the Old Walk and come up the street; and I'll go with Stubberd straight forward. By this plan we shall have 'em between us. Get their names only: no attack or interruption."

Thus they started. But as Stubberd with Mr. Grower advanced into Corn Street, whence the sounds had proceeded, they were surprised that no procession could be seen. They passed Farfrae's, and looked to the end of the street. The lamp flames waved, the Walk trees soughed, a few loungers stood about with their hands in their pockets. Everything was as usual.

---

*Kits: small fiddles; *crouds*: violins or fiddles; *humstrums*: hurdy-gurdies (instruments played by cranking a handle); *serpents*: coiled bass wind instruments.
†Suicide (Anglo-Latin); Stubberd means "murder."
‡Long wooden poles issued to constables as markers of their office.

"Have you seen a motley crowd making a disturbance?" Grower said magisterially to one of these in a fustian jacket, who smoked a short pipe and wore straps round his knees.

"Beg yer pardon, sir?" blandly said the person addressed, who was no other than Charl, of Peter's Finger. Mr. Grower repeated the words.

Charl shook his head to the zero of childlike ignorance. "No; we haven't seen anything; have we, Joe? And you was here afore I."

Joseph was quite as blank as the other in his reply.

"H'm—that's odd," said Mr. Grower. "Ah—here's a respectable man coming that I know by sight. Have you," he inquired, addressing the nearing shape of Jopp, "have you seen any gang of fellows making a devil of a noise—skimmington riding, or something of the sort?"

"O no—nothing, sir," Jopp replied, as if receiving the most singular news. "But I've not been far to-night, so perhaps——"

"Oh, 'twas here—just here," said the magistrate.

"Now I've noticed, come to think o't, that the wind in the Walk trees makes a peculiar poetical-like murmur to-night, sir; more than common; so perhaps 'twas that?" Jopp suggested, as he rearranged his hand in his greatcoat pocket (where it ingeniously supported a pair of kitchen tongs and a cow's horn, thrust up under his waistcoat).

"No, no, no,—d'ye think I'm a fool? Constable, come this way. They must have gone into the back street."

Neither in back street nor in front street, however, could the disturbers be perceived; and Blowbody and the second constable, who came up at this time, brought similar intelligence. Effigies, donkey, lanterns, band, all had disappeared like the crew of Comus.*

"Now," said Mr. Grower, there's only one thing more we can do. Get ye half-a-dozen helpers, and go in a body to Mixen Lane, and into Peter's Finger. I'm much mistaken if you don't find a clue to the perpetrators there."

The rusty-jointed executors of the law mustered assistance as soon as they could, and the whole party marched off to the lane of notoriety. It was no rapid matter to get there at night, not a lamp or glimmer of any sort offering itself to light the way, except an occasional pale radiance through some window-curtain, or through the chink of some door which could not be closed because of the smoky

---

*John Milton's 1634 masque, which features raucous revelers.

chimney within. At last they entered the inn boldly, by the till then bolted front-door, after a prolonged knocking of loudness commensurate with the importance of their standing.

In the settles of the large room, guyed to the ceiling by cords as usual for stability, an ordinary group sat drinking and smoking with statuesque quiet of demeanour. The landlady looked mildly at the invaders, saying in honest accents, "Good evening, gentlemen; there's plenty of room. I hope there's nothing amiss?"

They looked round the room. "Surely," said Stubberd to one of the men, "I saw you by now in Corn Street—Mr. Grower spoke to 'ee?"

The man, who was Charl, shook his head absently. "I've been here this last hour, hain't I, Nance?" he said to the woman who meditatively sipped her ale near him.

"Faith, that you have. I came in for my quiet supper-time half-pint, and you was here then, as was all the rest."

The other constable was facing the clock-case, where he saw reflected in the glass a quick motion by the landlady. Turning sharply, he caught her closing the oven-door.

"Something curious about that oven, ma'am!" he observed advancing, opening it, and drawing out a tambourine.

"Ah," she said apologetically, "that's what we keep here to use when there's a little quiet dancing. You see damp weather spoils it, so I put it there to keep it dry."

The constable nodded knowingly; but what he knew was nothing. Nohow could anything be elicited from this mute and inoffensive assembly. In a few minutes the investigators went out, and joining those of their auxiliaries who had been left at the door they pursued their way elsewhither.

XL

LONG BEFORE THIS TIME Henchard, weary of his ruminations on the bridge, had repaired towards the town. When he stood at the bottom of the street a procession burst upon his view, in the act of turning out of an alley just above him. The lanterns, horns, and multitude startled him; he saw the mounted images, and knew what it all meant.

They crossed the way, entered another street, and disappeared. He turned back a few steps and was lost in grave reflection, finally wending his way homeward by the obscure river-side path. Unable to rest there he went to his stepdaughter's lodging, and was told that Elizabeth-Jane had gone to Mrs. Farfrae's. Like one acting in obedience to a charm, and with a nameless apprehension, he followed in the same direction in the hope of meeting her, the roysterers having vanished. Disappointed in this he gave the gentlest of pulls to the doorbell, and then learnt particulars of what had occurred, together with the doctor's imperative orders that Farfrae should be brought home, and how they had set out to meet him on the Budmouth Road.

"But he has gone to Mellstock and Weatherbury!" exclaimed Henchard, now unspeakably grieved. "Not Budmouth way at all."

But, alas! for Henchard; he had lost his good name. They would not believe him, taking his words but as the frothy utterances of reck-lessness. Though Lucetta's life seemed at that moment to depend upon her husband's return (she being in great mental agony lest he should never know the unexaggerated truth of her past relations with Henchard), no messenger was despatched towards Weatherbury. Henchard, in a state of bitter anxiety and contrition, determined to seek Farfrae himself.

To this end he hastened down the town, ran along the eastern road over Durnover moor, up the hill beyond, and thus onward in the moderate darkness of this spring night till he had reached a second and almost a third hill about three miles distant. In Yalbury Bottom, or Plain, at the foot of the hill, he listened. At first nothing, beyond his own heart-throbs, was to be heard but the slow wind making its moan among the masses of spruce and larch of Yalbury Wood which clothed the heights on either hand; but presently there came the sound of light wheels whetting their felloes against the newly stoned patches of road, accompanied by the distant glimmer of lights.

He knew it was Farfrae's gig descending the hill from an inde-scribable personality in its noise, the vehicle having been his own till bought by the Scotchman at the sale of his effects. Henchard there-upon retraced his steps along Yalbury Plain, the gig coming up with him as its driver slackened speed between two plantations.

It was a point in the highway near which the road to Mellstock branched off from the homeward direction. By diverging to that village, as he had intended to do, Farfrae might probably delay his return by a couple of hours. It soon appeared that his intention was to do so still, the light swerving towards Cuckoo Lane, the by-road aforesaid. Farfrae's off gig-lamp flashed in Henchard's face. At the same time, Farfrae discerned his late antagonist.

"Farfrae—Mr. Farfrae!" cried the breathless Henchard, holding up his hand.

Farfrae allowed the horse to turn several steps into the branch lane before he pulled up. He then drew rein, and said "Yes?" over his shoulder, as one would towards a pronounced enemy.

"Come back to Casterbridge at once!" Henchard said. "There's something wrong at your house—requiring your return. I've run all the way here on purpose to tell ye."

Farfrae was silent, and at his silence Henchard's soul sank within him. Why had he not, before this, thought of what was only too obvious? He who, four hours earlier, had enticed Farfrae into a deadly wrestle stood now in the darkness of late night-time on a lonely road, inviting him to come a particular way, where an assailant might have confederates, instead of going his purposed way, where there might be a better opportunity of guarding himself from attack. Henchard could almost feel this view of things in course of passage through Farfrae's mind.

"I have to go to Mellstock," said Farfrae coldly, as he loosened his rein to move on.

"But," implored Henchard, "the matter is more serious than your business at Mellstock. It is—your wife! She is ill. I can tell you particulars as we go along."

The very agitation and abruptness of Henchard increased Farfrae's suspicion that this was a *ruse* to decoy him on to the next wood, where might be effectually compassed what, from policy or want of nerve, Henchard had failed to do earlier in the day. He started the horse.

"I know what you think," deprecated Henchard running after, almost bowed down with despair as he perceived the image of unscrupulous villainy that he assumed in his former friend's eyes. "But I am not what you think!" he cried hoarsely. "Believe me, Farfrae; I have come entirely on your own and your wife's account. She is in danger. I know no more; and they want you to come. Your man has gone the other way in a mistake. O Farfrae! don't mistrust me—I am a wretched man; but my heart is true to you still!"

Farfrae, however, did distrust him utterly. He knew his wife was with child, but he had left her not long ago in perfect health; and Henchard's treachery was more credible than his story. He had in his time heard bitter ironies from Henchard's lips, and there might be ironies now. He quickened the horse's pace, and had soon risen into the high country lying between there and Mellstock, Henchard's spasmodic run after him lending yet more substance to his thought of evil purposes.

The gig and its driver lessened against the sky in Henchard's eyes; his exertions for Farfrae's good had been in vain. Over this repentant sinner, at least, there was to be no joy in heaven.[24] He cursed himself like a less scrupulous Job,* as a vehement man will do when he loses self-respect, the last mental prop under poverty. To this he had come after a time of emotional darkness of which the adjoining woodland shade afforded inadequate illustration. Presently he began to walk back again along the way by which he had arrived. Farfrae should at all events have no reason for delay upon the road by seeing him there when he took his journey homeward later on.

Arriving at Casterbridge Henchard went again to Farfrae's house to make inquiries. As soon as the door opened anxious faces confronted his from the staircase, hall, and landing; and they all said in grievous disappointment, "O—it is not he!" The manservant, finding his mistake, had long since returned, and all hopes had been centred upon Henchard.

"But haven't you found him?" said the doctor.

"Yes. . . . I cannot tell 'ee!" Henchard replied as he sank down on a chair within the entrance. "He can't be home for two hours."

"H'm," said the surgeon, returning upstairs.

"How is she?" asked Henchard of Elizabeth, who formed one of the group.

"In great danger, father. Her anxiety to see her husband makes her fearfully restless. Poor woman—I fear they have killed her!"

Henchard regarded the sympathetic speaker for a few instants as if she struck him in a new light; then, without further remark, went out of the door and onward to his lonely cottage. So much for man's

---

*Job is silent for seven days before cursing his lot (Job 2:9–10 and 3:1–10).

rivalry, he thought. Death was to have the oyster, and Farfrae and himself the shells. But about Elizabeth-Jane; in the midst of his gloom she seemed to him as a pin-point of light. He had liked the look of her face as she answered him from the stairs. There had been affection in it, and above all things what he desired now was affection from anything that was good and pure. She was not his own; yet, for the first time, he had a faint dream that he might get to like her as his own,—if she would only continue to love him.

Jopp was just going to bed when Henchard got home. As the latter entered the door Jopp said, "This is rather bad about Mrs. Farfrae's illness."

"Yes," said Henchard shortly, though little dreaming of Jopp's complicity in the night's harlequinade, and raising his eyes just sufficiently to observe that Jopp's face was lined with anxiety.

"Somebody has called for you," continued Jopp, when Henchard was shutting himself into his own apartment. "A kind of traveller, or sea-captain of some sort."

"Oh?—who could he be?"

"He seemed a well-be-doing man—had grey hair and a broadish face; but he gave no name, and no message."

"Nor do I gi'e him any attention." And, saying this, Henchard closed his door.

The divergence to Mellstock delayed Farfrae's return very nearly the two hours of Henchard's estimate. Among the other urgent reasons for his presence had been the need of his authority to send to Budmouth for a second physician; and when at length Farfrae did come back he was in a state bordering on distraction at his misconception of Henchard's motives.

A messenger was despatched to Budmouth, late as it had grown; the night wore on, and the other doctor came in the small hours. Lucetta had been much soothed by Donald's arrival; he seldom or never left her side; and when, immediately after his entry, she had tried to lisp out to him the secret which so oppressed her, he checked her feeble words, lest talking should be dangerous, assuring her there was plenty of time to tell him everything.

Up to this time he knew nothing of the skimmington-ride. The dangerous illness and miscarriage of Mrs. Farfrae was soon rumoured through the town, and an apprehensive guess having been given as to its cause by the leaders in the exploit, compunction and fear threw a dead silence over all particulars of their orgie; while those immediately around Lucetta would not venture to add to her husband's distress by alluding to the subject.

What, and how much, Farfrae's wife ultimately explained to him of her past entanglement with Henchard, when they were alone in the solitude of that sad night, cannot be told. That she informed him of the bare facts of her peculiar intimacy with the corn-merchant became plain from Farfrae's own statements. But in respect of her subsequent conduct—her motive in coming to Casterbridge to unite herself with Henchard—her assumed justification in abandoning him when she discovered reasons for fearing him (though in truth her inconsequent passion for another man at first sight had most to do with that aban-donment)—her method of reconciling to her conscience a marriage with the second when she was in a measure committed to the first: to what extent she spoke of these things remained Farfrae's secret alone.

Besides the watchman who called the hours and weather in Cast-erbridge that night there walked a figure up and down Corn Street hardly less frequently. It was Henchard's, whose retiring to rest had proved itself a futility as soon as attempted; and he gave it up to go hither and thither, and make inquiries about the patient every now and then. He called as much on Farfrae's account as on Lucetta's, and on Elizabeth-Jane's even more than on either's. Shorn one by one of all other interests, his life seemed centring on the personality of the stepdaughter whose presence but recently he could not endure. To see her on each occasion of his inquiry at Lucetta's was a comfort to him.

The last of his calls was made about four o'clock in the morning, in the steely light of dawn. Lucifer* was fading into day across Durnover Moor, the sparrows were just alighting into the street, and the hens had begun to cackle from the outhouses. When within a few yards of Far-frae's he saw the door gently opened, and a servant raise her hand to the knocker, to untie the piece of cloth which had muffled it. He went across, the sparrows in his way scarcely flying up from the road-litter, so little did they believe in human aggression at so early a time.

"Why do you take off that?" said Henchard.

---

* The planet Venus, called the "morning star."

She turned in some surprise at his presence, and did not answer for an instant or two. Recognizing him, she said, "Because they may knock as loud as they will; she will never hear it any more."

XLI

HENCHARD WENT HOME. THE morning having now fully broke he lit his fire, and sat abstractedly beside it. He had not sat there long when a gentle footstep approached the house and entered the passage, a finger tapping lightly at the door. Henchard's face brightened, for he knew the motions to be Elizabeth's. She came into his room, looking wan and sad.

"Have you heard?" she asked. "Mrs. Farfrae! She is—dead! Yes, indeed—about an hour ago!"

"I know it," said Henchard. "I have but lately come in from there. It is so very good of 'ee, Elizabeth, to come and tell me. You must be so tired out, too, with sitting up. Now do you bide here with me this morning. You can go and rest in the other room; and I will call 'ee when breakfast is ready."

To please him, and herself—for his recent kindliness was winning a surprised gratitude from the lonely girl—she did as he bade her, and lay down on a sort of couch which Henchard had rigged up out of a settle in the adjoining room. She could hear him moving about in his preparations; but her mind ran most strongly on Lucetta, whose death in such fulness of life and amid such cheerful hopes of maternity was appallingly unexpected. Presently she fell asleep.

Meanwhile her stepfather in the outer room had set the breakfast in readiness; but finding that she dozed he would not call her; he waited on, looking into the fire and keeping the kettle boiling with housewifely care, as if it were an honour to have her in his house. In truth, a great change had come over him with regard to her, and he was developing the dream of a future lit by her filial presence, as though that way alone could happiness lie.

He was disturbed by another knock at the door, and rose to open it, rather deprecating a call from anybody just then. A stoutly built man stood on the doorstep, with an alien, unfamiliar air about his figure and bearing—an air which might have been called colonial by people of cosmopolitan experience. It was the man who had asked the way at Peter's Finger. Henchard nodded, and looked inquiry.

"Good morning, good morning," said the stranger with profuse heartiness. "Is it Mr. Henchard I am talking to?"

"My name is Henchard."

"Then I've caught'ee at home—that's right. Morning's the time for business, says I. Can I have a few words with you?"

"By all means," Henchard answered, showing the way in.

"You may remember me?" said his visitor, seating himself.

Henchard observed him indifferently, and shook his head.

"Well—perhaps you may not. My name is Newson."

Henchard's face and eyes seemed to die. The other did not notice it. "I know the name well," Henchard said at last, looking on the floor.

"I make no doubt of that. Well, the fact is, I've been looking for 'ee this fortnight past. I landed at Havenpool and went through Casterbridge on my way to Falmouth, and when I got there, they told me you had some years before been living at Casterbridge. Back came I again, and by long and by late I got here by coach, ten minutes ago. 'He lives down by the mill,' says they. So here I am. Now—that transaction between us some twenty years agone—'tis that I've called about. 'Twas a curious business. I was younger then than I am now, and perhaps the less said about it, in one sense, the better."

"Curious business! 'Twas worse than curious. I cannot even allow that I'm the man you met then. I was not in my senses, and a man's senses are himself."

"We were young and thoughtless," said Newson. "However, I've come to mend matters rather than open arguments. Poor Susan— hers was a strange experience."

"It was."

"She was a warm-hearted, home-spun woman. She was not what they call shrewd or sharp at all—better she had been."

"She was not."

"As you in all likelihood know, she was simpleminded enough to think that the sale was in a way binding. She was as guiltless o' wrongdoing in that particular as a saint in the clouds."

"I know it, I know it. I found it out directly," said Henchard, still with averted eyes. "There lay the sting o't to me. If she had seen it as what it was she would never have left me. Never! But how should she be expected to know? What advantages had she? None. She could write her own name, and no more."[25]

"Well, it was not in my heart to undeceive her when the deed was done," said the sailor of former days. "I thought, and there was not much vanity in thinking it, that she would be happier with me. She was fairly happy, and I never would have undeceived her till the day of her death. Your child died; she had another, and all went well. But a time came—mind me, a time always does come. A time came—it was some while after she and I and the child returned from America—when somebody she had confided her history to, told her my claim to her was a mockery, and made a jest of her belief in my right. After that she was never happy with me. She pined and pined, and socked* and sighed. She said she must leave me, and then came the question of our child. Then a man advised me how to act, and I did it, for I thought it was best. I left her at Falmouth, and went off to sea. When I got to the other side of the Atlantic there was a storm, and it was supposed that a lot of us, including myself, had been washed overboard. I got ashore at Newfoundland, and then I asked myself what I should do. 'Since I'm here, here I'll bide,' I thought to myself; ''twill be most kindness to her, now she's taken against me, to let her believe me lost; for,' I thought, 'while she supposes us both alive she'll be miserable; but if she thinks me dead she'll go back to him, and the child will have a home.' I've never returned to this country till a month ago, and I found that, as I had supposed, she went to you, and my daughter with her. They told me in Falmouth that Susan was dead. But my Elizabeth-Jane—where is she?"

"Dead likewise," said Henchard doggedly. "Surely you learnt that too?"

The sailor started up, and took an enervated pace or two down the room. "Dead!" he said, in a low voice. "Then what's the use of my money to me?"

Henchard, without answering, shook his head as if that were rather a question for Newson himself than for him.

"Where is she buried?" the traveller inquired.

"Beside her mother," said Henchard, in the same stolid tones.

"When did she die?"

"A year ago and more," replied the other without hesitation.

---

*Sighed deeply.

The sailor continued standing. Henchard never looked up from the floor. At last Newson said: "My journey hither has been for nothing! I may as well go as I came! It has served me right. I'll trouble you no longer."

Henchard heard the retreating footsteps of Newson upon the sanded floor, the mechanical lifting of the latch, the slow opening and closing of the door that was natural to a baulked or dejected man; but he did not turn his head. Newson's shadow passed the window. He was gone.

Then Henchard, scarcely believing the evidence of his senses, rose from his seat amazed at what he had done. It had been the impulse of a moment. The regard he had lately acquired for Elizabeth, the new sprung hope of his loneliness that she would be to him a daughter of whom he could feel as proud as of the actual daughter she still believed herself to be, had been stimulated by the unexpected coming of Newson to a greedy exclusiveness in relation to her; so that the sudden prospect of her loss had caused him to speak mad lies like a child, in pure mockery of consequences. He had expected questions to close in round him, and unmask his fabrication in five minutes; yet such questioning had not come. But surely they would come; Newson's departure could be but momentary; he would learn all by inquiries in the town; and return to curse him, and carry his last treasure away!

He hastily put on his hat, and went out in the direction that Newson had taken. Newson's back was soon visible up the road, crossing Bull Stake. Henchard followed; and saw his visitor stop at the King's Arms, where the morning coach which had brought him waited half-an-hour for another coach which crossed there. The coach Newson had come by was now about to move again. Newson mounted; his luggage was put in, and in a few minutes the vehicle disappeared with him.

He had not so much as turned his head. It was an act of simple faith in Henchard's words—faith so simple as to be almost sublime. The young sailor who had taken Susan Henchard on the spur of the moment and on the faith of a glance at her face, more than twenty years before, was still living and acting under the form of the grizzled traveller who had taken Henchard's words on trust so absolute as to shame him as he stood.

Was Elizabeth-Jane to remain his by virtue of this hardy invention of a moment? "Perhaps not for long," said he. Newson might

converse with his fellow-travellers, some of whom might be Casterbridge people; and the trick would be discovered.

This probability threw Henchard into a defensive attitude, and
instead of considering how best to right the wrong, and acquaint
Elizabeth's father with the truth at once, he bethought himself of
ways to keep the position he had accidentally won. Towards the
young woman herself his affection grew more jealously strong with
each new hazard to which his claim to her was exposed.

He watched the distant highway expecting to see Newson return
on foot, enlightened and indignant, to claim his child. But no figure
appeared. Possibly he had spoken to nobody on the coach, but buried
his grief in his own heart.

His grief!—what was it, after all, to that which he, Henchard,
would feel at the loss of her? Newson's affection, cooled by years, could
not equal his who had been constantly in her presence. And thus his
jealous soul speciously argued to excuse the separation of father and child.

He returned to the house half expecting that she would have vanished. No; there she was—just coming out from the inner room, the
marks of sleep upon her eyelids, and exhibiting a generally refreshed air.

"O father!" she said, smiling. "I had no sooner lain down than I
napped, though I did not mean to. I wonder I did not dream about poor
Mrs. Farfrae, after thinking of her so; but I did not. How strange it is that
we do not often dream of latest events, absorbing as they may be."

"I am glad you have been able to sleep," he said, taking her hand
with anxious proprietorship—an act which gave her a pleasant surprise.

They sat down to breakfast, and Elizabeth-Jane's thoughts reverted to Lucetta. Their sadness added charm to a countenance whose
beauty had ever lain in its meditative soberness.

"Father," she said, as soon as she recalled herself to the outspread
meal, "it is so kind of you to get this nice breakfast with your own
hands, and I idly asleep the while."

"I do it every day," he replied. "You have left me; everybody has
left me; how should I live but by my own hands."

"You are very lonely, are you not."

"Ay, child—to a degree that you know nothing of! It is my own
fault. You are the only one who has been near me for weeks. And you
will come no more."

"Why do you say that. Indeed I will, if you would like to see me."

Henchard signified dubiousness. Though he had so lately hoped that Elizabeth-Jane might again live in his house as daughter, he would not ask her to do so now. Newson might return at any moment, and what Elizabeth would think of him for his deception it were best to bear apart from her.

When they had breakfasted his stepdaughter still lingered, till the moment arrived at which Henchard was accustomed to go to his daily work. Then she arose, and with assurances of coming again soon went up the hill in the morning sunlight.

"At this moment her heart is as warm towards me as mine is towards her; she would live with me here in this humble cottage for the asking! Yet before the evening probably he will have come; and then she will scorn me!"

This reflection, constantly repeated by Henchard to himself, accompanied him everywhere through the day. His mood was no longer that of the rebellious, ironical, reckless misadventurer; but the leaden gloom of one who has lost all that can make life interesting, or even tolerable. There would remain nobody for him to be proud of, nobody to fortify him; for Elizabeth-Jane would soon be but as a stranger, and worse. Susan, Farfrae, Lucetta, Elizabeth—all had gone from him, one after one, either by his fault or by his misfortune.

In place of them he had no interest, hobby, or desire. If he could have summoned music to his aid his existence might even now have been borne; for with Henchard music was of regal power. The merest trumpet or organ tone was enough to move him, and high harmonies transubstantiated him. But hard fate had ordained that he should be unable to call up this Divine spirit in his need.

The whole land ahead of him was as darkness itself, there was nothing to come, nothing to wait for. Yet in the natural course of life he might possibly have to linger on earth another thirty or forty years—scoffed at; at best pitied.

The thought of it was unendurable.

To the east of Casterbridge lay moors and meadows through which much water flowed. The wanderer in this direction who should stand still for a few moments on a quiet night, might hear singular symphonies from these waters, as from a lampless orchestra, all playing in their sundry tones from near and far parts of the moor. At a hole in a rotten weir they executed a recitative; where a tributary brook fell over a stone breastwork they trilled cheerily; under an arch they performed a metallic cymballing; and at Durnover Hole they hissed. The spot at which their instrumentation rose loudest was a place called Ten Hatches, whence during high springs there proceeded a very fugue of sounds.

The river here was deep and strong at all times, and the hatches on this account were raised and lowered by cogs and a winch. A path led from the second bridge over the highway (so often mentioned) to these Hatches, crossing the stream at their head by a narrow plank-bridge. But after night-fall human beings were seldom found going that way, the path leading only to a deep reach of the stream called Blackwater, and the passage being dangerous.

Henchard, however, leaving the town by the east road, proceeded to the second, or stone bridge, and thence struck into this path of solitude, following its course beside the stream till the dark shapes of the Ten Hatches cut the sheen thrown upon the river by the weak lustre that still lingered in the west. In a second or two he stood beside the weir-hole where the water was at its deepest. He looked backwards and forwards, and no creature appeared in view. He then took off his coat and hat, and stood on the brink of the stream with his hands clasped in front of him.

While his eyes were bent on the water beneath there slowly became visible a something floating in the circular pool formed by the wash of centuries; the pool he was intending to make his death-bed. At first it was indistinct by reason of the shadow from the bank; but it emerged thence and took shape, which was that of a human body, lying stiff and stark upon the surface of the stream.

In the circular current imparted by the central flow the form was brought forward, till it passed under his eyes; and then he perceived with a sense of horror that it was himself. Not a man somewhat resembling him, but one in all respects his counterpart, his actual double, was floating as if dead in Ten Hatches Hole.

The sense of the supernatural was strong in this unhappy man, and he turned away as one might have done in the actual presence of an appalling miracle. He covered his eyes and bowed his head. Without looking again into the stream he took his coat and hat, and went slowly away.

Presently he found himself by the door of his own dwelling. To his surprise Elizabeth-Jane was standing there. She came forward, spoke, called him "father" just as before. Newson, then, had not even yet returned.

"I thought you seemed very sad this morning," she said, "so I have come again to see you. Not that I am anything but sad myself. But everybody and everything seem against you so; and I know you must be suffering."

How this woman divined things! Yet she had not divined their whole extremity.

He said to her, "Are miracles still worked, do ye think, Elizabeth? I am not a read man. I don't know so much as I could wish. I have tried to peruse and learn all my life; but the more I try to know the more ignorant I seem."

"I don't quite think there are any miracles nowadays," she said.

"No interference in the case of desperate intentions, for instance? Well, perhaps not, in a direct way. Perhaps not. But will you come and walk with me, and I will show 'ee what I mean?"

She agreed willingly, and he took her over the highway, and by the lonely path to Ten Hatches. He walked restlessly, as if some haunting shade, unseen of her, hovered round him and troubled his glance. She would gladly have talked of Lucetta, but feared to disturb him. When they got near the weir he stood still, and asked her to go forward and look into the pool, and tell him what she saw.

She went, and soon returned to him. "Nothing," she said.

"Go again," said Henchard, "and look narrowly."

She proceeded to the river brink a second time. On her return, after some delay, she told him that she saw something floating round and round there; but what it was she could not discern. It seemed to be a bundle of old clothes.

"Are they like mine?" asked Henchard.

"Well—they are. Dear me—I wonder if——Father, let us go away!"

"Go and look once more; and then we will get home."

She went back, and he could see her stoop till her head was close to the margin of the pool. She started up, and hastened back to his side.

"Well," said Henchard; "what do you say now?"

"Let us go home."

"But tell me—do—what is it floating there?"

"The effigy," she answered hastily. "They must have thrown it into the river higher up amongst the willows at Blackwater, to get rid of it in their alarm at discovery by the magistrates; and it must have floated down here."

"Ah—to be sure—the image o' me! But where is the other? Why that one only? . . . That performance of theirs killed her, but kept me alive!"

Elizabeth-Jane thought and thought of these words "kept me alive," as they slowly retraced their way to the town, and at length guessed their meaning. "Father!—I will not leave you alone like this!" she cried. "May I live with you, and tend upon you as I used to do? I do not mind your being poor. I would have agreed to come this morning, but you did not ask me."

"May you come to me?" he cried bitterly. "Elizabeth, don't mock me! If you only would come!"

"I will," said she.

"How will you forgive all my roughness in former days? You cannot!"

"I have forgotten it. Talk of that no more."

Thus she assured him, and arranged their plans for reunion; and at length each went home. Then Henchard shaved for the first time during many days, and put on clean linen, and combed his hair; and was as a man resuscitated thenceforward.

The next morning the fact turned out to be as Elizabeth-Jane had stated; the effigy was discovered by a cowherd, and that of Lucetta a little higher up in the same stream. But as little as possible was said of the matter, and the figures were privately destroyed.

Despite this natural solution of the mystery Henchard no less regarded it as an intervention that the figure should have been floating there. Elizabeth-Jane heard him say, "Who is such a reprobate as I! And yet it seems that even I be in Somebody's hand!"

XLII

BUT THE EMOTIONAL CONVICTION that he was in Somebody's hand began to die out of Henchard's breast as time slowly removed into distance the event which had given that feeling birth. The apparition of Newson haunted him. He would surely return.

Yet Newson did not arrive. Lucetta had been borne along the

churchyard path; Casterbridge had for the last time turned its regard upon her, before proceeding to its work as if she had never lived. But Elizabeth remained undisturbed in the belief of her relationship to Henchard, and now shared his home. Perhaps, after all, Newson was gone for ever.

In due time the bereaved Farfrae had learnt the, at least, proximate cause of Lucetta's illness and death; and his first impulse was naturally enough to wreak vengeance in the name of the law upon the perpetrators of the mischief. He resolved to wait till the funeral was over ere he moved in the matter. The time having come he reflected. Disastrous as the result had been, it was obviously in no way foreseen or intended by the thoughtless crew who arranged the motley procession. The tempting prospect of putting to the blush people who stand at the head of affairs—that supreme and piquant enjoyment of those who writhe under the heel of the same—had alone animated them, so far as he could see; for he knew nothing of Jopp's incitements. Other considerations were also involved. Lucetta had confessed everything to him before her death, and it was not altogether desirable to make much ado about her history, alike for her sake, for Henchard's, and for his own. To regard the event as an untoward accident seemed, to Farfrae, truest consideration for the dead one's memory, as well as best philosophy.

Henchard and himself mutually forbore to meet. For Elizabeth's sake the former had fettered his pride sufficiently to accept the small seed and root business which some of the Town Council, headed by Farfrae, had purchased to afford him a new opening. Had he been only personally concerned Henchard, without doubt, would have declined assistance even remotely brought about by the man whom he had so fiercely assailed. But the sympathy of the girl seemed necessary to his very existence; and on her account pride itself wore the garments of humility.

Here they settled themselves; and on each day of their lives Henchard anticipated her every wish with a watchfulness in which paternal regard was heightened by a burning jealous dread of rivalry. Yet that Newson would ever now return to Casterbridge to claim her as a daughter there was little reason to suppose. He was a wanderer and a stranger, almost an alien; he had not seen his daughter for several years; his affection for her could not in the nature of things be keen; other interests would probably soon obscure his recollections of her, and prevent any such renewal of inquiry into the past as would lead to a discovery that she was still a creature of the present. To satisfy his conscience somewhat Henchard repeated to himself that the lie which had retained for him the coveted treasure had not been deliberately told to that end, but had come from him as the last defiant word of a despair which took no thought of consequences. Furthermore he pleaded within himself that no Newson could love her as he loved her, or would tend her to his life's extremity as he was prepared to do cheerfully

Thus they lived on in the shop overlooking the churchyard, and nothing occurred to mark their days during the remainder of the year. Going out but seldom, and never on a market-day, they saw Donald Farfrae only at rarest intervals, and then mostly as a transitory object in the distance of the street. Yet he was pursuing his ordinary avocations, smiling mechanically to fellow-tradesmen, and arguing with bargainers—as bereaved men do after a while.

Time, "in his own grey style,"* taught Farfrae how to estimate his experience of Lucetta—all that it was, and all that it was not. There are men whose hearts insist upon a dogged fidelity to some image or cause thrown by chance into their keeping, long after their judgment has pronounced it no rarity—even the reverse, indeed; and without them the band of the worthy is incomplete. But Farfrae was not of those. It was inevitable that the insight, briskness, and rapidity of his nature should take him out of the dead blank which his loss threw about him. He could not but perceive that by the death of Lucetta he had exchanged a looming misery for a simple sorrow. After that revelation of her history, which must have come sooner or later in any circumstances, it was hard to believe that life with her would have been productive of further happiness.

But as a memory, notwithstanding such conditions, Lucetta's image still lived on with him, her weaknesses provoking only the gentlest criticism, and her sufferings attenuating wrath at her concealments to a momentary spark now and then.

By the end of a year Henchard's little retail seed and grain shop, not much larger than a cupboard, had developed its trade considerably, and the stepfather and daughter enjoyed much serenity in the pleasant, sunny corner in which it stood. The quiet bearing of one who brimmed with an inner activity characterized Elizabeth-Jane at this period. She

---

*Line 55 from Percy Bysshe Shelly's poem Epipsychidion (1821).

took long walks into the country two or three times a week, mostly in the direction of Budmouth. Sometimes it occurred to him that when she sat with him in the evening after these invigorating walks she was civil rather than affectionate; and he was troubled; one more bitter regret being added to those he had already experienced at having, by his severe censorship, frozen up her precious affection when originally offered.

She had her own way in everything now. In going and coming, in buying and selling, her word was law.

"You have got a new muff, Elizabeth," he said to her one day quite humbly.

"Yes; I bought it," she said.

He looked at it again as it lay on an adjoining table. The fur was of a glossy brown, and, though he was no judge of such articles, he thought it seemed an unusually good one for her to possess.

"Rather costly, I suppose, my dear, was it not?" he hazarded.

"It was rather above my figure," she said quietly. "But it is not showy."

"O no," said the netted lion, anxious not to pique her in the least.

Some little time after, when the year had advanced into another spring, he paused opposite her empty bedroom in passing it. He thought of the time when she had cleared out of his then large and handsome house in Corn Street, in consequence of his dislike and harshness, and he had looked into her chamber in just the same way. The present room was much humbler, but what struck him about it was the abundance of books lying everywhere. Their number and quality made the meagre furniture that supported them seem absurdly disproportionate. Some, indeed many, must have been recently purchased; and though he encouraged her to buy in reason, he had no notion that she indulged her innate passion so extensively in proportion to the narrowness of their income. For the first time he felt a little hurt by what he thought her extravagance, and resolved to say a word to her about it. But, before he had found the courage to speak, an event happened which set his thoughts flying in quite another direction.

The busy time of the seed trade was over; and the quiet weeks that preceded the hay-season had come—setting their special stamp upon Casterbridge by thronging the market with wood rakes, new waggons in yellow, green, and red, formidable scythes, and pitchforks of prong sufficient to skewer up a small family. Henchard, contrary to his wont, went out one Saturday afternoon towards the market-place, from a curious feeling that he would like to pass a few minutes on the spot of his former triumphs. Farfrae, to whom he was still a comparative stranger, stood a few steps below the Corn Exchange door—a usual position with him at this hour—and he appeared lost in thought about something he was looking at a little way off.

Henchard's eyes followed Farfrae's, and he saw that the object of his gaze was no sample-showing farmer, but his own stepdaughter, who had just come out of a shop over the way. She, on her part, was quite unconscious of his attention, and in this was less fortunate than those young women whose very plumes, like those of Juno's bird, are set with Argus eyes[26] whenever possible admirers are within ken.

Henchard went away, thinking that perhaps there was nothing significant after all in Farfrae's look at Elizabeth-Jane at that juncture. Yet he could not forget that the Scotchman had once shown a tender interest in her, of a fleeting kind. Thereupon promptly came to the surface that idiosyncrasy of Henchard's which had ruled his courses from the beginning and had mainly made him what he was. Instead of thinking that a union between his cherished stepdaughter and the energetic thriving Donald was a thing to be desired for her good and his own, he hated the very possibility.

Time had been when such instinctive opposition would have taken shape in action. But he was not now the Henchard of former days. He schooled himself to accept her will, in this as in other matters, as absolute and unquestionable. He dreaded lest an antagonistic word should lose for him such regard as he had regained from her by his devotion, feeling that to retain this under separation was better than to incur her dislike by keeping her near.

But the mere thought of such separation fevered his spirit much, and in the evening he said, with the stillness of suspense: "Have you seen Mr. Farfrae today, Elizabeth?"

Elizabeth-Jane started at the question; and it was with some confusion that she replied "No."

"Oh—that's right—that's right. . . . It was only that I saw him in the street when we both were there." He was wondering if her embarrassment justified him in a new suspicion—that the long walks which she had latterly been taking, that the new books which had so surprised him, had anything to do with the young man. She did not enlighten him, and lest silence should allow her to shape thoughts unfavourable to their present friendly relations, he diverted the discourse into another channel.

Henchard was, by original make, the last man to act stealthily, for good or for evil. But the *solicitus timor** of his love—the dependence upon Elizabeth's regard into which he had declined (or, in another sense, to which he had advanced)—denaturalized him. He would often weigh and consider for hours together the meaning of such and such a deed or phrase of hers, when a blunt settling question would formerly have been his first instinct. And now, uneasy at the thought of a passion for Farfrae which should entirely displace her mild filial sympathy with himself, he observed her going and coming more narrowly.

There was nothing secret in Elizabeth-Jane's movements beyond what habitual reserve induced; and it may at once be owned on her account that she was guilty of occasional conversations with Donald when they chanced to meet. Whatever the origin of her walks on the Budmouth Road, her return from those walks was often coincident with Farfrae's emergence from Corn Street for a twenty minutes' blow on that rather windy highway just to winnow the seeds and chaff out of him before sitting down to tea, as he said. Henchard became aware of this by going to the Ring, and, screened by its enclosure, keeping his eye upon the road till he saw them meet. His face assumed an expression of extreme anguish.

"Of her, too, he means to rob me!" he whispered. "But he has the right. I do not wish to interfere."

The meeting, in truth, was of a very innocent kind, and matters were by no means so far advanced between the young people as Henchard's jealous grief inferred. Could he have heard such conversation as passed he would have been enlightened thus much:

He.—"You like walking this way, Miss Henchard—and is it not so?" (uttered in his undulatory accents, and with an appraising, pondering gaze at her).

She.—"O yes. I have chosen this road latterly. I have no great reason for it."

He.—"But that may make a reason for others."

She (reddening).—"I don't know that. My reason, however, such as it is, is that I wish to get a glimpse of the sea every day."

---

*Anxious fear (Latin).

He.—"Is it a secret why?"

She (reluctantly).—"Yes."

He (with the pathos of one of his native ballads).—"Ah, I doubt there will be any good in secrets! A secret cast a deep shadow over my life. And well you know what it was."

Elizabeth admitted that she did, but she refrained from confessing why the sea attracted her. She could not herself account for it fully, not knowing the secret possibly to be that, in addition to early marine associations, her blood was a sailor's.

"Thank you for those new books, Mr. Farfrae," she added shyly. "I wonder if I ought to accept so many!"

"Ay! why not? It gives me more pleasure to get them for you, than you to have them!"

"It cannot!"

They proceeded along the road together till they reached the town, and their paths diverged.

Henchard vowed that he would leave them to their own devices, put nothing in the way of their courses, whatever they might mean. If he were doomed to be bereft of her, so it must be. In the situation which their marriage would create he could see no *locus standi** for himself at all. Farfrae would never recognize him more than superciliously; his poverty ensured that, no less than his past conduct. And so Elizabeth would grow to be a stranger to him, and the end of his life would be friendless solitude.

With such a possibility impending he could not help watchfulness. Indeed, within certain lines, he had the right to keep an eye upon her as his charge. The meetings seemed to become matters of course with them on special days of the week.

At last full proof was given him. He was standing behind a wall close to the place at which Farfrae encountered her. He heard the young man address her as "Dearest Elizabeth-Jane," and then kiss her, the girl looking quickly round to assure herself that nobody was near.

When they were gone their way Henchard came out from the wall, and mournfully followed them to Casterbridge. The chief looming trouble in this engagement had not decreased. Both Farfrae and Elizabeth-Jane, unlike the rest of the people, must suppose Elizabeth to be his

---

*Recognized position (Latin).

actual daughter, from his own assertion while he himself had the same belief; and though Farfrae must have so far forgiven him as to have no objection to own him as a father-in-law, intimate they could never be. Thus would the girl, who was his only friend, be withdrawn from him by degrees through her husband's influence, and learn to despise him.

Had she lost her heart to any other man in the world than the one he had rivalled, cursed, wrestled with for life in days before his spirit was broken, Henchard would have said, "I am content." But content with the prospect as now depicted was hard to acquire.

There is an outer chamber of the brain in which thoughts un-owned, unsolicited, and of noxious kind, are sometimes allowed to wander for a moment prior to being sent off whence they came. One of these thoughts sailed into Henchard's ken now.

Suppose he were to communicate to Farfrae the fact that his be-trothed was not the child of Michael Henchard at all—legally, no-body's child; how would that correct and leading townsman receive the information? He might possibly forsake Elizabeth-Jane, and then she would be her stepsire's own again.

Henchard shuddered, and exclaimed, "God forbid such a thing! Why should I still be subject to these visitations of the devil, when I try so hard to keep him away?"

XLIII

WHAT HENCHARD SAW THUS early was, naturally enough, seen at a little later date by other people. That Mr. Farfrae "walked with that bank-rupt Henchard's stepdaughter, of all women," became a common topic in the town, the simple perambulating term being used here-about to signify a wooing; and the nineteen superior young ladies of Casterbridge, who had each looked upon herself as the only woman capable of making the merchant Councilman happy, indignantly left off going to the church Farfrae attended, left off conscious manner-isms, left off putting him in their prayers at night amongst their blood relations; in short, reverted to their natural courses.

Perhaps the only inhabitants of the town to whom this looming choice of the Scotchman's gave unmixed satisfaction were the members of the philosophic party, which included Longways, Christopher Coney, Billy Wills, Mr. Buzzford, and the like. The Three Mariners having been, years before, the house in which they had witnessed the young man and woman's first and humble appearance on the Casterbridge stage, they took a kindly interest in their career, not unconnected, perhaps, with visions of festive treatment at their hands hereafter. Mrs. Stannidge, having rolled into the large parlour one evening and said that it was a wonder such a man as Mr. Farfrae, "a pillow* of the town," who might have chosen one of the daughters of the professional men or private residents, should stoop so low, Coney ventured to disagree with her.

"No, ma'am, no wonder at all. 'Tis she that's a stooping to he—that's my opinion. A widow man—whose first wife was no credit to him—what is it for a young perusing woman that's her own mistress and well liked? But as a neat patching up of things I see much good in it. When a man have put up a tomb of best marble-stone to the other one, as he've done, and weeped his fill, and thought it all over, and said to hisself, 'T'other took me in; I knowed this one first; she's a sensible piece for a partner, and there's no faithful woman in high life now;'—well, he may do worse than not to take her, if she's tender-inclined."

Thus they talked at the Mariners. But we must guard against a too liberal use of the conventional declaration that a great sensation was caused by the prospective event, that all the gossips' tongues were set wagging thereby, and so on, even though such a declaration might lend some *éclat* to the career of our poor only heroine. When all has been said about busy rumourers, a superficial and temporary thing is the interest of anybody in affairs which do not directly touch them. It would be a truer representation to say that Casterbridge (ever excepting the nineteen young ladies) looked up for a moment at the news, and withdrawing its attention, went on labouring and victualling, bringing up its children, and burying its dead, without caring a tittle for Farfrae's domestic plans.

Not a hint of the matter was thrown out to her stepfather by Elizabeth herself, or by Farfrae either. Reasoning on the cause of their reticence he concluded that, estimating him by his past, the throbbing pair were afraid to broach the subject, and looked upon him as an

---

*Malapropism for "pillar."

irksome obstacle whom they would be heartily glad to get out of the way. Embittered as he was against society, this moody view of himself took deeper and deeper hold of Henchard, till the daily necessity of facing mankind, and of them particularly Elizabeth-Jane, became well-nigh more than he could endure. His health declined; he became morbidly sensitive. He wished he could escape those who did not want him, and hide his head for ever.

But what if he were mistaken in his views, and there were no necessity that his own absolute separation from her should be involved in the incident of her marriage?

He proceeded to draw a picture of the alternative—himself living like a fangless lion about the back rooms of a house in which his stepdaughter was mistress; an inoffensive old man, tenderly smiled on by Elizabeth, and good-naturedly tolerated by her husband. It was terrible to his pride to think of descending so low; and yet, for the girl's sake he might put up with anything; even from Farfrae; even snubbings and masterful tongue-scourgings. The privilege of being in the house she occupied would almost outweigh the personal humiliation.

Whether this were a dim possibility or the reverse, the courtship—which it evidently now was—had an absorbing interest for him.

Elizabeth, as has been said, often took her walks on the Budmouth Road, and Farfrae as often made it convenient to create an accidental meeting with her there. Two miles out, a quarter of a mile from the highway, was the prehistoric fort called Mai Dun, of huge dimensions and many ramparts, within or upon whose enclosures a human being, as seen from the road, was but an insignificant speck. Hitherward Henchard often resorted, glass in hand, and scanned the hedgeless Via*—for it was the original track laid out by the legions of the Empire—to a distance of two or three miles, his object being to read the progress of affairs between Farfrae and his charmer.

One day Henchard was at this spot when a masculine figure came along the road from Budmouth, and lingered. Applying his telescope to his eye Henchard expected that Farfrae's features would be disclosed as usual. But the lenses revealed that to-day the man was not Elizabeth-Jane's lover.

It was one clothed as a merchant captain; and as he turned in his

---

*Highway (Latin).

scrutiny of the road he revealed his face. Henchard lived a lifetime the moment he saw it. The face was Newson's.

Henchard dropped the glass, and for some seconds made no other movement. Newson waited, and Henchard waited—if that could be called a waiting which was a transfixture. But Elizabeth-Jane did not come. Something or other had caused her to neglect her customary walk that day. Perhaps Farfrae and she had chosen another road for variety's sake. But what did that amount to? She might be here to-morrow, and in any case Newson, if bent on a private meeting and a revelation of the truth to her, would soon make his opportunity.

Then he would tell her not only of his paternity, but of the ruse by which he had been once sent away. Elizabeth's strict nature would cause her for the first time to despise her stepfather, would root out his image as that of an arch-deceiver, and Newson would reign in her heart in his stead.

But Newson did not see anything of her that morning. Having stood still awhile he at last retraced his steps, and Henchard felt like a condemned man who has a few hours' respite. When he reached his own house he found her there.

"O father!" she said innocently, "I have had a letter—a strange one—not signed. Somebody has asked me to meet him, either on the Budmouth Road at noon to-day, or in the evening at Mr. Farfrae's. He says he came to see me some time ago, but a trick was played him, so that he did not see me. I don't understand it; but between you and me I think Donald is at the bottom of the mystery, and that it is a relation of his who wants to pass an opinion on his choice. But I did not like to go till I had seen you. Shall I go?"

Henchard replied heavily, "Yes; go."

The question of his remaining in Casterbridge was for ever disposed of by this closing in of Newson on the scene. Henchard was not the man to stand the certainty of condemnation on a matter so near his heart. And being an old hand at bearing anguish in silence, and haughty withal, he resolved to make as light as he could of his intention, while immediately taking his measures.

He surprised the young woman whom he had looked upon as his all in this world by saying to her, as if he did not care about her more: "I am going to leave Casterbridge, Elizabeth-Jane."

"Leave Casterbridge!" she cried, "and leave—me?"

"Yes, this little shop can be managed by you alone as well as by us both; I don't care about shops and streets and folk—I would rather get into the country by myself, out of sight, and follow my own ways, and leave you to yours."

She looked down and her tears fell silently. It seemed to her that this resolve of his had come on account of her attachment and its probable result. She showed her devotion to Farfrae, however, by mastering her emotion and speaking out.

"I am sorry you have decided on this," she said with difficult firmness. "For I thought it probable—possible—that I might marry Mr. Farfrae some little time hence, and I did not know that you disapproved of the step!"

"I approve of anything you desire to do, Izzy," said Henchard huskily. "If I did not approve it would be no matter! I wish to go away. My presence might make things awkward in the future; and, in short, it is best that I go."

Nothing that her affection could urge would induce him to reconsider his determination; for she could not urge what she did not know—that when she should learn he was not related to her other than as a stepparent she would refrain from despising him, and that when she knew what he had done to keep her in ignorance she would refrain from hating him. It was his conviction that she would not so refrain; and there existed as yet neither word nor event which could argue it away.

"Then," she said at last, "you will not be able to come to my wedding; and that is not as it ought to be."

"I don't want to see it—I don't want to see it!" he exclaimed; adding more softly, "but think of me sometimes in your future life—you'll do that, Izzy?—think of me when you are living as the wife of the richest, the foremost man in the town, and don't let my sins, when you know them all, cause 'ee to quite forget that though I loved 'ee late I loved 'ee well."

"It is because of Donald!" she sobbed.

"I don't forbid you to marry him," said Henchard. "Promise not to quite forget me when——" He meant when Newson should come.

She promised mechanically, in her agitation; and the same evening at dusk Henchard left the town, to whose development he had been one of the chief stimulants for many years. During the day he had bought a new tool-basket, cleaned up his old hay-knife and wimble, set himself up in fresh leggings, knee-naps* and corduroys, and in other ways gone back to the working clothes of his young manhood, discarding for ever the shabby-genteel suit of cloth and rusty silk hat that since his decline had characterized him in the Casterbridge street as a man who had seen better days.

He went secretly and alone, not a soul of the many who had known him being aware of his departure. Elizabeth-Jane accompanied him as far as the second bridge on the highway—for the hour of her appointment with the unguessed visitor at Farfrae's had not yet arrived—and parted from him with unfeigned wonder and sorrow, keeping him back a minute or two before finally letting him go. She watched his form diminish across the moor, the yellow rush-basket at his back moving up and down with each tread, and the creases behind his knees coming and going alternately till she could no longer see them. Though she did not know it Henchard formed at this moment much the same picture as he had presented when entering Casterbridge for the first time nearly a quarter of a century before; except, to be sure, that the serious addition to his years had considerably lessened the spring of his stride, that his state of hopelessness had weakened him, and imparted to his shoulders, as weighted by the basket, a perceptible bend.

He went on till he came to the first milestone, which stood in the bank, half way up a steep hill. He rested his basket on the top of the stone, placed his elbows on it, and gave way to a convulsive twitch, which was worse than a sob, because it was so hard and so dry.

"If I had only got her with me—if I only had!" he said. "Hard work would be nothing to me then! But that was not to be. I— Cain—go alone as I deserve—an outcast and a vagabond. But my punishment is not greater than I can bear!"†

He sternly subdued his anguish, shouldered his basket, and went on.

Elizabeth, in the meantime, had breathed him a sigh, recovered her equanimity, and turned her face to Casterbridge. Before she had reached the first house she was met in her walk by Donald Farfrae. This was evidently not their first meeting that day; they joined hands without ceremony, and Farfrae anxiously asked, "And is he gone— and did you tell him?—I mean of the other matter—not of ours."

---

*Pads to protect the knees.

†In Genesis 4:13, Cain claims that his punishment is greater than he can bear.

"He is gone; and I told him all I knew of your friend. Donald, who is he?"

"Well, well, dearie; you will know soon about that. And Mr. Henchard will hear of it if he does not go far."

"He will go far—he's bent upon getting out of sight and sound!"

She walked beside her lover, and when they reached the Crossways, or Bow, turned with him into Corn Street instead of going straight on to her own door. At Farfrae's house they stopped and went in.

Farfrae flung open the door of the ground-floor sitting-room, saying, "There he is waiting for you," and Elizabeth entered. In the armchair sat the broad-faced genial man who had called on Henchard on a memorable morning between one and two years before this time, and whom the latter had seen mount the coach and depart within half-an-hour of his arrival. It was Richard Newson. The meeting with the light-hearted father from whom she had been separated half-a-dozen years, as if by death, need hardly be detailed. It was an affecting one, apart from the question of paternity. Henchard's departure was in a moment explained. When the true facts came to be handled the difficulty of restoring her to her old belief in Newson was not so great as might have seemed likely, for Henchard's conduct itself was a proof that those facts were true. Moreover, she had grown up under Newson's paternal care; and even had Henchard been her father in nature, this father in early domiciliation might almost have carried the point against him, when the incidents of her parting with Henchard had a little worn off.

Newson's pride in what she had grown up to be was more than he could express. He kissed her again and again.

"I've saved you the trouble to come and meet me—ha-ha!" said Newson. "The fact is that Mr. Farfrae here, he said, 'Come up and stop with me for a day or two, Captain Newson, and I'll bring her round.' 'Faith,' says I, 'so I will'; and here I am."

"Well, Henchard is gone," said Farfrae, shutting the door. "He has done it all voluntarily, and, as I gather from Elizabeth, he has been very nice with her. I was got rather uneasy; but all is as it should be, and we will have no more deefficulties at all."

"Now, that's very much as I thought," said Newson, looking into the face of each by turns. "I said to myself, ay, a hundred times, when I tried to get a peep at her unknown to herself—'Depend upon it, 'tis best that I should live on quiet for a few days like this till something turns up for the better.' I now know you are all right, and what can I wish for more?"

"Well, Captain Newson, I will be glad to see ye here every day now, since it can do no harm," said Farfrae. "And what I've been thinking is that the wedding may as well be kept under my own roof, the house being large, and you being in lodgings by yourself—so that a great deal of trouble and expense would be saved ye'—and 'tis a convenience when a couple's married not to hae far to go to get home!"

"With all my heart," said Captain Newson; "since, as ye say, it can do no harm, now poor Henchard's gone; though I wouldn't have done it otherwise, or put myself in his way at all; for I've already in my lifetime been an intruder into his family quite as far as politeness can be expected to put up with. But what do the young woman say herself about it? Elizabeth, my child, come and hearken to what we be talking about, and not bide staring out o' the window as if ye didn't hear."

"Donald and you must settle it," murmured Elizabeth, still keeping up a scrutinizing gaze at some small object in the street.

"Well, then," continued Newson, turning anew to Farfrae with a face expressing thorough entry into the subject, "that's how we'll have it. And, Mr. Farfrae, as you provide so much, and houseroom, and all that, I'll do my part in the drinkables, and see to the rum and schiedam*—maybe a dozen jars will be sufficient?—as many of the folk will be ladies, and perhaps they won't drink hard enough to make a high average in the reckoning? But you know best. I've provided for men and shipmates times enough, but I'm as ignorant as a child how many glasses of grog a woman, that's not a drinking woman, is expected to consume at these ceremonies?"

"Oh, none—we'll no want much of that—O no!" said Farfrae, shaking his head with appalled gravity. "Do you leave all to me."

When they had gone a little further in these particulars Newson, leaning back in his chair and smiling reflectively at the ceiling, said, "I've never told ye, or have I, Mr. Farfrae, how Henchard put me off the scent that time?"

He expressed ignorance of what the Captain alluded to.

---

*Dutch gin, named for a town near Amsterdam.

"Ah, I thought I hadn't. I resolved that I would not, I remember, not to hurt the man's name. But now he's gone I can tell ye. Why, I came to Casterbridge nine or ten months before that day last week that I found ye out. I had been here twice before then. The first time I passed through the town on my way westward, not knowing Elizabeth lived here. Then hearing at some place—I forget where—that a man of the name of Henchard had been mayor here, I came back, and called at his house one morning. The old rascal!—he said Elizabeth-Jane had died years ago."

Elizabeth now gave earnest heed to his story.

"Now, it never crossed my mind that the man was selling me a packet," continued Newson. "And, if you'll believe me, I was that upset, that I went back to the coach that had brought me, and took passage onward without lying in the town half-an-hour. Ha-ha!—'twas a good joke, and well carried out, and I give the man credit for't!"

Elizabeth-Jane was amazed at the intelligence. "A joke?—O no!" she cried. "Then he kept you from me, father, all those months, when you might have been here?"

The father admitted that such was the case.

"He ought not to have done it!" said Farfrae.

Elizabeth sighed. "I said I would never forget him. But O! I think I ought to forget him now!"

Newson, like a good many rovers and sojourners among strange men and strange moralities, failed to perceive the enormity of Henchard's crime, notwithstanding that he himself had been the chief sufferer therefrom. Indeed, the attack upon the absent culprit waxing serious, he began to take Henchard's part.

"Well, 'twas not ten words that he said, after all," Newson pleaded. "And how could he know that I should be such a simpleton as to believe him? 'Twas as much my fault as his, poor fellow!"

"No," said Elizabeth-Jane firmly, in her revulsion of feeling. "He knew your disposition—you always were so trusting, father; I've heard my mother say so hundreds of times—and he did it to wrong you. After weaning me from you these five years by saying he was my father, he should not have done this."

Thus they conversed; and there was nobody to set before Elizabeth any extenuation of the absent one's deceit. Even had he been present Henchard might scarce have pleaded it, so little did he value himself or his good name.

"Well, well—never mind—it is all over and past," said Newson good-naturedly. "Now, about this wedding again."

XLIV

MEANWHILE, THE MAN OF their talk had pursued his solitary way eastward till weariness overtook him, and he looked about for a place to rest. His heart was so exacerbated at parting from the girl that he could not face an inn, or even a household of the most humble kind; and entering a field he lay down under a wheatrick, feeling no want of food. The very heaviness of his soul caused him to sleep profoundly.

The bright autumn sun shining into his eyes across the stubble awoke him the next morning early. He opened his basket and ate for his breakfast what he had packed for his supper; and in doing so overhauled the remainder of his kit. Although everything he brought necessitated carriage at his own back, he had secreted among his tools a few of Elizabeth-Jane's cast-off belongings, in the shape of gloves, shoes, a scrap of her handwriting, and the like; and in his pocket he carried a curl of her hair. Having looked at these things he closed them up again, and went onward.

During five consecutive days Henchard's rush basket rode along upon his shoulder between the highway hedges, the new yellow of the rushes catching the eye of an occasional field-labourer as he glanced through the quickset,* together with the wayfarer's hat and head, and, down-turned face, over which the twig shadows moved in endless procession. It now became apparent that the direction of his journey was Weydon-Priors, which he reached on the afternoon of the sixth day.

The renowned hill whereon the annual fair had been held for so many generations was now bare of human beings, and almost of aught besides. A few sheep grazed thereabout, but these ran off when Henchard halted upon the summit. He deposited his basket upon the turf, and looked about with sad curiosity; till he discovered the road

---

*Hedge.

by which his wife and himself had entered on the upland so memorable to both, five-and-twenty years before.

"Yes, we came up that way," he said, after ascertaining his bearings. "She was carrying the baby, and I was reading a ballet-sheet. Then we crossed about here—she so sad and weary, and I speaking to her hardly at all, because of my cursed pride and mortification at being poor. Then we saw the tent—that must have stood more this way." He walked to another spot; it was not really where the tent had stood, but it seemed so to him. "Here we went in, and here we sat down. I faced this way. Then I drank, and committed my crime. It must have been just on that very pixy-ring* that she was standing when she said her last words to me before going off with him; I can hear their sound now, and the sound of her sobs: 'O Mike! I've lived with thee all this while, and had nothing but temper. Now I'm no more to 'ee—I'll try my luck elsewhere.'"

He experienced not only the bitterness of a man who finds, in looking back upon an ambitious course, that what he has sacrificed in sentiment was worth as much as what he has gained in substance; but the superadded bitterness of seeing his very recantation nullified. He had been sorry for all this long ago; but his attempts to replace ambition by love had been as fully foiled as his ambition itself. His wronged wife had foiled them by a fraud so grandly simple as to be almost a virtue. It was an odd sequence that out of all this tampering with social law came that flower of Nature, Elizabeth. Part of his wish to wash his hands of life arose from his perception of its contrarious inconsistencies—of Nature's jaunty readiness to support unorthodox social principles.

He intended to go on from this place—visited as an act of penance—into another part of the country altogether. But he could not help thinking of Elizabeth, and the quarter of the horizon in which she lived. Out of this it happened that the centrifugal tendency imparted by weariness of the world was counteracted by the centripetal influence of his love for his stepdaughter. As a consequence, instead of following a straight course yet further away from Casterbridge, Henchard gradually, almost unconsciously, deflected from that right line of his first intention; till, by degrees, his wandering, like that of the Canadian woodsman, became part of a circle of which

---

*Discolored circle in the grass, supposed to be caused by the dancing of fairies.

Casterbridge formed the centre. In ascending any particular hill he ascertained the bearings as nearly as he could by means of the sun, moon, or stars, and settled in his mind the exact direction in which Casterbridge and Elizabeth-Jane lay. Sneering at himself for his weakness he yet every hour—nay, every few minutes—conjectured her actions for the time being—her sitting down and rising up, her goings and comings, till thought of Newson's and Farfrae's counter-influence would pass like a cold blast over a pool, and efface her image. And then he would say of himself, "O you fool! All this about a daughter who is no daughter of thine!"

At length he obtained employment at his own occupation of hay-trusser, work of that sort being in demand at this autumn time. The scene of his hiring was a pastoral farm near the old western highway, whose course was the channel of all such communications as passed between the busy centres of novelty and the remote Wessex boroughs. He had chosen the neighbourhood of this artery from a sense that, situated here, though at a distance of fifty miles, he was virtually nearer to her whose welfare was so dear than he would be at a roadless spot only half as remote.

And thus Henchard found himself again on the precise standing which he had occupied a quarter of a century before. Externally there was nothing to hinder his making another start on the upward slope, and by his new lights achieving higher things than his soul in its half-formed state had been able to accomplish. But the ingenious machinery contrived by the Gods for reducing human possibilities of amelioration to a minimum—which arranges that wisdom to do shall come *pari passu** with the departure of zest for doing—stood in the way of all that. He had no wish to make an arena a second time of a world that had become a mere painted scene to him.

Very often, as his hay-knife crunched down among the sweet-smelling grassy stems, he would survey mankind and say to himself: "Here and everywhere be folk dying before their time like frosted leaves, though wanted by their families, the country, and the world; while I, an outcast, an encumberer of the ground, wanted by nobody, and despised by all, live on against my will!"

He often kept an eager ear upon the conversation of those who

---

*At an equal pace (Latin).

passed along the road—not from a general curiosity by any means—
but in the hope that among these travellers between Casterbridge and
London some would, sooner or later, speak of the former place. The
distance, however, was too great to lend much probability to his desire; and the highest result of his attention to wayside words was that
he did indeed hear the name "Casterbridge" uttered one day by the
driver of a road-waggon. Henchard ran to the gate of the field he
worked in, and hailed the speaker, who was a stranger.

"Yes—I've come from there, maister," he said, in answer to Henchard's inquiry. "I trade up and down, ye know; though, what with
this travelling without horses that's getting so common, my work
will soon be done."

"Anything moving in the old place, mid I ask?"

"All the same as usual."

"I've heard that Mr. Farfrae, the late Mayor, is thinking of getting
married. Now is that true or not?"

"I couldn't say for the life o' me. O no, I should think not."

"But yes, John—you forget," said a woman inside the waggon-tilt.
"What were them packages we carr'd there at the beginning o' the week?
Surely they said a wedding was coming off soon—on Martin's Day?"*

The man declared he remembered nothing about it; and the
waggon went on jangling over the hill.

Henchard was convinced that the woman's memory served her
well. The date was an extremely probable one, there being no reason
for delay on either side. He might, for that matter, write and inquire
of Elizabeth; but his instinct for sequestration had made the course
difficult. Yet before he left her she had said that for him to be absent
from her wedding was not as she wished it to be.

The remembrance would continually revive in him now that it
was not Elizabeth and Farfrae who had driven him away from them,
but his own haughty sense that his presence was no longer desired.
He had assumed the return of Newson without absolute proof that
the Captain meant to return; still less that Elizabeth-Jane would welcome him; and with no proof whatever that if he did return he would
stay. What if he had been mistaken in his views; if there had been no
necessity that his own absolute separation from her he loved should

*Martinmas, a November holiday.

be involved in these untoward incidents? To make one more attempt to be near her: to go back; to see her, to plead his cause before her, to ask forgiveness for his fraud; to endeavour strenuously to hold his own in her love; it was worth the risk of repulse, ay, of life itself.

But how to initiate this reversal of all his former resolves without causing husband and wife to despise him for his inconsistency was a question which made him tremble and brood.

He cut and cut his trusses two days more, and then he concluded his hesitancies by a sudden reckless determination to go to the wedding festivity. Neither writing nor message would be expected of him. She had regretted his decision to be absent—his unanticipated presence would fill the little unsatisfied corner that would probably have place in her just heart without him.

To intrude as little of his personality as possible upon a gay event with which that personality could show nothing in keeping, he decided not to make his appearance till evening—when stiffness would have worn off, and a gentle wish to let bygones be bygones would exercise its sway in all hearts.

He started on foot, two mornings before St. Martin's-tide, allowing himself about sixteen miles to perform for each of the three days' journey, reckoning the wedding-day as one. There were only two towns, Melchester and Shottsford, of any importance along his course, and at the latter he stopped on the second night, not only to rest, but to prepare himself for the next evening.

Possessing no clothes but the working suit he stood in—now stained and distorted by their two months of hard usage, he entered a shop to make some purchases which should put him, externally at any rate, a little in harmony with the prevailing tone of the morrow. A rough yet respectable coat and hat, a new shirt and neck-cloth, were the chief of these; and having satisfied himself that in appearance at least he would not now offend her, he proceeded to the more interesting particular of buying her some present.

What should that present be? He walked up and down the street, regarding dubiously the display in the shop windows, from a gloomy sense that what he might most like to give her would be beyond his miserable pocket. At length a caged goldfinch met his eye. The cage was a plain and small one, the shop humble, and on inquiry he concluded he could afford the modest sum asked. A sheet of newspaper was tied round the little creature's wire prison, and with the wrapped up cage in his hand Henchard sought a lodging for the night.

Next day he set out upon the last stage, and was soon within the district which had been his dealing ground in bygone years. Part of the distance he travelled by carrier, seating himself in the darkest corner at the back of that trader's van; and as the other passengers, mainly women going short journeys, mounted and alighted in front of Henchard, they talked over much local news, not the least portion of this being the wedding then in course of celebration at the town they were nearing. It appeared from their accounts that the town band had been hired for the evening party, and, lest the convivial instincts of that body should get the better of their skill, the further step had been taken of engaging the string band from Budmouth, so that there would be a reserve of harmony to fall back upon in case of need.

He heard, however, but few particulars beyond those known to him already, the incident of the deepest interest on the journey being the soft pealing of the Casterbridge bells, which reached the travellers' ears while the van paused on the top of Yalbury Hill to have the drag* lowered. The time was just after twelve o'clock.

Those notes were a signal that all had gone well; that there had been no slip 'twixt cup and lip in this case; that Elizabeth-Jane and Donald Farfrae were man and wife.

Henchard did not care to ride any further with his chattering companions after hearing this sound. Indeed, it quite unmanned him; and in pursuance of his plan of not showing himself in Casterbridge street till evening, lest he should mortify Farfrae and his bride, he alighted here, with his bundle and bird-cage, and was soon left as a lonely figure on the broad white highway.

It was the hill near which he had waited to meet Farfrae, almost two years earlier, to tell him of the serious illness of his wife Lucetta. The place was unchanged; the same larches sighed the same notes; but Farfrae had another wife—and, as Henchard knew, a better one. He only hoped that Elizabeth-Jane had obtained a better home than had been hers at the former time.

He passed the remainder of the afternoon in a curious high-strung condition, unable to do much but think of the approaching

---

*Iron shoe used as a brake.

meeting with her, and sadly satirize himself for his emotions thereon, as a Samson shorn.* Such an innovation on Casterbridge customs as a flitting of bridegroom and bride from the town immediately after the ceremony, was not likely, but if it should have taken place he would wait till their return. To assure himself on this point he asked a market-man when near the borough if the newly-married couple had gone away, and was promptly informed that they had not; they were at that hour, according to all accounts, entertaining a houseful of guests at their home in Corn Street.

Henchard dusted his boots, washed his hands at the river-side, and proceeded up the town under the feeble lamps. He need have made no inquiries beforehand, for on drawing near Farfrae's residence it was plain to the least observant that festivity prevailed within, and that Donald himself shared it, his voice being distinctly audible in the street, giving strong expression to a song of his dear native country that he loved so well as never to have revisited it. Idlers were standing on the pavement in front; and wishing to escape the notice of these Henchard passed quickly on to the door.

It was wide open; the hall was lighted extravagantly, and people were going up and down the stairs. His courage failed him; to enter footsore, laden, and poorly dressed into the midst of such resplendency was to bring needless humiliation upon her he loved, if not to court repulse from her husband. Accordingly he went round into the street at the back that he knew so well, entered the garden, and came quietly into the house through the kitchen, temporarily depositing the bird and cage under a bush outside, to lessen the awkwardness of his arrival.

Solitude and sadness had so emolliated† Henchard that he now feared circumstances he would formerly have scorned, and he began to wish that he had not taken upon himself to arrive at such a juncture. However, his progress was made unexpectedly easy by his discovering alone in the kitchen an elderly woman who seemed to be acting as provisional housekeeper during the convulsions from which Farfrae's establishment was just then suffering. She was one of those people whom nothing surprises, and though to her, a total stranger, his request must

---

*The biblical hero Samson loses his strength when Delilah cuts his hair as he sleeps (Judges 16:15–21).
†Softened.

have seemed odd, she willingly volunteered to go up and inform the master and mistress of the house that "a humble old friend" had come.

On second thoughts she said that he had better not wait in the kitchen, but come up into the little back-parlour, which was empty. He thereupon followed her thither, and she left him. Just as she had got across the landing to the door of the best parlour a dance was struck up, and she returned to say that she would wait till that was over before announcing him—Mr. and Mrs. Farfrae having both joined in the figure.

The door of the front room had been taken off its hinges to give more space, and that of the room Henchard sat in being ajar, he could see fractional parts of the dancers whenever their gyrations brought them near the doorway, chiefly in the shape of the skirts of dresses and streaming curls of hair; together with about three-fifths of the band in profile, including the restless shadow of a fiddler's elbow, and the tip of the bass-viol bow.

The gaiety jarred upon Henchard's spirits; and he could not quite understand why Farfrae, a much-sobered man, and a widower, who had had his trials, should have cared for it all, notwithstanding the fact that he was quite a young man still, and quickly kindled to enthusiasm by dance and song. That the quiet Elizabeth, who had long ago appraised life at a moderate value, and who knew in spite of her maidenhood that marriage was as a rule no dancing matter, should have had zest for this revelry surprised him still more. However, young people could not be quite old people, he concluded, and custom was omnipotent.

With the progress of the dance the performers spread out somewhat, and then for the first time he caught a glimpse of the once despised daughter who had mastered him, and made his heart ache. She was in a dress of white silk or satin, he was not near enough to say which—snowy white, without a tinge of milk or cream; and the expression of her face was one of nervous pleasure rather than of gaiety. Presently Farfrae came round, his exuberant Scotch movement making him conspicuous in a moment. The pair were not dancing together, but Henchard could discern that whenever the changes of the figure made them the partners of a moment their emotions breathed a much subtler essence than at other times.

By degrees Henchard became aware that the measure was trod by some one who out-Farfraed Farfrae in saltatory* intenseness. This was

---

*Pertaining to dancing or leaping.

strange, and it was stranger to find that the eclipsing personage was Elizabeth-Jane's partner. The first time that Henchard saw him he was sweeping grandly round, his head quivering and low down, his legs in the form of an X and his back towards the door. The next time he came round in the other direction, his white waistcoat preceding his face, and his toes preceding his white waistcoat. That happy face— Henchard's complete discomfiture lay in it. It was Newson's, who had indeed come and supplanted him.

Henchard pushed to the door, and for some seconds made no other movement. He rose to his feet, and stood like a dark ruin, obscured by "the shade from his own soul upthrown."[27]

But he was no longer the man to stand these reverses unmoved. His agitation was great, and he would fain have been gone, but before he could leave the dance had ended, the housekeeper had informed Elizabeth-Jane of the stranger who awaited her, and she entered the room immediately.

"Oh—it is—Mr. Henchard!" she said, starting back.

"What; Elizabeth?" he cried, as he seized her hand. "What do you say?—Mr. Henchard? Don't, don't scourge me like that! Call me worthless old Henchard—anything—but don't 'ee be so cold as this! O my maid—I see you have another—a real father in my place. Then you know all; but don't give all your thought to him! Do ye save a little room for me!"

She flushed up, and gently drew her hand away. "I could have loved you always—I would have, gladly," said she. "But how can I when I know you have deceived me so—so bitterly deceived me! You persuaded me that my father was not my father—allowed me to live on in ignorance of the truth for years; and then when he, my warm-hearted real father, came to find me, cruelly sent him away with a wicked invention of my death, which nearly broke his heart. O how can I love as I once did a man who has served us like this!"

Henchard's lips half parted to begin an explanation. But he shut them up like a vice, and uttered not a sound. How should he, there and then, set before her with any effect the palliatives of his great faults—that he had himself been deceived in her identity at first, till informed by her mother's letter that his own child had died; that, in the second accusation, his lie had been the last desperate throw of a gamester who loved her affection better than his own honour?

Among the many hindrances to such a pleading not the least was this, that he did not sufficiently value himself to lessen his sufferings by strenuous appeal or elaborate argument.

Waiving, therefore, his privilege of self-defence, he regarded only her discomposure. "Don't ye distress yourself on my account," he said, with proud superiority. "I would not wish it—at such a time, too, as this. I have done wrong in coming to 'ee—I see my error. But it is only for once, so forgive it. I'll never trouble 'ee again, Elizabeth-Jane—no, not to my dying day! Good-night. Good-bye!"

Then, before she could collect her thoughts, Henchard went out from her rooms, and departed from the house by the back way as he had come; and she saw him no more.

XLV

IT WAS ABOUT A month after the day which closed as in the last chapter. Elizabeth-Jane had grown accustomed to the novelty of her situation, and the only difference between Donald's movements now and formerly was that he hastened indoors rather more quickly after business hours than he had been in the habit of doing for some time.

Newson had stayed in Casterbridge three days after the wedding party (whose gaiety, as might have been surmised was of his making rather than of the married couple's), and was stared at and honoured as became the returned Crusoe* of the hour. But whether or not because Casterbridge was difficult to excite by dramatic returns and disappearances, through having been for centuries an assize town† in which sensational exits from the world, antipodean absences,‡ and such like, were half-yearly occurrences, the inhabitants did not altogether lose their equanimity on his account. On the fourth morning he was discovered disconsolately climbing a hill, in his craving to get a glimpse of the sea from somewhere or other. The contiguity of salt

---

*The shipwrecked-and-rescued hero of Daniel Defoe's novel *Robinson Crusoe* (1719).
†Town in which civil and criminal trials are held.
‡"Sensational exits from the world" is a reference to public executions; "antipodean absences" refers to banishments to penal colonies (often to Australia or the "antipodes").

water proved to be such a necessity of his existence that he preferred Budmouth as a place of residence, notwithstanding the society of his daughter in the other town. Thither he went, and settled in lodgings in a green-shuttered cottage which had a bow-window, jutting out sufficiently to afford glimpses of a vertical strip of blue sea to any one opening the sash, and leaning forward far enough to look through a narrow lane of tall intervening houses.

Elizabeth-Jane was standing in the middle of her upstairs parlour, critically surveying some re-arrangement of articles with her head to one side, when the housemaid came in with the announcement, "Oh, please ma'am, we know now how that bird-cage came there."

In exploring her new domain during the first week of residence, gazing with critical satisfaction on this cheerful room and that, penetrating cautiously into dark cellars, sallying forth with gingerly tread to the garden, now leaf-strewn by autumn winds, and thus, like a wise field-marshal, estimating the capabilities of the site whereon she was about to open her housekeeping campaign—Mrs. Donald Farfrae had discovered in a screened corner a new bird-cage, shrouded in newspaper, and at the bottom of the cage a little ball of feathers—the dead body of a goldfinch. Nobody could tell her how the bird and cage had come there; though that the poor little songster had been starved to death was evident. The sadness of the incident had made an impression on her. She had not been able to forget it for days, despite Farfrae's tender banter; and now when the matter had been nearly forgotten it was again revived.

"Oh, please ma'am, we know how that bird-cage came there. That farmer's man who called on the evening of the wedding—he was seen wi' it in his hand as he came up the street; and 'tis thoughted that he put it down while he came in with his message, and then went away forgetting where he had left it."

This was enough to set Elizabeth thinking, and in thinking she seized hold of the idea, at one feminine bound, that the caged bird had been brought by Henchard for her as a wedding gift and token of repentance. He had not expressed to her any regrets or excuses for what he had done in the past; but it was a part of his nature to extenuate nothing, and live on as one of his own worst accusers. She went out, looked at the cage, buried the starved little singer, and from that hour her heart softened towards the self-alienated man.

When her husband came in she told him her solution of the

birdcage mystery; and begged Donald to help her in finding out, as soon as possible, whither Henchard had banished himself, that she might make her peace with him; try to do something to render his life less that of an outcast; and more tolerable to him. Although Farfrae had never so passionately liked Henchard as Henchard had liked him, he had, on the other hand, never so passionately hated in the same direction as his former friend had done; and he was therefore not the least indisposed to assist Elizabeth-Jane in her laudable plan.

But it was by no means easy to set about discovering Henchard. He had apparently sunk into the earth on leaving Mr. and Mrs. Farfrae's door. Elizabeth-Jane remembered what he had once attempted; and trembled.

But though she did not know it Henchard had become a changed man since then—as far, that is, as change of emotional basis can justify such a radical phrase; and she needed not to fear. In a few days Farfrae's inquiries elicited that Henchard had been seen by one who knew him walking steadily along the Melchester highway eastward, at twelve o'clock at night—in other words, retracing his steps on the road by which he had come.

This was enough; and the next morning Farfrae might have been discovered driving his gig out of Casterbridge in that direction, Elizabeth-Jane sitting beside him, wrapped in a thick flat fur—the victorine of the period—her complexion somewhat richer than formerly, and an incipient matronly dignity, which the serene Minerva* eyes of one "whose gestures beamed with mind"† made becoming, settling on her face. Having herself arrived at a promising haven from at least the grosser troubles of her life, her object was to place Henchard in some similar quietude before he should sink into that lower stage of existence which was only too possible to him now.

After driving along the highway for a few miles they made further inquiries, and learnt of a road-mender, who had been working thereabouts for weeks, that he had observed such a man at the time mentioned; he had left the Melchester coach-road at Weatherbury by a forking highway which skirted the north of Egdon Heath. Into this road they directed the horse's head, and soon were bowling across that ancient country whose surface never had been stirred to a finger's depth,

---

*Roman goddess of wisdom.
†From Percy Bysshe Shelley's *The Revolt of Islam* (1818; canto 1, stanza 54).

save by the scratchings of rabbits, since brushed by the feet of the earliest tribes. The tumuli these had left behind, dun and shagged with heather, jutted roundly into the sky from the uplands, as though they were the full breasts of Diana Multimammia* supinely extended there.

They searched Egdon, but found no Henchard. Farfrae drove onward, and by the afternoon reached the neighbourhood of some extension of the heath to the north of Anglebury, a prominent feature of which, in the form of a blasted clump of firs on the summit of a hill, they soon passed under. That the road they were following had, up to this point, been Henchard's track on foot they were pretty certain; but the ramifications which now began to reveal themselves in the route made further progress in the right direction a matter of pure guesswork, and Donald strongly advised his wife to give up the search in person, and trust to other means for obtaining news of her stepfather. They were now a score of miles at least from home, but, by resting the horse for a couple of hours at a village they had just traversed, it would be possible to get back to Casterbridge that same day; while to go much further afield would reduce them to the necessity of camping out for the night; "and that will make a hole in a sovereign," said Farfrae. She pondered the position, and agreed with him.

He accordingly drew rein, but before reversing their direction paused a moment and looked vaguely round upon the wide country which the elevated position disclosed. While they looked a solitary human form came from under the clump of trees, and crossed ahead of them. The person was some labourer; his gait was shambling, his regard fixed in front of him as absolutely as if he wore blinkers; and in his hand he carried a few sticks. Having crossed the road he descended into a ravine, where a cottage revealed itself, which he entered.

"If it were not so far away from Casterbridge I should say that must be poor Whittle. 'Tis just like him," observed Elizabeth-Jane.

"And it may be Whittle, for he's never been to the yard these three weeks, going away without saying any word at all; and I owing him for two days' work, without knowing who to pay it to."

The possibility led them to alight, and at least make an inquiry at the cottage. Farfrae hitched the reins to the gate-post, and they approached what was of humble dwellings surely the humblest. The walls,

---

*Diana the Many-Breasted, the fertility goddess; in her temple at Ephesus, she is represented with many breasts.

built of kneaded clay originally faced with a trowel, had been worn by
years of rain-washings to a lumpy crumbling surface, channelled and
sunken from its plane, its gray rents held together here and there by a
leafy strap of ivy which could scarcely find substance enough for the
purpose. The rafters were sunken, and the thatch of the roof in ragged
holes. Leaves from the fence had been blown into the corners of the
doorway, and lay there undisturbed. The door was ajar; Farfrae knocked;
and he who stood before them was Whittle, as they had conjectured.

His face showed marks of deep sadness, his eyes lighting on them
with an unfocused gaze; and he still held in his hand the few sticks he
had been out to gather. As soon as he recognized them he started.

"What, Abel Whittle; is it that ye are heere?" said Farfrae.

"Ay, yes, sir! You see he was kind-like to mother when she wer
here below, though 'a was rough to me."

"Who are you talking of?"

"O sir—Mr. Henchet! Didn't ye know it? He's just gone—about
half-an-hour ago, by the sun; for I've got no watch to my name."

"Not—dead?" faltered Elizabeth-Jane.

"Yes, ma'am, he's gone! He was kind-like to mother when she wer
here, below, sending her the best ship-coal,* and hardly any ashes from
it at all; and taties, and such-like that were very needful to her. I seed en
go down street on the night of your worshipful's wedding to the lady
at yer side, and I thought he looked low and faltering. And I followed en
over Grey's Bridge, and he turned and zeed me, and said, 'You go back!'
But I followed, and he turned again, and said, 'Do you hear, sir? Go
back!' But I zeed that he was low, and I followed on still. Then 'a said,
'Whittle, what do ye follow me for when I've told ye to go back all these
times?' And I said, 'Because, sir, I see things be bad with 'ee, and ye wer
kind-like to mother if ye were rough to me, and I would fain be kind-
like to you.' Then he walked on, and I followed; and he never complained at me no more. We walked on like that all night; and in the blue
o' the morning, when 'twas hardly day, I looked ahead o' me, and I zeed
that he wambled, and could hardly drag along. By that time we had got
past here, but I had seen that this house was empty as I went by, and I
got him to come back; and I took down the boards from the windows,
and helped him inside. 'What, Whittle,' he said, 'and can ye really be

---

*Imported (thus high-quality) coal.

such a poor fond fool as to care for such a wretch as I!' Then I went on further, and some neighbourly woodmen lent me a bed, and a chair, and a few other traps, and we brought 'em here, and made him as comfortable as we could. But he didn't gain strength, for you see, ma'am, he couldn't eat—no, no appetite at all—and he got weaker; and to-day he died. One of the neighbours have gone to get a man to measure him."

"Dear me—is that so!" said Farfrae.

As for Elizabeth, she said nothing.

"Upon the head of his bed he pinned a piece of paper, with some writing upon it," continued Abel Whittle. "But not being a man o' letters, I can't read writing; so I don't know what it is. I can get it and show ye."

They stood in silence while he ran into the cottage; returning in a moment with a crumpled scrap of paper. On it there was pencilled as follows:

"MICHAEL HENCHARD'S WILL

"That Elizabeth-Jane Farfrae be not told of my death, or
    made to grieve on account of me.

"& that I be not bury'd in consecrated ground.

"& that no sexton be asked to toll the bell.

"& that nobody is wished to see my dead body.

"& that no murners walk behind me at my funeral.

"& that no flours be planted on my grave.

"& that no man remember me.

"To this I put my name.

"MICHAEL HENCHARD."

"What are we to do?" said Donald, when he had handed the paper to her.

She could not answer distinctly. "O Donald!" she said at last through her tears, "what bitterness lies there! O I would not have minded so much if it had not been for my unkindness at that last parting! . . . But there's no altering—so it must be."

What Henchard had written in the anguish of his dying was respected as far as practicable by Elizabeth-Jane, though less from a sense of the sacredness of last words, as such, than from her independent knowledge that the man who wrote them meant what he said. She knew the directions to be a piece of the same stuff that his whole life was made of, and hence were not to be tampered with to give herself a mournful pleasure, or her husband credit for large-heartedness.

All was over at last, even her regrets for having misunderstood him on his last visit, for not having searched him out sooner, though these were deep and sharp for a good while. From this time forward Elizabeth-Jane found herself in a latitude of calm weather, kindly and grateful in itself, and doubly so after the Capharnaum* in which some of her preceding years had been spent. As the lively and sparkling emotions of her early married life cohered into an equable serenity, the finer movements of her nature found scope in discovering to the narrow-lived ones around her the secret (as she had once learnt it) of making limited opportunities endurable; which she deemed to consist in the cunning enlargement, by a species of microscopic treatment, of those minute forms of satisfaction that offer themselves to everybody not in positive pain; which, thus handled, have much of the same inspiriting effect upon life as wider interests cursorily embraced.

Her teaching had a reflex action upon herself, insomuch that she thought she could perceive no great personal difference between being respected in the nether parts of Casterbridge and glorified at the uppermost end of the social world. Her position was, indeed, to a marked degree one that, in the common phrase, afforded much to be thankful for. That she was not demonstratively thankful was no fault of hers. Her experience had been of a kind to teach her, rightly or wrongly, that the doubtful honour of a brief transit through a sorry world hardly called for effusiveness, even when the path was suddenly irradiated at some half-way point by daybeams rich as hers. But her strong sense that neither she nor any human being deserved less than as given, did not blind her to the fact that there were others receiving less who had deserved much more. And in being forced to class herself among the fortunate she did not cease to wonder at the persistence of the unforeseen, when the one to whom such unbroken tranquillity had been accorded in the adult stage was she whose youth had seemed to teach that happiness was but the occasional episode in a general drama of pain.

---

*A Galilean town; in the biblical account (Matthew 4:16), when Jesus preached there "the people which sat in darkness saw great light" (King James Version).

ENDNOTES

1. (p. 17) *the Seven Sleepers had a dog:* Seven third-century Christians of Ephesus (in present-day Turkey) sought refuge from the persecutions of the Roman emperor Decius in a cave. After sleeping there for 300 years, guarded by a dog named Katmir, they awoke to find Christianity the accepted religion.

2. (p. 25) *folly to think of making Elizabeth-Jane wise:* Thomas Gray's "Ode on a Distant Prospect of Eton College" (1747) ends with the lines: "where ignorance is bliss, / 'Tis folly to be wise."

3. (p. 38) *He was ruddy and of a fair countenance:* In the Bible (1 Samuel 16:12), David is described as "ruddy, and withal of a beautiful countenance" (King James Version; henceforth, KJV). David is first Saul's friend and later his rival. Hardy's allusion here foreshadows the tensions that will emerge between Henchard and Farfrae.

4. (p. 50) *"It's hame, and it's hame, hame fain would I be. . . . The lark shall sing me hame to my ain countree":* The lines are from a popular Jacobite folk song, referring to the return of the exiled Prince Charles Edward Stuart (1720-1788) to the English throne.

5. (p. 55) *"we rebelled against the King one or two hundred years ago, in the time of the Romans":* Buzzford is referring to the Duke of Monmouth's unsuccessful attempt in the seventeenth century to seize the throne from the Roman Catholic James II. However, Buzzford confuses James's Roman Catholicism with the ancient Roman occupation of the British Isles.

6. (p. 59) *Cranstoun's Goblin Page:* In Sir Walter Scott's poem *The Lay of the Last Minstrel* (1805), Lord Cranstoun's dwarf servant plays cruel, unperceived practical jokes.

7. (p. 63) *the quicker cripple at Bethesda:* In the biblical story of the pool at Bethesda (John 5:29), diseased people immerse themselves in hope of a cure; the pool performs this miracle for the first to enter after an angel disturbs the surface and so gives "quicker cripples" an advantage.

8. (p. 68) *in 1705 a woman who had murdered her husband was half-strangled and then burnt there in the presence of ten thousand spectators:* Hardy refers here to

the public execution of Mary Charming, which he discussed in 1908 in a *Times* article titled "Maumbury Ring."

 9. (p. 74) *like leafy Laocoöns*: Virgil's *Aeneid* describes the death of the Trojan priest Laocoön and his sons when they are attacked by sea serpents. A well-known classical sculpture, on display in the Vatican, depicts the event.

10. (p. 83) *never—to paraphrase a recent poet—never a gloom in Elizabeth-Jane's soul but she well knew how it came there*: In his essay "Wordsworth," English poet and critic Matthew Arnold (1822-1888) remarks, "No line in Goethe's poetry . . . but its maker well knew how it came there."

11. (p. 91) *the prophet Baruch's sly definition: "The virgin that loveth to go gay"*: Hardy here refers to the apocryphal biblical book of Baruch (6:9). The quoted words are those of Jeremiah, who is castigating the Babylonian's habit of making gold crowns for their idols.

12. (p. 91) *the "delicate imposition" of Rochefoucauld*: François, duc de la Rochefoucauld (1613-1680), wrote a well-known book of Maxims; maxim 289 reads "Affected simplicity is a delicate fraud."

13. (p. 109) *Like Jacob in Padan-Aram, he would no sooner humbly limit himself to the ringstraked-and-spotted exceptions of trade*: This is a reference to the biblical story of Jacob, who serves his father-in-law Laban in Padam-Aram (present-day Syria) for years, receiving inferior-quality ("ringstraked-and-spotted"—that is, discolored) cattle as wages. Despite this unfair bargain, Jacob is able to use sorcery to ensure that his cattle reproduce at a faster rate than Laban's (see Genesis 30:30-43).

14. (p. 109) *Character is Fate, said Novalis*: German Romantic poet Baron Friedrich Leopold von Hardenburg (1772-1801) wrote under the name Novalis. The quotation, from Novalis's posthumously published novel *Heinrich von Ofterdingen* (1802), was used in George Eliot's novel *The Mill on the Floss* (1860); it is from this source that Hardy knew the aphorism.

15. (p. 116) *like the brethren at the avowal of Joseph*: The Bible (Genesis 45:3) tells of the discomfiture of Joseph's brothers when they recognize him years after selling him into slavery.

16. (p. 119) *Like Prester John's, his table had been spread, and infernal harpies had snatched up the food*: Ludovico Ariosto's epic *Orlando furioso* (1532) tells the story of how the Ethiopian king Prester John is punished for his ambition: God blinds him and has a group of harpies (beasts with

women's heads and vulture's bodies) steal his food from his plate every time he tries to eat.

17. (p. 126) *men who held in their mouths coins of Hadrian, Posthumus, and the Constantines:* The three names are of emperors during Rome's occupation of Britain. The Roman dead were buried with coins in their mouths to pay for their passage to the underworld.

18. (p. 167) *"meaner beauties of the night":* The words are from the opening line of "Elizabeth of Bohemia," by Sir Henry Wotton (1568-1639): "You meaner beauties of the night, / That poorly satisfy our eyes / More by your number than your light, / You common people of the skies; / What are you when the moon shall rise?"

19. (p. 178) *follow the triumphal chariot of this man to the Capitol:* The Capitol is the hill in Rome where the Temple to Jupiter stood. It was the site of triumphal processions in which successful generals gave thanks for their victories; their vanquished enemies followed them in the procession.

20. (p. 186) *where the clouds drop fatness:* The line from the biblical book Psalm (65:11) is "Thou crownest the year with thy goodness, and thy paths drop fatness" (KJV). Hardy's implication is that the woman's bonnet is greasy.

21. (p. 198) *like John Gilpin:* In the poem "The Diverting History of John Gilpin," by William Cowper (1731-1800), a merchant delays celebrating his wedding anniversary to attend to customers. "Although it grieved him sore, / Yet loss of pence, full well he knew, / Would trouble him much more."

22. (p. 200) *'Video meliora proboque, deteriora sequor':* Elizabeth-Jane quotes from book 7 of the *Metamorphoses* of Ovid (43 B.C-A.D.17). "I see and approve the better course; I follow the worse." The words are spoken by Medea about her passion for Jason.

23. (p. 212) *"Yes, she was wise, she was wise in her generation":* In a biblical parable (Luke 16:1-13), a crafty steward manages to thrive even after he is dismissed for cheating his master. Christ remarks, "The children of this world are in their generation wiser than the children of light" (KJV).

24. (p. 264) *Over this repentant sinner, at least, there was to be no joy in heaven:* Hardy refers to Luke 15:7, in which Jesus says, "Joy shall be in heaven over one sinner that repenteth, more than over ninety and nine just persons, which need no repentance" (KJV).

25. (p. 269) *"She could write her name, and no more"*: This is a mistake by Hardy, or Henchard, since Susan has written a letter to Henchard. Alternatively, she could have learned to write after her sale by Henchard.

26. (p. 279) *Argus eyes*: In classical mythology, the one-hundred-eyed Argus is sent by Juno to guard a white cow (in fact, the beautiful Io, whom Juno's husband, Jove, covets). When Jove has Argus killed, Juno sets his hundred eyes into the tail of the peacock in tribute of his service.

27. (p. 299) *"the shade from his own soul upthrown"*: This is a quotation from Percy Bysshe Shelley's *The Revolt of Islam* (1818): "Some moonstruck sophist stood / Watching the shade from his own soul upthrown / Fill Heaven and darken Earth, and in such mood / The Form he saw and worshipped was his own" (canto 8, stanza 6).

INSPIRED BY THE MAYOR OF CASTERBRIDGE

Film

Hardy's novel has inspired two television movie productions and one feature film adaptation. In 1978 the BBC aired a seven-part miniseries of *The Mayor of Casterbridge* that starred Alan Bates as Henchard. The straight-shooting, faithful remake was directed by David Giles from a screenplay by playwright Dennis Potter. In 2003 Ciaran Hinds starred in the version aired on A&E, directed by David Thacker. Ted Whitehead, who wrote a television version of the Hardy novel *Tess of the D'Urbervilles* (1998), wrote the screenplay.

Director Michael Winterbottom adapted *The Mayor of Casterbridge* to the cold mountains of gold rush California in *The Claim* (2000). Featuring the bleak, snowy landscape as prominently as its main actors, this austere film has a practiced sadness that pervades every slow, dream-like shot. Peter Mullen stars as Irish immigrant Daniel Dillon, who sells his wife and daughter to a prospector in order to stake a claim on gold-rich land. Dillon then builds the busy mining town of Kingdom Come, where he rules with an iron fist. To further boost his economic prospects, he must convince the railroad surveyor Dalglish, played by Wes Bentley, to direct his tracks through the town. At the same time, Dillon's wife and daughter return to Kingdom Come, and the twin pressures prove to be his unraveling.

While *The Claim* succeeds in retaining the tragic spirit of its predecessor, at times it tends too far toward subtlety and obtuseness, needlessly masking key plot details and relationships between characters. Likewise, in its obscurity and meditative nature the film lacks the punch of the novel: The wife-auction scene that opens Hardy's novel does not appear until a full thirty minutes into *The Claim*. Winterbottom adapted Hardy's *Jude the Obscure* into *Jude* in 1996; as in *The Claim*, he takes great liberties with the plot, excising the last seven chapters, while retaining the soul of the novel.

Fiction

J. K. Rowling borrows from *The Mayor of Casterbridge* for the names of two characters in her popular *Harry Potter* novels. Soon after Henchard reveals to Elizabeth that he is her father, he criticizes her use of regional dialect; to Henchard, the use of such language signifies low breeding. He complains, "Good God, are you only fit to carry wash to a pig-trough, that ye use such words as those?" Rowling borrows two of these vernacular terms to name characters in her novels: "dumbledores" and "hag-rid." In Hardy's lexicon, the words mean bumblebees and indigestion, respectively. Rowling uses them to name Dumbledore, the master of Harry's school, and Hagrid, the Keeper of the Keys and Grounds.

COMMENTS & QUESTIONS

In this section, we aim to provide the reader with an array of perspectives on the text, as well as questions that challenge those perspectives. The commentary has been culled from sources as diverse as reviews contemporaneous with the work, letters written by the author, literary criticism of later generations, and appreciations written throughout the work's history. Following the commentary, a series of questions seeks to filter Thomas Hardy's The Mayor of Casterbridge *through a variety of points of view and bring about a richer understanding of this enduring work.*

Comments

THE SPECTATOR

Mr. Hardy has not given us any more powerful study than that of Michael Henchard. Why he should especially term his hero in his title-page a "man of character," we do not clearly understand. Properly speaking, character is the stamp graven on a man, and character therefore, like anything which can be graven, and which, when graven, remains, is a word much more applicable to that which has fixity and permanence, than to that which is fitful and changeful, and which impresses a totally different image of itself on the wax of plastic circumstance at one time, from that which it impresses on a similarly plastic surface at another time. To keep strictly to the associations from which the word 'character' is derived, a man of character ought to suggest a man of steady and unvarying character, a man who conveys very much the same conception of his own qualities under one set of circumstances, which he conveys under another. This is true of many men, and they might be called men of character *par excellence*. But the essence of Michael Henchard is that he is a man of large nature and depth of passion, who is yet subject to the most fitful influences, who can do in one mood acts of which he will never cease to repent in almost all his other moods, whose temper of heart changes many times even during the execution of the same purpose, though the same ardour, the same pride, the same wrathful magnanimity, the same inability to carry out in cool blood the angry re-

313

solve of the mood of revenge or scorn, to swing back to an equally hasty reasonableness, distinguish him throughout. In one very good sense, the great deficiency of Michael Henchard might be said to be in 'character.' It might well be said that with a little more character, with a little more fixity of mind, with a little more power of recovering himself when he was losing his balance, his would have been a nature of gigantic mould; whereas, as Mr. Hardy's novel is meant to show, it was a nature which ran mostly to waste. But, of course, in the larger and wider sense of the word 'character,' that sense which has less reference to the permanent definition of the stamp, and more reference to the confidence with which the varying moods may be anticipated, it is not inadmissible to call Michael Henchard a 'man of character.' Still, the words on the title-page rather mislead. One looks for the picture of a man of much more constancy of purpose, and much less tragic mobility of mood, than Michael Henchard. None the less, the picture is a very vivid one, and almost magnificent in its fullness of expression. The largeness of his nature, the unreasonable generosity and suddenness of his friendships, the depth of his self-humiliation for what was evil in him, the eagerness of his craving for sympathy, the vehemence of his impulses both for good and evil, the curious dash of stoicism in a nature so eager for sympathy, and of fortitude in one so moody and restless,—all these are lineaments which, mingled together as Mr. Hardy has mingled them, produce a curiously strong impression of reality, as well as of homely grandeur.

—June 5, 1886

WILLIAM DEAN HOWELLS

I came rather late, but I came with all the ardor of what seems my perennial literary youth, to the love of Thomas Hardy, whom I first knew in his story *A Pair of Blue Eyes*. As usual, after I had read this book and felt the new charm in it, I wished to read the books of no other author, and to read his books over and over. I love even the faults of Hardy; I will let him play me any trick he chooses (and he is not above playing tricks, when he seems to get tired of his story or perplexed with it), if only he will go on making his peasants talk, and his rather uncertain ladies get in and out of love, and serve themselves of every chance that fortune offers them of having their own way.

—from *My Literary Passions* (1891)

JOYCE KILMER

According to the Hardy philosophy, implicit in his tales and explicit in his poems, sorrow is the rule and joy the exception. In no other writing is he more clearly a fatalist than in "The Mayor of Casterbridge"; in no other book does he urge more unmistakably his belief that men and women are but helpless puppets in the hands of mischievous fate, that good-will and courage and honesty are brittle weapons for humanity's defense.

—from *The Circus, and Other Essays and Fugitive Pieces* (1921)

VIRGINIA WOOLF

Henchard is pitted, not against another man, but against something outside himself which is opposed to men of his ambition and power. No human being wishes him ill. Even Farfrae and Newson and Elizabeth-Jane whom he has wronged all come to pity him, and even to admire his strength of character. He is standing up to fate, and in backing the old Mayor whose ruin has been largely his own fault, Hardy makes us feel that we are backing human nature in an unequal contest. There is no pessimism here. . . . The true tragic emotion is ours.

—from *The Second Common Reader* (1932)

Questions

1. William Dean Howells wrote, "I love even the faults of Hardy." What are Hardy's faults as a writer?

2. Is Hardy a misogynist?

3. "In no other book does [Hardy] urge more unmistakably his belief that men and women are but helpless puppets in the hands of a mischievous fate," writes Joyce Kilmer. Do you agree? Is this "fate" imposed upon a character, or does it originate from within? In other words, is fate's operative agency human or supernatural?

4. Does love exist in the universe of *The Mayor of Casterbridge*, or only sex?

5. In what ways do the settings of the book—natural, human, and man-made—determine the actions of the main characters?

FOR FURTHER READING

Biographies

Gibson, James. *Thomas Hardy: A Literary Life*. Basingstoke, England: Macmillan, 1996.

Hands, Timothy. *A Hardy Chronology*. Basingstoke, England: Macmillan, 1992.

Seymour-Smith, Martin. *Hardy*. London: Bloomsbury, 1994.

Turner, Paul. *The Life of Thomas Hardy*. Oxford: Blackwell, 1998.

Critical Studies

Bayley, John. *An Essay on Hardy*. Cambridge and New York: Cambridge University Press, 1978.

Daleski, H. M. *Thomas Hardy and Paradoxes of Love*. Columbia and London: University of Missouri Press, 1997.

Garson, Marjorie. *Hardy's Fables of Integrity: Woman, Body, Text*. Oxford and New York: Oxford University Press, 1991.

King, Jeanette. *Tragedy in the Victorian Novel: Theory and Practice in the Novels of George Eliot, Thomas Hardy, and Henry James*. Cambridge and New York: Cambridge University Press, 1978.

Kramer, Dale, ed. *Critical Approaches to the Fiction of Thomas Hardy*. London: Macmillan, 1979.

Lawrence, D. H. *Study of Thomas Hardy and Other Essays*. Edited by Bruce Steele. Cambridge and New York: Cambridge University Press, 1985.

Miller, J. Hillis. *Thomas Hardy: Distance and Desire*. Cambridge, MA: Harvard University Press, 1970.

Williams, Merryn. *Thomas Hardy and Rural England*. London: Macmillan, 1972.

Contemporary Reviews of Hardy

Cox, R. G., ed. *Thomas Hardy: The Critical Heritage*. London: Routledge and Kegan Paul, 1970.

Lerner, Laurence, and John Holmstrom, eds. *Thomas Hardy and His Readers: A Selection of Contemporary Reviews*. New York: Barnes and Noble, 1968.

Other Works Cited in the Introduction

Gittings, Robert. *Young Thomas Hardy*. London: Heinemann, 1975.

Guerard, Albert J. *Thomas Hardy: The Novels and Stories*. Cambridge, MA: Harvard University Press, 1949.

Hardy, Thomas. *The Life and Work of Thomas Hardy*. Edited by Michael Millgate. London: Macmillan, 1984.

———. "The Dorsetshire Labourer." In *Thomas Hardy's Personal Writings: Prefaces, Literary Opinions, Reminiscences*, edited by Harold Orel. London: Macmillan, 1967.

Howe, Irving. *Thomas Hardy*. New York: Macmillan, 1967.

Millgate, Michael. *Thomas Hardy: His Career as a Novelist*. London: Bodley Head, 1971.

Moody, Rick. "Introduction." In *The Mayor of Casterbridge*, by Thomas Hardy. Oxford: Oxford University Press, 2003.

Saintsbury, George. *Saturday Review* (May 29, 1886).

Showalter, Elaine. "The Unmanning of the Mayor of Casterbridge." In *Critical Approaches to the Fiction of Thomas Hardy*, edited by Dale Kramer. London: Macmillan, 1979.

Woolf, Virginia. "The Novels of Thomas Hardy." In *The Second Common Reader*. New York: Harcourt Brace, 1932.

we have Hardy's impression of life as it came to him without conscious ordering."

What he managed to do in *The Mayor of Casterbridge* was to keep the balance between free will and determinism, possibility and fatalism, an open question for as long as possible. This is largely because of his forceful, dynamic, and resourceful main character, who is not so easily crushed by fate. We feel the volitional air go out of Jude and Tess, and their life forces winding down, long before their respective novels end, whereas Henchard faces a serious choice of whether to reinvent himself once again, only ten or so pages from the end. Working on a Wessex farm, still in his forties:

> Henchard found himself again on the precise standing which he had occupied a quarter of a century before. Externally there was nothing to hinder his making another start on the upward slope, and by his new lights achieving higher things than his soul in its half-formed state had been able to accomplish. But the ingenious machinery contrived by the Gods for reducing human possibilities of amelioration to a minimum—which arranges that wisdom to do shall come *pari passu* with the departure of zest for doing—stood in the way of all that. He had no wish to make an arena a second time of a world that had become a mere painted scene to him (pp. 293).

If he does not reinvent himself yet again, it is because the bitter wisdom he has acquired points him in another direction. The dark laughter of the Gods has arranged life's experience in the form of a figure-eight, with wisdom and ambitious energy touching for only a moment before they cross, pass, and part. This figure of the do-si-do movement is peculiarly Hardyesque, like the zigzagging circle of centrifugal and centripetal forces invoked to show Henchard's conflicted pull toward and away from town. If it was Thomas Hardy's particular genius as a novelist to fuse character with place, in *The Mayor of Casterbridge* he hit upon a story that could sustain all the well-intentioned and intemperate wanderings, all the back-and-forth divagations of the human heart.

Phillip Lopate, a professor at Hofstra University, is a recipient of a John Simon Guggenheim Fellowship, two National Endowment for the Arts grants, and a New York Public Library Center for Scholars and Writers Fellowship. He is best known for his essays, which are collected in *Bachelorhood*, *Against Joie De Vivre*, and *Portrait of My Body*. He is the editor of the anthology *Art of the Personal Essay* and has written a novel, *The Rug Merchant*; a book of poetry, *The Daily Round*; and, most recently, *Waterfront: A Journey Around Manhattan Island*.